Camille wasn't drawn to over-endowed men, especially since she worked in testosterone central where muscles were the norm, but holy moly! This man, probably no more than thirty, was the epitome of sex on the hoof.

She licked her lips and forced herself to calm down. *I look like hell,* she reminded herself. *On a good day, this superior male specimen wouldn't give me a passing glance. After three failed near-marriages, I do not need another complication. Wash your mind, girl. While I'm at it, I better check to make sure I'm not drooling.*

She took the hand that Harek extended to her as he said, "I've heard so much about you that—"

They both froze, extended hands still clasped. A sensation, like an electrical shock, except softer and coming in waves, rippled from his fingers into hers, then rushed to all her extremities. It was like having world-class sex without all the bother . . .

By Sandra Hill

Deadly Angels Series
EVEN VAMPIRES GET THE BLUES
VAMPIRE IN PARADISE
CHRISTMAS IN TRANSYLVANIA
KISS OF WRATH • KISS OF TEMPTATION
KISS OF SURRENDER • KISS OF PRIDE

Viking Series I
THE PIRATE BRIDE • THE NORSE KING'S DAUGHTER
THE VIKING TAKES A KNIGHT • VIKING IN LOVE
A TALE OF TWO VIKINGS
MY FAIR VIKING (formerly THE VIKING'S CAPTIVE)
THE BLUE VIKING • THE BEWITCHED VIKING
THE TARNISHED LADY • THE OUTLAW VIKING
THE RELUCTANT VIKING

Cajun Series
THE LOVE POTION (Book One)

Viking Series II
HOT & HEAVY • WET & WILD
THE VERY VIRILE VIKING • TRULY, MADLY VIKING
THE LAST VIKING

Creole-Time Travel Series
SWEETER SAVAGE LOVE • FRANKLY, MY DEAR

Others
LOVE ME TENDER • DESPERADO

SANDRA HILL

A DEADLY ANGELS BOOK

EVEN VAMPIRES GET THE BLUES

AVONBOOKS

An Imprint of HarperCollins*Publishers*

This is a work of fiction. Names, characters, places, and incidents are products of the author's imagination or are used fictitiously and are not to be construed as real. Any resemblance to actual events, locales, organizations, or persons, living or dead, is entirely coincidental.

AVON BOOKS
An Imprint of HarperCollins*Publishers*
195 Broadway
New York, New York 10007

ISBN 978-0-06-235652-9
www.avonromance.com

First Avon Books mass market printing: September 2015

Avon Trademark Reg. U.S. Pat. Off. and in Other Countries, Marca Registrada, Hecho en U.S.A.
HarperCollins® is a registered trademark of HarperCollins Publishers.

Printed in the U.S.A.

10 9 8 7 6 5 4 3 2 1

This book is dedicated to my two daughters-in-law, Kimberly Kohler and Bethany Stough, both of whom are strong women like those I like to portray in my books. Kim is an experienced special education teacher, now working on her doctorate degree. Bethany is a full-time emergency room nurse with plans to further her education, as well. How these two manage to do the work they do, and excel, at the same time raising a family, is beyond me. I am so proud of them. They make me work harder with my books to keep up with the high bar they set for women.

Author's Note

I have often said that there's a great similarity between Vikings, Navy SEALs, and, yes, even Viking vampire angels, all of which are featured in this book. It struck me especially when listening to Shane Patton (actor Alexander Ludwig) recite this "poem" as a young Navy SEAL in the movie *The Lone Survivor*. (And, by the way, did you know that Ludwig plays Bjorn, Ragnar Lothbrok's son, in the History Channel's *Vikings* series? Talk about coincidence!)

Variations on this anonymous ballad have been around for years, and it seems to me that, with a little word substitution, it could just as well be "The Navy SEAL Ballad," or "The Viking Ballad," or "The Vangel Ballad." *Long-boatin'* for *parachutin'*. *Fang-mouthed* for *hairy-chested*. *Hit a battle-axe warrior with a small hatchet* for *shoot a large caliber man with a small caliber bullet*. *Been to three pygmy picnics* to *Been a-Viking three times*.

Enjoy!

THE FROGMAN BALLAD

Been around the world twice, talked to everyone once,

I've seen two white whales hump, been to three pygmy picnics, I even know a man in Thailand with a wooden dick.

I've pushed more peter, more sweeter, and more completer than any other peter-pusher around.

I'm a hard-bodied, hairy-chested, rootin, tootin, shootin', parachutin', scuba-diving, KA-BAR-carrying, Rolex-wearing FROGMAN, last of the bare-knuckled webfoot warriors. There ain't nothing I can't do. No sky too high, no sea too rough, no muff too tough.

Learned a lot of lessons in my life. Never shoot a large caliber man with a small caliber bullet.

Drove a lot of trucks. Even those big mothers that bend and go CHOOSH CHOOSH when you step on the brakes.

Anything in life worth doing is worth over-doing. Moderation is for cowards.

I'm a lover, I'm a fighter, I'm a UDT/SEAL diver. I'll wine, dine, intertwine and then sneak out the back door when the refueling is done. If you're feeling froggy, then you better jump because this Frogman has been there, done that and is going back for more.

Hoo-yah!

EVEN VAMPIRES GET THE BLUES

Prologue

Hedeby, A.D. 850

You could say he was a Viking wheeler dealer . . .

Everything he touched turned to gold, or leastways a considerable profit, and thank the gods for that, because Harek Sigurdsson was a brilliant Viking with an insatiable hunger for wealth and all its trappings.

It didn't matter that he had vast holdings in the Norselands, an estate in Northumbria, several *hird*s of warriors who served under him when called to battle by one grab-land king or another (Harek was a much-sought battle strategist), amber fields in the Baltics, trading stalls in the marketplaces of Hedeby, Kaupang, and the Coppergate section of Jorvik, a fleet of twelve longships and two knarrs, and numerous chests filled with coins, jewels, and rare spices. It was never enough! Not to mention three wives and six concubines . . . or was it seven?

Not that he wanted or needed any more wives or concubines. Like many Viking men (hah! men of all lands, truth to tell), he was betimes guided by a body rudder known for its lackwittedness when it fancied a woman. The Wise Ones had the right of it when they proclaimed: A cock has no brain. Well, at the ripe old age of twenty and nine, he had finally taken a sip from Odin's famed well of knowledge. In future, when he came upon a comely woman, he would bed her, not wed her, then send her on her merry way with a pat on the rump and a pouch of gold coins. Cheaper that way and lots less trouble!

Harek had just completed a meeting with Toriq Haraldsson, his agent here in Hedeby. Toriq had once been a *hersir* overseeing Harek's Norse housecarls. Unfortunately, the fierce swordsman had lost an arm in battle. Harek had no qualms about hiring the handicapped man as his business representative. Loyalty and honesty were more important in that role than fighting skills. Besides, Toriq had once saved Harek's life in battle at a time when Harek had been young and not yet so adept in fighting. A berserk Dane had been about to lop off Harek's very head. Suffice it to say, the wergild for a highborn man's head was enormous.

As they walked side by side on the raised plank walkways that crisscrossed the busy market center, men and women alike glanced their way, not just because of their impressive Norse height and finely sculpted features. Their attire—fur-lined cloaks, gold brooches fastening shoulder mantles, soft leather half boots—could support a tradesman's family for years.

Unaware or uncaring of the attention, Toriq scowled and grumbled under his breath. Toriq was not happy with Harek today.

"Spit it out, man. What troubles you?"

"This latest venture of yours . . . it ill-suits a man of your stature," Toriq said, but then he had to step aside to accommodate a crowd that had gathered to watch a craftsman blowing blue glass into a pitcher. Other artisans were hammering gold and silver into fine jewelry. In fact, Harek noticed an etched armband he might purchase later. In other stalls, workers could be seen carving wood and ivory, or firing clay pots in kilns behind the trading tables.

Hedeby was an exciting city, always something going on. To Harek, the bustle of commerce, the sounds of money being made, were like music to the ears. There wasn't anything that couldn't be purchased here, from the prized walrus rope that was cut in a single spiral strip from shoulder to tail, to—well—to his latest venture.

"Slave trading, that is what rubs you the wrong way?" Harek asked, now that he and his agent could walk side by side once again.

"Yea, and it should rub you the same, boy." Toriq always referred to Harek in that way, even though Harek had long since been blooded in battle and it had been thirteen years since Toriq had saved his bloody head. Toriq himself had not yet seen forty winters.

"'Tis just another way of amassing a fortune."

Harek shrugged, not taking offense. After all, Toriq was a free man, welcome to voice his opinion. Still, it did not hurt to remind him of certain facts. He glanced pointedly at the massive gold ring that adorned Toriq's middle finger, a writhing dragon design with ruby eyes, worth a small fortune. "My ventures helped make you a wealthy man, Toriq."

"That they have, and most appreciative I am."

"And your eight children, as well?" Harek mentioned, trying to lighten the mood. "How else would you dower all those daughters?"

Toriq was always complaining about how expensive it was to support females, much as he loved his six daughters and his lone wife, Elsa. "All boys need is a sword and occasional change of braies and boots, but girls want gunnas and hair beads and slippers and brooches for every occasion and all the household fripperies that are a seeming necessity" was Toriq's usual refrain.

Not today, though. He just shook his head sadly at Harek.

"I am always looking for new ways to earn still more gold. Slave trading is no different than trading in amber or moneylending, both of which have been our mainstay. I'm only surprised I haven't tried it afore."

"There is a vast difference, Harek."

"How so? In every country, there are thralls. You have thralls yourself."

"Nay. I have indentured servants. Due to their own circumstances, some folks are forced to sell themselves, but only for a time. Then they are free."

"You are splitting hairs, my man. Vikings are known to free thralls if they are well-pleased. Some even wed their thralls or take them as concubines. Slavery is a fact of life. Why should I not profit from it?"

Toriq threw his arm out in frustration . . . and almost knocked over a plump maiden. After apologizing profusely, he turned to Harek once again. "You have riches enough to buy a small kingdom. Why can you not be satisfied with what you have?"

Harek was approaching frustration himself now, and he bristled. Criticism, even from a friend, could go too far. "A man cannot have an excess of gold. All the sagas say 'tis best to save for rainy days."

"Pfff! It could rain for forty days and forty nights, like it did for that Noah character the Christians babble on about, and you would still stay afloat. On the other hand, you would probably fill your Ark—rather, longship—with gold, and it would sink from its very weight. Then where would you be? Sunk by your own greed."

Realizing the inadvertent humor in his remark, Toriq laughed and squeezed Harek's forearm. "Peace, my friend. You gave me back my life when I thought I no longer had worth as a man. You know I will do whate'er you ask."

"Even if it leaves a bad taste in your mouth?"

"Even then."

They had almost arrived at the harbor when a horn blared, announcing the arrival of yet another sea vessel. Hopefully, it would be *Silver Serpent*,

Harek's largest longship, which was expected any day from the eastern lands. With its human cargo.

Anyone entering or exiting Hedeby, located at the junction of several major trade routes, had to do so by foot or horse or cart through one of three gateway tunnels built into the massive semicircular ramparts of the fortified city. Once they passed through into the bright light onto the wharves, Harek surveyed the seventy or so ships and boats, with flags of many colors denoting family or business or royal allegiance, that were tied at anchor or beached farther on for repairs.

The new arrival was indeed Harek's slave trader. To his dismay and Toriq's horror, they could practically smell the "cargo" afore the passengers even alighted.

And what a motley bunch they were! More than fifty men, women, and children of various nationalities, from ebony to white skin, wobbled on shaky sea legs over the wide gangplank onto the dock. There should have been a hundred. Harek bristled with anger, wondering what had happened to the others. Even a dimwit could see that this was a disaster that meant money lost. Even the most tightfisted farmer knew that you did not starve a pig before market.

As a whole, the starveling group, wearing raggedy garments, was filthy, some covered with dried vomit and other body emissions. Scabs, bruises, and lice were in clear evidence. Their eyes as they passed by Harek and Toriq were dead, except for a few in shackles who held his stare with murderous intent.

"The reeking ship will have to be scrubbed down with lye afore used again for any purpose," Toriq noted, as if Harek had not already come to the same conclusion.

"I want these thralls bathed, fed, and clothed. A healer will have to be called to treat some, I warrant," Harek told Toriq.

"It will be a sennight or more before any of them are fit for the auction block."

"And time wasted means less profit," Harek repeated one of his favorite proverbs.

"Precisely."

"Meanwhile, I have a thing or two to say to the captain of this floating cesspit."

"Where shall I take them?" Toriq studied the individuals, some of whom were shivering despite the summer heat. Obviously, they could not be housed in the slave quarters where goods and persons were stored before auction, not in this condition. If naught else, there would be fear of contagion. Odin only knew what diseases bred on these sorry bits of humanity.

"I have no idea where to house them. To Muspell, for all I care, at this point."

Toriq tapped his chin thoughtfully, then said, "I will take them to the storage building behind the amber trading stall. It is mostly empty now. Elsa will know what to do about delousing these people and fattening them for market, though she will not thank me for the task." That was as close as Toriq went to taunting him with I-told-you-so's.

"Buy her a new gold neck torque with my regards," Harek advised.

"You do not know women if you think that will suffice," Toriq told him.

"Do whate'er you must then."

It was, in fact, three sennights afore Harek returned to Hedeby from a brief trip home to his Norse estate where he'd been summoned to handle a crisis involving a neighboring chieftain with a land dispute. The lackbrain Viking would think again afore trying to steal property from Harek in his absence, especially in his present mood.

His first wife, Dagne, resided there, and what a shrew she'd turned out to be! Now that the first bloom of youth had passed Dagne at twenty and five, Harek could scarce bring himself to give her a conjugal duty swive. 'Twas hard to find her woman place in all that fat, Dagne now being as wide as she was tall. But did she appreciate his husbandly attentions? Nay! She was too busy complaining:

"There is not enough wood for the hearth fires."

It is summer. You do not need to keep all the hearth fires burning.

"The cook is too mouthy and disrespectful."

Probably because you invade her domain too much.

"One of the privies needs cleaning."

Then clean it.

"Why can't we have a beekeeper in residence?"

Because you would tup him, as you did the blacksmith, the shipwright, the horse breeder, and the monk.

"The rushes in the great hall are flea ridden."

Um, I can tell you where we keep the rakes, my dear.

"Your mustache is too bristly."

Then stay away from my damn mustache.

"I heard that Queen Elfrida has a new silver fox-lined cloak. Why can't I have one, too?"

Because three dozen foxes would have to die to cover your bulk.

"There is a black bear in the north wood needs killing."

I can think of something else that needs killing.

"I might be increasing again."

And yet I have not been home for nigh on ten months. How do you explain that, my halfbrained wife?

There was a good reason why Norsemen went a-Viking so much.

In the end, Harek left his Norse estate, with good riddance, vowing to himself not to return for a good while. And renewing his vow never to wed again.

To his relief, Toriq had already handled the thrall situation in his absence. Not only cleaning and feeding them, but selling them at the slave mart the day before. "Four thousand mancuses of gold for fifty slaves! That is wonderful!" Harek exclaimed, doing a quick mental calculation. "Even with expenses—initial purchase price to the slavers, sixty seamen's wages for one month, food and clothing for the thralls during the voyage, medical care where needed, the auctioneer's commission, and a goodly bonus for you—there has to be a clear profit of at least twenty-five hundred mancuses."

Toriq nodded. "A few of the skilled slaves—a carpenter, a farrier, a wheelwright, a weaver, and a beekeeper—brought a goodly amount by themselves."

Good thing Dagne, with her sudden yen for a beekeeper, did not hear of the beekeeper.

"And, of course, the younger, more attractive women raked in considerable coin. I saved one especially nubile Irish wench from the bidding block. For your bedplay, if you choose. Otherwise, my Elsa says she must go." He waggled his eyebrows at Harek.

He slapped Toriq on the shoulder in a comradely fashion. "A job well done, my friend! Already I can see the possibilities for the future. Longships sent to different ports to gather new cargo. The Rus lands, Byzantium, Norsemandy, Jorvik, Iceland. With more selective purchases and better treatment, I guarantee there will be even better returns on investment."

"Cargo? Cargo?" Toriq sputtered. "You are speaking of human beings, Harek. Many of whom are stolen from their homes."

"You still object?" Harek was surprised. "I thought . . . I mean, you did such a good job. I thought you now accepted the wisdom of slave trading as a side business."

Toriq shook his head vigorously. "I mean no insult, Harek, but you will have to find another man to handle this business. I did it this once, but no more."

"No offense taken," Harek said, but, in truth, he *was* offended. Perhaps that was why he was so dissatisfied with the Irishwoman in his bed furs that night. Beautiful, she was, but Toriq had failed to mention that she could not stop weeping for her young son who had been sold to a Frankish vintner and a husband who had been left behind on a poor Irish farm. Never mind that it had been the husband who'd sold her and his youngest son into thralldom. Harek wished he could sell Dagne so easily.

Disgusted, Harek made his way to the sleeping quarters on his largest knarr anchored at the docks. There, instead of celebrating a new, successful business venture, he succumbed to a long bout of sullen mead drinking, which led to alehead madness. Leastways, it had to be madness, for the *drukkinn* apparition that appeared to him out of the darkness was not of this world.

A misty, white shape emerged. Ghost-like.

"Harek Sigurdsson!" a male voice yelled out of the mist, so loud that Harek jerked into a sitting position on the pallet in the alcove of his enclosed space and almost rolled off to the floor. He blinked and tried to see the hazy blur standing in the open doorway leading to the longship's deck. The only light came from the full moon outside.

He stood, and at first he was disoriented. Who wouldn't be with a head the size of a wagon wheel, with what felt like a battle-axe imbedded in his skull?

A man . . . He could swear it was a man he saw standing there, and yet at the same time, there was no one there. Just a swirling fog.

"Who goes there?" he yelled out, thinking it must be one of the crew stationed on board overnight.

Silence.

Now he was starting to be annoyed. "Present yourself, man, or suffer the consequences."

No one answered. Good thing, because he realized he had no weapon in hand. Should he grab a knife? What kind of weapon did one use with a ghost? Would a blade even suffice?

He shook his head to clear it, to no avail. He was still under the influence of ale. Or something.

He could see clearer now, and it was a tall, dark-haired man wearing a long gown in the Arab style who beckoned him outside. The gown in itself was not so unusual but the broadsword he held easily in one hand was, especially since it was his own pattern-welded blade. Then, there were the huge white wings spread out from his back.

What? Wings? Huh? It couldn't be possible. He closed his eyes and looked again. Definitely wings.

Was it even a man? Or some kind of bird?

He had heard of shivering men suffering from wild dreams of writhing snakes or even fire-breathing dragons, but usually it was men trying to wean themselves away from years of the addictive brews or opium. Harek rarely drank to excess and never had an interest in the poppy seed.

But Harek had a more important issue at the moment. His bladder was so full he would be pissing from his ears if he didn't soon relieve himself. Making his way through the now empty doorway, he staggered over to the rail. Undoing the laces on his braies, he released himself and let loose a long stream of urine. When he was done—shaking his cock clean, then tucking it back into his braies—he breathed a sigh of relief, then belched. Which was a mistake. His breath was enough to gag a maggot.

Which cleared his head enough to let him know he still had company. The man-bird stood there, scowling at him with contempt. The wings were folded so that he could scarce tell they were there.

"Who . . . what are you?"

"Michael. The Archangel."

Harek knew about angels. In his travels, he had encountered many a follower of the Christian religion, and a pathetic religion it was, too. Only one God? Pfff! "I am Norse."

"I know who you are, Viking."

He did not say "Viking" in a complimentary manner. And, really, Harek needed to get to his bed and sleep off this alehead madness. Best he get this nightmare over with as soon as possible. "And you are here . . . why?"

"God is not pleased with you, Harek. You are a dreadful sinner, as are your brothers, as are many of your fellow Norsemen. 'Tis time to end it all."

"End it? Like, death?"

"You say it."

"All of us?" he scoffed.

"Eventually."

"We all must pass to the Other World *eventually*."

"That is not what I meant. Life as you know it will end shortly for you and your brothers; in fact, it has already for some of you. And the Viking race as a whole will dwindle away gradually over the centuries until there is no country that will claim you."

Huh? "That requires an explanation. Are you threatening me and my family?" Was this apparition implying that some of his brothers were already dead? Harek tried to recall the last time he had made contact with or heard from any of his family and realized it had been months. Inching backward from the looming figure, he hoped to reach a nearby oar, which he could use as a makeshift weapon. But he felt dizzy and wobbly on his feet. "I need to sit down."

"What you need, fool, is to pray."

What a ridiculous conversation! He could not wait to wake up and tell his friends about this strange dream. It would be fodder for the skalds who ever needed new ideas for their sagas. "Pray? For my life?" he scoffed.

"No. For your everlasting soul. Your death is predetermined."

Enough! This madness had gone on long enough! "Speak plainly," Harek demanded.

"Thou art a dreadful sinner, Harek. Dreadful! Your greed is eating you alive, and you do not even know it."

He must have appeared confused. Bloody hell, of course he was confused. "What have I done that is so bad?"

The man-thing—an archangel, he had called himself—shook his head as if Harek were a hopeless case. "Your most recent activity is so despicable. How can you even ask?"

"Oh! The slave trading! That is what this is about." Harek was disgusted up to his very gullet with all the sanctimonious condemnation of his business dealings. First Toriq. Now some angel with flea-bitten wings trying to lord over him.

"I do not have fleas."

That was just wonderful. The creature could read minds.

"And I am not a creature."

Harek inhaled deeply for patience and almost fell over. He reached the rail for support. "In truth, what is so wrong with thralldom? Your own biblical leaders—Abraham, David, Moses—had slaves." On occasion, Harek's father had hired monk scholars to tutor his sons, and, being a merchant, Harek had often traveled to Christian lands where the inhabitants considered it their mission in life to convert those "heathen Vikings." He knew more than most Christians about their book of rules and sagas.

"You dare to compare yourself to such great men!" The angel pointed a forefinger at Harek, and Harek felt a jolt of sharp pain shoot through him.

"I only meant—"

"Silence! For your sins, you will die, taking your mortal form with you. For the grace of God, you are being given a second chance to redeem yourself."

That caught Harek's attention, but he was an astute businessman. He knew no great prize came without a price. A second chance was going to cost him, sure as . . . well, sin. "And what must I do to redeem myself?"

"You will become a vangel—a vampire angel—one of the troops being formed to fight Satan's evil Lucipires, demon vampires."

Harek had no idea what a vam-pyre was. Sounded like something to do with fire. But angels . . . that, he did understand. "I am a Viking. I hardly think I am the material for saintly angelhood."

"You will not be that kind of angel."

"For how long would I be required to fight these . . . um, demons?" He was still not convinced this wasn't just a bad dream.

"As long as it takes. Seven hundred years at first. Longer, if you fail to follow the rules."

"Whoa! Seven hundred years?"

"Or longer."

"And there are rules?" *What am I . . . a youthling who needs to be told when he can do this or that? We shall see about that.*

"No great prize comes without a price?" Michael told him, repeating his own thoughts back at him. Again. "Do you agree?"

"Do I have a choice?"

"There is always a choice."

What did he have to lose? Besides, he was an intelligent man. He would find a way to reverse the decision later, if he so chose. Harek nodded, and before he had a chance to change his mind, the archangel pressed the tip of the broadsword against Harek's chest, causing him to lean backward, farther and farther, until he fell over the rail into the water.

It should have been no problem. He was a leather-lunged swimmer when need be, but his body was suddenly riddled with excruciating pain. His jaw felt as if it were being cracked, then forced back together with an iron vise. In fact, it felt as if he had long, fang-like incisors now. And his back! His shoulder blades seemed to burst open. The place where wings should go, he presumed, but no; a quick pass of his fingers over those spots revealed that the skin had healed into raised knots. All this happened in the matter of seconds as he sank deeper and deeper into the murky depths. Choking on the briny water. Fighting to swim upward against a force determined to hold him down. His ears began to ring, and a sense of lethargy overcame him. Drowning. He no longer fought his fate.

Even so, Harek had time and brains enough left to realize that he'd forgotten to ask one important question:

What exactly was a vangel?

Chapter 1

Somewhere in Siberia, A.D. 2015

The weather outside was frightful . . .

Harek was bundled up to his eyeballs, wearing three pairs of socks, lined boots, long johns, snow pants, a red and black wool jacket over a turtleneck sweater, thermal gloves, and a hunter's cap with ear flaps. But still he shivered as he attempted to thaw the ice-frozen lock on the door of his friggin' car, which probably wouldn't make it down the friggin' driveway to the friggin' one-lane highway that led to the nearest friggin' store where he could buy twenty-seven different kinds of bait, vodka by the gallon, but only one kind of friggin' beer.

Not that he had any interest in fishing or numbing his senses with the Russian alcohol, which was clear as water but as destructive as a Saxon's mace to the head. His brain was still his best asset. Besides, after one thousand, one hundred, and sixty-five years as a vangel, his job was still to kill Lucipires and to save humans on the verge of being taken by the demon vampires. And, yes, his initial "penance" as a vangel had been for seven hundred years, but every time he, or his brothers, committed some little, or big, transgression, like fornication (celibacy came hard for virile Vikings, *hard* being the key word), or excess drinking (these modern folks did make incredibly good beer), or gambling (his weakness), more years would be piled on. At this rate, they would be vangels until the Final Judgment.

"What in bloody hell are you doing?"

Harek glanced up to see a big black bear standing in his driveway. A *talking* bear!

He yelped with surprise and held up the whirring object in his hand as a weapon—a blow dryer attached to multiple extension cords leading into the garage electrical outlet. He'd forgotten to put his vehicle in said garage last night after a night of *drukkinn* gambling. Well, that sounded worse than it had been. A little beer and poker, that had been all. And today, all the car doors were frozen shut, the price of living in this godforsaken land in the middle of godforsaken nowhere where it was dark almost all the godforsaken time! No wonder the Russians drank so much! If only he had an AK–47! He could shoot the beast and have bear stew for a month. *Yuck!* If only the damn car doors would open, he could hop in and hope the animal would saunter away looking for a meal elsewhere. *Yeah, like that's going to happen!*

But then he realized that the bear was laughing. A talking, *laughing* bear?

"Is that the latest weapon here in Siberia?" the bear chortled. A bear with a voice very like his brother Vikar's. Harek narrowed his eyes and peered closer, difficult with the dim light coming from the open garage. It *was* his brother Vikar! Dressed in a black fur cloak that covered him from hooded head down to his boots.

"Very funny! I was trying to unfreeze the locks on my vehicle with a blow dryer, if you must know," he said, turning off the gun-like object and laying it on the hood of the car.

"You own a blow dryer?"

"Of course. Don't you?" Viking men were vain about their appearance, especially their hair. He would bet his last poker chip that Vikar used one for his long locks on a regular basis.

Vikar's shrug was his answer. And then he shivered. "It's colder than a witch's tit here. How do you stand it?"

"Not well," Harek admitted, not about to confess his latest lapse into gambling the night before. He turned and walked through the garage and into the house, where the blasting furnace provided some welcome warmth. A dozen vangel men resided here with him. By the sound of the television at the other end of the house, he could tell that at least some of them were watching yet another rerun of *The Walking Dead*, that ghoulish show about zombies. Thank God for satellites, which allowed them some limited television reception. Otherwise, they would probably have all turned to vodka by now.

Harek took the last two beers from the fridge in the kitchen and handed one to Vikar. His brother shoved the hood back on his cloak, which indeed seemed to have been made of bearskin, and took a long draw on the bottle.

"What are you doing here, Vikar? I mean, it's great to have the company, but even I wouldn't come here if I didn't have to."

"I've been sent to summon you."

"By whom?" *Dumb question.*

"Mike." That was the rude nickname the vangels had given their heavenly mentor/tormentor.

"Why didn't you just call me? You didn't need to come in person."

"I tried, but I kept getting a 'no service' message, even on our secure satellite phone."

Harek nodded. Reception here was erratic. "Why does Mike want me?"

"I have no clue. Maybe he has a mission for you."

Harek's spirits brightened immediately. Maybe he was forgiven. Maybe this would be his chance to leave his dark, freezing, godforsaken abode. "Let me go change. I'll see if I can schedule a flight."

"No time. Mike will only be in Transylvania for a few more hours. We have to teletransport."

Headquarters for the vangels was a creepy castle in the mountains of Transylvania, Pennsylvania. Not Romania. Teletransport was something vangels did only in emergencies.

"How about the vangels I have stationed here with me?"

"Just you, for now."

Thus it was that Harek found himself standing minutes later under a warm, eighty-degree sun next to the blue water of an in-ground swimming pool beyond the back courtyard of the castle, looking like an absolute fool in his arctic attire. The pool was a new addition to the run-down castle Vikar had been renovating for the past three years—a never-ending job, or so he claimed. Vikar had disappeared, probably to change his clothing. Yes, there he came from the back door wearing naught but a thigh-length, flowered bathing suit, grinning at him.

"Since when do Vikings wear flowers?" Harek grumbled.

"It's Hawaiian," Vikar said, as if that made a difference.

A few children—Vikar and Alex's little ones, the "adopted" Gunnar and Gunnora, along with Sigurd's stepdaughter, Isobel—were swimming at one end of the pool like little ducks. Vikings were known to take to the water, any water, from a young age. But everyone else was gawking at him. His six brothers, in and out of the water, including Vikar, who dived neatly into the pool splashing everyone within ten feet, and some enjoying cold brews in frosted bottles. Their wives, those who had them, sat about under umbrella tables, sipping from tall glasses sporting skewers of fruit. And several dozen vangels basked in the sun and hot tub. Lizzie Borden, their cook (yes, *that* Lizzie Borden), scurried back and forth between the kitchen and the patio carrying trays of snacks.

There was also a tub of ice holding bottles of Fake-O, the synthetic blood vangels needed in between the real blood gained from fanging saved humans or by destroying Lucipires. Without it, vangel skin would become lighter and lighter, almost transparent, especially in sunlight. With it, their skin glowed with seeming suntanned health.

"Oh, this is fair! I'm off to Arctic Neverland freezing my arse off while you all enjoy a pool party!" Harek yanked off his cap, uncaring that his hair probably stood up on end, making him look even more ridiculous, and shrugged out of his jacket.

Behind him he heard a voice say, "Art thou speaking to me, Viking?" The voice did not say "Viking" in an endearing manner.

It was Michael, of course. Not in the white robes typical of an archangel, or of the warrior attire often seen in Michael the Archangel statues, but good ol' faded Levi's with a white T-shirt and Nikes, his long, dark hair flowing down to his shoulders. Despite the modern garments, there was no mistaking that this was a celestial being, even without the sunshiny halo that surrounded him. At least he wasn't wearing swimming trunks. Harek didn't think he was up for viewing hairy angel legs . . . if they were, in fact, hairy.

Before Harek had a chance to respond, Michael asked, hands on hips, "Do you have my home site ready to load up on the computer highway for me?"

Harek barely restrained himself from rolling his eyes. Michael tried to be modern by using contemporary language, but he frankly didn't know a computer mouse from a rodent. He'd been wanting Harek to set up an archangel site for him on the Internet, in keeping with social networking of the times, but he kept changing his mind about what he wanted. First, it was going to be an information place, which Harek had told him was too boring and would get no traffic. Then it was going to be a blog, but Michael could never decide what subjects to discuss first. Then it was going to be an advice column, questions sent in by viewers and answered by himself, but Harek had warned him that he might not like the questions he would be asked. Truth to tell, an angelic presence on the Internet was a good idea, if only Michael could make up his mind exactly what he wanted.

"Um . . ." Harek answered.

"I would have thought with all the extra time thou had there in the colds of Siberia it would be done by now," Michael remarked. "It is not as if you have rid the Russian lands of all Lucipires. Yakov still flourishes, I understand."

Yakov, a former Russian Cossack, was one of the high haakai demon vampires on the council headed by Jasper, king of all the Lucipires. Yakov's home base was somewhere in Siberia, in a place called Desolation, a site Harek had not yet been able to locate, precisely, although he was close.

"That is unfair! I have destroyed many of Yakov's minions and saved many of his victims during my exile. I have fought beside my brothers on every mission to which I've been called. My kill and save records are nothing to scoff at."

"Exile, is it now?" Michael homed in on that one, insignificant part of what he'd said.

But Harek recognized immediately that his word had been ill-chosen, and he, whose intelligence was his greatest asset, was at a loss for a better word. *What in bloody hell am I doing, arguing with an archangel?* He could tell by the silence around him and the disbelieving expressions on his brothers' faces that they were stunned by his audacity.

"As for your sudden emphasis on fairness," Michael went on. "If life were fair, you would be roasting on a spit in that Other Place."

"Sorry," Harek murmured, and raised his chin, waiting for whatever punishment would be doled his way.

But then Michael smiled.

He is smiling.

At me?

When an angel smiled, a heavenly warmth enveloped the recipient. When an archangel smiled, an indescribable sensation of peace flowed forth. It was like a blessing.

Huh? Harek was confused.

"In truth, we are pleased with your work, Harek. Why else would I have summoned you to head this new mission?" He put a hand on Harek's shoulder and squeezed. "Come. We have much to discuss."

Dazed, Harek followed Michael into the castle, through the back doors leading into the massive kitchen (Lizzie's domain), down a long corridor (sporting murals depicting angels, what else? Angels with cute little fangs!), past a dining room (that could seat fifty in a crunch), a chapel (with hard-as-stone pews and kneelers), an office (where Vikar pissed and moaned about all his work leading the vangels; like herding cats, he claimed), a computer center (Harek's pride and joy), salons converted into family and television rooms (vangels had a lot of time to pass between missions; there probably wasn't a G-rated movie they hadn't seen, and, yes, R-rated ones, too, for their sins), then into the front, formal living room. His brothers and several of the more experienced vangels, like Karl, Svein, and Jogeir, followed after Harek and Michael. Chairs had already been set up in a half circle with a high-backed upholstered chair in its center.

Michael started the meeting in his usual manner, with a prayer. "Lord, bless and protect your warrior vangels as they embark on a new mission." When they were all seated, Michael addressed Harek. "Are you familiar with Boko Haram in Nigeria?"

The Islamic extremists best known for abducting young girls for sex slaves and forced child brides. Harek nodded. This was his expertise. Intelligence information. Despite his living at the end of beyond, he had spotty Internet access to the latest news. He wished he'd been forewarned and could have gathered more data, but still he could say, "The terrorist cell Boko Haram, or BK, started as a religious insurgency movement fighting to make it 'haram' or 'forbidden' for Muslims to engage in any political or social activity associated with Western culture, like the education of girls, but it has escalated into a militant insurrection intent on atrocities, sometimes for mere shock value. It has been in operation for more than five years, but the mass kidnappings became one of their prime tactics a year or so ago. Despite worldwide condemnation, especially when they took captive almost three hundred schoolgirls from Chibok in Nigeria, they are getting stronger and bolder. Bombing towns, setting fire to huts and businesses, stealing animals and what little food there is, in essence making thousands of people homeless."

Michael exchanged looks with some of the others, as if to say, *That Harek! A walking encyclopedia, he is.*

"What? Is intelligence a sin now, too?"

"Only when it is accompanied by greed. Do not be so sensitive, Harek," Michael admonished. Then, "Cnut, tell us what you know. And, please, spare us the lecture."

Cnut was their security expert, head of a company called Wings International Security. Most of the vangels held outside jobs—doctor, Navy SEAL, prison chaplain, whatever—as a front for those times when they were not involved in vampire angel business. Lately, Cnut had taken to a strange hairstyle, strange even for a Norseman, based on that Ragnar Lothbrok character on the History Channel's popular *Vikings* series. It was shaved on either side of his head, with intricate braids forming a sort of scalp lock through the center, from forehead to nape and down to his shoulders.

But that was neither here nor there.

"I've been in Nigeria for the past few months, primarily around Maiduguri, and the tangos are amping up for an operation that might very well outdo the atrocities of the Chibok school attack." *Tango* was a term they'd learned, and adopted, from their brother Trond, a Navy SEAL. It meant terrorist or bad guy. "Jasper is in the area and Lucies are infiltrating their ranks, right and left."

That was news to most of them. Truly, the Lucies were like cockroaches; annihilate their nests in one area and they pop up in another. It wasn't surprising, though, that Jasper would target such evil men. Hell, it might even have been Lucies who started the organization to begin with. Evil begets evil, or something like that.

Cnut set up an easel and put a large map of Africa on it that could be seen by all of them. "Everywhere you see an X indicates a place where an attack has taken place in the past two years. You can see how their range of operation is expanding. I've been able to pinpoint the location of some of their cells; those are indicated with a checkmark. There's no main headquarters to target because they keep moving, especially in the dense Sambisa Forest area. But here's the thing. They're planning something big in the next few weeks. Really big. Possibly hitting the Global School in Kamertoon, where there are multinational students. It's located halfway between the capital of Abuja and the Sambisa Forest. Or they could aim for several of the Global Schools for girls, located throughout Africa, all at one time. The Global Schools are particularly repugnant to Boko Haram because they're privately owned by an American conglomerate."

"What do you want us to do?" Harek asked.

"I'll need help," Cnut said, waving a hand around the room. "Even with the two dozen vangels I have there with me, it's not enough. Initially, though, I think it should be a three-pronged effort. Harek, if you and your team would come back to Nigeria with me, I can familiarize you with the situation, firsthand. With your trusty laptop, you could probably get better intelligence than I could in half the time." That was true. Harek knew more about computers than Bill Gates, if he did say so himself. "Then you'll travel to Coronado, California, where you'll be our link with Trond and the Navy SEALs."

Trond, who was a member of those elite special forces, sat up straighter. Apparently, this was the first he'd heard of his involvement.

Harek frowned with confusion. "Why would we involve the SEALs?" Usually, vangels worked alone. There was always the danger of discovery. He could see the headline now, "Vampire Angels Help Navy SEALs Save the Day." Or vice versa.

"It is not the job of vangels to save innocents,"

Michael answered for Cnut. "Let the human heroes rescue those children who have been abducted or are about to be taken. Vangels will destroy the Lucipires and save any evil humans who choose to repent."

"What makes you think the Navy will welcome any outside involvement?" Trond asked, looking at Cnut and Harek.

"Even the Navy will appreciate the intelligence Harek will bring them, hitherto unknown information about the terrorists," Michael said. "It will be up to you, Harek, to imply that Wings works for the Nigerian government,"

"A lie? You are encouraging me to lie?" Harek inquired of the archangel, going for a bit of levity.

Michael didn't even smile; in fact he frowned, and his brothers rolled their eyes at Harek's mistake.

"Is Harek going to become a Navy SEAL, too?" Trond asked hopefully. "I can't wait to see him go through Hell Week. He'll probably puke his guts out the first time he's put through drownproofing."

"I do not think that will be necessary," Michael said, frowning at Trond, too, for his teasing in the midst of a serious discussion. "As I said, Harek can be at the SEAL compound as a representative of a private security company with information on one of their targets . . . Boko Haram," Michael explained. "In the past, before 9/11, SEALs operated mainly on their own, but with terrorism rising by the day, and not enough time to train a corresponding number of new SEALs, they have had to work with other special forces and agencies."

"Other countries even send their best soldiers to train with us, to learn the Navy SEAL way," Trond added. "So outside persons on the compound aren't unknown."

Harek nodded, and could feel excitement begin to pump through his veins. It was always an adrenaline rush when a new mission began. Besides, the climate in California was warm. Anything was better than freeze-your-arse Siberia. And maybe, if he completed this mission well, he would no longer be exiled. Maybe he would even be sent somewhere pleasant, like the Caribbean, where he had a hidden retreat, earned with his stock market winnings. Maybe the powers-that-be, i.e., Mike, would realize that his talents were better used far from the frozen north. Maybe he would even be permitted to form his own technology company, for the good of the vangel cause, of course.

He could swear he heard laughter in his head.

His head shot up, and sure enough, Michael was looking directly at him, his eyebrows arched.

On the other hand, maybe not.

Chapter 2

Roses are red, violets are blue, she stunk, all right, pee-you! . . .

Camille Dumaine was dragging her feet as she walked from the beach at the Coronado Navy SEAL training compound, her almost-thirty-year-old bones feeling every jarring step of her just completed six-mile jog in heavy boots on wet sand under a bright, ninety-degree California sun. Fun, fun, fun!

Didn't help that she was sweating like a pig or that one of the swabbies in the newbie class had barfed all over her during "sugar cookies," an exercise designed to punish. Also didn't help that she heard a male voice call out, "Yo, Camo! The CO wants to see you."

It was Trond Sigurdsson, whose Navy SEAL nickname was Easy. All SEALs got appropriate, and not-so-appropriate, nicknames when they first entered BUD/S training, Basic Underwater Demolition SEAL. Goose, Whiz, Stud, Dog, K–4, Geek, Spidey, Zombie, F.U., JAM, Slick. Trond, or Easy, was a mite lazy, known to always look for the easy way.

Same nicknaming was true of the elite WEALS, Women on Earth, Air, Land, and Sea, the sister unit to the SEALs, of which Camille was a charter member, two years of training and five years on duty now. Thus Camille's nickname of Camo, which wasn't a play on her name, or not totally, but was based on her ability to camouflage herself, no matter the setting. Being invisible in a crowd could be invaluable for a special forces operative, male or female, she'd learned on more than one occasion. It was one of the prime reasons she'd been recruited to begin with.

A chameleon, that's what she would put on her résumé, if she had one. Who knew, growing up in New Orleans's upscale Garden District, that being of average height and weight, with plain brown hair and eyes, and just a touch of Creole coloring in her skin, would be such an asset? Certainly not her, and definitely not her father and mother, Dr. Emile Dumaine and Dr. Jeannette Dumaine, world-renowned professors of Southern studies at Tulane University and authors of numerous books on the subject, or her overachieving brother, Alain Dumaine, who was a NASA rocket scientist—(*No kidding! There really are rocket scientists.*)—currently teaching at Princeton University. But she had learned early on that, with the aid of makeup, clothing, a wig, even something as simple as posture or hand gestures, she could change herself into whatever she wanted to be. (*Honest, Mother, I wasn't in the French Quarter after midnight. You heard the police description of those underage kids, "drunk as skunks." And they thought one was me? Blond, six foot tall, boobs out to here. Ha, ha, ha.*)

"I need to shower first," she told Easy.

"I think Mac means *now.* They've been holding off the meeting 'til you got back from your run." He sniffed the air and took a step back, even as he spoke, and then grinned. Easy knew well and good that SEALs and WEALS had to work just as hard, physically, after they'd earned their trident pins, to keep in shape. Smelling ripe was not so unusual. "The more you sweat in training, the less you bleed in battle" was a familiar mantra. "Just make sure you stand downwind," Trond suggested.

A meeting? He mentioned a meeting? She went immediately alert. Rumors had been circulating for weeks about a new mission. One that involved taking down those African scumbags who had been kidnapping young girls for sex slaves. Boko Haram, or whatever terrorist-du-jour group felt compelled to perform atrocities for some self-professed higher good. Camille felt passionately about what was being done to these innocent children in the name of religion, and she wanted in on this mission. Partly she was infuriated by a women's rights issue, but it was also her history as a Creole that fueled her fire. Camille's great-grandmother many times removed—her namesake, actually—had been "sold" at one of the famous pre–Civil War Quadroon Balls when she was only fifteen.

She watched as another man joined Easy. The similarities, and the differences, between the two men were immediately apparent. Both were very tall, probably six foot four, lean, and well muscled, but whereas Easy's attire—athletic shorts, drab green SEAL T-shirt, and baseball cap, socks, and boondockers—said military to the bone, this guy wore a golf shirt tucked into khaki pants with a belt sporting an odd buckle in the shape of wings, designer loafers without socks, and a spiffy gold watch. Whereas Easy looked as if he was about to work the O-course, the other man carried an over-the-shoulder, high-end, leather laptop case, more suited to Simi Valley. The most dramatic difference was between Easy's dark high-and-tight haircut, and the new guy's light brown hair spritzed into deliberate disarray. The pale blue eyes they both shared were the gravy on this feast for the eyes.

Camille wasn't drawn to overendowed men, especially ones who were so vain they moussed their hair in the morning, especially since she worked in testosterone central where muscles were the norm, but holy moly! This man, probably no more than thirty, was the epitome of sex on the hoof.

She licked her lips and forced herself to calm down. *I look like hell,* she reminded herself. *On a good day, this superior male specimen wouldn't give me a passing glance. After three failed near-marriages, I do not need another complication. Wash your mind, girl. While I'm at it, I better check to make sure I'm not drooling.* "Your brother, I presume?" she said to Easy.

"How could you tell?" Easy said with a laugh. "Camo, this is my brother Harek Sigurdsson. Harek"—he nodded his head in her direction—"this is Camille Dumaine, the female Navy SEAL I told you about."

Why would Easy be discussing me with his brother? Definitely not proper protocol for secretive special forces members to be made known to civilians, even a family member. *And why do the SEALs continually refer to the WEALS as female SEALs, as if they aren't a powerful force on their own? So irritating!* She frowned at Easy, who just grinned. The idiot! Even if he was married to a fellow WEALS member and a good friend of Camille's, Nicole Tasso, his charm was wasted on her.

His brother, on the other hand . . . whoo boy!

She took the hand that Harek extended to her as he said, "I've heard so much about you that—"

They both froze, extended hands still clasped. A sensation, like an electrical shock, except softer and coming in waves, rippled from his fingers into hers, then rushed to all her extremities. It was like having world-class sex without all the bother.

"What is that odor?" Harek asked, as if stunned.

Talk about an instant lust destroyer! "Vomit," she disclosed.

He shook his head. "No. Roses." He closed his eyes, leaned forward slightly, and inhaled deeply. "Hundreds and hundreds of roses." Turning to his brother, he asked, "Can't you smell it?"

"Are you demented? She smells like she's been rolling in . . ." Easy's voice trailed off as something seemed to occur to him. "The mating scent! Finally! You've been bitten! Oh man! Oh man! Mike swore a moratorium on any more human mating. I can't wait to tell Vikar and the others."

"No! That's impossible!" Harek stared at her now like she was some strange, repulsive creature. And what was it with those slightly elongated incisors of his? She hadn't noticed them at first. Not that they looked bad. It was just that today, with all the modern orthodontics, folks, especially male ones pretentious enough to get designer haircuts (she would bet his cost at least a hundred dollars at some high-priced unisex salon), would have corrected the imperfection.

"What scent? What bite?" *Did he say something about mating? Human mating? Huh? As compared to nonhuman mating? And mating crap? Is that code for sex?* "Oh hell! I don't have time for this nonsense. I need to see what the CO wants." She tugged her hand out of Mr. Sexy's continued clasp and was about to walk away.

Easy, who had been bent over laughing, raised his head and said, "'Tis the musk men and women in my, uh, family give off when they meet their destined life mates."

Well, that was clear as mud, especially since Harek was muttering, "No, no, no! Not now. Not her! I just got back from Siberia. I haven't thawed out yet."

"You come from Siberia? Nobody comes from Siberia."

"Well, I came from Siberia originally, by way of Pennsylvania, and then Nigeria . . . all those -ia places."

Is he trying to be funny? Dolt! No, he seems to be serious. Idiot, then.

"Harek is always being sent to Siberia as a punishment," Trond told her.

"By whom?"

"Our . . . uh, employer." Trond's blue eyes darted right and left, as if recognizing he'd revealed something he shouldn't have.

"Your employer is Uncle Sam," she pointed out.

"Another, higher authority," Trond said enigmatically.

"No, I don't *come* from Siberia. I come from Transylvania," Harek replied distractedly, still shaking his head as if to ward off some repulsive thought. Her.

"Romania? You live in Transylvania, Romania?" Why she fixated on this irrelevant fact in the midst of all the other stuff was a puzzle, one she would consider . . . later.

"He means Transylvania, Pennsylvania. Our hometown," Trond explained, since his brother seemed speechless except for the continual muttering, "Life mate? No way! Not now. Not her."

"What the hell is a life mate? And why not me? Forget I asked that." As for thawing out from Siberia, or Transylvania, or the frickin' moon, if he was any hotter, Harek would combust. She gave the obviously distressed man a glare and turned on Trond. "As for musk and your family, in case you need a reminder, Easy, I am not a member of your family."

"Yet," Easy said ominously.

Harek looked as if he was going to throw up.

Welcome to my life, Camille thought.

Chapter 3

Date with a vampire?...

"Well, that was humiliating," Harek said once he and Trond were seated in the command center's conference room, where several dozen military types, mostly male, milled about, waiting for the meeting to start.

"Humiliating for whom? You or Camo?"

"Me, of course. I behaved like a pathetic moron."

"Yep. Lost your Viking charm somewhere along the way. Probably frozen in a Siberian tundra. Do they have tundra in Siberia?"

Harek ignored Trond's question, musing that he would probably have to apologize to the woman. He wasn't exactly sure what he had said while in that rose-infused haze, but he was fairly certain he'd said something about her not being suitable as life mate for his far superior self, or some such thing. Which was true, but not what one said to a woman. Even he, Viking to the chauvinistic core, knew that. Besides, he hadn't meant "suitable" precisely. More like not now, not in this place, not with a female warrior woman. Not ever.

Well, that was better.

Not.

He took his laptop out of its case, along with some printouts he'd made of his BK findings, in addition to Cnut's initial assessment. Harek loved modern technology, and he was good at it. Passionate to always learn more. Luckily, it was one passion that wasn't deemed sinful.

Meanwhile, Trond's wife, Nicole, who was also one of those WEALS, came in and sat on Trond's other side. Harek had stayed with them last night in their Coronado apartment, which was one night too many. With his years of forced celibacy, he did not need to hear energetic bedplay from down the hall, *all night long*. It was a wonder the two of them could stand without toppling over. When Harek had remarked just so to Trond this morning and said he would be looking for a hotel room for the remainder of his stay, Trond had just graced him with a lackwit grin. In fact, all five of his married brothers—Vikar, Trond, Ivak, Mordr, and Sigurd—walked around with the selfsame lackwit grins all the time. It was disgusting, really, and pitiful for Viking men who were accustomed to excessive bedsport. Leastways, they had been in the old days, especially during the long Norse nights, which were almost as cold as bloody Siberia.

His reverie was broken as Camille walked in with two other women—a tall, majestic-looking black beauty, and a shorter blonde with the biceps of a weightlifter. They all wore similar workout attire: T-shirts, shorts, and boots. Camille had changed to a clean shirt, scrubbed her face, and pulled her shoulder-length hair into a ponytail in the short time since he'd met her.

He no longer smelled roses, thank the Lord. Of course, the woman was across the room from him, but still he didn't feel that odd, magnetic pull he had earlier. Trond was wrong about the life mate crap. Harek must have overdeveloped olfactory senses, like his sharp intellect, and the floral scent must have emanated from some distant flower garden, carried on the breeze. Leastways, that was his theory, and he was sticking to it.

Besides, she was not at all his type of woman. Not that she was bad-looking, now that she was somewhat cleaned up. But she was plain. Harek, on the other hand, was an exceedingly good-looking Viking man in his prime. Because of his appearance—and his wealth, he had to admit—he'd always had the pick of the litter when it came to women. Even his first wife, Dagne, had been a spectacular beauty before she'd turned fat and shrewish. Women had a tendency to do that, lure a man in with outward glitter, sweet as honey in the beginning, which ended up being mere brass, not gold, and sour as pickles. Bait and switch, in modern terminology. Mayhap a plain woman would make the better life mate, if a man were dumb enough to be looking for a partner locked to his side forevermore.

No, no, no! I am not looking for a partner, plain

or otherwise. This is my chance to prove myself with Mike, to get my stupid arse out of freezing Siberia, for good. If I start getting carnal thoughts, and acting on them, heaven forbid, I'll be growing ice crystals on my testicles forever.

Not that he was having carnal thoughts about Camille, who sat down in one of the front rows with her female companions.

Yet, he thought he heard a voice in his head say.

It was probably his conscience. He hoped it was his conscience.

If he was going to have carnal thoughts, it wouldn't be about a female whose goal in life was to prove she could do everything a man could. It would be about someone like that Lagertha, the Norse princess in the History Channel's *Vikings* series. Now, there was a woman! Actually, Lagertha was a female warrior, too, but when she leaped into the bed furs with Ragnar, she was all woman. Betimes a woman being the aggressor was a good thing. A very good thing! *I wonder if Camille . . .*

No, I am not wondering anything about her.

Anyhow, forget Lagertha. Harek much preferred a wench with a body like that singer Jennifer Lopez. He liked a well-formed woman with an ample—but not too ample—arse.

There was another worrisome thing. Harek's deadly sin was greed, and he had come to accept the truth of his dark compulsions. He was indeed greedy about all things, not just wealth or stature or physical trappings. What if he were given free rein with a woman—a life mate, for cloud's sake!—how might his greed manifest itself in sex after all these years of being reined in? He could only imagine the kinds of things he would do.

"Harek!" His drifting thoughts were interrupted by a man in a dull beige military uniform, seated at a table on the low dais at the front of the room, waving him forward. It was Navy SEAL Lt. Darryl "Geek" Good, whom he'd met on several occasions in the past.

He and Darryl had much in common, in addition to both being geeks of a sort. Geek, once an insult, was now modern slang for "very intelligent person." Darryl had the face of a baby, or untried youthling, but the brain of a genius, which was deceptive. The "boy" had not only been around the block a time or twenty, he knew things the average man did not. *Like me,* Harek thought with a shameless pat on his own back. Darryl's IQ was almost as high as Harek's and his computer skills on a par with Harek's, too.

In addition, Darryl was probably a millionaire due to his invention of something called a penile glove, which he sold on the Internet. Enough said! Unlike Harek, Darryl's entrepreneurial skills were not impeded by celestial interference. Talk about unfair! Truth to tell, Harek had hidden assets that . . .

Harek immediately tried to wipe that last thought from his mind, just in case you-know-who was "listening" in. He was not in the mood for yet another "Life Is Not Meant to Be Fair" lecture. Gathering up his laptop, paperwork, and carry bag, he walked up to the dais to join Darryl, who stood and shook hands with him. "Good to see you again, man! Did you get that rough draft I sent you last night?"

"I did. Thank you. Did my BK slides convert into your system?"

"Like a wet dream. Where'd you get that Powerfont program?"

"Developed it myself. Couldn't find anything on the market that combined dimensional PowerPoint with subtext and algorithms."

"Ah." The gleam in Darryl's eyes was pure geekful. It took a geek to understand how another geek could get turned on by a new technological invention. Darryl added, "I could show you how to market that program if you want."

Like Mike would ever allow that! Besides, I do not want to know what he'd have to say about Darryl's penile glove enterprise. "No time for that at the present, but thanks for the offer."

He opened his laptop on the table next to Darryl's and pointed out some new information, which the SEAL immediately began to copy to a flash drive. He and Darryl had been working together, via e-mail, the past few days, trying to combine and collate Wings International Security intelligence with that of the Navy SEALs, related to Boko Haram.

While Darryl was busy tapping away on his computer, Harek glanced around the room and noticed Camille staring at him with raised eyebrows. Apparently, she was surprised to see him here, participating in a mostly SEAL meeting. She'd probably thought he was on the base just visiting his brother.

He winked at her.

Whaaat? Why he would do such an asinine thing in a professional setting, he had no idea. But then he was behaving like an ass today.

She blushed and shook her head, as if he was a hopeless idiot. Which he was. Today, leastways.

Commander Ian MacLean called the meeting to order. "We are here today to discuss a new mission. Deadly Wind."

Everyone sat up straighter, interested.

MacLean paused for dramatic emphasis, then explained, "The Islamic extremists in Nigeria are spreading, like an ill wind, to use a poor cliché, and it will be our job to not only rescue the victims already in their captivity, but to destroy the tangos, once and for all."

Applause greeted his words, and a communal shout of "Hoo-yah!" That was SEAL talk for "Hell, yeah!" or some such thing.

"You're probably wondering, why now? Everyone expected SEALs to come to the rescue, guns blazing . . . as if that's ever the case, or hardly ever."

Laughter greeted those words. Everyone in the world had heard about that incident in Mosul last year.

"But thus far our government's stance has been to provide only technical assistance. In other words, consultants," MacLean continued, that last word said with a sneer. "Now, they want our help, especially because of the international outcry at the BK group's atrocities. Many Muslim sects practice Sharia law, but BK carries it to an extreme not seen, at least in the public eye, for centuries."

Sharia was an ultraconservative interpretation of Islamic law that included, among other things, honor stonings of women for adultery, and harsh punishments of even small children. One little boy accused of stealing bread had to have his hand crushed by holding it under the wheel of a moving dump truck. Mostly, Sharia was anti-women to an extent that females were considered nothing more than possessions. No wonder they could justify kidnapping schoolgirls!

"This will be a joint JSOC effort of SEALs, Rangers, Delta Force, AFSOP, and Wings International Security, a private security firm we've worked with in the past," MacLean said. "Wings has crucial and credible intel on BK's current location and plans." He nodded toward Harek at that last remark. "We will be boots on the ground in Africa in two weeks. In the meantime, you operatives will be working your butts off in preparation. If you're in this room now, you are Chosen." The commander grinned.

To their credit, not one of the three dozen or so SEALs or WEALS appeared reluctant at being called to duty. In fact, they were excited, if the expressions on their faces were any indication, including Miss Dumaine, who smiled widely, exposing rows of even white teeth, a sharp contrast against her lightly tanned skin.

(Harek had been yearning for *even* teeth for many years, by the by. Fangs got in the way, even when retracted, for lots of things, like eating corn on the cob, sipping through a straw, blowing up a balloon, going down on . . . Never mind. Even kissing, an activity sorely lacking in his life for a looong time.)

Harek noted that Camille wasn't so plain when she smiled. Not that it mattered. Just . . . interesting.

The commander called Lieutenant Luke "Slick" Avenil up to the dais and deferred to him as leader of this mission. Avenil, whose dark hair was sprinkled with strands of silver on the sides, was older than most of the SEALs, at close to forty. Aside from being a highly decorated military man, Avenil was street-smart from a young age. A good man to have at your back. As Harek recalled from talks with Trond, Avenil was a long-divorced man whose ex-wife's sole goal in life seemed to be taking him back to court for more and more alimony.

Once the commander left the stage, Avenil introduced about a dozen of the non-SEAL folks in the room. Two CIA agents, a Department of Defense deputy secretary of something or other, reps of Army and Air Force special forces, a member of the ruling council of Nigeria, and then Harek, who would be the liaison with Wings, which already had "boots on the ground" in Nigeria, meaning Cnut, although his name wasn't mentioned specifically. Avenil also introduced Lieutenant Darryl Good, and motioned for both Harek and Darryl to stand and present the initial data for the mission.

Darryl used a remote device to lower a large screen from the ceiling. On it, the two of them began projecting graphics from their high-tech computers, a running slide show of geography, including thermal imaging, where the terrorists were believed to be hiding out, places they had targeted in the past, new sites they were believed to be aiming for in the future. There were also photographs of some of the leaders, with bios. A short lesson on the history of the Boko Haram organization, how it had started as a religious fight against encroaching Western culture, such as educating girls, and escalated into an all-out bloody insurrection of terror.

Harek and Darryl worked well together. While one spoke, the other operated the computers, then vice versa. For more than an hour they gave the attentive audience all the data they needed to begin to plan their mission. Questions were tossed out intermittently and answered as best they could. When the two of them were stumped, the commander or some of the government folks spoke up. Sometimes there were no answers. This vile group, Boko Haram, wouldn't have managed to continue with its atrocities for so long if they weren't able to maintain secrecy.

When one man complained, "I'll never remember all this crap," Avenil interjected, "You better remember, F.U., or you could drop off this mission."

Avenil wasn't being crude, or out of order, when he told the SEAL to F.U.; it was actually the nickname for the man who'd spoken up, Frank Uxley, Harek recalled now. A highly skilled soldier, but with the personality of a toad.

"In any case, printouts of all this data will be in

folders at your seats by this afternoon. However, you are to study them here. Nothing leaves the command center. Is that clear?" He was speaking to the entire room, not just Uxley. "Secrecy is essential. Paperwork has a way of getting lost or stolen."

Everyone nodded in understanding.

"Now, let's break for lunch. For those of you not familiar with the base, just follow the crowd to the chow hall. Everyone, report back to the command center at fourteen hundred hours. If any of you have reservations or reasons for not participating in this mission, you can speak to me or the commander now. If you have questions about the mission itself, I prefer you save them for Darryl or Harek in the afternoon session. Do not discuss details outside this room in a public place, even among yourselves. And, yes, the chow hall is a public place."

As people began shuffling out of the room, laughing and talking in small groups, he heard Camille address MacLean. "Commander, sir, I want very much to be part of this mission, but as you recall, I have liberty next weekend to attend my brother's wedding in Nawleans. I was supposed to be leaving day after tomorrow, Friday night."

"Oh, that's right. Damn! I really wanted you to participate . . . maybe even infiltrate the school as a student, but . . ." He shrugged. "Family is important, too."

Harek, who was blatantly eavesdropping, couldn't imagine in a million years how Camille, close to thirty years old, could ever pass for a schoolgirl.

"No, no, no," Camille quickly put in. "I don't want to be excused. If it comes to a choice, I'll blow the wedding." By the flush on her face, he could tell that would be harder than she let on. If it was her brother who was being married, she was probably in the wedding party. Women cared overmuch about such things. "I was just wondering if I could be excused for those two days. It's early in the planning stages for this op, and I could have someone bring me up to speed Sunday night on what I missed over the weekend."

"I don't know," MacLean said, obviously not convinced.

"I could go with her to Louisiana and drill her on all the intel," Harek offered. "In private, not public places," he quickly added, recalling Avenil's admonition about secrecy. "Besides, Geek and I won't be starting our presentation until Monday. And . . . uh . . . I have a brother who's a chaplain at Angola Prison that I wouldn't mind visiting."

No one was more shocked by the offer than Harek himself. *What in bloody hell am I thinking? Go with a woman—even a plain one, such as her—for two whole days? I am a Viking, not a eunuch.* On the other hand, after the bone-deep cold of Siberia, the steam heat of the South would be a welcome change for Harek.

"Oh no, that wouldn't be necessary," Camille demurred, and shot him a glare for having made the suggestion.

"I didn't realize you two knew each other." MacLean studied them suspiciously.

"We don't," Camille said.

"We met earlier," Harek blurted out, fool that he was, "but Camille is right. We don't really know . . ."

But MacLean was already nodding. "Good, good! Not ideal, but that could work. Mostly we'll just be going over and over the data presented today, and engaging in physical training. The real work begins Monday with a trip a few days later down to San Clemente Island for jungle survival training. And, actually, Camo, you'll probably learn more from Harek than you would here in a boring classroom."

"That's what I'm afraid of," he heard her mutter.

Hey, he was the one being inconvenienced here. She should be thankful. Instead, once excused, she said, rather ungraciously, "I'll give you the details about the wedding later." And a piece of her mind, Harek was sure. "Do you own a tux?" she added.

"Sure," he said.

Once she stomped off, Trond stepped up. "That was nice of you."

"Bullshit!" Harek replied.

"Still smelling roses?"

"Bite me."

"Nah. I think I'll leave that to your weekend date."

"It is not a date."

"Seriously, Harek, what were you thinking?"

"I wasn't."

They both frowned at each other, and said as one, "Mike!"

It had to be Michael, their celestial pain in the arse, who'd planted the idea in his head. Why, he hadn't a clue, but it was exactly the way the archangel worked. Putting them in inexplicable situations, and leaving it to them to figure out why. Like they were puppets and he pulled their strings, giving them just enough leeway to fall on their faces.

"Are you coming to the chow hall with me?" Trond asked. There were only a few people left in the room now.

"No, I'm not hungry. Besides, I have to find someplace to rent a tux."

Chapter 4

Some folks get their chocolate fix with candy, others . . .

The first chance Camille had to talk with Harek, who was obviously avoiding her since putting her in an uncomfortable situation with the commander yesterday, was mile four of their six-mile warm-up exercise the next morning, just after dawn. He was trailing at the end of the twenty members of the Deadly Wind team jogging along the sandy beach of the Pacific Ocean. She had to slow herself down to keep pace with the idiot.

Active participation in the SEAL physical training during this two-week pre-op period was considered optional for the outside folks, though highly recommended. The Justice Department reps were certainly not about to exert themselves in this way. And she'd noticed the CIA guys showed up only midway through the run, having probably had a leisurely breakfast at the Hotel Del beforehand. A logical deduction since they were soon hurling the contents of their stomach along the way. Everyone knew you should eat after a long run, not before. Jeesh!

Harek was wearing only running shorts and boots with white socks rolled over the top, like many of the men. She and the other five women out this morning wore the same, except covered on top with WEALS T-shirts.

Despite being in seemingly good physical condition—in fact, really good physical condition, as evidenced by the striated six-pack in his abdomen and long, extended muscles in his legs—Harek was huffing away like a locomotive. Visitors to Coronado were always asking to run with the SEALs—congressmen, celebrities, even presidents—not realizing just how difficult a workout it would be. They rarely finished any particular rotation.

Rivulets of sweat soaked Harek's hair, which had lost its mousse about mile two, and ran down his face and over his chest. His face was flushed as he concentrated on placing one foot after another.

"Why don't you quit before you have a heart attack?" she suggested. "You have nothing to prove here."

"Go. Away," he gasped out, and didn't even look at her.

"Only trying to help."

He grunted.

"Like you helped me. Yesterday."

Nothing.

"You know, with the commander. Intruding into my personal life by inviting yourself to my brother's wedding."

Nothing.

"What's with that anyhow? Most men have to be dragged kicking and screaming to a wedding. Are you gay or something? Like Julia Roberts's gay friend Rupert Everett in *My Best Friend's Wedding*."

That at least drew a killing glance that pretty much said, *Not fucking gay!*

"I don't even know you. Why would you pull that kind of crap?"

He increased his stride. Since he had about eight inches in height on her, she had to zip up her own pace to catch up.

"What's your game anyhow?"

He turned her way without breaking stride. Maybe he wasn't as out of shape as she'd first thought. "Can't a guy"—pant, pant—"just be nice"—pant, pant—"without ulterior"—pant, pant—"motives?"

"Mr. Nice Guy, huh? Nope. Not buyin' it. And forget that life mate crap. Not buyin' that, either. There's something really weird about you, and I'm gonna find out—"

"Spare me." Pant, pant. "If you don't want me"—pant, pant—"to go with you"—pant, pant—"I won't." The hopeful expression on his face was almost funny. The jerk was regretting his impulsive offer.

"Like that'll work after you planted the idea in the CO's head."

"Unplant it."

Definitely having second thoughts. Big deal! "Oh no! You're not getting out of this now."

He rolled his eyes, which were probably burning from the salty perspiration dripping into them, along with the mousse. "A perfect example"—pant, pant—"of female illogic." Pant, pant. "Do you want me"—pant, pant—"to accompany you"—pant, pant—"or not?"

Actually, though she hated the intrusion by a virtual stranger into her personal space, after she'd had a chance to think about it, having a date for the wedding was a good idea. Harek would be a buffer between her and her parents, who were constantly nagging her about doing something important with her life—translated: formal education, preferably with a doctorate degree in academia. They were purebred intellectual snobs. The most recent idea was a fast track to a doctorate in theoretic behavioral science recently developed by Tulane University. Not that she even had a clue what theoretic behavioral science was. But everyone in the Dumaine family had a doctorate, even her aunts and uncles and cousins. Her lack of even a bachelor's was a huge embarrassment.

And there was another reason why having Harek for a "date" wouldn't be so bad. Her third ex-fiancé, Dr. Julian Breaux, a heart surgeon and brother to the bride, Inez Breaux, would be there with his highly pregnant wife, Justine, Camille's once-upon-a-time best friend. *And isn't that just the cutest thing in the world. Julian and Justine. Gag me with a stethoscope.* Camille had broken up with

Julian six months ago. Justine was eight months' pregnant. *You do the math!*

Chalk up another disappointment to Camille's parents, that she hadn't been able to hold on to the most eligible bachelor in the Crescent City. *A doctor, for heaven's sake! Even if I never got a doctorate myself, maybe marriage to a doctor would satisfy them. At least that's what I must have been thinking. Why else would I have put up with Julian's egotistical crap? The douche bag!*

"Yes, I want you to come with me to Nawleans," she finally replied to his question, "now that it's been forced on me."

They had finished the run and someone handed both of them chilled bottles of water. Harek chugged his down, then bent over at the waist, trying to get his breathing back to normal.

"You should walk around, to slow your heart rate gradually," she suggested.

He cut her another go-away scowl.

Not a chance! She had things to say. "We can hop a military flight from the base to Fort Polk on Friday at five. I've arranged for a rental car to be there for the drive to Nawleans. We might be able to hit the tail end of the rehearsal dinner at Alcide's. I should be there since I'm a bridesmaid. You can stay with me at my parents' house in the city. Don't give me that look. In a guest room. I'll fill you in on other details later."

"Is that all?" he asked, his voice reeking with sarcasm, or maybe it was amusement.

"One more thing. No hitting on me. If you lay one hand on me, I'll cut off your balls with a sharp blade, and, believe me, we have tons of those around my parents' house. My father collects Civil War swords." She paused. "Am I clear?"

He laughed. "For a woman who's being dealt a huge favor, you sure know how to lay down the rules. Here's a news flash, sweetling—"

She noticed that he was no longer panting. That was some quick recovery, or maybe he'd been pretending to be overwinded for some crazy reason. Hmm. "And no phony baloney endearments, either. No sweetheart, darling, sugar, cupcake, honey, lover, and especially not babe. I hate that word."

He arched a brow. "As I was saying . . . here's a news flash, *babe*. I don't do rules well, as evidenced by my long, long walk on this earth. No, I am not going to explain that comment. As for hitting on you, don't you think you should wait until I show even a spark of interest? I can stay in a hotel. In fact, I prefer the privacy. And if you dare to put your hands on my balls, it better be for carnal purposes." He paused. "Am I clear?"

She could feel herself blush. "I was just trying to—"

He waved a hand dismissively. "I know what you were trying to say. Believe me, I have no designs on your virtue."

Her face heated even more. "You don't have to be insulting."

The expression on his face immediately changed to one of regret. "Did I give offense? I did not mean to. Oh, I really am a pitiful lackwit these days. I did not even apologize for my other bad behavior with you yet."

"Huh?" This was a reversal. But she had no idea what he was talking about. "What *other* bad behavior?"

"The day we met. Outside the command center. What I said about your being unsuitable life mate material."

Oh, that.

"Forgive me, m'lady. I have not had good woman luck in the past, as evidenced by three bad marriages, and the last thing I need is another."

Whoa! Who said anything about marriage?

As if reading her mind, he continued, "Not that you were referring to marriage, but everyone knows that bedplay leads to wedlock, if a man is not careful. Not that you offered bedplay, but you did mention touching body parts. I mean . . ."

She laughed. "Did you ever hear the expression: 'When you're in a hole, stop digging'?"

"We had a similar saying back in my . . . uh, country. 'When you find yourself buried in a pile of shit, keep your mouth shut.' "

"Exactly. So, you've been married three times, huh? How old are you?"

"Twenty and nine years . . . *or so.*"

"Same as me. And I've had three bad near-marriages. What a coincidence!"

"Near-marriages?"

"Engagements."

"Ah, that makes as much sense of Trond's famous near-sex."

She wasn't about to ask what he meant by that. "You talk really funny. I mean, you use archaic words like *sweetling, lackwit, m'lady, woman luck.*"

He shrugged. "I am a Viking. Even after all these centuries, a Viking is a Viking."

They were almost back at the command center, their run having involved three miles in one direction down the beach, then a hairpin loop back. A BUD/S class sat, arms linked, along the water's edge engaged in an exercise called "surf appreciation." Every time a wave came in, they got soaked. Every time a wave went out, their shorts, and underwear, in fact, every bodily crevice, was filled with rough, wet sand. Despite the already warm sun, the water was icy cold. The sand abraded the skin. Torture, Navy SEAL style.

"Are we good now?" she asked Harek. "I mean, no hard feelings or anything? We're just teammates for this mission. You're doing me a favor. I'm grateful. Yada, yada."

"If you say so."

She reached out to shake his hand.

His warning of "No, no, no!" came too late.

Later, she wondered if it was she who grasped his hand or Harek who locked on hers, palm to palm, or some weird magical force, but locked they were. For a brief second that felt like hours, incredible sensations rippled out from their joined hands. A combination of electric shock and tickles that flowed in soft waves out to all her extremities and lodged in every erotic spot in between, and, whoo boy, there were lots of those. Despite her heightened arousal, she tried to yank her hand free, to no avail. If she didn't stop this madness now, she was going to have an orgasm, right here on the Coronado beach, with a bunch of horny Navy SEALs watching.

"Harek," she pleaded.

His head was thrown back, and he was breathing through his open mouth, where she could see slightly extended incisors. The fool was about to get his rocks off, just holding her hand. So was she.

"Harek!" she said, louder now.

His blue eyes opened slowly, and they were more silver than blue now. He licked his lips and looked at her, jerking to attention as he recognized immediately what the problem was. "Bloody damn hell!" he muttered, and managed to disengage himself from her.

"What the hell was that all about?" she asked, once they had both gotten themselves back under control.

"You do not want to know," he grumbled.

"By the way, you smell like chocolate. Did you have some sickeningly sweet cereal for breakfast? No wonder you—"

"I have no idea what you are talking about. I do not smell like anything other than sweat. And, no, I did not eat breakfast. Do you take me for a total fool? No, do not answer that."

He stomped away then, as if she was to blame for everything. His grueling morning run, the weekend wedding, the erotic handshake, his Godiva chocolate body odor.

"Just so you know, bozo," she said to his back, in a voice too low for him to hear, "I'm a chocoholic."

Chapter 5

Julia Roberts had nothing on her . . .

Varek was cooling his heels in a tavern on the outskirts of New Orleans, wondering what the hell he was doing there, for about the fiftieth time. It was already eight p.m., and the rehearsal dinner had presumably started a half hour ago.

He was wearing a gray Hugo Boss suit with a pale blue dress shirt and silver angel wing cuff links. Black Gucci loafers and a black and gray striped, silk Armani tie completed his outfit. His hair was slicked back off his face in a sophisticated style, not the usual deliberate disarray. He looked good, if he did say so himself, and definitely out of place in this blue-collar neighborhood bar reeking of stale beer and greasy hamburgers.

To his chagrin and embarrassment, Camille had been wearing jeans, a denim jacket, and a baseball cap when they'd boarded the military plane in Coronado. His attire stood out like a wart on a witch's nose, compared to his date's. He'd felt like the dork his brothers were always saying he was.

He knew it was only a rehearsal dinner, not the wedding itself, but it was being held in that famous Alcide's Restaurant, and he'd assumed it would require more than casual attire. When he'd hissed his irritation to the woman, "I thought this was a formal affair," she'd replied, "It is. You look fine."

Fine? What kind of half-arsed compliment was that? I look better than fine, he'd thought. "Then why are you wearing *that*." He'd given her clothing a scornful glance. "Oh, is this a rebellious statement of some kind to your family? Weddings bring that out in some folks. I sensed discord when—"

"Sit down and shut up."

Whoa! I hit a sore spot there. Definite family issues. But more important to him, she'd been ordering him around already, and he was not pleased, especially when she'd added, "Do you buy mousse by the gallon?"

"Huh?"

"Hair mousse."

He'd put a hand to his head. "Gel, not mousse."

She'd shrugged. "Big difference."

He'd bristled. If there was one thing Viking men were vain about, it was their hair. Well, there were many things they were vain about, but hair was one of them. And even though Harek did not wear his hair long in the Viking style, he still took special care with it. "What is wrong with my hair?" he'd asked.

"Nothing. Just that you seem to take more time with it than most women I know. What do you do when you are out on an op? Go into mousse withdrawal?"

"Very funny. And it is gel, not mousse. A men's hair product."

She'd shaken her head, failing to see the distinction.

He and Camille hadn't talked much on the short flight or since then in the rental car, which she'd insisted on driving, until she told him she needed to stop at this tavern and suggested he have a beer while she visited the ladies' facility. Why she needed to take her overnight bag with her defied explanation, but then women were often strange about their bathroom visits. Unlike men, who just said, "I have to piss." Much simpler.

That had been fifteen minutes ago. And now he sat here, sipping at a bottle of Dixie beer, fuming. Already, he'd had to fend off the overtures of two women and one man: the waitress with the impressive bosom; a harlot who walked the streets of New Orleans selling her wares, although she'd offered him a discount; and a man whose braies were so tight his cock stuck out like the figurehead on the bow of a longship.

He was about to raise his hand for another beer when his attention was caught by a woman emerging from the ladies' room. She wore a tight red dress held up by two thin straps and ending just above her knees. Her shoulders and arms were deliciously bare, as were her long legs, which led to black, strappy shoes with four-inch heels. Her light brown hair was a mass of curls reminiscent of the bed muss after energetic bedplay. Her pouty lips were scarlet red. From her ears dangled long, filigreed silver chains that swayed as she walked. Her neck bore no adornment, and he felt a lurch of excitement when he imagined he could see the deep vein at its curve, the most enticing temptation to a vampire, even a vampire angel.

Harek shifted uncomfortably on his bar stool, thankful for his jacket, which would hide his hair-trigger arousal.

Now, this was a woman whose overtures he would not turn away. Or, leastways, he would have difficulty turning away, he immediately amended, just in case you-know-who, the Big M, was listening in to his thoughts.

He noticed two things at once. First, the woman was carrying Camille's carry bag. Oh no! Had this woman accosted Camille in the ladies' room? Was Camille lying on the floor, the victim of an assault?

He began to rise, and felt for the weapons under his jacket. A vangel always carried at least a knife or pistol, often a retractable sword in secret pockets.

But then, almost at the same moment, he realized something else. The closer she got, the stronger the scent of roses that assailed his senses.

The woman winked.

His jaw dropped.

It was Camille. Smiling at him with a "gotcha!" kind of smile.

At just that moment, the sound system in the

bar, which had been playing country music, blasted out with that old Roy Orbison song "Pretty Woman," and Camille walked to the beat of the music. In truth, she strutted her stuff, as modern folks said. And she did it damn well, and knew it, too.

This weekend was going to be a lot more interesting than Harek had thought. That was for damn bloody sure, Harek told himself. Or was it a promise?

When she got closer, she said in a sex-husky voice, "You smell good enough to eat."

Huh? The only thing he smelled was roses. "I beg your pardon," he choked out, her words planting a picture in his head that caused his already interested, favorite body part to lurch.

"You're like a just-baked chocolate cake with dark cocoa butter icing and white chocolate sprinkles. Three layers."

Oh. The chocolate nonsense again. He'd heard his brothers' wives claim their spouses exuded a particular life mate scent, but they were manly odors like pine or sandalwood. Not candy. Besides, I am not, not, not in the market for a life mate.

"All that sinfully good sweetness," she purred, "that melts on the tongue. A person could get a chocolate high just breathing you in. Bet a dime you taste divine." She licked her lips, causing them to glisten.

Definitely an interesting weekend ahead.

Oh, he was not so vain as to believe her flirting meant she was attracted to him. The wench was goading him.

So, she's not as plain as I thought. Or she knows how to earn her nickname of Camo . . . camouflage. Either way, she made a fool of me, or more likely, I made a fool of myself, with her help.

"What are you standing there for? You'll make us late," she said, tapping him on his still gaping jaw, then handing him her small luggage to carry.

"Me? You're the one who insisted on—"

But she had already passed him by, and for a moment Harek just watched as her hips swayed in the tight red dress. Everyone else in the bar watched, too. All to the beat of "Pretty Woman."

And then, just before she reached the exit door, she wiggled her butt. Just a little wiggle. But it was enough for Harek to recognize what it was. A challenge.

He smiled. And followed after her.

If this wench thought she could issue him a challenge like that and escape unscathed, she had another think coming. There was nothing a Viking loved more than a good challenge.

Let the games begin, Harek thought, licking his suddenly extended fangs. *The Viking vangel games, that is.*

He didn't ride a horse, but he was a prince . . .

They arrived at the world-famous Alcide's Restaurant in the French Quarter about nine p.m. Turned out they wouldn't be very late, after all. Camille had called her mother's cell a short time ago and learned that the wedding rehearsal at St. Louis Cathedral had been delayed by more than an hour due to a wedding party before them, which had been "rudely unprepared."

Her mother also considered it rude of Camille not to have come home earlier for her brother's pre-wedding festivities, like maybe a week ago. When Camille had explained, many times, that the military didn't make allowance for such things, her mother had declared, "Well, that's just rude."

"Tell it to Uncle Sam."

"Uncle who?"

That about summed up her mother's understanding of Camille's work.

Harek had insisted on taking the wheel of her rental car on the last leg of their journey here, and he'd driven like a NASCAR maniac, no doubt due to his annoyance with her over her chameleon routine back at the tavern. She loved people's reactions when she pulled off one of her transformations, but men didn't like being fooled by a woman. Then there had been her totally immature and highly satisfying butt wiggle. Some statements were made without words.

Their thirty-minute drive should have been a time when he could have tutored her on aspects of the Deadly Wind mission, but she hadn't been about to distract him with talk. You'd think he was driving a Ferrari, not a boring Toyota Camry.

She had to give him credit for finding a parking space on one of the side streets off tourist-packed Bourbon and being able to maneuver into the tight slot. And he not only didn't make a snide remark about the several hookers who gave him the eye, but he barely seemed to notice them.

She also had to give him credit for his appearance. The boy did clean up well. Not that he hadn't looked good in casual attire, but in a pewter-gray suit (undoubtedly designer quality), a pale blue dress shirt (that complemented his compelling blue eyes), with silver cuff links (face it, there was something incredibly sexy about good old-fashioned cuff links on a man, especially when he took them off, with slow intent).

He was steaming hot.

Instead of its usual spiky disarray, his dark blond hair was slicked off his face tonight, giving him a sophisticated edge. Add his subtle chocolate body odor, and whoo boy! The Big Easy just got a whole lot easier.

The minute they entered the restaurant, she was assailed by the wonderful scents of the French-Creole cuisine. Her stomach growled in response, and she realized that she hadn't eaten since this morning.

"Have you been to Alcide's before?" she asked Harek as they waited their turn for the maître d'.

He shook his head. "The fanciest I got last time I was here was a po-boy food truck."

"Hey, a good po-boy is nothing to scoff at."

Just then, the maître d' said to them, "Monsieur? Mademoiselle?"

"We're with the Breaux party. The rehearsal dinner," she said.

"Ah." He motioned for a hostess to lead their way through the busy restaurant to one of the many private dining rooms. "Have a good evening."

Camille sniffed the air appreciatively again as they walked among the diners, noticing every kind of seafood imaginable, from bayou crawfish to the Gulf's redfish. She hoped the restaurant's signature Oysters Rockefeller was on their menu tonight.

Harek put his hand to the small of her back, an ingrained male gesture of protection that she found oddly endearing, and whispered in her ear, "You keep sniffing the air like a bloodhound. If you mention my chocolate body odor one more time, I'm going to pinch your jiggly arse."

She was about to correct him, that it was the restaurant fare that she was sniffing, but, instead, told him, "I do not jiggle. And what's with this 'arse' business?"

"Arse, ass, butt, booty, whatever. On you it definitely jiggles," he said with a laugh, "and I do not just mean that exaggerated ploy back in the dive."

She glanced at him over her shoulder. Physical fitness was a requirement for Navy WEALS, and she'd sweated gallons these past few years to get in such shape, or as Southern belles were wont to say, ladies did not perspire, they glistened. "My butt does not jiggle! I might have deliberately wiggled it, once, but it does not jiggle on its own, like freakin' Jell-O. Furthermore—"

He put a fingertip to her lips to stop her tirade. "Not to worry. I like Jell-O."

Oooh, he was pushing all her buttons tonight. And she wasn't thinking straight, to give him such openings. "I thought I told you not to make familiar remarks while we're here."

"No. When you were reciting your rules, you told me not to call you sweetheart, darling, sugar, cupcake, honey, lover, or babe. There was naught mentioned of jiggling arses . . . or Jell-O."

She could tell by the grin twitching at his lips that he found her "rules" amusing, and he had no intention of abiding by them.

But they'd arrived at the open double doors of the dining room where the Breaux dinner was being held, an elaborately decorated space with Audubon prints and framed scenes of old New Orleans adorning the burgundy walls. The cypress wainscoting shone with an aged patina. Several crystal chandeliers hung from the crown medallions in the ceiling. Alcide's was a family-owned restaurant that had been around since the 1840s, and it did its best to maintain its historic details, despite Katrina and other natural disasters.

In fact, her namesake ancestor, Camille Fontenot, the one who'd been "sold" at a pre–Civil War Quadroon Ball, mentioned in one of her diaries being taken to this very restaurant by her protector. And, damn, but that was a touchy subject for her. Touchy, hell! More like a jab in the heart. A fifteen-year-old mistress! But she couldn't think about that now.

Inside the large room, two dozen well-dressed guests stood about talking in clusters, drinking cocktails, while the waitstaff was pouring ice water into goblets on the long table for their formal, sit-down dinner. Conversation buzzed, along with occasional laugher, and a soft jazz instrumental provided a pleasant background through an invisible sound system.

"Are you good to go?" Harek asked, using the hand at the small of her back to squeeze her waist in support, a surprising gesture, and words more in line with the military lingo soldiers employed just before a live op. He seemed to understand how difficult this family affair was going to be for her. Definitely a live op. Maybe even a few explosions.

In fact, as if reading her mind, he explained, "I come from a large family. Six brothers. Five sisters-by-marriage, and dozens of extended . . . um, family. Believe you me, I understand the strife of blood kin."

She put her hand over his, at her waist, and squeezed her thanks. Instead of the electrical zing she'd felt previously when she touched him, this time there was a feeling of warmth. Peace.

A thin, wiry man in a dark suit with an MIT tie was the first to see them. Her brother, Alain. He was only an inch or two taller than her five foot eight, but next to Harek's six foot four, he seemed short. Everybody did.

Alain smiled and took the hand of his fiancée, Inez Breaux, walking toward them. Inez was a petite woman, even in high heels, wearing a royal-blue, knee-length sheath with short sleeves and a sweetheart neckline. Alain was five years older than Camille, as was his bride-to-be.

"Alain," Camille said, stepping forward to

kiss him on the cheek, "Congrats, big brother. Finally!" He and Inez had been engaged for about ten years.

"Glad you could come, Cam. Mother can concentrate on you now, instead of driving me crazy." He did look rather dazed, as he often was in a social setting, more at home in his labs. She hadn't seen her brother in three years, and she noticed that his hair was receding prematurely. That was something new. And he blinked nervously behind his wireless glasses, a longtime habit. Still, he was a nice-looking man, and he looked good in what was probably a new suit from Armand's men store, where Dumaine men had been clothed for two hundred years. "She gave two honors lectures today, in between delivering a luncheon address to a Newcomb College alumnae group, which left me to fight with the florist over the colors of the roses on my ushers' boutonnieres. Did you know there are seventeen different colors of white roses?" He blinked at Camille. "I'm not making that up. Mother picked Ivory Cream, but they mistakenly made them up with Ivy Dream. Horrors!"

Inez rolled her eyes at Camille in the age-old "Men!" manner. Then, she stepped closer. "Hello, Camille. I'm glad you made it."

Camille hugged Inez, who smelled like Joy, a perfume she'd been using as long as Camille could remember. "You look wonderful. Grand-mère Octavie's earrings are perfect with that dress."

Inez put her fingertips to the sapphire stones surrounded by tiny diamonds, which were part of a parure, which also included a necklace, a bracelet, and a brooch. "I chose this dress specifically to match." She held out her hand to show the sparkling jewels at the wrist. "The necklace and pin seemed too much, though. What do you think?"

"Perfect," she said. "Grand-mère only wore the complete set on formal occasions, like Mardi Gras."

"You don't mind my getting the set, do you?" Inez asked. "I could give you the bracelet."

Camille fisted her hands behind her back, reflexively. Transforming her overall appearance at the last minute had been easy-peasy, but there was nothing she could do for her rough skin and blunt nails, a casualty of special warfare. Besides, her grandmother would roll over in her raised tomb at Lafayette Cemetery at the thought of breaking up the parure. "No, no. I don't mind. Not at all. And I wouldn't think of breaking up the set. Besides, it wouldn't match my camouflage suit." Since neither Alain nor Inez got the joke, just staring at her blankly, Camille went on, "Besides, I get the pearls, and everyone knows they go better with drab green." Again, no reaction.

A slight coughing noise at her back rescued her. Harek.

She turned to him and said, "Harek, I'd like you to meet my brother, Alain. Dr. Alain Dumaine. He's was a rocket scientist at NASA."

"Tsk, tsk. Camille loves to say that," he told Harek with a shake of his head. "I'm an aerospace engineer specializing in lunar atmospheric modules. I'm currently a professor at Princeton, on loan from NASA."

"Jeesh! That's what I said. And this is my, um, friend, Harek Sigurdsson. He does hush-hush work for Wings International Security."

Harek shot her a scowl before extending a hand to her brother, "Pleased to meet you. Your sister has a warped sense of humor."

"You noticed that, did you?" Alain said with a laugh. "You won't believe what Camille did for a Halloween costume when she was fifteen. About put our mother in cardiac arrest."

Here we go, already! It was Camille who was shooting scowls now. What she didn't need was a family member reciting a litany of all her antics over the years. It usually started with "You won't believe what Camille . . ."

Before Alain could elaborate, Camille continued with the introductions, "And this is Alain's fiancée, Dr. Inez Breaux, a professor of genetic research at Johns Hopkins."

Instead of shaking Inez's hand, Harek lifted it and kissed the knuckles in the cosmopolitan style. The show-off! But Inez obviously liked the gesture, if her out-of-character giggle was any indication.

"Perhaps you know my brother Sig . . . Dr. Sigurd Sigurdsson. He was a physician at Johns Hopkins until recently," Harek said to Inez. "But then, it's such a big place that—"

"Actually, I do know Dr. Sigurdsson. We shared some research a few years back. He's a brilliant physician. Where is he now?"

"On some island off the Florida Keys, starting a pediatric oncology clinic, or some such thing."

"Really?" Inez was genuinely interested. "Perhaps you can give me his contact information later?"

"Sure."

Alain and Inez moved on to mix with their other guests, and a waiter passing with a tray of stemmed glasses offered them a choice of red or white wine. Camille drank her dry Chablis down in one gulp when she saw her mother and father approaching.

"Liquid courage?" Harek asked, sipping at his red Merlot.

"You have no idea." She plastered a big smile on her face and said, "Mother! Daddy!"

"Darling!" her mother said, giving Camille an air kiss on either side of her head.

Camille wasn't offended by the lack of a maternal hug. Her mother's face was impeccably made up with foundation, mascara, lip gloss, and rouge, and her short salt-and-pepper hair was styled perfectly. She wore a rose silk dress with a matching silver braid–trimmed jacket. There were diamond studs in her small shell-like ears and a ruby and diamond butterfly brooch on her jacket lapel. The subtle scent of Chanel No. 5 wafted around her. The epitome of smart middle-aged woman!

Her father, an older version of Alain with pure white hair and blinking eyes, was not so reticent. He hugged her warmly and whispered against her ear, "I missed you, *chaton*." Her father had been calling her his kitten as an endearment since she was a child, always clinging to him, like a . . . well, cat.

"I missed you, too," she said, kissing his cheek. She introduced both parents to Harek then. "Harek, this is my mother, Dr. Jeannette Dumaine, and my father, Dr. Emile Dumaine. Mother, Father, this is Harek Sigurdsson, a friend from Coronado. He's in the security business."

Several pleasantries were exchanged then, mostly related to their trip there, but already her mother had dismissed Harek as unimportant, Camille could tell. The lack of a doctorate before his name, no doubt. And, although his assessment was not so blatant, her father's attention was diverted by a call from some colleagues on the other side of the room, who said, "Come, Emile, come. We need your opinion." It probably had something to do with General Robert E. Lee, her father's special interest. There wasn't anything her father didn't know about the famous general, right down to his shoe size, no doubt. Her mother, on the other hand, was an expert on the role of Southern women during the Civil War.

Her mother was about to leave, too. Some last-minute detail she needed to discuss with the mother of the bride. Before she left, she told Camille, "Dr. Solic from Tulane is here tonight. Make sure you discuss that new program with him, the one I wrote you about. Your father and I have discussed it, and we both agree that it would be perfect for you. It's not too late to start over, darling."

Her mother was referring to that fast track to

a doctorate in theoretic behavioral science. So much more appropriate than a grubby military career!

She bristled.

But did her mother notice, or care? No, she was adjusting the straps on Camille's dress in a futile motherly attempt to raise the bodice.

Camille was tempted to swat her mother's hands away.

"Be nice, Camille," her mother said, patting her on the bare shoulder. "You will at least talk to him, won't you? I've already told him you're interested."

"I already told you—" Camille started to say, but her mother was giving a little wave to more late arrivals at the door. Before leaving, her mother flashed Camille a pointed look of warning related to the newcomers, Dr. Julian Breaux, brother of the bride, and his very pregnant wife, Justine.

Her parents, and their friends, were academic snobs. They measured success not by wealth, but the number of degrees a person held. By their standards, she was an utter failure. Never mind that she was fighting to give them the freedom to pursue schooling to the nth degree. That was irrelevant.

As for her ex-fiancé, what did her mother think she was going to do? Dump a glass of wine in Julian's too-pretty face? She'd already done that. Besides, her wineglass was empty. She set it on the tray of a passing waiter and took another. As for her former best friend, did her mother think she was going to karate chop her baby bump? Justine was history to Camille. Still her BFF, but instead of Best Friend Forever, she was now Bitch of a Former Friend. In Camille's mind.

Taking a sip of the cool beverage for fortification, Camille sighed, then shrugged.

"What?" Harek asked.

"Huh?" She'd forgotten he was there. That's how screwed up she was.

"You just muttered something about, 'It is what it is.' "

"I did?"

"You did." He asked something odd then. Well, odd to her. "Are you wealthy?"

"Me, personally? Hardly."

"Your family. This little affair has to be costing twenty thousand dollars, and I've never seen so many Rolexes or expensive jewelry in one place. I get high just smelling all the gold here."

It bothered her that Harek would be impressed by such things, but some men were like that. If he was looking to cash in with her, he was in for a rude awakening. She lived on a second lieutenant's salary. "Wait until you see the wedding reception being planned by the bride's family. Now, *they* are probably, as you say, reeking of gold. My parents are wealthy, too, depending on your definition of wealthy. Millionaires are a dime a dozen these days, I've been told."

He nodded. "I recall a time when a handful of gold coins could buy a longship."

"What?"

"Never mind." He was still surveying the room, probably mentally tallying the net worth of the whole gathering. Maybe he was really poor and unaccustomed to such excess.

She shouldn't be so judgmental.

Maybe she was more like her parents than she'd thought.

"Listen, Harek, don't be offended by my parents or some of the others here."

"Because I am not wealthy?"

She shook her head. "No, the money is inherited. They're intellectual snobs."

He frowned in confusion. "I'm intelligent."

"Yeah, but you don't have doctor in front of your name, or a bunch of letters after your name."

He was still obviously confused. "Why would that matter? Degrees are easy enough to obtain. I have an IQ of 200, but do you see me proclaiming that fact to the world? Why would I? My brothers would clout me aside the head with the flat side of a broadsword if I did."

"Nobody has an IQ of 200," she remarked with boozy irrelevance. She was beginning to feel the effect of her one glass of wine on an empty stomach.

He arched his brows at her in disagreement.

Despite herself, Camille kept looking over at Julian and Justine, who had garnered a small crowd, the men shaking his hand in congratulations and the women patting Justine's big belly.

"Can I assume that is one of your near-husbands?" Harek asked, following the direction of her stares. He was too perceptive, or else she was too transparent. Probably the latter.

"Yes. Dr. Julian Breaux, a heart surgeon, is

my third ex-fiancé. And that's Julian's wife, Justine. She used to be my best friend, since nursery school."

"The third, huh? How long ago did you end the engagement?" he asked.

It was nice of him to assume that she was the one who'd broken the engagement, which she had been. With cause. But Camille didn't want to talk about it. In fact, if it wouldn't be too obvious, she'd like to slip out of the room and go somewhere to get drunk, or at least mind-numbing buzzed. None of this was Harek's fault, though, and she didn't want to be rude to him. "Six months ago," she replied.

"Six . . . ?" Harek looked at Julian, Justine, and then Camille. "Ah!"

It didn't take an IQ of 200 or even 100 to figure that one out.

"And they expect you to stand here and pretend naught is wrong?" he asked.

She wasn't sure who the "they" was that he referred to, but she nodded.

"I do not think so," he said. He placed his half-empty wineglass on a sideboard and took hers out of her hand, as well. Then he took her in his arms and kissed her soundly, long and openmouthed and wet—there might have been tongues involved—until her knees started to buckle. The silence around them was loud as cymbals clashing. Even the music seemed to have paused. Only then did he wrap an arm around her shoulders and lead her toward the still open doorway.

"Prince Charming to the rescue?" she inquired. When he didn't respond, she asked, "Are you going to be my Prince Charming, or something?"

"Or something." She could see that anger simmered just beneath the surface of his stony face. On her behalf? That was nice. Not necessary, but nice.

"Where are we going?" she whispered, trying not to notice the stunned guests they passed. Or Julian, the louse.

"Does it matter?"

She thought only for a second before answering, "Hell, no!"

Chapter 6

The morning-after blues . . .

At five-thirty the next morning, Harek was sitting on the back verandah of Evermore, a historic Greek Revival home in the old Garden District of New Orleans—a home with a name, for cloud's sake—watching as dawn emerged over the formal gardens spread out before him. Magnolias, lilies, dahlias big as saucers, roses . . . all contributed to the explosion of color.

His brother Ivak, who was renovating a rundown plantation in Terrebonne Parish known by the oxymoronic title of Heaven's End, ought to see this; it would give him some good ideas for his own overgrown landscape. Not that Ivak didn't have enough on his plate just removing snakes and kudzu and such.

This was the kind of place Harek would like to own. Old architectural details, but modern amenities. Understated elegance. Rare examples of antique Newcomb pottery made by eighteenth-century New Orleans artists were displayed throughout, but top-of-the-line appliances shone with stainless steel polish in the kitchen. The gleam of old patina showed in the grain on the mantels of many cypress fireplaces, even though the house boasted full-house air-conditioning. A home, or estate, with a name. He figured the house must be worth at least two million dollars, and if you added in some of its museum-quality oil paintings, double that.

Of course, a modern penthouse in a Manhattan skyscraper would be welcome, too.

Or a chateau in the French wine region.

But he would never get away with such blatant displays of wealth with Michael looking over his shoulder. If the archangel said once, he said a thousand times, "Poverty is next to godliness," to which Harek usually replied, "I do not see the logic in that," to which Michael usually replied, "Live with it!"

Truth to tell, Harek owned a discreet hideaway on a Caribbean island, which he'd managed to keep a secret for more than a year. It was only a matter of time before Michael found out, and Harek's punishment would be immense. Betimes a pleasure was worth the pain, he had decided. *Besides, it is a good investment,* Harek declared to himself. He wondered if Michael would buy that defense.

He'd learned about the property from Zebulan, who was, of all things, a demon vampire, who happened to own a Caribbean island hideaway himself. Which was odd . . . that a devil would do a favor for an angel. The only thing a Lucipire gave a vangel under normal circumstances was trouble. Well, actually, Zeb was a double agent of sorts for Michael, but that was another story.

Harek held a mug of strong chicory coffee cradled between both palms. His laptop was open on a low table in front of his chair, along with a china plate holding a half-eaten beignet, still warm from the oven. He'd already eaten one of the delicious New Orleans confections. When he'd crept barefooted down the wide staircase of the silent house a short time ago, wearing only jeans and a white T-shirt, he'd fully expected to make his own cup of coffee, but there had been a servant in the kitchen already—the cook, Tenecia—preparing for what would be a busy wedding day in this household of the groom. In fact, there were several uniformed servants moving quietly about the house, polishing silver, dusting furniture. Although they didn't refer to them as servants, or even "the help," like that telling book of the same title a few years back. Too politically incorrect. They were household professionals.

The church wedding wouldn't start until five p.m., and the reception was being held afterward at General's Palace, right here in the Garden District, but there was still much activity that would be going on here. That was the reason for the early activity. Harek planned to be gone by then, and stay away most of the day. The less he was under the eagle eye of Camille's mother, the better. Best not to raise too many questions about who, or what, he was. Besides, the woman annoyed him, especially the way she treated her daughter. It was none of his business, of course, but that didn't mean he had to willingly expose himself to such condescension.

"You're up early," he heard a voice say behind him.

He half turned to see Camille standing in the doorway, holding a mug of coffee to her chest like it was the Holy Grail. Where was the beauty of last night? This creature was barefooted, like himself, wearing shorts with a matching tank top of a bright neon green color that hurt his tired eyes. No bra as far as he could tell, and he could tell things like that, not because he was a vangel, but because he was a man, a Viking man. Men had supersonic vision when it came to even the hint of a female nipple. Her makeup was smeared, creating a raccoon effect about the eyes and a smudged red, bruised effect on her lips. Her hair was a tangled mess, lopsided, where she must have been sleeping. She still wore one dangling silver earring. The other was in his suit pocket; she'd dropped it in one of the bars they'd visited in the French Quarter.

The last he'd seen of her, she'd still been wearing the sexy red dress, and she'd been plastered face-first on her bed where he'd delivered her about two a.m. She'd been deep in what they called in the old days "alehead madness." In other words, schnockered.

"You're up early, too. I thought you'd stay in

bed all morning. You've only had three hours' sleep," he replied, watching as she managed to sink down into the chair next to him with a groan, being careful not to spill her coffee. She eyed the half-eaten beignet on his plate with distaste, and groaned when a bird chirped in a nearby tree.

Can anyone say hangover?

"Pfff! I have to be at the dressmaker's by eight to have a first and final fitting for my bridesmaid dress." Her upper lip curled with disgust as she added, "It's pink." She informed him of the color as if that should have some meaning to him.

It didn't.

"Actually, its color is described as blush, but it's been my experience that blush is just a bridal shop's way of luring a customer into a putrid pink bridesmaid-from-hell confection. They have a surplus of these monstrosities they've been trying to unload for a hundred years. Just like celery means baby-poop green, and tangerine means screaming Halloween orange." She sipped at her coffee after expounding that bit of female wisdom, which meant absolutely nothing to him. "I think Inez has lost her mind, having such a big wedding. At one point she even wanted a Southern belle theme. Hoop skirts, mint juleps, the works. Really, weddings turn even the most intelligent women into dingbats. I told her that, if she thought my brother was suddenly going to morph into Rhett Freakin' Butler, I had a plantation called Tara I could sell her. Luckily she saw reason. The wedding reception will still be a bigass extravaganza, but at least I won't have to wear hoops. Just pink."

Camille's woozy spiel amused Harek. She was probably still a little bit drunk.

"Well, you could go back to bed after the fitting, couldn't you?"

"Are you kidding? I intend to be out of here for the rest of the day. My mother has lined up hairdressers, manicurists, makeup artists, a masseuse, and God only knows who else coming to the house to prepare us for the wedding. Did I tell you there are three hundred invited guests for the reception? I could puke."

"Please don't."

"I already did."

Too much information. "Where will you go?" *Maybe she has a hideaway, like I do.*

"I could take you sightseeing in Nawleans or on a swamp tour."

Her offer was made so reluctantly that he had to laugh. "No need to entertain me. I intend to go visit my brother at his plantation outside Houma. Don't worry. I'll be back in time for the festivities."

She looked at him with such yearning that he asked, "Would you like to go with me?"

"Yes! Could you wait 'til after my fitting? I'll be done before nine."

He tried to school his face not to show his disappointment. He'd been looking forward to this time alone, away from her tempting, troubling floral aura. And, yes, the air reeked of roses now, and not from the gardens, either.

"You'll probably be bored. My brother Ivak and his wife, Gabrielle, have a child, and all they talk about is Mikey-this, Mikey-that."

She smiled. "I like children."

"Why don't you have some of your own?"

"Why don't you?"

I did. Once upon a time. Not all it's cracked up to be, fatherhood. But then, I was not a good father. I wonder if I would be different now. Hah! No use wondering about that. Vangels were sterile. Across the board, none of them could breed children. Except for Ivak, who was the exception. A mistake. A blessed mistake, Michael was always quick to add, especially since the child was named after him. Ivak ever was a suck-up, always had been, in Harek's opinion.

But all he replied to Camille was "Touché!"

"I'll let you drive my Benz convertible if you take me with you?"

"You have a Mercedes Benz?" This woman never ceased to surprise him.

She nodded. "A gift when I graduated from high school. In hopes, no doubt, that I would go to college and excel academically and make my family proud of me. Especially my father, the cheater, who has two families and sees no irony in dishonoring his wife, and my mother, who puts up with the insult. Great role models!"

Huh? He could tell Camille immediately regretted her words, and Harek wasn't about to delve into that personal family minefield. Instead he asked, "Are they not proud of you for your military career?"

"Not even a little."

He could tell that was a sore subject, as well; so, he changed it. Even Vikings could be sensitive when they wanted to be. "If you own a luxury vehicle, why are we driving a Toyota?"

"I keep my car here. Can you imagine how I would be razzed back on the base if I rode around in a seventy-thousand-dollar vehicle? Actually, there are four Benz out in the garage. Mine, my mother's, my father's, and Alain's. And probably his other . . . never mind. Suffice it to say, we're a Benz family." She waggled her eyebrows at him.

More examples of a wealth he yearned to have once again. And he wouldn't even need a Mercedes Benz. A BMW would do.

"You might want to shower and change before your fitting." He glanced at his wristwatch. "We'll have to leave in an hour."

She put a hand to her unruly hair and grimaced. "What? You're embarrassed to be seen with me?"

"No. You can stagger along looking like you barely survived a longship ride on a stormy North Sea, for all I care, but if you run into your mother, she will never let you leave the house." Actually, he was really glad that she looked so bad this morning. It took the edge off the dangerous attraction he'd been feeling toward her. Life mate? Hah!

"Oh Lord! You're right. And I probably smell, too."

"That you do," he said. "Like a rose. A vomity rose." He smiled at her to lessen the insult and did a mental high-five. Vomity roses held no appeal. He'd escaped a bullet this time, and he knew it.

The laughter he heard then probably came from some distant place in the house. Not in his head.

The ghosts of brides past . . .

The bridesmaid dress wasn't as bad as Camille had expected and it hadn't required much in the way of alterations. Definitely blush-colored, not pink-pink, it was a short-sleeved, figure-hugging silk gown, much like that worn by Pippa Middleton in the royal wedding. Unlike the notorious Pippa gown, Camille's had a deeply scooped neckline, exposing some cleavage, not a draped one, and there were lots of tiny buttons in back, but instead of leading from the neck, Camille's started mid-back and ended mid-butt. That's all she needed, folks staring at her butt, not that she didn't have a great butt, thanks to all those forced crunches. The finished product would be delivered to Evermore this afternoon. She could have done without the matching blush-colored high heels, but all in all, she felt as if she'd dodged a bullet.

Now she had to face the other bullet in her life. The chocolate-scented one that was screwing up her hormones and turning her brain to mush. Why else would she have invited herself along on his trip to visit his brother? And even worse, she'd almost jumped the man's bones last night, and she couldn't even blame it on the alcohol.

Time to put the skids on this out-of-control train of temptation. You'd think after three near-marriages she would have learned, but she was a pathetic romantic at heart. What she needed more than anything was to get through this wedding and concentrate on her WEALS work, not necessarily in that order. Instead of cruising off to the bayou, she was going to suggest to Harek that they find a quiet place to go over the Deadly Wind mission details.

He was waiting for her down the street at the Roux on Orleans Restaurant in the historic Bourbon Orleans Hotel, where he said he would have a cup of coffee and check e-mails. Camille loved New Orleans and all its history, but she hated this particular hotel with a passion because of its very history. It was close to the bridal shop, though, and it would have taken too much of an explanation if she'd urged Harek to wait for her somewhere else.

He stood when he saw her. "Finally! I just got an e-mail from Ivak. They're expecting us to stay for lunch." He was already closing his laptop and putting it, along with some paperwork, into his carry bag.

So much for her plan to get out of a day together. "Um . . . I was beginning to think maybe we should just go to a library or the park or something and go over the mission details. You know, like the CO recommended."

He gave her suggestion serious thought, his head cocked to the side, and she noted, once again, just how attractive Harek was. Even today, wearing faded jeans and a ratty old gray T-shirt with the logo "Mensas Do It Smarter," he was sex on a stick. Add to that the subtle scent of chocolate, and she was facing a sexy Fudgsicle.

"No. Let's put the top up on the Benz, and you can drive while I grill you on mission details.

That will give us roughly an hour going and an hour coming back. And, actually, it's a good idea for us to do some 'homework' today. I just got some alarming updates that you'll want to know about." He glanced meaningfully down at his laptop case.

How could she argue with that? She nodded and they walked out of the restaurant side by side. As they approached the ballroom, which was set up for some kind of formal reception with floral centerpieces on the round tables and silver flatware bracketing china plates, she stiffened, as she always did, and a wave of nausea swept over her.

"Hey! What's the matter?" Harek asked, taking her by the forearm to prevent her keeling over.

"Don't worry about it. I have this reaction every time I enter this hotel, and pass that room." She waved a hand toward the ballroom.

He frowned with confusion.

"This hotel—that ballroom, in particular, the Orleans Ballroom—has a lurid history. It was the scene of the famous Quadroon Balls where free women of color entered into a sort of servitude to white men of that time. One of my ancestors—my grandmother, about ten times removed, another Camille; I'm named after her—stood on this very spot and became a sex slave to a man who was a sugar planter. She was fifteen years old." Truth to tell, Camille had come to love James Bellefleur and bore him two bastard children, joyfully. Probably some Stockholm syndrome kind of thing, or another emotional aberration psychologists would have a name for today.

"You know all this from history books?"

"Not exactly. There's plenty of historical detail on the Quadroon Balls and *plaçage,* but my ancestor's story I know from her diaries," she explained. "I swear, though, that I have a genetic memory of the event. Or maybe it's true that the ballroom is haunted. The ghosts of all those slave brides, who weren't really slaves or brides."

"Slavery!" he muttered. "A thousand years, and I am still being harangued over my sin."

Harek's reaction was not what she had expected. "What? What did you say?"

"Nothing of import. I do not understand by half what you said. Are you a quadroon?"

"Hardly. A quadroon is one-quarter black. I do have a minuscule amount of color in my blood, though. Does that bother you?"

"No. Why should it?"

She shrugged. "Bothers some men, believe me. I know from experience."

"Your ex-fiancé?" he guessed.

"One of them. Not Julian. He's Creole himself."

Harek still seemed confused.

"Anyhow, *plaçage* was a recognized practice here in the South long before the Civil War," Camille said, and gave Harek her short lecture on the subject. "Woman of color, the lighter the better, would enter into an agreement with a white man she met at one of the Quadroon Balls, essentially becoming his common-law wife—his *placée*—for life, or as long as he wanted her. In the best of circumstances, the women were given homes, usually on Rampart Street, money to live on, and their children would be free. Meanwhile, he had his own family back on the plantation and legitimate children."

"They were mistresses, then?"

"No!" she said, more vehemently than was warranted, she supposed. "They called themselves concubines, not prostitutes, but to me, it was slavery pure and simple. The women did it for survival, not by choice, and it was a despicable practice." She looked at him. "You don't seem shocked."

He shrugged. "Camille, thralldom has been around since the beginning of time. Even the Bible mentions slavery, and there were certainly such practices in Viking times," he said, his face oddly red, as if he had a personal interest in the subject.

"Are you defending slavery?" she spat out.

"Whoa!" he said, putting up his free hand. "I never said any such thing. I was merely pointing out that slavery was a part of many cultures at one time. Yes, it was a sinful custom, but it must be judged through a historical prism."

"Bullshit!"

He laughed. "You are right, of course. My boss would certainly agree with you, though he would use a different word."

"Your boss? At the security company?"

"No, a higher-up boss."

They had arrived at the car; he handed her the keys and she used a remote button to put up the soft top. Then she slid into the driver's seat, and Harek arranged himself on the passenger side, after sliding the seat back as far as it would go, with the laptop on his raised thighs.

"So, what's the big news?" she asked as she eased the car through downtown traffic and then onto I–10.

"Boko Haram has taken an entire village. Killed a hundred adults, men *and* women, and abducted fifty girls and a dozen boys."

Camille's face took on a grim expression. "Slaves. They're going to make those poor children into slaves."

"That's why it's so important to you to be part of this mission, isn't it? The slavery aspect?"

She nodded, banking down the emotion that would have her either weeping with sorrow or shouting with outrage. WEALS learned early on to keep personal feelings at bay lest they act irrationally and satisfy those chauvinists who still felt women didn't belong in the military.

He reached over and squeezed her right hand, which was on the steering wheel. "We will conquer these terrorists and bring back the kidnapped children, that I promise you."

"You can't know that."

"I have insider information," he told her, "or you could say, higher information," he added, under his breath.

"Higher than what?"

"Higher than hell," he said, which made no sense at all.

"Sometimes you are really weird," she commented.

"You have no idea."

Chapter 7

The best things, and trouble, come in small packages . . .

Now Harek understood why he had been assigned to this particular mission.

Michael delighted in placing the vangels in impossible situations related to the most heinous sins they'd committed in their human lives. Vikar's pride was tested by being forced to live in a run-down castle in a little town in the middle of nowhere. Trond's sloth was surely tested as a Navy SEAL whose least strenuous exercise involved six-mile runs before breakfast. Ivak's lust had nowhere to go in an all-male Louisiana prison. Mordr had to control his wrath in a Las Vegas home full of children. Sigurd didn't have much to envy in his island hospital.

And now Harek, the greedy one, who had dared to venture into slave trading, was practically joined at the hip with a woman who loathed slavery in any form. How would she react if she found out about his history? Probably shoot him with an AK–47, or cut off his balls with a KA-BAR knife.

"You're muttering to yourself," Camille pointed out.

"Must be a sign of old age."

"How old are you?"

"Older than you could ever imagine."

She arched her brows at him.

"Watch the road," he warned. Then, "Twenty-nine human years."

"Just like me," she noted. Then, "As compared to nonhuman years?"

"Something like that."

"See. That's what I mean about your being weird. You're always saying things like that." In a surprisingly good masculine voice, she mimicked him, "I answer to a higher authority. Older than you can imagine. Nonhuman years, baby."

"I didn't say 'baby.' "

"It was implied. And what's with those pointy teeth, anyhow? Trond has them, too. Is it a family characteristic? Seems to me it would be easy enough for a dentist to file them down."

"You don't like my fangy teeth?"

"I didn't say that." She blushed. "I was being rude, wasn't it?"

"Very."

"It's just that you're so vain in other ways that I would think you'd go for perfection."

"In what ways am I vain?"

"The mousse."

He groaned. That again! "It's not mousse. It's gel. And besides, I didn't use anything today."

"I noticed."

She noticed too damn much. "We were going to be riding in an open convertible, and I didn't want bugs clinging to my hair." He smiled at her.

"Good thinking." She smiled back at him.

He felt a little warm jolt, not down below, but in the region of his heart. From a shared smile? "If we're going to be rude, let me ask you this, m'lady. Why do you downplay your looks?"

She passed a driver in a minivan that was going too slow, then eased back into the right lane before answering him. "What makes you think I downplay my looks, *m'lord*?" She put emphasis on that last word, just to show that she'd noticed his "m'lady" slip of tongue.

He must be more careful with her. "That woman last night could have any man she wanted. Then today . . . well . . . look at you." Now that *was* rude. But, truth to tell, he was a bit irritated that she hadn't taken any trouble with her appearance to go with him today. She wore beige linen slacks with a darker beige, short-sleeved blouse, and brown sandals. Her beige—all right, brown—hair was pulled back into a ponytail. (What happened to the golden highlights?) And on her face was not a speck of makeup, not even a swipe of gloss, let alone that fuck-me red lipstick. Drab colors.

But she didn't seem to mind his rude perusal. In fact, she grinned. "What makes you think I'm looking for a man? Step out of the Dark Ages, my friend. Women do not need men today."

If she only knew! He really did come from the Dark Ages. "You need us for some things," he argued, and realized he had veered into a subject area that could be dangerous as quicksand for a celibate like himself. "Let's get down to business," he said, and opened his laptop. "The thing you have to understand about BK is that they have a deep-rooted religious conviction that compels them to declare jihad against Christians, especially American Christians. In fact, not just Christians. Any non-Muslim people."

"They aren't the first people to use religion to justify evil."

He nodded. "To them, we're a threat to their culture and way of life. One example is the education of women."

She rolled her eyes.

"Face it, we're not going to change their beliefs or actions by declaring them terrorists."

"They *are* terrorists."

"Of course they are. But let me give you an example. Suppose there were people in this country—vigilantes of a sort—who went after people who perpetrated atrocities on black people, Ku Klux Klansmen of the vilest sort. Would you frown on the vigilantes' methods, but secretly applaud their ends? Left-handed justice?"

"That's an unfair comparison."

"Maybe so, but you need to go into this mission understanding that the Muslim extremists believe they have a moral obligation to preserve their society in the old ways. Leastways, some of them do. Diplomacy is not going to work. Violence is the only thing they understand, and even then, when we kill them, they will consider themselves martyrs for a holy cause."

"I find it hard to believe that rape and sexual slavery of women or forcing young boys to become soldiers and kill their own families fall under the umbrella of any religion."

"You're right. While the group's original intent was merely to change Nigeria's practice of allowing girls to go to school, it has snowballed into something way bigger. A political rebellion. And, of course, when a group grows the way BK has, there are bound to be rebels with their own causes and practices, like rape." He could have expounded further on the subject of soldiers at war and rape, but he did not think she would appreciate his telling her that, from the beginning of time, warriors had considered rape one of the prizes of victory, a salve to the adrenaline rush of battle. Not that he condoned, or had ever allowed his troops to do such, but many had, and still did.

"Do you have any idea what our role will be there on this mission? I mean, specific jobs?"

He shook his head. "All I know for sure is that Wings is interested in taking out the terrorists"—especially the Lucipires, and saving those evil ones willing to repent—"but the SEALs are most interested in rescuing the captives. The duties will overlap, of course, but we won't know until we get back on base exactly how the mission will be executed." He had ideas, of course, and suggestions, but that info could wait.

"How long do you think the mission will last?"

"Probably only a few days, from insertion to extraction. The longer we're there, the greater chance of BK noticing our presence and moving their operation. Or attacking."

For the next half hour or so as Camille drove expertly off I–10, onto I–310, and then the longer trek on US–90, he told her all he knew about the region they would be visiting, its language, terrain, and customs. And he gave her up-to-date figures on the terrorist membership, its kills, and atrocities.

His lesson was interrupted by Camille exclaiming, "Holy moly! You didn't tell me your brother owned one of the grand old sugar plantations."

"I'd hardly call it grand." The sign for Heaven's End had been painted and rehung, and the roadway, or *allée,* leading up through a corridor of live oak trees had been cleared, somewhat, but it was still a run-down plantation in much need of TLC. Or a demolition.

"It was grand at one time," Camille said in a steely voice.

He glanced at her to see what had brought on that reaction. "Heaven's End was built by my grandfather many times removed . . . the one who 'bought' my grandmother Camille at a Quadroon Ball. It was here that he lived with his *real* family."

Oh crap! "Wow! Talk about coincidence," Harek said, but what he thought was *Michael! How could you?*

He could swear he heard a voice in his head say, *How could I not?*

The last time Harek had been here, it had

seemed more like a tropical jungle with huge trees barely peeking out here and there from the overgrown foliage. Now, the kudzu and wildness had been cut back, exposing ancient oaks, tupelo, chinaberry, willow, and sycamore, and, in the distance, he could see an orchard brought back to life, bearing blossoms of what he supposed would be cherries, figs, apples, pears, plums, and peaches. Flowering bushes, like bougainvillea and magnolia, were enormous with age. Their scent was almost overpoweringly sweet.

Despite all the improvements, the roughly two-hundred-year-old main house was still a major work in progress, as evidenced by the scaffolding around all parts of the mansion. Workmen were repairing the hipped roof, which had caved in here and there, and painters were sanding down the many layers of peeling paint off the exterior. It was a raised, Creole-style house, the kind where the main living area was on the second floor, and the ground floor had been used for kitchen and storage rooms in ages past. There were three-story columns that rose all the way to the top floor; those, too, had been sanded down, preparatory to being primed and painted. Once gracious galleries that surrounded all sides of the house were filled with comfortable chairs and rockers and colorful potted flowers. Thankfully, the wide steps—about twelve feet wide—that led from the front drive up to the second floor entry had been repaired. Harek had almost broken a leg falling through the rotten boards when he was here last time. Broken glass had been replaced in the floor-to-ceiling windows, a necessity when snakes had been a huge problem in the beginning.

If Çamille was upset about this being the former home of her grandfather, so to speak, wait until she saw what Ivak was doing with the slave quarters. He'd turned the cottages into living quarters for his vangel workers.

"Have you been here before?" he asked her.

"Once. About ten years ago. But it was vacant and overgrown. A tear-down, I would have thought."

"Ivak said that it's been vacant since the 1970s. He bought it two years ago. His wife, Gabrielle, is a lawyer, and they have a little boy, about a year old. So, progress has been slow, as you can see." He was blathering to fill the silence.

She nodded, hearing but not really hearing him, her gaze rapt on the scenery they passed.

"Are you okay? Do you want to go back to New Orleans?"

Camille had pulled up to the front of the mansion, and although she had stopped the car, the motor was still idling. She appeared angry, or sad, as she stared out at the plantation house and grounds.

She shook her head. "No. It's just a building, a piece of land. It has no meaning to me."

Her flushed face and white-knuckled fists on the steering wheel gave lie to her statement. It had meaning, all right. To her. Even though it happened long ago, it must represent rejection . . . a father who favored one family over another. And slavery, of course. A plantation this size couldn't have prospered without slave labor in those pre–Civil War days.

The decision was taken out of their hands by the man who walked around the side of the building, his long blond hair hanging smoothly to his shoulders, his handsome face framed by thin war braids intertwined with crystal beads the same shade of blue as his eyes. It was Ivak, coming from what appeared to be a rose garden. He carried a shovel in one hand and a headless snake in the other. Smiling, he said, "Welcome to the Garden of Not-So-Eden, brother. Do you think Adam had this problem?"

"Probably," Harek said through the open window, laughing.

At his side, he heard Camille murmur, "More pointy teeth."

"Who would have thought that a Viking warrior would be reduced to warring with reptiles?" Ivak said to him. "No matter how many I kill, they keep multiplying. Like Saxons. Or loaves and fishes. Yeech!" He tossed the creature off into some bushes and wiped his hand on his denim braies. The shovel he propped against a tree.

Camille turned off the engine, and they both emerged from the low-slung car.

Ivak shook his head, then arched his eyebrows at Camille. "Is this the life mate?"

Harek could see the disbelief in Ivak's quick assessment, and somehow that bothered him. It was acceptable if Harek criticized her plainness, but he did not want others to do the same. Besides, she was not, not, not his life mate.

"Trond has a big mouth," Harek commented, and motioned for Camille to come closer. "Ivak, this is Camille Dumaine. Camille, my brother Ivak."

She extended a hand for Ivak to shake, which rather jarred Ivak, who was more accustomed to women hugging him, or other things. Ivak was the best-looking of all the brothers, which was saying a lot, and he milked it for all it was worth. Harek could see that Camille shared all womankind's appreciation of Ivak's charm, because she was smiling.

She didn't look half bad when she smiled, by the by. In fact, she was halfway to pretty. More than halfway. There was a certain appeal in unadornment, he was beginning to see.

Then, surprising them both, she said to Ivak, "And, no, I am not his life mate, or soul mate, or even girlfriend. I'm just the driver."

"Ahhhh," Ivak said, and winked at Harek. If there was anything a Viking man appreciated, it was a woman with spirit.

"Hawk, Hawk," a childish voice squealed as a little person waddled out the front door and across the upper verandah, followed by his mother, Gabrielle. Hawk was the closest the toddler could come to pronouncing Harek.

Harek took the steps two at a time before the child would topple over the edge and raised the child high in the air over his head. "Hey, Mikey, who's a big boy? Walking already! I'll bet you can run, too."

Mikey giggled, and drool dripped down onto

Harek's forehead. He squirmed out of Harek's embrace, then showed just how well he could waddle/run from one end of the verandah to the other. Over and over.

Harek smiled at Gabrielle and said, "Bet he wears you out."

"You have no idea," she said, and hugged Harek warmly. "I'm so glad you came. We missed you at Easter."

"I was in Siberia."

"I know," she said with a laugh.

Everyone thought it was funny, that he was sent repeatedly to such a cold, dismal place. It was not funny. Suddenly he had an epiphany. Maybe Mike knew about his Caribbean hideaway, and that's why he kept sending him to icy regions. Naw! If Mike knew, he'd turn his island into a pillar of salt, or a volcano, or something.

Ivak was coming up the steps with Camille.

Harek introduced Camille to Gabrielle and said, "One of Camille's ancestors lived here at one time," which was all Gabrielle needed to hear. She took the still-running Mikey by the hand, promising him a cookie and milk, and led Camille through the open, double front doors, which were framed on either side by tall, narrow, etched glass windows. "You have to tell me everything you know. I have old pictures I can show you, but there's so much we can't find out about the plantation's history."

Camille gave Harek a frown over her shoulder, probably because he'd disclosed her connection to Heaven's End, but she followed Camille inside.

"I doubt I can add much," she said, which was a whopper of a lie if he ever heard one.

"We'll be eating in an hour," Gabrielle called back to her husband.

"Good. Can you send out a couple of beers, sweetling?"

"Sure thing, honey." The look Ivak and Gabrielle exchanged then was one he noticed among all his brothers and their spouses, and often at the most inappropriate times. Like now. It was none he'd ever experienced himself. One of such incredible intimacy. Love, but more. 'Twas enough to make a grown man gag.

He and Ivak sat down in the low rockers and propped their long legs on the rail. Now that he was up on the verandah, he could see all the numerous five-gallon cans of paint and drywall compound, along with brushes and rollers. They were soon enjoying cold long-neck bottles of Dixie beer brought by a female ceorl, who nodded mutely when they thanked her.

"Cnut told me more about your mission," Ivak said right off. "Will you be needing me and my vangels?"

"Possibly. I should know more in the next few days."

"Are you sure Lucies are involved with Boko Haram?"

"Seems likely, considering the depravity of some of their actions. Beheadings. Mass murders. Rape. Unspeakable torture."

Ivak nodded somberly. They all knew of Jasper's talent for inventing new methods of gaining information from captives. Even vangels shuddered with fear.

"It's going to be touchy, working so closely with the SEALs and other operatives, keeping your vangel identity secret."

"Tell me about it," Harek said. "But we'll manage. We always do." He glanced around the seemingly peaceful setting. "Are you rid of Lucies at the prison?"

"Most of them. Especially with Dominique gone." A few years back, they'd managed to annihilate one of Jasper's high haakai, Dominique Fontaine, who had operated out of a New Orleans restaurant headquarters called Anguish and had even infiltrated Angola Prison, where Ivak was a chaplain. "Every once in a while, a stray one wanders in. Be careful in New Orleans. There's likely a few rogue demons still remaining."

That made sense. The evil in Angola would lure a Lucipire, as would the decadence of the Crescent City, even when there was no major Jasper mission involved.

A honking horn drew their attention then. Coming to a brake-screeching halt, right behind Camille's Benz, was a lavender, 1960s-vintage, Chevy Impala convertible. Driving it was a grinning Leroy Sonnier, Gabrielle's ex-con brother. Riding shotgun was the Cajun midget troublemaker—okay, that was politically incorrect—the petite Cajun matchmaker/folk healer Louise Rivard, best known up and down the bayou as Tante Lulu. She was as old as dust, but that didn't stop her from having bright red hair, or from wearing hot pink biking shorts and a T-shirt with the glittery logo, "Let the Fun Begin."

Before, Harek had suspected he was in trouble.

Now, Harek knew he was in trouble . . . *big* trouble. Michael was sending in the big guns.

Chapter 8

Stormy weather on the horizon . . .

Camille was a mess, and not just her hair, which tended to frizz after a day in this humid heat with no air-conditioning. AC was about number seventeen on the list of priorities for the Heaven's End restoration project, Ivak had told them, unapologetically, as they ate lunch under a whirring ceiling fan. He had installed a historically incorrect rain forest shower in an upstairs bathroom, though, he'd added, also unapologetically, in case anyone needed to "cool off."

"Does Mike know about that sybaritic addition?" Harek had asked. He often used big words, Camille had noticed, and not for particular effect. He seemed to think in dictionary mode when he wasn't sounding like a character from a medieval movie.

"Mike was the first one to try it out," Ivak had

replied. At Harek's dropped jaw, Ivak had hooted, "Just kidding."

"Who's Mike?" Camille had asked.

"Our boss," they both said at the same time.

"You both have the same boss?" That was odd. A security specialist and a prison chaplain working for the same company?

"Don't try to figure it out," Gabrielle had interjected. "It's a family thing."

That was clear as bayou mud.

In any case, it wasn't the heat and humidity that was causing Camille's problems. No, she was an emotional wreck from all the shocks of the day. She should have just rented a hotel room after her fitting this morning and slept the day away, her head covered by a blanket, until it was time for her bridesmaid obligations. She got a headache—another headache—just thinking about the evening to come.

Sadly, Camille felt safer and more at peace as a special forces agent back at Coronado and on live ops abroad than she did here in the South, fighting her past. A psychiatrist would have a heyday analyzing her screwed-up psyche.

It was bad enough that she was strolling around the plantation where her ancestor, *a slave owner,* had raised his legitimate family, which felt like a betrayal of sorts to her namesake grandmother, but she was nodding and smiling until her jaw hurt at the renovations being made to the old mansion (did she really need to see the bedroom where dear ol' granddad slept with his wife?). Next, she would be dropping by her father's "other" home in Lafayette to visit his longtime mistress, the floozy (a romance author, for heaven's sake!), and hanging with her twin half sisters, whom she had never met in person and vowed she never would. They were—surprise, surprise—grad students in philosophy, or French literature, or something else equally esoteric, at Harvard University. Her father must be very proud. Her brother had met them at one time, when the girls were in high school, and said they seemed nice. Camille had told her brother he was an idiot.

She couldn't dwell on her father's not-so-secret life, or she really would go off the deep end. Not really, but she might scream or growl or punch something, which would call attention to herself, and she'd really rather be invisible, one of her greatest assets in WEALS.

Back to Heaven's End. She should have been appalled at the old slave quarters, but she couldn't fault what they were now . . . charming cottages to house Ivak's staff, who, incidentally, had the same pointy incisors as Harek and Ivak and Trond, and they weren't even blood relatives. Weird, that's what it was. She sensed a mystery here that she needed to figure out. Later. Maybe they were some kind of cult who filed their teeth that way? Modern-day vampires?

A chocolaty vampire at that, in Harek's case. If she wasn't so full from the delicious lunch of shrimp étouffée, lazy bread, tomato salad, and the sinfully decadent Peachy Praline Cobbler Cake that Tante Lulu had brought, she would probably be licking Harek up one side and down the other. She still might.

I really am losing my mind.

And speaking, rather thinking, of that friend of the Sigurdsson family, Tante Lulu . . . holy moly! The dingbat old lady voiced an opinion on everything, especially her favorite saint, Jude, whom she worked into every conversation thread. He was apparently the patron saint of hopeless cases, and Camille could have sworn that Tante Lulu looked directly at her when she'd imparted that fact. But then Harek had exclaimed, "Are you saying I'm hopeless?" Maybe Tante Lulu had strange eyes, like those portrait paintings that, no matter where you stood, the person seemed to be staring at you.

"We're all hopeless, at one time or another," Tante Lulu had replied in all her homespun wisdom. "Truth ta tell, *cher,* I come t'day 'cause St. Jude whispered in mah ear that there was someone in need of our help."

Harek had about choked on the beer he'd been sipping at as they'd relaxed around the dining room table. (And that was another thing. In between beers, Harek and Ivak had been quaffing down cardboard containers of something called Fake-O, which they drank with grimaces on their faces. Odd!) But then Tante Lulu's rheumy eyes turned to Camille, and she knew it was she that the old lady had in her crosshairs. Camille was hopeless, all right, hopeless as a hooker in a Junior Miss pageant.

Harek sat next to Camille on one side of the

table, facing Leroy and Tante Lulu on the other side, with Ivak and Gabrielle at either end. Tante Lulu sat on two cushions to compensate for her height. The child Mikey had been put down for a nap, kicking and screaming, a while ago by his nanny, Elsa, another pointy-teeth person. Like a little Energizer bunny, Mikey kept going and going, tiring everyone out and eventually himself. He was adorable.

Gabrielle's brother Leroy, who'd recently gotten his master's degree in social work from the University of Tennessee and was about to start a job running a halfway house for Angola parolees, had been flirting with Camille ever since he arrived. Probably because she was the only single female there. And she'd been flirting back at him, mostly because it seemed to annoy Harek, and she was annoyed at Harek for blurting out her dubious connection to Heaven's End.

Actually, Leroy was a fascinating person, having served time in prison for murdering his abusive father. Tante Lulu, who was a friend of a friend of practically everyone in Louisiana, had helped procure his release. In any case, Leroy seemed to have a genuine interest in her work with WEALS.

"Would you like to come see our operation?" Leroy asked her. "We're having an open house at Gateways on Monday."

"We're leaving tomorrow," Harek answered for her.

She kicked his leg under the table. "I'd love to see it, Leroy. Maybe next time I'm back in

Nawleans." Not that she intended to come back anytime soon, but if she did, she would.

"Give me your e-mail address and cell number, and we can keep in touch," Leroy suggested. "Maybe I can come out to Coronado sometime, get the grand tour."

"No, no, no. Camille will be too busy. An upcoming mission and all that. Very hush-hush." Harek was repeating her exact words, the ones she'd used last night to describe his work to her brother.

She stamped his foot with her foot. Hard.

He winced, but smiled warmly at her. Fake warmness. What was up with that?

"Harek and Camille are soon-to-be life mates," Ivak blurted out. He was leaning back in his chair, enjoying the interplay.

"We are not!" she and Harek said at the same time.

"I doan know," Tante Lulu interjected. "I'm thinkin' St. Jude mus' have somethin' in mind fer you two, ta have me skedaddlin' over here t'day."

The old lady had already given Camille a St. Jude medal on a silver chain, a plastic statue that would fit in her purse, and a prayer card.

Tante Lulu glanced sideways at Leroy beside her. "Or mebbe it's you he has in mind fer Camille."

Leroy pretended delight and said, "Yippee!"

Gabrielle giggled, "You better beware, Camille. When Tante Lulu decides to matchmake, you are a dead duck. I know from experience."

"A very pretty dead duck," Ivak added, winking at his wife. "I enjoyed plucking you as I recall."

"Tsk, tsk!" Tante Lulu said with a grin at the sexual innuendo.

Harek grumbled, "Bloody hell!"

"Camille, I could call mah niece Charmaine over at her beauty shop in Houma and get ya in fer a last-minute appointment if ya want. She'd get ya gussied up real good fer the weddin'."

"Uh, thanks, but no thanks," Camille answered. "I can handle it myself." If Tante Lulu's red-dyed hair, heavy foundation complete with rouged cheeks, and the purple enameled nails were any indication, she could definitely do better *gussying* herself.

Even though lunch had been early, it was already one p.m. and they needed to head back to the city. Camille glanced at Harek and he nodded, understanding her silent message.

"Hate to eat and run, Ivak, but Camille and I need to hit the road. She has a lot of gussying to do back at Evermore."

"Evermore?" Ivak asked.

"That's the name of Camille's family home," Harek informed his brother, and the two of them exchanged a look.

"Leave it to you!" she thought Ivak murmured to Harek. "Be careful."

"Be careful of what?" she asked Harek.

"Riches," he said enigmatically.

Camille nudged Harek with her knee. "My mother's already sent me thirteen text messages. If I don't return soon, she'll be sending out a posse."

He nudged her back and added a quick pass

of his palm over her thigh, up high. When she glanced his way, he just waggled his eyebrows.

"Are you two playin' hanky-panky under the table?" Tante Lulu inquired. "No singin' hymns afore the gospel!"

"I'm a great singer," Harek told Camille.

"Get real," she said, and stood.

"I think she likes me," Harek confided loudly to Ivak, as he stood, too, along with all the others at the table.

"Hey, you're a Viking. Women can't resist Vikings," Ivak reminded his brother.

"Puh-leeze! Not the Viking stuff again," Gabrielle said with a groan.

" 'Tis true, heartling," Ivak told his wife. "In the old days, back in Viking times, women from all countries invited Norsemen into their bed furs because we were more handsome and brave and virile than their men, even on their best days."

Gabrielle laughed. "And because Viking men bathed more often than others."

"That, too," Ivak agreed, coming around the table to give his wife a quick kiss.

Harek turned to Camille, as if about to give her a kiss, too.

"Don't even think it," she warned, although when he smiled like that, the smell of chocolate was overpowering.

"I swear, you are so hot, you could make my hard drive melt, and, believe me, my hard drive is very hard at the moment," Harek whispered in her ear.

The fool! Even knowing that he was just teasing, Camille felt a flush of warmth rush through her body.

"I'm 'spectin' the thunderbolt any minute now," Tante Lulu announced, staring at her and Harek.

"What?" Camille said. "The sun is shining brightly, not a cloud in sight." That's all she would need, rain to make this wedding nightmare complete.

"Not that kind of thunder," Tante Lulu explained. "Nope, it's the thunderbolt of love. Do ya have yer hope chest yet, honey?"

"Are you talking to me?" Camille asked. Really, the old lady's mind jumped from one subject to another like popcorn on a hot griddle.

"I was talkin ta Harek about the hope chest," Tante Lulu said. "Not ta worry, mah boy. I'll have one made fer ya, lickety-split. All the men in mah family, and all the male friends of the family, gets hope chests. No, no, ya doan have ta thank me. A man's gotta have a place ta store his linens and doilies and such before the weddin'."

"There. Is. Not. Going. To. Be. A. Wedding," Harek said.

Camille laughed, not because she disagreed with him, but the red color in his face was so satisfying. She didn't know what it was about his discomfort that entertained her. Immature of her, she recognized. But funny, dammit.

Suddenly, off in the distance, the sound of thunder could be heard. Very distinctly.

Camille stopped laughing.

Weddings were the bane of most men . . .
more so if they were Vikings . . .

Once again, four hours later, Camille had the last laugh. On him.

Harek groaned on first seeing Camille come down the stairs of her parents' home wearing a long, slim gown of pure silk temptation. It wasn't white and it wasn't rose-colored, something in between that made her skin appear creamy smooth, dusted with honey. Not that the dress was sluttish, not at all. It was sex on a sophisticated, subtle level. The worst kind. Or the best kind, depending on your point of view.

The front of the dress was cut in a wide half circle, barely caught off her shoulders by short cap sleeves and almost but not quite exposing the tops of her breasts. A tease. Behind, there wasn't much skin exposed, but there were twenty-seven tiny buttons . . . *Yes, he counted them as she turned halfway down the staircase to pose and show him all sides of the gown.* The buttons led from below her shoulder blades down, down, down to the middle of her derriere. It was the fabric, though, that was the killer. Some kind of clingy silk stuff that moved when she did, cupping her breasts and her buttocks.

"Oops, I forgot my purse." She went back upstairs.

And he got a hard-on just watching the movement of her arse. Up, down, up, down. Like a longship on the high seas. Holy frickin' waves!

She was back, carrying a small gold mesh bag the size of a piece of toast. It had a long gold chain that she'd looped over her shoulder.

Which caused him to notice her neck that was bared by her upswept hair, hair that had miraculously turned blondish, or maybe it was the glittery stuff she seemed to have dusted herself with. It was going to be a constant struggle for him to keep his fangs retracted lest he pounce on her and take a bite, right where the curve of her neck seemed to throb with sweet blood close to the surface.

It was troubling, this growing need he had to feed. More than once in the past year, he'd felt vampire-ish in his hunger for blood, and not just to save sinners or destroy Lucies. Was it possible that his vampire side was overtaking his angel side? Not that he ever felt very angelic.

Down, Dracula, down, he joked with himself.

Her only jewelry was a pair of pearl stud earrings that called attention to her small shell ears, the whorls of which he would love to lick. He had a particular skill in ear play that he hadn't practiced in more than a century. Perhaps it was time to . . .

No, no, no. No ear sex. No bloodsucking. No arse watching.

"You look very nice," he said, taking Camille's hand as she stepped off the last step. She was wearing high heels that matched her dress, so her height was enhanced by a good four inches. He liked that she didn't have to crane her neck to look up at him. *Necks again! I have got to stop thinking about necks.*

"You look pretty good yourself." She stepped closer and flicked a speck of lint off the lapel of his black tux jacket, then smoothed out the fabric.

"You smell like chocolate," she said.

"You smell like roses," he said at the same time.

"Chocolate roses? That's some combination."

"Works for me." He gave a rueful laugh and considered for a brief instant of insanity that it wouldn't hurt to lean in and taste her lips, just to see if there was such a thing as chocolate roses.

He was saved by the bell, or rather the belle, who made a very unladylike snort of disgust as she approached, coming from a downstairs bathroom in a wave of some sophisticated perfume with tones citrusy floral. Dr. Jeannette Dumaine was wearing a pale blue gown with about a million sparkling crystals, not to be outdone by the diamond necklace and earrings that could very well be worth a million dollars. "Camille, darling, let me see how you look." Camille's mother shoved him aside—she blamed him for Camille being gone all day—and inspected her daughter with a critical eye.

"The gown fits perfectly," she conceded. A bone of contention had apparently been Camille's refusal to come back to New Orleans weeks ago for a proper fitting, "but why aren't you wearing the pearls?"

"It seemed like too much. The dress speaks for itself, don't you think?" Camille patted her mother on the arm and said, "You look very elegant, Mother. Too young to be the mother of the groom."

Jeannette preened at the compliment.

At fifty-something, the lady did look much younger, probably due to some work being done on her face and neck. Modern men had no way of knowing for sure how old women were, with all the sly artifices available, including plastic surgery. And don't even think about bosoms with silicone or enhancing bras to fool clueless men. Not that he was looking at Camille's mother's breasts. Jeesh! He was just saying . . . thinking.

"Is everyone ready?" Dr. Emile Dumaine asked, coming out of the library with Alain. Both of them wore similar white tuxedo jackets over black formal pants, and Harek wondered briefly if he should have gone for the lighter color. But, no, even if he was half angel, he rarely wore white because his skin was pale when he'd gone too long without feeding.

Dr. Dumaine wore a subtle clove/citrus-embued cologne that hit Harek like a silent punch. Harek was being assaulted by all these conflicting scents. Roses, spices, fruit. Whew!

Emile and Alain were both carrying tumblers of an amber liquid. Bourbon, would be his guess. He could have used a glass himself. That, or a gallon of Fake-O. Yeech!

"You look lovely, Jeannette," Emile said, kissing his wife lightly on the cheek in an oddly formal fashion. Then he turned to Camille and said, "You, too, sweetheart."

"That color suits you, Cam," Alain added. Apparently, Camille had been complaining to him about the "pink" gown.

Camille made a face at her brother.

Harek reached out and shook Alain's hand. "Good luck tonight, man."

"Thanks. Sorry we didn't get a chance to talk more while you were here," Alain said.

"How could you? They were gone all day," Mrs. Dumaine pointed out.

"Now, Jeannette. Let's not spoil the happy occasion," Emile chastened.

To Harek's surprise, the usually strong-minded harpy zipped her mouth into a tight line, then said, "The limo is waiting outside. Are we ready?"

They all nodded, and Harek whispered to Camille, "I'll follow in your car. That way we can leave when we want."

"Good thinking," she whispered back.

The wedding went off as planned at St. Louis Cathedral. Beautiful setting. Beautiful bride. Beautiful music. Beautiful church rituals.

Ho-hum.

Harek hated weddings.

He amused himself by watching Camille's ass in the clingy dress during the processional. Then he amused himself by watching Camille's ex-fiancé, who was one of the groomsmen, watching Camille's ass. Further bored, he amused himself by singing along when the organist played "Ave Maria" for a small choir, until he realized that people were turning to look at him, even Camille from up on the altar where she stood, gaping. What? Other people were singing, too. But then, he realized he'd called attention to himself because he was so good. Vangels had remarkably good singing voices.

He made a rueful shrug of apology to Camille and those closest to him while the choir continued until the end of the song. Finally, it was the time for the exchange of vows. *Will this service never end? I need a beer, or something stronger, or a swig of Fake-O, or a combination of both. Yeah, that would be good. I could create my own mixed drink. Bottle it up. Make a million bucks. Scotch and blood on the rocks. Blood-tini. Bloody Sour. Blood Bliss. Drac's Fang. Fuzzy Fang. Fangs for the Memories. A Fanger, instead of a Banger. Or maybe the emphasis should be on angels. Something like Angel Blood, Heavenly Hooch, or a Dirty Angel.*

I'm losing my mind here.

He cursed under his breath, and the heavyset lady in the pew in front of him, wearing a black straw hat the size of an umbrella dripping with purple flowers, turned and hissed at him.

He did another shrug-apology, and tried just twiddling his fingers while the ceremony went on endlessly. Was he the only one who had to piss? The only one bored, bored, bored?

Taking out his cell phone, which was on silent mode, he checked for text messages. There was one from his brother Vikar.

Call me

Well, he couldn't very well call now, so he texted back.

In church. can't talk. what's up?

Almost immediately, there was a response.

WTF! U, in church? Roof fall in?

LOL. 4 a wedding.

Even better. Or worse.

U better not say that around Alex.

Having fun?

Yeah, like root canal on angel fang.

Ouch. I hear u found life mate. Not ur wedding, is it? Knowing u, texting during marriage wouldn't be odd. U always have cell phone or computer glued 2 ur arse or other body parts. Do you sleep w/laptop, btw?

No, haven't found a life mate. No, not my wedding. No, I don't sleep w/computer. U contact me just 2 annoy me?

Cnut called. Something big coming down, as suspected. Suggests 4 of VIK, including u, come 2 his aid with team of vangel warriors. ASAP.

Myself & . . . ?

Mordr, Ivak & me w/troops, 2nite. Trond w/u & SEALs.

He nodded to himself. A good combination. And just the right number since he and Trond would be unable to bring their own vangel fighters without risking secrecy of the group.

Be back in Coronado 2moro. Prob won't be in Nigeria 'til next week.

Just then, Black Hat Lady made a tsking sound, and Harek figured he was on her shit list, again, this time for texting in church. But when he looked up, he saw that it was the woman next to her, cell phone at her ear, who was getting the dirty eyeball. The woman, a pretty blonde wearing a tiny feathered hat with fake rosebuds, glanced his way, and he winked conspiratorially at her. She grinned and winked back.

For a moment, he thought he detected fangs, but she'd turned back to face the altar. He was probably wrong. He seemed to have fangs on the brain at the moment. *Fang Me. Bang Me.* Yep, he was losing it.

That little bit of flirting occupied at least a half minute.

At the same time, a foul odor filled the air. Had someone farted? In church? It was probably Big Hat. Phew!

He signed off with Vikar and breathed a sigh of relief—actually, he released the breath he'd been holding in the wake of the gas lady—when the priest told Alain he could kiss the bride, a sure sign that the wedding was over. Soon the recessional started and Harek got another gander at Camille's ass in the clingy gown. The other bridesmaids wore similar gowns, but none of them had Camille's posterior curves to carry them off in quite the same way. No doubt all the WEALS exercises—crunches and squats and the lot—developed muscles in that area that some women yearned to have. Not a bad side advantage, from his viewpoint, anyhow.

It annoyed the hell out of him to see Julian glance Camille's way repeatedly. A bit of dog in the manger on Julian's part, if you asked Harek, which no one did. Julian didn't want her and yet he did. And, besides, it was dog in the manger-ish for him, too. He didn't want her, *that way* . . . well, yes, he did, but not as a life mate. At least he wasn't married like good ol' Julian.

Harek slipped out the side door and was about to head for the Benz when he got another whiff of that stinky odor. Something unpleasant, like sulfur. That meant there was a Lucie in the area. Just one, by the strength of the odor, Harek guessed, already reaching inside his tux jacket for several throwing stars, which had been cured in the symbolic blood of Christ. He placed them in his outside tux pockets. He scanned the area. Someone in the church or just outside must be a really bad sinner, or about to commit some major transgression to lure a lone Lucie out in the open like this.

Almost immediately, he realized that the Lucie in question was the blond woman with the cell phone. So it hadn't been gas he'd smelled, and blamed on the lady in the black hat, but the rotten egg odor of a demon vampire. And the Lucie was staring directly at Camille's father.

Huh?

What kind of great sin had Dr. Emile Dumaine committed, or was he planning to commit? And why hadn't Harek detected a lemon scent on Camille's father? There had been that citrusy clove cologne he wore, but it had been subtle, not overpowering, like a sin scent. It must be something bad Emile was contemplating, then, not yet a sin set in stone, brimstone, so to speak.

More important, why hadn't Harek detected a Lucie sitting right in front of him? Had he been distracted by boredom, less than diligent? If so, he would hear about it soon enough from Michael. Usually Harek could spot a Lucie from half a mile away, though this one was a lowly hordling, not a powerful haakai. And why hadn't the Lucie known he was a vangel . . . a high VIK, for cloud's sake? Perhaps a church setting diffused the odors of demons and angels. He would have to check on that. Good info to have, if true.

People were exiting the church now, heading toward their vehicles, while the bridal party hung behind for pictures. Camille hadn't noticed him yet. In fact, she appeared to be fending off advances from that horndog Julian. Harek would have something to say to the man. Later.

Moving quickly, he placed himself midway between the Lucie and Emile, forcing the demon vampire to notice him. His eyes were probably already turning from blue to silver, and he could feel his fangs elongating. Her eyes went wide with recognition and immediately began to redden as she began to morph into demonoid form, which she could not—should not—do in public. Scales were breaking out on her skin. Soon a tail would appear and deadly mung would seep from her demon pores. Her size would increase for combat.

But she had to know she was no match for a vangel of his powerful lineage. He might be a computer geek in present times, and he might have been a merchant in the old days, but at heart he would always be a Viking warrior.

In a rush, she dashed for a back door of the cathedral. He followed her into a storage room where priestly vestments hung on padded hangers, and jars of holy water and anointing oils were lined up on built-in shelves.

The Lucie was now in full demonoid form complete with clawed hands and three-inch fangs, and, yes, breasts. Big, red, scaly breasts and black nipples. Its mons was covered with long, straggly, black hair, though the hair on its head was still blond and oddly beautiful. Seeing there was no escape, the demon lunged for him. Mung flew off its scaly skin and hit the walls, as well as some of the priestly garments. Luckily, he was able to jump aside and avoid both being clawed and having his tux get stained. Mung could be poisonous if it got into an open wound, and if demon fang juice entered the body of either a vangel or a human, it was a sure ticket to Lucipiredom. *Not to be confused with any of the Magic Kingdoms, believe you me,* he joked with himself.

Stay alert, Harek, he chided himself. *Never turn your back on a Lucipire. Never underestimate your enemy, though they be Saxon or Satan's minion. Get the bloody damn job done.*

Outraged at being thwarted, the Lucie spun awkwardly and raised high a long hatpin, of all things. Not to be dismissed, of course, since it had probably been treated with some vile substance. A pin that size must have been stuck not just in her feathered hat, but all the way through her evil, dumb blond head. Amazing the things a Lucie would do for Jasper.

The Lucie backhanded him across the face, catching him by surprise, and causing Harek to fly against the wall. Harek swiped blood from his lip with the back of his hand and glared. No way would he let himself be bested by a mere hordling.

With his agility restored, Harek jumped to his feet. Before the Lucie could pierce him with the sharp hatpin, he took one of the throwing stars out of his pocket. He aimed it at the Lucie's left thigh, causing the creature's knee to buckle, and it went down to the floor with a heavy thud, the pin rolling out of its hand. Immediately, Harek followed with another star to the wretch's neck, causing it to claw with both hands, trying to pull it out. The Lucie fell backward, growling with pain, furious with frustration.

Both of those wounds would cause the demon vampire to die, eventually, but that would only send it back to Jasper's lair. The weapon had to pierce the heart in order to destroy the Lucie for good, condemning it to hell for all eternity.

He did not want this Lucie dead yet, thus his

well-aimed hits. He needed to know why Camille's father was in the demon's crosshairs.

"Are you here alone?" he asked the dying demon as it writhed on the floor, its blood seeping from both wounds, especially the neck.

The demon refused to answer.

So Harek stepped on the star in her thigh, causing the sharp edges to go deeper.

The demon screamed.

"Tell me, are you here alone?"

She nodded. "My partner . . . killed in Angola last year . . . I . . . I have been wandering."

"Why are you following Dr. Dumaine?"

The Lucie blinked at him, surprised that he knew the target.

"What great sin has he committed?" When the Lucie didn't immediately reply, he added, "Or is he about to commit?"

Blood oozed out of the demon's mouth and nose. It would not be long now. Harek had to act quickly. "Tell me," he demanded, "and I will make your passage quicker."

"Murder. His wife. Has mistress. Money." On those words, the demon's eyes began to close and a gurgling sound came from its open mouth, the death rattle. Even so, it rose to its knees.

Harek could have poured a jar of holy water over the demon, but that would only cause its skin to burn off. An ugly sight, but not fatal. No, Harek needed to do more. Without delay, he drew a long switchblade from an interior pocket of his jacket, popped it open, and swiped wide, catching the Lucie's arm through flesh and bone, above the elbow. The demon looked with horror at the severed arm, which hung by a scrap of skin. Given an opening, Harek thrust the blade through the beast's heart. Immediately, the Lucie fell backward again and began to dissolve into a puddle of odorsome slime.

Harek went over to one of the wide, narrow-depth drawers in the built-in storage units and took out what appeared to be linen napkins. He used one to wipe the blade of his knife and return it to his jacket. Another he used to pick up the hatpin, which he in turn used to lift the throwing stars from the slimy, disintegrating mass on the floor. He placed those in a third clean napkin, which he wrapped tightly and placed with the knife in the interior pocket. He would clean them all later.

"What are you doing?" he heard behind him.

Camille.

Without turning, he said, "I was looking for a men's room. That was a bloody long service, and I had to piss."

"I saw you follow a woman in here. Where is she?"

"Uh. I didn't see any woman," he lied, already having kicked aside her dress, shoes, and feathered hat so they were under the garment rack. "Shouldn't you be in the limo, on the way to the reception?"

"I decided to go with you. What is that mess on the floor?"

"What? Oh? One of the bottles of holy oils must have spilled."

"It stinks. I've never known church oils to smell like that."

"Maybe it was spoiled." He turned then.

And she gasped, clapping both hands to her face in horror.

Realizing that his fangs were still extended, he ran his tongue over his front teeth, and the fangs retracted, but it was too late. She'd seen.

"Who are you?" she asked then. "*What* are you?"

"The better question is," he said, with weary resignation, "why would your father want to kill your mother?"

Chapter 9

She was all shook up, but not by Elvis . . .

An hour later, sitting at the head table with the rest of the bridal party in the Garden Room of General's Palace, Camille was still shaken. And scared.

Camille had grown up in a city known for its bizarre people and happenings. Think voodoo. A creepy wax museum. Ghost sightings. Mardi Gras excesses. Sex out the wazoo, some of it weird, to say the least. Anne Rice, with her *Interview with the Vampire* nonsense, had lived in this very Garden District at one time. But Camille had never been afraid. Instead, she was mostly amused.

Besides, danger was a fact of her life in the WEALS. Face it, the terrorists she was committed to destroying were some of the scariest folks on earth.

But this was different.

Who was this man she'd brought with her to New Orleans? She was almost positive that she'd seen fangs on him. Real, honest-to-goodness fangs, not fake French Quarter plastic trinkets. Forget Tom Cruise as Lestat. Harek had seemed to be the real deal, handsome-as-hell, sexy-as-sin vampire. If one had a thing for vampires, that was. She didn't. Not before, anyhow.

And a woman had gone into the cathedral storeroom ahead of him, no matter what Harek said. In fact, Camille had seen a lady's feathered hat peeping out from under the hanging church vestments. The slime, or oil, or whatever it was on the floor, had evaporated before her very eyes, like magic. And what had Harek meant about her father murdering her mother?

What did it all mean?

"I can explain," he'd assured her.

"I doubt it," she'd said.

His shoulders had sunk as he'd exhaled with disgust, and the oh-fuck! expression on his face belied any confidence he'd proclaimed of being able to explain diddly-squat. Before he could try, she'd backed up toward the still-open doorway of the storeroom. "I'm going to the reception in one of the limos, after all," she said. "You can go in my car, and we'll talk later. Or maybe it would be better if you didn't come at all."

"Oh, I'll be there. Count on it. And we will talk."

"Whatever. I can't deal with this now."

"I owe you an explanation, Camille," he'd said, "but more than that, I have to save your father from what he's planning to do."

On those ominous words, he'd walked past her, through the doorway. Instead of the stinky slime odor, all she'd noticed then was chocolate.

Talk about bizarre!

She'd managed to avoid talking with Harek during the cocktail hour while a jazz quartet played subdued, traditional blues numbers. Several hundred people had stood about drinking Inez's signature punch, Mint Buzz, which had miniature heart-shaped ice cubes floating on top. *Gag me with a cocktail stirrer.* Those so inclined got hard liquor, wine, or sodas at the bar. And a few, like Harek, had nursed bottles of beer.

She wasn't drinking anything at all, except for the occasional sip of Perrier, because she had to stay alert. Harek was watching her. All the time. And if that wasn't bad enough, Julian kept trying to get her alone. "I never stopped loving you," Julian whispered in her ear at one point.

Puh-leeze! Talk about tacky. His very pregnant wife was sitting on a chaise in the lounge because her ankles were swollen from standing so long in church. He probably wasn't getting any at home the past few weeks and figured Camille would be desperate for his touch. The delusional dog! She hadn't been getting any for a long time, either, but she'd rather crawl, alone, through Lafayette Cemetery on All Souls' night, than let him touch her again. And, yes, she'd done that once, the woo-woo cemetery visit, but she'd been with a group of friends, and they'd been only twelve years old and fearless at the time.

Camille tried to maintain a bright face, she

really did. Inez made a lovely bride in her antique lace gown, and Alain looked so happy. Camille didn't want to spoil the day for them. And so she made her way through the appetizer stage of dinner, where turtle soup was finished with great flair tableside with aged sherry, not a small feat considering the number of tables in the large room. She barely tasted the main course, even though it was one of her favorites: filet of beef covered with lump Crab Imperial, served over a bed of baby white asparagus, with a side of buttery truffled grits. She noticed that Harek, sitting at one of the front tables with, among others—*could you believe the irony?*—Julian's wife, Justine, didn't seem to have any trouble scarfing down the delicious food, in between smiling and talking to Justine. *About what?* she wondered.

Worst of all, or among the worst things, Camille kept finding herself staring at her father and noting his interactions with her mother. It was preposterous to think the thin academic whose head was usually buried in a book could ever think of murdering his wife. But . . . had he always been so cold toward her mother? They were never the perfect couple. How could they be with her father's double life? Even though they were never openly affectionate, they'd seemed committed to each other at the very least as professional colleagues who lived together. Comfortable with their upscale standard of living among the elite of the Crescent City. They'd been married for more than thirty-five years. There must be some affection between them.

A blip of memory tugged at Camille's brain. A long time ago, soon after she'd learned about her father's mistress and other family, she'd overheard some ladies in her mother's garden club speaking about Sonja Nance, her father's lover. "She'll be mistress of Evermore one day, mark my words."

Which was impossible. Evermore belonged to Camille's mother, and it had been passed down through two generations of females. In fact, the majority of money in the family belonged to dear old Mom. The house, the antiques, the paintings. Drs. Emile and Jeannette Dumaine had very good jobs at the university, but their salaries combined could never support a house of this size in this location. The taxes alone would . . .

No, it was a ridiculous idea. Damn Harek for even planting these seeds of suspicion in her mind. It must be a warped kind of joke that Harek was playing on her.

For what purpose, though?

And he hadn't seemed a cruel kind of person.

Still . . .

Her attention was brought back to the present by a new band setting up on the small stage, and the center of the room being cleared for dancing. "Let's all stand for the bridal dance," the leader announced as the band segued into that Etta James classic "At Last." Which caused everyone to laugh because Alain and Inez had had an over-long engagement.

They looked beautiful together, and for the moment, Camille forgot all the worries weighing her down.

Then the band moved slowly into another song, Billie Holiday's "Our Love Is Here to Stay," and the bride's and groom's parents joined them on the dance floor. Camille studied her parents, who danced well together. Nothing intimate, but then this would not be the place for intimacy. They appeared to be talking intently about something, probably related to the wedding details. Her father's head was cocked to the side as he listened to something her mother was telling him. Then he frowned.

Hmm.

They switched partners to Adele's "Make You Feel My Love," and the bride danced with her father, the groom with his mother, and so on. This particular band was known for its mixture of modern and traditional music, to please both the young and old in the crowd. And then the bridal party joined them on the dance floor to Nat King Cole's "Unforgettable." Camille had been partnered with Julian and had to warn him once they started dancing, "Get your hand off my butt, or I'll cut that silly smirk off your face with my KA-BAR knife."

"Ooh, I love when you go all tough girl on me."

"Really? As I recall, you wanted me to quit the teams and go back to school, like my parents wanted."

"I was just getting on their good side." He shrugged and flashed her what was, in his own esteemed opinion, a boyish grin.

Where is that KA-BAR knife?

His hands were playing with the buttons on

the back of her dress now. He might have even undone one.

She made a hissing sound and tried to knee him in the groin.

He was quicker, anticipating her move, and he twirled her in an intricate dance step under his arm, then back in his embrace, tighter now.

"You are a flaming asshole, Julian."

"And you are flaming beautiful." He laughed. "I can't help myself, darlin'," he said against her ear. "You are irresistible in that gown."

"I was pretty resistible about nine months ago." Enough was enough! She stepped deliberately on his foot so that she could get some space between them.

"Now, sweetheart, I've explained how that happened."

"Um, I think this is my dance," Harek said, tapping Julian on the shoulder and literally shoving him aside.

"You didn't have to do that," she said once Julian stalked off and Harek took her into his arms.

"You wanted him pawing you in front of his wife?"

"Of course not."

"Just say, 'Thank you, Harek.' "

"Thank you," she said grudgingly, "even though I could have handled the shithead myself."

"M'lady, chivalry is not dead in some quarters. Betimes, a damsel must let her knight do his knightly things for her." Laughing, he drew her tightly against him, his hard parts pressed into her softer ones, her face resting on his wide shoulder.

"Do all knights smell like the richest warm chocolate?" Ironically, the band was playing that old James Taylor song, "How Sweet It Is." For sure!

"Only the best ones. Truth to tell, only me. Leastways, I've never heard of any other sweet knights." She could tell he was smiling against her hair.

"Lucky me!" she muttered, and nuzzled his neck, barely restraining herself from taking a lick, just to see how he tasted. "You should know I'm a chocoholic," she confessed.

"Lucky me!" he muttered back, and tugged her even closer. "Have I told you how much I like your gown? Especially the back."

She refused to ask what he meant by that. She suspected she knew, having caught several men checking out her backside when she'd been walking down the aisle, especially The Louse.

"Are you wearing undergarments?"

"Of course!" she said indignantly.

His palm swept over her bottom, so quickly she was probably the only one who noticed. "Are you sure?" he asked, then guessed, correctly, "A thong, then," and he groaned.

Before she could protest, he said, "I'm going to explain everything to you, Camille, about me and what you think you saw at the church."

She was trying to concentrate on what he said, but his chocolate scent was enveloping her, and she felt all warm and gooey, like his hot chocolate was melting her ice cream. Oh, that was bad! She couldn't explain it, but without him doing anything overt, there was this melting sensation passing over her. Like a warm, streaming fondue fountain.

"You won't like what I have to tell you, of course, but I will tell you the truth."

Huh? Her mind was still back on chocolate fondue, or was it chocolate body paint?

"But for now, let's just dance a little and enjoy the party."

And they did. Harek was a good dancer. She was, too. They moved together like a couple accustomed to each other's moves. She wondered . . . No, she was not going to wonder.

When the band played the Frank Sinatra song "The Best Is Yet to Come," she sincerely hoped that was true, because right now she was feeling damn good. And she hadn't even had a drink yet, except for short sips of champagne during the toasts to the wedding couple. She felt surprisingly dazed as Harek led her into an anteroom during an intermission, almost like she was buzzed with booze, though it had to be passion. Drunk on love, she almost giggled aloud. He encouraged her to sit on a plush velvet chair and went down on one knee beside her so that he was eye level with her.

"What? You going to propose or something?" she joked, suddenly uncomfortable.

"Hardly." He shook his head and took one of her hands in his. He was looking so serious that any further jokes she might have been considering faded away.

"Who are you, really, Harek?"

"There is no way to ease into telling you who I am, Camille."

Uh-oh!

"I am a Viking vampire angel," he told her.

Camille burst out laughing. So much that people kept poking their heads into the anteroom to see what was going on.

"You're making a scene," Harek said with disgust. "Let's get out of here."

"Sure thing, angel baby." She pressed her lips together and almost choked on a giggle.

"Very funny. I am not an angel. I am a *vampire* angel." He elongated his fangs slightly.

Instead of being frightened, she remarked, "Cute!"

Cute? Cute! Fangs are not cute. If he didn't know better, he would think Camille was drunk. She was probably in shock. Poor thing!

Then she added, "Don't forget Viking." At his puzzled frown, she explained, "Viking vampire angel, that's what you said. Ha, ha, ha. 'I am Thor, hear me roar.'" The last she said in a fake male voice that sounded a little like Arnold Schwarzenegger in *The Terminator.*

Poor thing, my ass!

"Are you going to bite me?" she asked.

"Only if you ask."

She shook her head. "I don't think so. I don't like blood."

"I do."

"Are you trying to scare me?"

"Yes. No. C'mon, let's go." He stood and held out a hand to help her rise from her chair. "Do you have any more bridesmaid duties?"

"Not that I know of. Not that I care." Ignoring

his hand, she stood on her own. Then she tilted her head to the side, staring at him. "Where do you fang people? In the neck?"

"Usually. But, in that gown, I am much more tempted by your ass."

"You don't have to be crude."

He shrugged. "It is what it is. In that clingy fabric, your bottom is like a blinking neon sign of temptation."

She made a tsking sound of disapproval . . . at his continuing crudity, he supposed. Then she asked, laughing again, "Do you sleep in a coffin or on a cloud?"

She didn't believe a word he'd said.

It was going to be a long night.

Chapter 10

She wasn't laughing for long...

Camille was still laughing in the passenger seat of her Benz as a stony-faced Harek drove them back to Evermore.

She continued to laugh as he unlocked the door of the house with the key she handed him.

Her laughter began to taper off as he stomped through the silent house and into the library. She followed him and saw that he'd flicked on a lamp and was helping himself to a heavy crystal tumbler of her father's aged bourbon. He tossed a half glass back in one gulp, then poured another. In fact, he poured the amber liquid into two tumblers and handed one to her.

She took it and sank down into a wingback chair in front of the cold fireplace. She sipped slowly, appreciating the smoky flavor as it burned a path down her throat.

Harek sat down in the matching chair, facing her, his long legs extended, the heavy crystal glass cupped in both hands, resting on his lap. He'd removed his bow tie in the car and opened the first couple buttons of his dress shirt. With his designer disheveled hair and the healthy, deeper tan he'd somehow gotten since this afternoon, he looked good enough to eat. And she wasn't thinking that just because he smelled like chocolate. Bourbon and chocolate. Yum!

"Are you done laughing like a hyena?" he asked, his blue eyes piercing her with intensity.

"You have no sense of humor at all, Harek. Honestly. You tell me you're a frickin' vampire angel and expect me not to laugh? What alien world do you come from? Oh, wait. You do come from an alien word, so to speak. Heaven. Or is it Hell?"

"I don't come from either place. I come from the Norselands of 850 A.D. where I died after committing a grave sin. Well, many grave sins, but one really big one. Each of my brothers and I are guilty of one of the Seven Deadly Sins."

"Eight-fifty," she scoffed. "That would make you"—she did a quick mental calculation—"about a thousand years old."

"Add a century or so."

Holy moly! And he actually expects me to believe this crap? "And your big sin was?"

"Greed," he said without hesitation. At her arched brows, he explained, "I like gold and riches. I have a talent for gaining wealth, at any cost, truth to tell."

"So you're a time traveler, like Michael J. Fox in *Back to the Future*?"

He shook his head. "We vangels—Viking vampire angels—used to time travel, back and forth through the eras, but the last few years Michael stationed us here, permanently, in your time."

"Michael?"

"St. Michael the Archangel."

She rolled her eyes. This just got better and better. She took another sip of bourbon and waved for him to continue.

"Because God was disgusted with us Vikings—too vain and vicious, He claimed—'twas decided that the Viking race would fade into extinction. You will notice there is no Viking nation today. Not Norway, or Sweden, or Denmark. The closest there is to a Norse culture is Iceland. In any case, God decided to wipe us all out by having us absorbed into other societies, and as for us seven Sigurdsson brothers in particular, we were given a second chance to make amends by becoming vampire angels to fight against the Lucipires."

"I'm afraid to ask, what are Lucipires? Some kind of scary beasts?"

"Worse than that. Lucipires are Satan's demon vampires, led by Jasper, worst of the fallen angels. The Lucies roam the earth, taking terrible sinners before their destined time, giving them no chance to repent before dying. Their fate is almost worse than Hell for those who die normally in some grave state of sin. These victims go to Horror, Jasper's domain in the far North, where they are turned into demon vampires."

"Seriously, Harek? Seriously? You expect me to believe this crap?"

"'Tis the truth, Camille. I wish it were not so, but . . . no, I take that back. If it were not so, I would be one of Satan's minions for all these years toasting my toes in his hellish fires." He grinned then and added, "Marshmallow toes."

She was not amused. "So, you're a fighter in God's army?"

"You could say that."

"Like a priest?"

"Hardly. I am a Viking. Purity is not one of our strong points."

"You know that this is impossible to believe."

He emptied his glass, then set it on a table next to his chair. "So be it," he said, and waved a hand, back and forth like a windshield wiper in front of the fireplace. Immediately, a hazy cloud appeared, and in it, she could see a huge beast with red scales and red eyes. It looked like a man, and yet not human at all with its clawed hands and long tail, not to mention fangs, really big fangs. The beast was fighting with a man with wings . . . well, not really wings, they were more like hazy blue appendages coming out of his back. The beast and the angel man, who also had fangs, fought with swords. When the victor's sword pierced the demon's heart, it began to dissolve into a puddle of . . . slime.

As the mind picture, or whatever it was, began to fade, her gaze shot to Harek. "The cathedral? That slimy substance on the floor?"

He nodded. "The woman back at the cathedral

that you saw . . . she was a demon vampire. Her target was your father."

Camille let out a little whimper of distress. "I think I need another drink." When he refilled her glass, she said, "Are you saying there are creatures like that roaming the earth? Demons, I mean."

He nodded. "Actually, there was a large nest of Lucies living in New Orleans until about two years ago. They worked out of a restaurant called Anguish."

"Eeew! I've eaten there. Before it burned down." She shivered with distaste at the prospect of having been surrounded by demons. Not that she believed Harek, of course.

An uncomfortable thought occurred to her then. "The SEALs? Coronado? What are you doing there? Oh God! I'm going to have to tell the CO that we're being infiltrated by . . . by some people? Terrorists, maybe."

"No, no, no! You cannot repeat what I've told you. Vangels are good guys. Most of the time. Our job with the SEALs is to help eradicate Boko Haram. They are evil personified. Some of them are—"

"Lucipires," she finished for him.

"Precisely."

She put a hand to her aching head. Her brain was going to explode with all this information Harek was filling it with. "Exactly how old are you?"

"If you count my almost thirty human years, eleven hundred and ninety-five years old."

"Oh my God!"

He winced. "I really wish you wouldn't swear like that."

"Huh? I distinctly heard you use the F word this morning when that truck driver pulled in front of me."

"The F word is allowed . . . well, not allowed, but not as bad for vangels as using the Lord's name as an expletive."

"Oh good Lord!"

He made an oddly adorable tsking noise.

Just then, they heard the sound of an engine pulling into the driveway and the garage door opening. They both sat up. That would be her parents. Earlier than expected. It sounded like they were arguing.

"Camille," he said, "I can explain this better. Later. But I need to spend some time alone with your father tonight."

"What are you going to do to him?" she asked with sudden alarm. She wasn't very close to her father, but she wouldn't want him hurt, either.

"Hopefully, save him. And your mother. I need you to go upstairs once he comes in."

"Why can't I stay?"

"'Tis a private matter. Go."

"I don't know."

"Trust me," he said.

And, strangely enough, she did.

A vangel's work is never done . . .

Harek was still in the library, but he could hear Camille talking to her parents in the hallway.

"You're home early," Camille said.

"Not really," Jeannette disagreed. Did she ever have a warm tone of voice when speaking to her daughter? "It's close to midnight. Besides, the band was playing that loud modern music, and some of the dancing was rather obscene."

"I would have stayed," Emile told Camille, "but your mother wanted to leave. I rather enjoyed watching the dancers."

Jeannette made a sound of disgust.

Meanwhile, Harek was rummaging around the room, sniffing and exploring. Searching. In a cabinet, under the liquor bar, behind an impressive array of bottles, he found what he was looking for. A quart bottle of antifreeze. Poison. And for a college professor with his research skills, not all that original. With a nod of satisfaction at the quickness of his discovery, Harek closed the cabinet doors and placed the plastic container behind some books on a nearby shelf. He sat down again, whiskey glass in hand.

"It was a beautiful wedding," Camille remarked, probably to calm the waters of what had been sounding like the beginning of a domestic argument.

"Yes. Yes, it was. Everything was perfect. Inez's cousin from Biloxi caught the bridal bouquet." Jeannette's voice was almost accusatory.

"What? You wanted me to catch the thing?" Camille laughed. "One of the reasons I left early was to avoid just that. Harek would have had a heart attack if I caught the bouquet."

"Where is your young man?" her father asked.

Hardly hers, but now is not the time for arguing semantics. "In the library, having a drink."

"Wonderful. I could use a good bourbon myself."

"Hah! Seems to me you had more than—"

"That will be enough, Jeannette. This is not the time or the place," Emile interrupted his wife sternly.

"Whatever," Jeannette said. "I'm off to bed. It's been a long day, a long week, and we still have the brunch we're hosting tomorrow afternoon."

"Good night, Jeannette. Good night, Camille. What time will you be leaving?"

"Around noon."

"Plenty of time for us to talk. Dr. Solic said he never got a chance to discuss the new curriculum with you."

Camille had told Harek about her parents wanting her to enter some fast-track, higher degree program at Tulane. That's probably what he was referring to.

There was more murmuring, then the sound of high heels climbing the stairs and Emile walking toward the library.

When he entered, Harek said, "Lock the door, please."

"I beg your pardon," Emile said.

"You should." Harek stood and walked over to the shelf, where he picked up the antifreeze and raised it for Emile to see. Harek said nothing, just arched his brows.

Emile's face turned red, infused with anger. The lackwit didn't know yet just how much trouble he was in. But he had the good sense to lock the door. "You had no right to go through my private property."

"We both know why you purchased antifreeze."

Emile shrugged as if he owed him no explanation. With a pretended calm, the man walked over to the cabinet and poured himself a large glass of bourbon. Harek noticed that his hands shook, and he cupped the glass in both hands to prevent it spilling as he sank into one of the wingback chairs, the one Camille had just vacated.

Harek took the other chair, again.

Ironic, wasn't it, Harek noted suddenly, that here was an angel, so to speak—*that would be me*—in a winged chair. *Angel, wings. Get it.* Of course, there was a potential demon—*that would be Emile, if he didn't change his ways*—sitting in a winged chair, too. Harek shook his head to clear it of such nonsense. Then, *Focus, man, focus. You have work to do.*

Emile sipped at his drink with a sigh of appreciation. The specially aged brew probably cost ten dollars a swallow. "If you're thinking of blackmail, forget about it. I'm not the one holding the purse strings in this family." Emile was calmer now, with booze courage. He probably thought he could bluff his way out of this. "Does Camille know what a lowlife you are?"

"Does Camille know what a *nithing* you are?" Harek countered.

"What? A nothing? I'll have you know I am

an esteemed professor. My research books are read worldwide. My reputation as an academic is excellent. If you think to intimidate me with insults—"

"Blah, blah, blah. I said *nithing,* not nothing. A *nithing* is less than nothing."

Emile raised his chin haughtily. "Your manners are atrocious, even for a Northerner."

What a pompous ass! Thinks he can get away with murder! Thinks he can turn the tables on a vangel! Little does he know how far north I come from.

"What is it you want from me?" Emile demanded to know.

"'Tis not what I want from you, but what I can do for you."

"And what is that? Sell me a high-priced home security system? Provide me with unnecessary bodyguard services? Insure my home or antiques?" The snideness of his remarks was a cover-up for nervousness, Harek realized.

"I can save your soul."

"Pfff! As if you could! Besides, I'm not ready to die yet."

"You are in danger of a fate worse than death, my friend."

Emile bristled at Harek's referring to him as a friend, but his innate good breeding, even in this unusual situation, prevented him from saying so. A lowlife, yes. But friend, no. "Isn't that what they say about women and rape? A fate worse than death?" Emile continued to sip at his drink.

Now he was making Harek angry. "It is what they say when Satan's minions are circling a sinner, fool. Do you not sense the immortal danger your soul is in?"

"Oh please! I don't believe in all that Heaven-Hell nonsense."

"You did at one time," Harek reminded him. Between the cathedral where Harek had killed the Lucipire and the reception, Harek had pulled over to the side of the road and used his laptop in the car to research Emile Dumaine's history. Amazing what you could find out when you had the skills. Emile had grown up in a strong Catholic family. They'd been poor as church mice, but Emile was bright and ambitious and he'd earned scholarship after scholarship until he had a doctorate degree and had married into money. Jeannette's family money. "In fact, you once considered the seminary."

"How did you know that? Never mind. That was before I grew up and got enlightened. I only would have attended seminary to get an education. No way would I have taken final vows."

Harek sighed. "Just when did you start down the path of sin?"

"What have I done that is so wrong?" He waved a hand at the antifreeze that sat on the liquor bar. "I haven't used that. Yet. Maybe I never would."

"And maybe you would. Besides, for more than twenty-five years, you have lived a double life. No, I do not want to hear your excuses for infidelity and illegitimate children and hidden expenses and deceit, deceit, deceit. I can tell you without a doubt that God is not pleased with you. If you died today of some natural cause, you would go to Hell, or some holding place until the Final Judgment, but that is not why I am here. 'Tis what you are contemplating"—he pointed at the antifreeze—"that will take you to a place far worse than Hades if you are not careful. You, my friend—and believe me, I am the only friend you have at the moment—are in the crosshairs of an evil far greater than you could ever contemplate with all your book learning."

"Who the hell are you?"

"More like, who in heaven am I? I am Harek Sigurdsson, born in the year 820, died in the year 850, when I became a Viking vampire angel, one of God's vangels."

"An angel? Ha, ha, ha."

"Not an angel. A vangel."

Emile blinked at him. "Are you crazy?" He was eyeing the locked door now like it had been a mistake and wondering how he was going to escape.

"Your sinful state has come to the attention of the Lucipires."

"Oh good Lord!"

"Not the Lord, but the other guy. In this case, Jasper, king of all the Lucipires, which are demon vampires. They are sent to take the gravest of human sinners before their time, sucking the life out of them before they have a chance to repent, as they might have done during a normal life span. Sinners, those whose souls are not yet totally black, always figure they can commit the bad deed and repent later. Fools, one and all!" *Myself included.*

Emile flushed guiltily. That's just what he'd

done, convinced himself that he could commit murder and make up for it later. Must mean he still had a speck of conscience.

"The place these victims are taken is called Horror," Harek continued, "and it is just that. A horrible place where people are tortured endlessly until they agree to join the ranks of the Lucipire undead. That, my friend, is the fate worse than death."

"This is absolutely ridiculous."

"I wish it were," Harek said sadly, and felt his incisors extending.

"You . . . you have fangs and blue wings," Emile sputtered.

"The fangs are real. The wings are just fog . . . an impression of something that might be there one day. Back to the Lucipires . . ." Harek planted a mind picture in Emile's head and showed him the woman who had followed him into St. Louis Cathedral, the one who had morphed into a huge fanged creature dripping mung from its scales and drool from its fangs.

Emile recoiled and dropped his glass to the floor, where the liquid splattered and the glass splintered into many pieces. Neither of them paid any attention to the mess.

"How'd you do that? Is it a magic trick? Or some new electronic marvel connected to your cell phone or something? Camille said you're some kind of technological genius, but . . ." Emile continued to gape at the cloudy picture.

Camille said that about me? Before she knew who I really am? Well, well. Good to know. "No, it is not a trick or some gadget that can be scientifically explained."

But Emile was not listening to him. "I've seen that woman several times the past few days. At the Faculty Club. At a gas station. Standing in front of this very house."

Harek nodded. "She was following you, waiting for the right moment."

"I don't understand. Is she a stalker?"

"If only that was all she had been! But she is no longer of any importance. I killed her."

"You . . . *what*?" Emile recoiled, finally beginning to realize the dangerous person he was with. A murderer, he would be thinking.

"When were you going to start the poison?" Harek asked, done with all this sidestepping of the real issue.

"Tonight," Emile confessed, clearly confused. "I am tired of the double life. Sonja is badgering me to marry her. More and more every day. She wants to live in this house and enjoy the lifestyle my wife has always had. I keep telling her, Evermore and everything in it belongs to Jeannette. The only way I can get it is . . ." He didn't have to finish the sentence for Harek to know what he meant.

"Excuses, Emile? Sonja made me do it?"

Emile raised his chin haughtily. "It's what I want, too."

"Is that *really* what you want?"

Emile thought for a long moment, then shook his head. "No. Everything has gotten out of hand."

"If you are that unhappy with Jeannette, why not just leave?"

"I wasn't always unhappy. It's true, I married Jeannette for her money and social status, but I grew fond of her. Maybe even a little bit in love for a while. Then I met Sonja and . . ." He shrugged.

"So, it's all the fault of your mistress?"

"Yes. No." He rubbed his face between both hands. When he glanced up again, his face looked haggard. "What can I do . . . what should I do?"

"I can help you if you truly want help."

"I do, but . . ." He hesitated, unsure of what that help would entail.

"You will need to say a few simple words, and then I will fang you."

"What?" Emile stared pointedly at Harek's extended incisors. "For the love of God!"

"Precisely," Harek said. "For the love of God, and in your wish to repent, you will allow me to give you a bite and take a small amount of your blood into my mouth. At the same time, a drop or two of fluid from my fangs will go into your body."

"And that's all?"

He nodded. "The rest will be up to you. A new beginning."

"This is the strangest thing I've ever heard of, and there are lots of strange happenings in Nawleans. I need to think about this."

Harek shook his head. "The time for thinking is over. You are already in the Lucipires' crosshairs. The woman—the demon—at the cathedral today would have alerted others of her kind. Your sin taint reeks and will act as a lure for others to come after you. 'Tis only a matter of time."

"I reek?" Emile once again raised his snooty nose, but then his nostrils flared as he no doubt smelled what Harek did. "Lemons?"

Harek nodded.

"I don't understand."

"You do not need to understand. All you need to do is repent."

"But fanging and blood and . . ." Emile shivered with distaste.

"It is what it is. Take it or leave it. The decision is yours. If you do not accept my offer, nothing will be done to stop your murderous plan. I will not be going to the police. The decision is yours," he repeated.

After a long pause, Emile sighed. "Just do it."

Harek stood and motioned for Emile to stand in front of him. Harek made the sign of the cross across his chest and then Emile's. "Say after me: For the love of God, I am sorry for my sins and promise to do better."

Emile's eyes widened at the simplicity of what he was being asked to do. He repeated the words. Then, without being told to do so, he arched his neck to the side.

It took only a minute for the fanging to take place, and, really, there was not much pain involved, just a momentary jab, like a needle. Once completed, there was an immediate transformation, for both parties. Harek was filled with warmth and his skin heated into a healthy tan complexion, that on top of the jolt he'd gotten from destroying the Lucie at the cathedral. Emile's eyes went wide with wonder before his legs buckled and Harek had to help him back to his chair. Tears streamed from his eyes. Not an unusual reaction, but Harek had to ask, "Are you all right?"

Emile nodded and took a white linen handkerchief from the breast pocket of his tuxedo. He used it to wipe away the wetness on his face. "It felt like an electric shock passing through my body, but not in a bad way. I can't explain it, but somehow I feel lighter, from the inside out. And clean. And warm, like I might be oozing heat from every pore of my body, but not heat-heat, more like a glow." He glanced down at his hand, probably checking to see if he was turning into a light bulb, or something, which he wasn't, of course. "This is amazing," Emile said with a child-like laugh. "Tell me everything."

Harek got Emile a new glass of bourbon, then sat down once again in the other wingback chair. He didn't need any more alcohol himself tonight. In fact, a fanging gave him a sort of adrenaline rush, not unlike a liquor high.

"You've lost your blue wings and fangs," Emile remarked.

"Yes, though they are not wings exactly, as I said. More like the promise of wings."

"And your eyes are back to being blue. They were silver there for a while, you know."

"I know." In any time of high emotion, his eyes changed color. Damn inconvenient it was betimes, too, especially when he was being aroused by a woman and didn't want her to know.

For the next half hour, he gave Emile the short

version of Vangel History 101. The academic in Emile required the asking of many questions. So fascinated was Emile that he barely sipped from his drink. You'd think he had discovered alien life on another planet, and he was the only one who'd been given the opportunity to interview his very own Mork. Interview with a Martian.

That was proven true in the end when Emile said with excitement, "This will make a wonderful article. Even the *New York Times* will be interested. Hah! Any magazine would jump on the story. And the TV networks, too. Maybe I could get a book deal. Publish or perish is the rule for most professors. This would take that rule to a whole other level."

And they would probably pay big money, too. Damn, but there are so many ways to gain great wealth in this new world, and I'm prevented from having more than a dollar in my pocket, practically. Ah, I guess 'tis better to be poor than to have crispy toes. "No," Harek said emphatically.

"Not even the *Times-Picayune*?"

"No."

"Well, a scholarly journal, then."

"No."

"Nothing? I can tell no one?"

"Not a soul."

"Not even Jeannette? Or Sonja?"

"No and no."

"How will I explain my sudden change of mind? Hell, my sudden change of life?"

Harek shrugged. Not his problem.

Emile rose from his chair. "I should go upstairs and begin to make amends to my wife. You know, I haven't slept in the same room as Jeannette for years."

Too much information.

"She will probably kick me out."

"Maybe. Maybe not. She has stuck with you for all these years, Emile. There has to be a reason for that."

"Hmm." Emile stared at Harek for a long moment, seemingly searching for the right words. Then all he said was, "Thank you."

"It is only my duty," Harek replied. *And my penance.* "Go and sin no more."

Harek was alone then, and he just sat, enjoying the silence, except for the loud ticking of a mantel clock. He couldn't deny that it felt good to do good. A vangel wasn't supposed to enjoy his work. It was supposed to be a punishment, a penance. Just a job. Still, betimes there was job satisfaction, nonetheless.

He smiled to himself, then yawned widely. It had been a long day, and would be even longer tomorrow when they headed back to Coronado. Soon after, he would be in Nigeria on the mission from Hell, literally.

Just a job.

Yeah, right.

Chapter 11

Sin on the rocks . . .

Far away, in the cold, cold North, in a mansion called Horror, Jasper, king of the Lucipires, was watching CNN. It was a breaking news story on the latest "atrocities" being committed by the terrorist group Boko Haram in Nigeria.

Jasper loved a good atrocity. And he loved terrorists, too, especially when they were so creative in their tortures and random in their killings. Of course, many of them were his very own demon vampires, who were increasing their ranks within the organization day by day. This world didn't know how bad terror could become. Yet.

With him was the powerful Arab haakai Haroun al Rashid, one of his council members, who was in charge of infiltrating terrorist networks in his part of the world. They sat on reclining leather chairs called La-Z-Devils, not unlike the human La-Z-Boys, except these were specially designed with holes in the posterior region to accommodate a Lucipire's massive tail. They were in humanoid form at the moment, though, so they could enjoy the special almas caviar that Haroun had brought with him, knowing of Jasper's passion for the rare delicacy. It was hard to eat fish eggs on toast points with claws and mung from their scales dripping onto the food. Alma translated to diamond in Persian, but in the case of caviar, referred to the eggs taken from white sturgeon that were a hundred years old. Expensive, to say the least.

"That's him. That's the American I told you about," Haroun exclaimed, pointing at the TV screen. "David Baxter, from Denver. I recruited him myself."

Jasper looked at the screen where a balaclava-clad man had just beheaded two missionaries from Khartoum. With the knitted black hood covering his entire head, except for the eyes, it would be difficult for the average viewer to determine his nationality, but those damn CIA forensics experts in the United States were getting too good at gaining information from the smallest detail, like height, and posture, and accent if the terrorist spoke.

Jasper chewed the last of his appetizer and followed it with a long swallow of Blood on the Rocks . . . vodka, seltzer, and human blood over crushed ice. Yum! "I am well pleased with the work you are doing with the terrorists," he told Haroun.

"Thank you, master. It was your suggestion that we bring in more foreign sympathizers. We have so many volunteers now, we cannot train them all, or turn those ready into Lucipires."

"I understand. Really, the world is in such chaos now—thanks be to Satan—that people, especially vulnerable, young, extremist Muslim men, jump at the chance to be part of a greater cause."

"Yes, yes." Haroun wrung his hands with glee. "Fighting against democracy appeals to those wanting a return to the old ways. Of course, it is a ruse, this recruitment process. What we really want is evil men to become Lucipires who in turn recruit more men to join the cause who in turn become Lucipires."

"Be careful that in the midst of this influx of new members there are not vangels trying to undermine your efforts."

"Of course. They are sneaky angels, ha, ha, ha."

Jasper smiled at Haroun's jest, although it wasn't all that funny. Haroun had been a Silk Road merchant at one time, best known for his ruthless slave trading. In many ways, he had not caught up with the twenty-first century. Unlike Jasper who prided himself on being a modern man . . . rather demon. He even carried a cell phone these days and played Dungeons and Dragons on the Internet, and, yes, he'd been known to check out some of the porno sites. And people thought demons were depraved!

"Now, tell me about this upcoming event," Jasper encouraged Haroun.

"We would love nothing more than a terrorist

attack on American soil, but hiding any young people we would kidnap would be difficult there. The next best thing will be an attack on one of those Global Schools in Nigeria, housing children of Americans and Europeans who work there. Perhaps the one in Kamertoon. It is not that far from the Sambisa Forest which BK has found to be a particularly good hiding place."

Jasper was familiar with the Sambisa Forest, once a nature preserve. It was now a neglected, overgrown jungle.

Jasper nodded and listened attentively as Haroun outlined the details of the new mission.

"Here is the best part," Haroun said. "The Kamertoon facility is a boarding school for girls, ages ten to fifteen. We will take the children, but we will lock the teachers in the building and set it afire with explosives."

"I love it!" Jasper said, licking his lips. Not that he had any interest in innocent children. So sickeningly sweet! Yuck! But the evil ones who would capture and torture them? Yes, yes, yes!

"As appalled as the world has been with young African girls being kidnapped and sold into forced marriages or prostitution, imagine the horror at these mostly white girls facing such fates! Such is the bigotry of the world. Don't you love it, master?"

"Just don't go overboard," Jasper cautioned. "We have learned, to our regret, to make our missions short and unremarkable. In and out, like we did on the casino project. Greed is a sin, and who doesn't love a good sin? But greed is also a weakness we cannot afford. It could make the difference between a successful mission and utter failure."

"Agreed."

There was a loud, agonizing scream then.

Jasper and Haroun jerked to attention, almost spilling their drinks.

The screaming continued, joined in with others.

Beltane, Jasper's hordling assistant, ducked his head inside the open doorway and said, "Forgive my intrusion, master, but they have just begun torture on the latest arrivals. You have to see this. Craven has invented a new tool called the Wire Impaler."

Jasper stood and set his glass aside. "Will you join me?" he asked Haroun. "This should be fun."

Caviar, bloody cocktails, and torture . . . could life get any better than this?

A funny thing happened on the way to . . .

Camille was lying on the top of her coverlet in her old high school nightshirt. On it was Snoopy wearing a tutu and the logo, "I'm a Smart Person, I Just Do Stupid Things." The story of her life.

She'd been listening for a long time for her father and Harek to come upstairs so that she could find out what had happened with the cleansing, or whatever the hell it was called, but she must have fallen asleep. Checking her bedside clock, she saw that it was 1:10 a.m., an hour since she'd come upstairs.

She got out of bed and tiptoed downstairs and went toward the library, where a lamp still burned, but no one was there. Backtracking upstairs, she heard the light murmur of voices from the master suite. Her mother and father? Wow! That must mean something. They hadn't slept in the same room since she was a child, as far as she knew.

Moving barefoot over the Oriental carpet, she made her way to the guest room at the end of the hall. She thought she heard movement, maybe water running, but then silence. She considered knocking but didn't want to alert her parents to her whereabouts. How silly was that for an almost thirty-year-old woman? Worrying that she'd be caught in the sack with a boy? Jeesh!

Opening the door slowly, she sidled inside the room. The bed was empty, although the covers had been turned down. A light emanated from the adjoining bathroom, where the door was half open. And then, there stood Harek with a towel wrapped around his middle, low down. He was using another towel to dry his hair.

Startled, he just gaped at her, but then he took in her nightshirt and bare legs, from mid-thigh downward, and smiled, adding his own Snoopy-ism, "Good grief!"

"You were supposed to stop at my bedroom and tell me what happened," she said quickly, trying to hide her embarrassment. All her good parts were covered, but she somehow felt naked under his perusal.

"I was?"

She nodded. Then she added her own "Good grief!" when she noticed how tan he was, more so than earlier this evening. How could that be? Surely he wasn't using a self-tanning product, along with mousse. On the other hand, men could be so vain that way, sometimes more so than women. "Been out in the sun since I saw you an hour ago?"

"Oh," he said, and put a hand to his face, realizing to what her "Good grief!" had been directed. He'd probably thought it was because of his hot body, which, incidentally, was very hot, what she could see of it, which was a lot. Even his muscled calves and narrow feet were kind of sexy. And his blond happy trail? She would fan herself if it wouldn't be too obvious. And chocolate! She could gain five pounds just inhaling the air in this room. Sinfully sweet!

"A vangel tans after killing a Lucie or removing a sinner's blood taint."

Damn! The vangel nonsense again! "Did you talk to my father?"

"I did."

"And?"

"He won't be harming your mother, and, if my guess is correct, I believe he will be recommitting himself to his marriage."

"Really? Just like that? Twenty years of cheating and he's suddenly a changed man?"

Harek shrugged. "God works in wondrous ways."

"Oh good Lord!"

"Exactly."

"Do you really expect me to believe that?"

"You asked and I told you. 'Tis up to you to believe or not."

Great! Make me feel like the bad guy. "And Sonja?"

"A thing of the past."

What? Is he serious? Yes, he looks serious. This is amazing. Unbelievable. But amazing, if true. "And his children with Sonja?"

"Do not push it, Camille. They will always be his daughters."

Camille sank down to the side of the bed, trying to take in these new happenings, including the events of the day.

"Do you really think that is a good idea?" he asked in a choked voice.

She glanced up to see what he meant.

"Sitting on my bed, wearing naught but a wanton shirt, smelling like roses."

"Huh? This shirt is not naughty."

"I didn't say naughty. I said wanton."

"Same thing."

She realized that he'd meant *naught*, as in "nothing but." "How did you know I'm not wearing a bra or panties? Do you have Superman vision or something on top of everything else?"

"Super . . . super . . . ?" An odd gurgling noise came from his throat. "You're not wearing undergarments? Oh, I am lost. Fifty years of celibacy, and I am felled by roses and a Snoopy dog."

Fifty years . . . How could he be celibate for fifty years if he was only thirty? Oh, wait, there was that thousand-year-old stuff. She felt a giggle of hysteria bubble up in her, which she quickly stifled. Good thing, too, because while she'd been distracted, Harek had dropped his towel, and not just the one he'd been using to dry his hair.

Holy.

Mother.

Of.

God!

Camille had seen a few erections in her time, but this was different. Harek was different. Magnificent seemed too small a word—*ha, ha, ha, small, hardly!*—for the way he looked to her. Like the statue of David, but better. All well-defined muscles and bones, from wide shoulders, to narrow hips, to lean-sinewed thighs, all a framework for his penis that was veined marble, standing out from his body, signaling his attraction—his need—for her.

How heady a compliment was that?

She didn't look down, but there was a good chance Snoopy was doing the happy dance, just looking at Harek.

Or should she be insulted? No, she was the one who'd come, uninvited, into his bedroom in the middle of the night. But that's not why she'd come. Was it? No, of course not.

"I'm feeling kind of lonely, standing here naked," he said.

"What do you mean?"

"Lose Snoopy."

Oh. "Oh." *Yikes!*

"No, wait. Let me unwrap you. Like a present." Before she could guess what he meant, he knelt before her and placed a palm on each of her thighs, under the hem of her nightshirt. The tips of his fingers almost, but not quite, touched her pubic hair.

Blood rushed to that region, and the pleasure was so intense she felt herself sway.

Harek righted her and then somehow got his hands under her bottom and lifted the shirt, but only waist-high. At the same time, he spread her knees wider so that she was fully exposed to him.

"So pretty!" he said, sitting back on his heels and staring at her there. "Look at yourself, Camille. See how pretty you are."

She didn't want to, but she did. And what she saw was not herself. Correction, she saw herself, all right, wide open for business and practically waving a welcome sign, but what she homed in on, instead, was that part of Harek, big and hard, and pointing at her like a heat-seeking missile, and, boy, did she have the heat, or was that the hots, for him.

My brain is melting from hormone overload.

"Are you wet for me, Camille?" he asked silkily.

How did she answer a question like that? "Probably."

"You better check."

Huh? "Could we just get on with it, Harek. I'm not good at games."

"Lucky for you, I am. Touch yourself, Camille," he ordered.

She bristled. Camille was in the military. She was accustomed to taking orders, but not from men in her personal life.

"Do not try to deny that you know how."

Of course she knew how. She was almost thirty years old. She had read *Cosmo* as a teenager. She'd read *Fifty Shades* as an adult. She put a finger, just one, her middle finger, to herself. And, yes, there was dampness. "Are you satisfied?"

"Not even a little," he said with a laugh. "I am a greedy bastard."

But when she looked at him, she saw that his silvery blue eyes were half slitted with passion, and his lips were parted, showing the pointy incisors. *So, he likes looking at me there, and he likes watching me touch myself.* She did it again, this time going deep, just as a test, and he barely caught the gasp of surprise that escaped his lips. *Oh yeah, he likes it. He likes it!*

"Witch," he murmured, and kissed the fingertip she'd just put to herself. "Roses. More bloody roses!"

Women had a thing about body odor, especially down there. And she knew for a fact that she didn't smell like roses there. Even so, she took a surreptitious sniff, and holy hell! She did detect a slight scent of roses.

But Harek had moved on to something else. "Take off the garment, sweetling. Slowly." Meanwhile he was running his fingertips up the backs of her legs, from her ankles to her butt, then back again. If she hadn't just shaved her legs that day, she would have guessed that every hair follicle was standing on end, waving, *Me, me, me!* Her pubic hairs definitely were.

"Sweetling? That's a new one," she said with horny irrelevance. "Well, since you ask you so nicely . . ." She crisscrossed her arms and tugged at the hem by her waist, raising it higher. And higher. And higher. Then over her head, tossing it to the floor.

He studied her body in infuriating silence. "You've been hiding a lot, Camille," he told her then. "A lot."

She did have a good body. A healthy metabolism and hard exercise guaranteed that. Her breasts weren't big, but they were proportional to the rest of her body, and, since she'd never had children, the nipples were pink and smallish.

He touched her nipples, lightly, and smiled when her lower body jolted in reaction. Her dampness was becoming a flood.

"We are going to have such fun," he promised then, and put both hands on her waist, lifted and tossed her onto the middle of the bed, following after her. With a sensual hum of approval he arranged himself over her with his hard part pressed into the V of her widespread thighs. If she was the violin and he was the bow (*She'd moved on from rockets to musical instruments. So, sue her!*), they were already making sweet music, *down there.* In the pit (*Don't have a dirty mind!*) . . . the orchestra pit.

Holy frickin' cow! I didn't know I could move from inside out, without actually trying.

Move over Beethoven. Mama's got a brand-new song, she thought, then giggled at the idiocy of her musing.

"You think my agony is funny, do you, wench?"

She opened her eyes, which she hadn't realized were scrunched tightly closed. Harek was arched over her on braced arms, and he actually did appear to be in agony. The best possible kind. Good! Welcome to the club. Even knowing, she asked with mock innocence, "What's wrong?"

"I want you so bloody damn much, I'm having trouble controlling my enthusiasm, that is what is wrong."

"Enthusiasm?"

He shrugged. "Viking for arousal."

She smiled.

"You are enjoying my discomfort!"

"No. I like that you're attracted to me."

"Attracted! Any more attracted and I will be plowing a furrow in this mattress."

"You have a charming way with words." She put a hand to his chest, just to see if his skin was as warm as it appeared. It was. "Do you know that your eyes have turned silvery, and you have blue wispy wings coming out of your shoulders?"

"Not wings. No wings! Not when I am feeling so unangelic."

"They sure look like wings."

"'Tis probably smoke coming out of my ears from all the heat you are stoking in me."

"Are we going to make love?"

"I do not know about making love, but I intend to sate my lust on you fifty ways to Valhalla."

"You believe in Valhalla?"

"No, but I didn't want to say that other word."

"Heaven?"

"Hell."

"You think you're going to Hell for making love."

"No, but I will be punished."

"I don't underst—"

He put his fingertips to her lips. "Enough talking." Then he replaced his fingertips with his mouth, and she felt herself melting into a kiss so chocolaty sweet and sexually explicit that she was drowning in sensuality. Every erotic spot on her body was connected by thin threads of sensitivity to her lips. She vibrated with each brush of his lips, each lick of his tongue, each nip of his teeth. When she tasted him with her own tongue, brushing against his pointed incisors, he groaned low and deep in his throat.

A sudden alarming thought occurred to her. "Do you fang during sex?"

"I can, but I won't, unless you want me to." He was still braced over her body, but he was rubbing his silky chest hairs over her nipples, causing them to be engorged and aching for more. She arched up and did her own abrading, harder.

He chuckled.

"Why would I want that? Fanging?" she gasped out.

"It enhances the sexual pleasure for the woman a hundredfold, I have heard."

"And for the man?"

He grinned. "A thousandfold."

Of course, the idea was planted in her fool head now. "I don't want to," she lied.

"You don't have to," he replied. "There are plenty of other things we can do. Like . . ." He proceeded to do the most incredible things to her ears, first one, then the other. Using his lips and wet tongue and teeth and warm breaths, he aroused every nerve ending in her body, just by making love to her ears. And in between, he whispered words of encouragement to her, some of them wicked, not usually spoken aloud.

She used her hands to explore his shoulders and back and buttocks, but she couldn't move her lower body, as she wanted to, because he had her pinioned to the bed with his hips. "I'm ready," she finally said with exasperation.

"For what?"

"You."

"Where?"

"Inside me."

"It's too soon."

"Screw soon. I want you. Now. There are condoms in the bedside drawer in my bedroom. Oh damn, I wasn't planning this when I came to your room."

He arched a brow at her. "Condoms? You have condoms?"

"I wasn't anticipating this. But the Navy makes us WEALS put protection in our toiletry kits. Just in case."

"I don't need a condom. Vangels are sterile."

"Your brother . . ."

"Except for Ivak."

In a momentary lapse from talking, Harek had raised himself slightly and Camille managed one quick thrust of her hips, causing him to slide inside her, to his surprise. It was always good to surprise a man in bed. But, truth to tell, *slide* wasn't the right word. Because he was big, and she hadn't had sex in a while, her slick channel was welcoming him with fierce spasms that moved him higher, inch by blissful inch. *Holy frickin' sex machine!* A wave of orgasms swept over her, so intense she might have blacked out for a moment. Her eyes were probably rolling back in her head.

When she was able to glance up—he was still embedded in her, unmoving—she saw that his teeth were gritted and sweat beaded his forehead. He was clearly fighting his own climax. A strange haze seemed to surround them, like a cocoon, and it smelled, surprise, surprise, like chocolate roses. She was going to bottle the scent and make a million dollars, if she ever survived this awful/wonderful sexual experience.

Harek seemed to be watching her, waiting for something. "Are you ready?"

She tried to laugh, but it came out as a gasp.

"I take that for yes," he said with a smile, and began to slowly, very slooooooowly, draw himself out of her body until only the head of his penis was inside her. The friction was pleasure and torture so intense that she let out a long moan and raised her knees, spreading herself even wider.

He took his time going back in again, too. She wanted to beat his back with her fists and scream, *Faster!* But her tongue seemed to be stuck to the roof of her mouth as she panted for breath. She did put her hands on his hard butt cheeks, though, trying to encourage him.

The stubborn man took his slow good time.

In.

Out.

In.

Out.

Innnnnnn.

Ouuuuuut.

She was dying and having dozens of mini orgasms while he stroked her inner walls with frustrating slowness. Once he stopped when he was in her fully and rubbed his pubic bone against her clitoris, back and forth, back and forth, 'til she exploded in a full-blown climax of shuddering spasms.

"Are you done now?" she asked, though she couldn't see for the exploding stars that blinded her. Okay, that was an exaggeration, but not by much. Down below, she was one shattering mess of sensations. Hard to tell what was going on in sex central, too many things at one time.

He laughed. "I've barely begun."

That cleared her vision fast.

"Hold on to the headboard, sweetling," he advised then. "This is going to be a rough ride."

What a corny cliché, she thought as she grabbed for the wood spindles. Almost immediately, she revised her thinking to *Go, cowboy, go!*

He slammed into her, over and over and over. And each time he hit her clitoris, just so, only for a brief second, but more arousing because it was so brief. In and out, he stroked her, long and hard. 'Til she barely stifled a scream.

Looping her legs over his shoulders, he hit her from a different angle, and the inner convulsions started all over again. She was grasping and ungrasping him in a rhythmic dance as old as time, but unlike anything she'd ever experienced before.

She almost screamed again, and this time he reared his head back and gritted out his own climax before falling heavily onto her body. Only belatedly, she worried that her parents might have heard her, but there appeared to be silence in the house. Thank God she hadn't actually screamed. But a loud whimper could be heard in the quiet, couldn't it? She listened some more. Just silence, except for the ticking of the grandfather clock downstairs. Whew!

Like a rag doll, she lay splayed out, with him still semisoft inside her body, his face resting against her neck. She could feel his fangs pressing against her skin, but he made no move to bite her. Thank God! She wouldn't have the strength to fight him off. Nor would she want to.

"Sorry I am, Camille," he said against her ear.

"Why?"

"I did not spend nearly enough time in foreplay. Next time I will do better."

"Next time?" she choked out.

"Did I not mention that I am a greedy man?"

She began to laugh then. The man had that effect on her. Better? That was impossible. That was the best sex she'd ever had. The best sex anyone had ever had. With an angel, yet! She doubted Adam and Eve had had such good sex. Or Samson and Delilah. As for his vampire half—*and wasn't that an interesting question, which part of Harek was vampirish?*—good ol' Drac had nothing on him, Impaler or not!

Unfortunately, or fortunately, her laughter extended to all parts of her body. Even down below. And that semisoft part of his body was clearly enjoying the humor with growing—what was it Harek had called it?—enthusiasm.

Chapter 12

Vikings and cowboys, same thing!...

"Your vagina is laughing," Harek grumbled, but he wasn't really displeased.

"My lady parts are not laughing," she asserted.

"I beg to differ, m'lady. But not to worry. Your happy lady parts are making my man parts happy, too."

"I noticed," she said, and gave a little wiggle to demonstrate that she was aware of his growing appreciation, still inside her.

It was true, though. He could feel the residual ripples of her humor throughout the muscles of her body. In her breasts, which were flattened against his chest; in her arms, which encircled his shoulders; in her thighs, which were wrapped around his hips; and, yes, those interior muscles surrounding his own Mr. Happy. It was the strangest aspect of the female anatomy he'd ever experienced, and he'd experienced some really strange ones, like the woman in Vestfold with labia so long she could tie a knot there, which her husband sometimes did when he had to be off a-Viking for months at a time. A chastity belt, you could say.

From the light streaming through the open bathroom door, he saw the sex flush that infused her face and neck and parts of her chest. Her lips were bruised by his earlier kisses. Her hair was bed mussed from flailing about. In essence, she looked like a well-sated woman. Gorgeous. Well, she was still plain, in a way, but gorgeous at the same time. And the scent of roses—and chocolate now, too—was almost overpowering. Like an aphrodisiac.

He leaned down and kissed her lightly on the lips. "That was wonderful. Spectacular." Then he eased himself out of her, inch by torturously erotic inch, and rolled over onto his side, taking her with him so they were facing each other.

Blinking with surprise, she said, "Oh. I thought . . . you're right. It's late. We should go to sleep."

He blinked back at her, not understanding, at first. Oh. She thought he'd withdrawn from her body because he was done. Hah! He ran a fingertip from the center of her neck, over her shoulder, and down one well-toned arm to her wrist, where he lifted her hand and kissed the inside of her wrist, where a pulse beat strongly.

She shivered, then faked a yawn.

"Nice try!" He was the one laughing now as he swatted her lightly on the rump.

"But you . . ." She waved a hand downward.

"I didn't pull out because I'm done. I want to start all over again and enjoy every bit of the present you've handed me. Believe me, I'm going to savor every sexual, greedy moment until my chain gets yanked."

"What present?"

"You."

He could tell his answer pleased her. "What chain?"

"The one Mike is going to pull when he finds out what I'm doing."

"Mike?"

"The archangel."

"Oh, that again."

"Always that, dearling. You still aren't convinced, hmm?"

"Not even a little. Well, maybe a little. How can—"

He put a fingertip to her lips to stop further questions and eased her to her back. Leaning over her, he promised, "I'll explain anything you want. Later. But for now, I want to taste your skin. Especially here." He licked her lips. "And here." He licked his way around and over a nipple. "And here." He dipped his tongue into her navel. "And here." He leaned toward her curly hairs.

But she took his face in her hands pulling him upward. "Not there. I need to go wash up first. I'm . . . messy."

He shook his head. "I like you wet and messy from my climax and yours. We can bathe together afterward."

For the next half hour, he did in fact check out every part of her body, front and back. He especially liked the way he could turn her pink nipples rosy red with flicks of his tongue and soft, then hard suckling that had her arching her back off the bed and ordering him not to stop, "Don't you dare damn stop now!" She'd come to a peak just from his ministering to her breasts.

Then there were the backs of her knees, which were especially sensitive. When he licked her there, she nigh shot up off the bed and squealed like a pig . . . a cute pig. Maybe that wasn't the best comparison; best he keep that thought to himself.

He tried sucking on one of her toes, but she kicked him in the groin. He decided to save that particular sex play for later. It was a well-honed taste that had to be developed.

He liked the curve of her buttocks and the sweet crease that separated them, and he told her so repeatedly. She was uncomfortable with his attentions there, like many women were. If he had more time, which he was almost certain he would not, he could teach her not to be so squeamish.

She told him, "Move on!"

Of course, her nether hairs and woman's channel merited much savoring. Her unhooded clitoris was standing at full attention by the time he was done with her. Not that he was done by any means, but she was keening with need and he had pushed himself beyond the limits of his own self-control.

"Do it," she demanded finally, "or I'm going to lop off that tree between your legs."

Camille had a way with compliments betimes.

He rolled onto his back and arranged her on top of him. "Do you want me, Camille?" he asked.

"You know I do," she snapped, rather dazed with overarousal.

"Do you ride?"

She smiled, the kind of smile Eve invented and Mona Lisa perfected. "Do I ever!"

"Show me."

And she did.

Holy clouds! Did she ever!

Then Brad and Angelina walked in . . .

Camille slept late the next morning. Well, eight o'clock. Which was not surprising because Harek, who snored beside her, hadn't let her rest until close to dawn.

The man had been insatiable.

Who was she kidding? She'd been insatiable.

She slid quietly off the bed and looked down at Harek, who was splayed out on his back, arms above his head, legs spread, sleeping the deep sleep of the well-satisfied male. His limp penis, which looked darn good even at half-mast, lay spent on his balls. She went into the adjoining bathroom and splashed water on her face. She wasn't about to take a shower, not right now here in the guest bathroom, lest she awaken the monster in the bed, who would no doubt be ready to go another round, limp willy or not. She'd heard what they said about Navy SEALs and their staying power, but whoever said that had never shaken the sheets with a Viking.

She pulled her Snoopy shirt over her head and went back to her bedroom, where she donned a belted, pink candy-striped cotton robe, another legacy from her teen years. She could smell fresh coffee brewing before she even got to the kitchen, which was empty except for Tenecia, their long-time cook.

After exchanging some warm hugs and inquiries about her family—Tenecia had a son who owned an auto body shop and a daughter who worked as a special ed teacher—Camille asked, "Mom and Dad not down yet?"

"Oh, they be down, all right. Went fer a walk, they did."

"Together?"

Tenecia laughed, putting both hands over her apron-covered belly. "Yep. Holdin' hands 'n everythin'." Tenecia rolled her eyes meaningfully.

Could Harek have really worked his magic on her father? He'd certainly worked some kind of magic on her.

Tenecia handed her a steaming cup of coffee, and Camille took a welcoming swallow. There was nothing anywhere else in the world like strong Creole coffee, the chicory mellowed by Tenecia's own secret of crushed eggshells and a pinch of salt in the water.

Camille glanced around the large, sunny kitchen. Every one of the six burners on the commercial gas stove had pots or frying pans bubbling away with a wonderful-smelling concoction, and both ovens were lit up with baked goods. Caterers were outside setting up tables and tents for the brunch to be held here early this afternoon. Household staff could be seen in the dining room polishing silver.

"What's on the menu for today?"

"Three kinds of quiche, smoked ham, thick sliced bacon, eggs Benedict, scrambled eggs, fresh fruit salad, Waldorf salad, banana puddin', sweet rolls, lazy bread, biscuits, okra jelly, my grandma's special relish with watermelon pickles, beignets, of course, cain't have no meal in Loo-zee-anna without beignets." She took a deep breath and continued, "Boudin sausage, crawfish and shrimp omelettes, an' that's jist fer starters."

"Good Lord! You must have been working for weeks on this."

"I have, though some of it's gonna be made, on the spot, by that fancy-pancy chef out in the yard," Tenecia told her with disapproval in her voice. "I coulda done it myself with a helper 'r two. Don't know why yer mama had to hire no fancy chef who cooked for Emeril one time. If he says 'Bam!' jist one time, I'm gonna show him, 'Bam!' "

Camille smiled and helped herself to a beignet that had not only been sprinkled with sugar but drizzled with chocolate. The first bite was like an explosion of taste in her mouth, and she moaned her appreciation. You'd think after all the "chocolate" last night, she'd be stall fed with the taste. Instead, her appetite had increased.

"Not again," she heard a male voice say behind her.

Harek had come in wearing jeans, a T-shirt, and athletic shoes. His usually meticulous hair was rumpled, and not designer rumpled. More like I've-just-had-some-badass-sex rumpled. He grinned at her and kissed her cheek.

"Not again what?" she asked.

"The moaning. I don't think I could survive any more of your moaning."

Tenecia giggled, and Camille gave Harek an admonishing frown.

He said hello to Tenecia, whose acquaintance he'd apparently made the day before, as evidenced by his saying, "You made beignets again, Tenecia. A woman after a man's heart. Your husband is a lucky man."

"I got no husband."

"Will you marry me?"

Tenecia giggled, again, and Harek helped himself to a beignet and a cup of coffee. When Tenecia bustled off to speak to the caterers about some mistake they were making with the placement of steam tureens, Harek sat down at the table next to Camille. Real close. "Hi," he said, and waggled his eyebrows at her.

"Don't 'hi' me. The last time you said hi to me, I ended up with my face in a pillow and my rear in the air."

"You don't need to thank me."

"I wasn't thanking you."

"You did at the time. As I recall, you kept saying—"

"Don't remind me."

"Don't go all morning-after-ish on me, Camille. Last night . . . this morning was too good. Don't spoil it with regrets."

"It was good for me, too," she admitted.

They smiled at each other, and the warmest feeling suffused her. It wasn't sexual, more like loving.

Whoa! Nobody said anything about love. Before you know it, she'd be planning another wedding and then having a fourth ex-fiancé to contend with.

Another Whoa! That was some leap. From good sex to bad breakup all in one breath.

Just then, her mother and father walked in, and, yes, they were holding hands and grinning at each other like teenagers who'd just discovered French kissing. Camille would bet her WEALS medallion that they'd made love last night. Yeech! Not a picture she wanted in her head.

Her mother wore white sneakers and neatly pressed capris topped by a lightweight aqua sweater set and Great-Aunt Effie's opal and diamond earrings. Her father wore white deck shoes and Bermuda shorts, also neatly pressed, topped with an aqua Bayou DeSiard Country Club golf shirt. They looked like senior citizen dress-alikes. Wannabe twins. Camille didn't think her father had played golf a day in his life. These clothes must have been packed away from when they were lots younger. In fact, the two of them looked lots younger this morning. Amazing what good sex could do for appearance, like a shot of Botox to the libido. *No, no, no, I am not thinking that. Otherwise, I'd have to admit to being ten years younger myself after last night.*

"Good morning, sweetheart," her father said, leaning down to give her a kiss on the top of her head and a pat on the shoulder.

"It's a beautiful day," her mother added, actually hugging Camille from behind. A real hug, not one of those fly-by hugs Camille had become accustomed to. "Are you sure you can't stay another day, dear? With all the wedding madness, we haven't had a chance to catch up."

Catch up on what? Camille almost asked. Since when was her mother interested in Camille's life?

"No, sorry, I have to be back at the base this afternoon."

"I could call that commander person and ask for a special excuse for you to stay over," her father suggested.

"Good idea, Emile," her mother said, and the two of them exchanged more sappy grins.

But what had her father said? Special excuse? Did he think the military was like grade school where all he had to do was send a note excusing her from class for the day because she had a tummy ache?

"And you, too?" her father said to Harek. "I could request a dispensation for you, as well."

A dispensation now? Here's a news flash, Papa, the CO is not like a pope.

"Uh, no thanks," Harek said. "I actually have a different commander."

Does he mean God? Or St. Michael? Oh Lord!

"Well, give me his name and number and I'll make the call," her father offered magnanimously, while her mother beamed at him with pride.

"Uh, my boss has an unlisted number," Harek mumbled, looking to Camille for help.

Forget that. He was the one who'd turned her parents into a bleepin' newlywed couple. A regular Brad and Angelina. If they started adopting kids from third world countries, Camille was going to puke, or throttle someone's neck. That someone was concentrating on his coffee now like the secrets of the universe were hidden in its black depths.

"What is that delicious smell in here?" her mother asked.

"Tenecia has been cooking up a storm," Camille said, as if her mother didn't already know that.

Her mother was checking the various pots to make sure all her directions had been followed. Camille was sure the menu had been put together by her mother, who had many years' experience as a hostess for faculty parties.

"No, it's chocolate I smell, and not just that itty-bitty drizzle over the beignets."

"I don't smell chocolate," her father said. "I smell roses. Lots of roses. Are your roses in bloom now, honey? They must be. Or the florist delivered more flowers. It's beginning to smell like a funeral parlor, ha, ha, ha."

Her father cracking a joke?

Camille and Harek exchanged glances. Chocolate and roses. Were they giving off scents to other people now, too, not just to each other?

Camille felt as if she'd fallen into some Alice

in Wonderland rabbit hole, and all the characters were not what they appeared to be.

"Well, I need to take a shower and get dressed," her mother said brightly. "We can talk more when I come back down. Will you bring two coffees up with you, darling?"

At first, Camille thought her mother was asking her to bring the coffees, but then she realized that it was darling dad she'd been addressing. He was already at the counter, placing two cups and two beignets on a tray.

"By the way, Harek," her mother said, causing Harek's head to jerk up. "Thank you." There were tears in her mother's eyes as she addressed Harek. "I don't know what you did, but Emile tells me that I have you to thank for . . ." She shrugged at her unfinished statement.

But Harek nodded in understanding.

"Yes. I owe you . . . we owe you," her father attempted to speak in a choked voice. "If there's ever anything we can do for you . . ."

"No. This is my job. Your job is to . . . you know," Harek said enigmatically to her father.

What? What job? Camille wasn't sure she wanted to know.

Once she and Harek were alone again in the kitchen, she stared at him. "You really are one of those things, aren't you? A vangel."

"For my sins, yes."

"Wow!"

"Is that a good wow or a bad wow?"

"I'm not sure. A vangel, for heaven's sake. I had sex with a vangel!"

"Hot vangel sex, I might add." He smiled at her, and whoo boy, his smiles were hard to resist. "Wouldst thou consider a quick return to your bed furs and some more hot vangel sex?"

"You're kidding, right?"

"Not a bit. If we hurry, I might have time to show you the famous Viking S-spot."

She shouldn't ask. She really shouldn't. "Is that the same as the G-spot?"

"No. The S-spot is far better." The smile on his face was pure wickedness.

What kind of angel was he anyway? A wicked angel, for sure!

"Where is . . . No, don't tell me," she said, then flashed her own wicked smile back at him. "Show me."

Chapter 13

Surprise, surprise!...

Harek's sexual relationship with Camille, if it could be called a relationship, was short-lived. In fact, the casualness with which she had treated him since they left New Orleans yesterday bordered on sexist.

The more she treated him like a friend, or a professional colleague, the more he wanted to show her just how friendly he could be. To think, he'd even gone to the trouble of showing her the famous Viking S-spot! *Talk about ingratitude!*

For the first time in his life, Harek felt like he was the one-night stand. *Face it, I've been used. And I don't like it. Not one bit.*

Harek had been working out with the Deadly Wind mission participants all morning, starting with the obligatory six-mile run in heavy boots before a six a.m., or 0600 (*whoopee-dam-militaryspeak-dee!*) breakfast of "doggie dicks," a Navy name for small sausages, powdered eggs, referred to as "yellow puke," and black coffee thick enough to hold a standing spoon, so loaded with caffeine it ought to be called "black bull." Beignets and specially brewed chicory coffee were a thing of the past. Lunch in the chow hall had been no better. The only good thing Harek could say was there was plenty of it, especially carbs to build up energy. *Can anyone say SPAM?* And he didn't mean the Internet kind.

Harek was in prime physical health, but this was hard. His brother, guilty of the sin of sloth or laziness, had the energy of a, well, sloth. "How do you do it?" he'd asked Trond at one point.

Trond had just grinned. He was enjoying Harek's discomfort way too much. "Mayhap you need a break, little brother. There's a rocking chair in the lounge, I believe."

"Rock my ass," Harek had replied.

"Seems to me your ass was already rocked enough this past weekend."

It was useless complaining to his brother.

The morning had been filled with physical exercises that bordered on torture. Really. The O-course or obstacle course of workout rotations was also called the Oh-my-God course, for good reason. As for the grinder—the concrete arena where many of the maneuvers took place, surrounded by buildings, much like a penitentiary yard—it did indeed grind away at the poor saps, male and female, who participated. And people signed up for this crap, willingly? And they thought Vikings were unbalanced!

Harek would hurl his guts out before he quit now, in light of Trond's challenge—rocking chair, indeed!—even though he, as an outsider, was not required to complete all the grueling drills. Besides, Camille seemed to have no trouble climbing the cargo net like a friggin' monkey or freezing her pretty butt off in "surf appreciation" nonsense. He would be damned if he would cry off.

As a result, Harek was practically limping as he entered the classroom for the afternoon tactical session. It had about fifty of those school chairs in it, the ones with a small desk attached. Harek sat in the back row next to an FBI agent, Henry Rawlings, who was hurting as much as Harek, as evidenced by the groan as he adjusted himself on the hard chair.

"Can you believe these SEALs? They either have a God complex or a Rambo fixation," Henry muttered.

"Well, they say there are three reasons why anyone would become a SEAL. To prove something to themselves, to prove something to someone else, or because they're crazy," Harek commented. *Or because they're ordered to by none other than St. Michael the Archangel.*

"I vote for crazy."

"Ditto."

"That F.U. character said I run like a girl. I told him to suck my dick and he said he'd rather suck his own, and claimed he could, if he wanted, it was that big."

The SEALs *were* rather full of themselves, some more than others. F.U. was known to be particularly obnoxious.

Lieutenant Avenil, Slick, came in then and strode up to the front. "Time to get down to the nitty-gritty," he said right off. "Open the folders on your desk. On top, you'll see a schedule for the next week. There will be some modifications as we go."

Paper rustled as occupants of the room did as they were told, followed by a few groans.

That afternoon they would be engaged in CQ, or close quarter training, in simulated settings, mock-ups of the Nigerian school complex they were targeting. Tomorrow they were off to San Clemente Island for a jungle survival rotation, followed by a day of skydiving at Camp McCall. Everyone on this team was jump qualified, including Harek, or they wouldn't have been accepted for the mission. There would be instructions regarding the culture that would involve body posture, treatment of women, deference to authority or religious figures. Plus a short course on jungle animals and pests. The Sambisa Forest region was primitive, to say the least.

Harek was coming to realize, if he didn't know already, that many of the SEALs were highly intelligent, even with master's degrees. When out on an op, they were often called upon to be not just commando warriors, but also doctors, engineers, mechanics, and survivalists, not to mention a bit of "rootin'-tootin'-parachutin'" rodeo cowboy.

"Now, you all know that language is often a problem when we are OUTCONUS," Slick said.

"The bad news is that there are more than five hundred different languages and dialects spoken in Nigeria by the two hundred and fifty different tribes."

FU exclaimed, "Oh crap!"

Slick ignored FU and went on, "The good news is that English is the official language of Nigeria due to its early colonization. If all else fails, many people there speak a form of pidgin or broken English. Cage and even Camille will give us tips on that vernacular since Cajun and Creole languages utilize forms of pidgin English." Navy SEAL Justin "Cage" LeBlanc and Marie Delacroix were Cajuns from Louisiana, Harek already knew from Trond; so Camille must be Creole.

"What the hell is pigeon English?" someone called out.

"Not pigeon. Pidgin," Slick corrected.

Cage stood and turned to face the class. "Di ting wey mai eyes see, mi mouth no fit talk abo. If I said that to you, it would mean something like, Words fail me. I read that somewhere on the Internet."

"Oh crap!" F.U. said again. "Now we gotta learn redneck."

"Not redneck, asshole." Cage glared at F.U.

"Enough, boys!" Slick said. "In between our other drills, there'll be a shortcut language course to give you, not a proficiency in the local dialect, but a feel for key words and phrases."

Communal groans followed. If there was anything SEALs and other warriors hated, it was classroom work.

"Back to your folders," Slick directed them then. "Timing is everything, especially on this mission. As a result, a group of you, Team Red, will go out on Saturday. These will be the ones who will be openly infiltrating the school and community."

Harek checked the sheet in front of him and saw that Camille Dumaine would go in as a student. How the hell she would manage that, Harek had no idea. In addition, SEAL Sylvester "Sly" Simms, a former black underwear model for *GQ* and other magazines, with his wife, Donita Leone, an ebony-skinned ex-Olympic swimmer, would be newly hired as assistant principal and teacher, respectively. Omar ben Sulaiman, aka Teach, a rare Arab–Native American SEAL—forget rare, the only one of his kind—would pose as a new janitor at the school. Those would be the only inside contacts.

Harek felt an odd chill of foreboding go up his spine at the prospect of Camille placing herself in the midst of so much danger. If she were caught . . . well, her fate did not bear thinking about. He shouldn't be concerned. She was a trained soldier, after all. God forbid that he should place undue emphasis on her being a woman in such a situation. Still . . .

"The following Monday, Team Yellow will go into the LZ marked on the map behind me. It will be a nighttime drop from a lights-out C–147. The aircraft will be in and out of the zone within five minutes. From then, you're on your own. Covert and quiet are the key. Do not engage the enemy, unless absolutely necessary. The longer the tangos are unaware of our presence, the better. That's the reason for the sporadic insertions.

"As you can see, Team Green will enter here." He pointed to a spot on the map about a football field away from Insertion Point B. "That will be two days later. The drop will be a fast rope down from a copter. Again, quick entry and exit. By Friday, Teams Blue and White should be in place. No more than ten operatives per team. Each with the appropriate specialists: snipers, explosives, communications, recon, etc. I realize that this is a large number. We SEALs operate best in small units of less than five. The logistics of this project are different, though. Any questions so far?"

"I sense a goat fuck coming on, with us tripping over each other," Geek said.

"It will be your job with logistics to make sure that doesn't happen," Slick told Geek.

"Great!" Geek muttered.

There was silence for a moment as everyone searched the lists to see where they, or their comrades, were on the teams. Harek was on Team Yellow, along with Henry, the FBI guy next to him; a CIA agent, Brad Omstead; and SEALs Jacob Alvarez Mendoza, or JAM, the team leader; and Justin "Cage" LeBlanc; F.U.; and Geek. Trond was on Team Green. Slick was leading the last unit, Team White, in, which would allow them to cover the four corners of the square perimeter, about one mile on each side.

SEAL Torolf Magnusson spoke up, probably expressing the opinion of some others in the room, "Man, I don't like the timing on this. Flash and dash, quick in and out is more our speed." Magnusson was a Viking whom Harek had met several times before. No, he was not a vangel. He was from the Norselands, though. The tenth-century Norselands! But that was another story. "The longer we're in hostile territory, the more we become targets," Magnusson pointed out. "The more time for shit to go wrong."

"I understand your concern, Max, but we're dealing with a whole other animal here. BK is expecting shock and awe. We have to give them the unexpected. Silent but deadly."

"It's not called unconventional warfare for nothing," someone remarked.

"Right," Slick agreed. "This mission will be well-orchestrated down to the last detail. No blind date here. In the most successful mission, no shots are fired; we had that message hammered into us throughout BUD/S. That will not be the case here, I damn-fucking-guarantee. But let's make sure there are no mistakes. We do not want another ISIS debacle." Slick's warning referred to the failed attempt to rescue one of the American captives in Iraq, who later had been beheaded.

"We go in as ghosts. Full-ruck ghosts," he added with a smile. The backpacks and weaponry SEALs and other military carried often weighed as much as seventy-five pounds and contained everything from camelback water packs to night-vision goggles to KA-BAR knives to medical kits to breacher bars to heavy radio equipment or collapsible machine guns. "Now, you may have noticed that some mission-essential people are absent this afternoon."

Harek glanced around quickly. He hadn't realized . . .

"Let me introduce you to Desmond Buhari and Fatima Tinibu, the new assistant principal and the language arts teacher at the Global School in Kamertoon." Sly and his wife Donita came out, dressed in traditional African professional attire. They nodded to the group and stood to the side.

"And this is Abdul-Karim, a new janitor at the school. He is an Arab Muslim, new to the country, interested in joining Boko Haram."

Omar came out wearing regular clothing, but a checkered cloth was wrapped around his head, Middle Eastern style. A *keffiyeh*.

"Next up," Slick said, "is the new assistant attaché at the American embassy in Abuja, Mr. Gerald Larson and his wife, Sally Larson, from Alexandria, Virginia." Out came Kevin "K–4" Fortunato and Trond's wife, Nicole. K–4 wore a tan business suit with a brown and white striped dress shirt and a solid brown tie. Nicole, who must have dyed her hair red since he'd seen her this morning, wore a conservative green sheath dress with medium height, darker green high heels. Both K–4 and Nicole seemed to have aged by ten years, due to makeup or something.

"And their daughter, Linda Larson, who is about to enroll at the Global School, a fifteen-year-old ninth grader. The school only goes up to grade nine. We had originally planned for three students, but decided later that three would be pushing it. So, only four bodies inside the school. The KISS principle."

That would be: Keep It Simple, Stupid.

"As few operatives in plain sight as possible."

Out came a slightly pudgy young girl in a school uniform of short-sleeved, white blouse tucked into a navy-blue, pleated, knee-length skirt, white anklet socks, and loafers. She had frizzy red hair, the same color as her mother's, and a light smattering of freckles. No breasts at all, to speak of. And knobby knees. The sulky expression on her face was typical of young teens, and her posture was pure hunched-shoulders, insecure-pubescent girl child.

Holy frickin' clouds!

It was Camille.

Harek blinked several times to make sure his eyes weren't betraying him.

There was a ripple of applause at Camille's appearance, and she did a little bow, immediately resuming her young girl posture.

"As usual, Camille has earned her WEALS nickname of Camo for camouflage. Those of us who know her have witnessed her transformation in the past to Persian crone, Iraqi boy, beauty pageant contestant . . . some say the movie *Miss Congeniality* was based on one of her experiences. I'm not saying that's true. I'm just sayin'." Slick winked at Camille.

Harek didn't like Slick winking at Camille. In fact, he didn't like the too-handsome SEAL knowing her better than he did. *Not that I have any proprietary rights. I'm just sayin', or thinkin'. Or going out of my blippin' mind.*

How was he going to focus on killing Lucipires in Nigeria when Camille was walking around like a blinking neon sign to Boko Haram? *Take me, take me!*

He wondered for one brief moment if he could "take her" to his private island and hide her for the duration.

A voice in his head asked, *What island?*

"Um."

Thou art a fool.

"A fool in love?" he jested, a lame attempt to divert attention away from his careless mention—rather thinking—about the island.

Can anyone say Siberia?

Archangels had no sense of humor.

Wet T-shirts, wet panties, same thing!

By Friday evening, Camille was alternately bone-weary with physical exhaustion and pumped with adrenaline about the upcoming mission.

Also, scared spitless.

A person would have to be brain dead not to fear these radical extremists. What they did with women captives didn't bear imagining. What they would do with an American girl would probably be even worse.

The answer is, don't get captured, Camille, she told herself. She was sitting at the desk in her bedroom of the small cottage she shared in Coronado with her WEALS roommates Marie Delacroix and Bobby Jo Franklin. Marie, a Cajun from Louisiana, was a former Marine who'd joined WEALS after 9/11. Bobby Jo was a lesbian bodybuilder and looked like it. Entering the service under its "don't ask, don't tell" policy a few years back, Bobby Jo rarely discussed her sexual orientation, and, as far as Camille knew, she didn't date, but the SEALs, known for their political incorrectness, liked to tease Camille and Marie about apples in a shared barrel and nonsense like that. They even had the nerve to give Bobby Jo the nickname Butch. The women just ignored the teasing, most of which was harmless. Besides, Bobby Jo could probably arm wrestle a few of them to the ground.

Following a late-afternoon dismissal back at the base, Camille showered, ate a quick dinner, and packed her bag for the trip. While her red hair dried into a frizzy mess, she sat at her desk "taking care of business," as special ops soldiers were told to do before any mission. Last wills and testaments updated, bills paid, family good-byes, that kind of thing. She'd even called her parents, who were blissfully happy and planning a cruise. A themed cruise with some academic purpose. Instead of shuffleboard, there would be lectures. Yippee!

They hadn't seemed worried about Camille, but then she'd made it sound like this was a routine mission. In fact, she might have said she was going to France, not Nigeria.

Tomorrow morning, Camille would board a military transport to Dallas with K–4 and Nicole.

From there, they would take a commercial flight to Nigeria. All day in the air! She'd downloaded *Game of Thrones* onto her Kindle and planned to start the series, if she didn't conk out and sleep. Sunday they would settle into the embassy housing, and Monday morning, Camille's "parents" would take her to the boarding school. She was on her own after that, except for Sly, Donita, and Omar, who should already be in place, having arrived over the weekend.

"Hey, get a move on it, darlin'. Good times t'night down on the bayou . . . uh, bay." A head popped into the half-open doorway. It was Marie who hadn't lost her Cajun accent even after all these years on the West Coast. And, yes, she was dressed for a night out, in her favorite skinny jeans and scoop-neck T-shirt.

"I don't think I want to go out tonight," Camille said.

"C'mon, *chère*, the Wet and Wild is callin' your name."

Camille laughed. The Wet and Wild was a bar that catered to military personnel from the naval base, including SEALs and WEALS. It was traditional to down a few the night before a live op, for the single folks, anyway.

"Look at me," Camille said, waving a hand toward her wild hair. "The only way I could tame this frizz is by putting it into pigtails."

In the end, Camille agreed to join both Marie and Bobby Jo for a few hours, and she didn't look too bad, if she did say so herself. She'd managed with a little gel to draw all of her hair up onto the top of her head, where she held it all together with one of those claw thingies. This only drew attention to the semipermanent freckles on her face (they would wear off in time, or by using some potent chemicals), but a little makeup covered them. Mascara and red lip gloss, and she was good to go. She, too, wore jeans. Not skinnies, in her case. She had a little too much butt for those. But they were tight and black, like her tank top. With her red high heels and hair piled atop her head, she looked taller than her five-eight.

"I'm going to lose my gay creds by hanging out with you two," Bobby Jo complained as they crossed the parking lot. Camille and Marie had talked her into ditching her cargo shorts and man's dress shirt for a "Walking Dead" T-shirt and white capri pants and sandals. There wasn't much that could be done with her short, short hair, but she had agreed to a small amount of blue eye shadow, which made her eyes look huge.

The three of them opted out of the politically incorrect, wet T-shirt spraying machine at the entrance, a longtime fixture at the Wet and Wild, which meant they had to pay a small cover charge. Friday nights meant a live band, and this was how the owners paid for it. Plus it was a big attraction for certain folks.

It was eight o'clock and the place was already crowded and loud with laughter and conversation and the clinking of glasses, not to mention the country music band, which was just tuning their instruments, about to start playing. Camille was glad she'd come, suddenly. It would be nice to relax with friends. Morbid as the thought was, you never knew who might be missing the next time they met.

They were wending their way train-style through the crowd toward a table on the far side where Marie recognized some people. Being the caboose, Camille couldn't see much.

But then she did.

Two tables had been pushed together. Sitting there were several WEALS, and SEALs: K–4, JAM, Geek, F.U., an FBI agent who was part of the Deadly Wind mission, and several others.

Including Harek Sigurdsson.

All week she'd been pretending that they were just pals, that the mind-blowing (and other body parts–blowing) night she'd spent with him hadn't meant anything. How was she going to keep up the pretense when he stood and stared at her like she was the answer to his prayers? Or at least the answer to his lust.

He wore a pure white T-shirt, untucked, over faded jeans. His dark blond hair had been spritzed into that ridiculous designer disarray. A gold watch on his left wrist sparkled with richness (could that be a Rolex?) against his tan skin. His blue eyes sparkled with something else. And even from ten feet away, even with the stale beer/perfume/body heat stink of the dive, Camille smelled chocolate.

She was wet before he even said hello.

And she hadn't needed any frickin' spray machine to get that way, either. Just a hot-as-hell Viking with chocolate body odor.

Then he smiled.

One!

Two!

Three!

She was down for the count.

Chapter 14

Love was in the air, or something . . .

Harek knew Camille had arrived before he saw her. Those fucking roses!

And he meant that literally. He got a hard-on every time he smelled roses these days. Case in point: He'd been ready to jump the bones of a woman coming out of the supermarket the other day before she turned and he realized she was eighty years old and carrying a jumbo bouquet of cellophane-wrapped roses.

Talk about embarrassing. And, just his luck, Trond had been with him at the time. They'd stopped on the way home to buy some feta cheese for the Greek salad Nicole was making. (Yes, Harek was still staying at Trond and Nicole's house, but he'd bought a pair of earplugs to wear at night.) Trond had been calling out older woman/younger man jokes and ribald limericks ever since, some of them rather creative. "There once was a youth with big feet, who had a taste for old meat . . ." That kind of nonsense. Trond must be getting them from the Internet. And the gossip hound told every vangel in the world about the incident. Vikings did love to gossip, being confined together for months at a time in a longship when they went a-Viking. Vangels were even worse, having so much spare time between missions.

But no mistake this time. It was Camille arriving in a cloud of essence of roses, apparent even in a room more noted for essence of stale beer.

Camille had that silly red hair piled on top of her head and the silly freckles, but she didn't look silly to him, and not at all like a fifteen-year-old schoolgirl. Not in skin-tight black jeans and a tank top, both of which outlined every curve of her luscious body. And he knew just how luscious it was—lucky him!—from personal experience. The interesting thing to Harek was how Camille could change her appearance so dramatically. It was an aspect of her persona that would always keep a man on his toes. Among other things.

His only saving grace at the moment was that he probably smelled, too. Like a bleepin' chocolate bar. Forget that. He was a whole supersize Whitman's Sampler, and Camille didn't have a clue what she was going to get. Yet.

He smiled.

And she tripped, just catching herself.

Good! No, bad. Bad, bad, bad! Holy smokin' clouds! Did she have to wear those sinfully sexy red high heels? Roses and red high heels. Sounded like the title of a romance novel. He might as well throw in the towel right now.

Without being asked, Henry, his new FBI friend, moved over a seat to make room for Camille. When Harek raised his brows in question, Henry, who was closing in on forty, twice-divorced, and as cynical as an atheist at a revival meeting, sang in a quite good baritone, especially considering he was on his fourth beer, "Love Is in the Air." Then added, "Or something."

"Or something," Harek muttered. But he wasn't so sure.

He waved for Camille to come sit beside him. He saw her hesitate for a second, then sigh with resignation and head his way.

He wasn't going to get bent out of shape over that hesitation. He'd been waiting all week to corner her, and his window of opportunity here might be too short for quibbling over small stuff. *Pick your battles, soldier,* he told himself. "I was hoping you'd come tonight so I could say a proper good-bye," he said when she sat down.

"Were you?"

He had always been of the opinion that sarcasm ill-suited women, but perhaps he shouldn't share that sentiment with her just yet, or ever.

She nodded when JAM asked if she wanted him to fill a glass for her from the pitcher of beer on the table. "A proper good-bye, huh?" she asked after taking her first sip of beer and licking the foam off her upper lip.

He didn't care at all about her licking the foam off her upper lip. He wasn't even looking there.

"Would that be as a friend?" She was circling the rim of her glass with a forefinger as she asked the question.

He wasn't watching the movement of that finger. He wasn't imagining it circling something else.

"Because friends are all we are, right?" she added.

"Not a chance," he muttered.

"What did you say?"

"Not a thing." He took a sip of his own beer and asked, "What's with all this friend crap? Ever since we returned from New Orleans you've been giving me the cold shoulder."

"Have I? I didn't mean to."

Liar!

"Don't you want to be my friend?" She batted her reddish-brown lashes at him.

He wondered irrelevantly if she'd dyed them, as well as her hair. She must have. Which, of course, made him wonder if she'd dyed her nether hair, too? Of course she had. And freckles . . . oh damn! She'd probably painted freckles on other parts of her body, besides her face. Would she have some on her chest, near her breasts? On her belly? And how about her butt?

"Am I boring you?" she asked, interrupting his fantasy.

Not even a little.

"You didn't answer me. Don't you want to be my friend? I figured after spending a weekend in my home, and all you did for my parents, and everything we know about each other now, well, you know. We should be friends, at least."

He could tell that she realized her mistake with those last two words, and he immediately pounced, before she had a chance to retract them. "At least, sweetling. At the very least."

"Let's cut the crap here, Harek. What do you want from me?"

"Do you have to ask?" He put an arm around her shoulder and squeezed.

"And that's all?"

Jeesh! Women! Did they have to make a big deal out of everything? "For now," he said, which was a load of bullshit. All he had was now. Already, he could sense Mike moving in. Any second he would be pulling the plug, and Harek didn't mean *that* plug. He meant the end to any contact with Camille. Like, "Siberia, here I come!"

Any further conversation was postponed by F.U. and Geek getting into an argument over bombs versus intelligence in combating terrorism. F.U. claimed that the military needed to give the tangos more "shock and awe," as in blowing their asses to smithereens, and he was just the explosives expert to do it, while Geek said intelligence gathering and covert operations were the way to go. No need for a big-bang show of force. JAM, who had been a Jesuit in training at one time, said that a little prayer helped, too.

"That's the problem," Marie interjected. "Everyone thinks that God is on their side."

Harek knew whose side God was on, but he

wasn't about to call attention to himself with that kind of religious discussion.

"Are you ready to deploy on Monday?" Camille asked him, while around them people were giving food orders to the waitress. Hot wings, nachos, pretzels, that kind of thing.

He nodded. "How about you? You leave in the morning, don't you?" He knew that because Nicole would be traveling with her, and Trond had started saying good-bye to his wife at three this afternoon. Can anyone say "horny Viking"?

"Yep. At five a.m.," she said, and licked the salt off a pretzel stick that she took from a basket placed in front of them.

That lick was appreciated by his chocolate stick.

Between the beer foam and the salt, he felt like he was being assaulted. By licking. He groaned.

She smiled.

The witch!

"I'm worried for you," he blurted out . . . without thinking, obviously.

"Why?" She cocked her head to the side and crunched on her pretzel. Crunch, crunch, crunch.

Who knew crunching could be sexy? "The danger."

"I won't be out in the field, like you and the others."

"Just as dangerous. More so, in some ways."

"Harek, this is what I do."

"I know." Didn't mean he had to like it.

"Besides, I'm not your concern."

"I beg to differ. Unfortunately. I suspect Mike sent me here to protect you, as well as kill some

Boko Haram Lucipires and save those who can still repent."

"Whoa, whoa, whoa. Are you saying that Boko Haram are demon vampires?"

"Some of them are."

She rolled her eyes. "And you'll try to save them?"

"Those that are not entirely black of soul have to be offered the opportunity. Most, if not all, will be too far gone, though."

"Un-be-freakin'-lievable!"

"It is what is."

"And you think the archangel had me in his crosshairs, too, when he sent you here?"

"It would seem so."

"What? You gonna save me, like you did my father?"

Between the sarcasm and now the scoffing, he should have been put off. He wasn't. "You don't need that kind of saving."

"What kind of saving, then?"

He shrugged. "I don't know. It'll come to me eventually."

"Pfff! Let me know when you figure it out."

"You'll be the first to know." He grinned. *Best to show her my sunny side when she continues to jab at me with her snide remarks. Olaf Hairy Arms had the right idea. Cut off his wife's nagging tongue. No, that wouldn't be a good idea. No licking then.*

"Just out of curiosity, is your brother Trond a vangel, too?"

Blather, blather, blather. "He is."

"And Nicole."

"No. She is just his mate for life . . . *his* life. No, I don't want to explain now. Let's dance."

The band, which had been playing rowdy country songs, like "I Love This Bar," and "Boot Scootin' Boogie," segued into a poignant, slow ballad, something about, "I Need You Now."

For sure.

"Do you think this is a good idea?" she said, even as she stood and dusted pretzel salt off her shirt.

Add salt dusting to licking as carnal triggers.

As to her question, dancing was the best idea he had, barring sex in the backseat of Trond's Jeep, which he'd driven over here and which was outside in the parking lot. "Do you have any better ideas?" he asked, following her to the tiny dance floor and opening his arms to her.

Camille put her arms around his shoulders and nuzzled her face into his neck. He put his palms on her buttocks and yanked her tight into the cradle of his hips, then looped his hands loosely around her waist. With her high heels, she fit perfectly against him.

Harek wasn't crazy about dancing. Seemed a wasted form of foresport to him. Why not just do the real thing? But he liked dancing with Camille. Especially when she snuggled closer and made a little kittenish mewl against his ear. Especially when his denim-clad crotch brushed her denim-clad crotch with every sway of the dance. Especially when the aura of roses surrounded them, as if they were all alone, swaddled in an erotic cocoon, not in the middle of a crowded dance floor with a bunch of horny sailors.

They danced and danced, saying nothing, to one "crazy"-themed song after another. Patsy Cline's "Crazy," Johnny Cash and Waylon Jennings's version of "I Wish I Was Crazy Again," the more recent "Redneck Crazy" by Tyler Farr, and then the far-from-country Queen's "Crazy Little Thing Called Love." He knew because the singer made an announcement before each song. Maybe he was going a little crazy himself. He knew he was when he realized he was slow dancing with Camille to that fast, very fast song, "The Devil Came Down to Georgia." The band must have moved on from crazy to frenzied. Folks around them were laughing.

"Let's get out of here," he said, and began to lead Camille off the dance floor. Thankfully, she didn't protest. In fact, she muttered, "You better buy me a chocolate bar real soon, or I'm going to start nibbling on your skin."

"Damn, I hope so!"

Between the front door and the Jeep, about fifty feet, he must have kissed Camille twenty times, sometimes not even stopping as they kissed. It was a wonder they didn't trip over the gravel or bump into a vehicle. When they were in the car, he asked, "Where to? Can't go to Trond's house. He and Nicole started saying their good-byes this afternoon, and they'll probably still be going at it by the time you leave in the morning."

Camille laughed. He'd already told her, back in

New Orleans, what living with Trond and Nicole was like.

"How about that Motel 6 down the road? It doesn't look too bad," he said.

"No, let's go back to my place. Marie and Bobby Jo probably won't be back until two, and you'll be gone by then. I have to get up by four. We go boots off the ground at five."

He glanced at his watch . . . a Rolex his brothers had given him for Christmas, sort of a joke related to his sin of greed. He loved the watch, which Mike would no doubt confiscate once he got a gander at it. Harek enjoyed the luxury while he could.

It was only ten p.m. Hah! Camille had another think coming if she thought they'd be nearly satisfied in less than four hours. He was no dummy, though. He kept his mouth shut, and just nodded.

When they got to the cottage on a Coronado side street, he grabbed his backpack from the rear seat. It contained his laptop that he didn't like to risk, even in a locked car; his secure cell phone; and some other items.

Once inside the small house, whose ceilings seemed almost too low for his six-foot-four frame, Camille asked, "Would you like something to eat, or drink?"

He shook his head and just stared at her. She knew what he wanted.

"C'mon," she said, taking his hand and leading him upstairs.

He wanted to ask her why she'd changed her mind about having sex with him. He didn't, though, fearing she would give him that friends-with-benefits crap. He didn't know why, but he resisted the idea of mere friendship with Camille.

At the end of the hall, they entered a small bedroom that held a double bed, a bedside table with a low-wattage lamp, a dresser with a mirror on top, and a desk. There was an adjoining bathroom that appeared to be small, too. A packed suitcase stood on the floor at the foot of the bed. She closed and locked the door, then leaned back against it.

He liked the sound of that lock. It gave a sort of mental high five to what was to come.

"I wondered where you slept," he said.

"I pictured you here," she said.

"What was I doing?"

"Just what you're doing now, staring at me with smoldering blue eyes and a hard-on that could drill cement."

Smoldering eyes and a hard cock, what more could a guy ask for? He laughed and shook his head at her. "Have I told you that you have a way with words?"

"A time or two. This is just about friends, right?"

Damn, damn, damn. "I'm feeling very friendly."

"You never give me a straight answer."

"Here's straight for you. I want you so much my heart is racing and my hands are shaking. I'm afraid to step closer to you because my knees might buckle. I'm one thousand, one hundred, and ninety-five years old, and I have never felt this way about a woman before."

"Is that the truth?"

"The God's honest truth."

"I feel the same way," she confessed, "although I don't have that many years under my belt. What do you suppose it means?"

Did Eve talk so much in the Garden of Eden? No wonder Adam ate the friggin' apple! "I'm afraid to guess."

"Not the life mate nonsense?"

He shrugged. What else could it be?

"What should we do?"

Now, *that* he had an answer to. "Carpe diem. Seize the day. Live for the moment and let the chips fall where they fall."

"You're full of clichés today, aren't you?"

Either that or I'm full of shit. I'm a grown man, experienced, intelligent even beyond my years, but I feel like an untried youthling with his first maid. And if she doesn't stop chattering, I'm going to pull out my hair, one gelled strand at a time. Aaarrgh! He sat on the edge of the bed and toed off his athletic shoes. Then he leaned back on the stacked pillows and folded his hands behind his neck, extending his long legs and crossing them at the ankles, tapping the footboard. "Take off your clothes, sweetling. Slowly. But don't put those shoes away. I have plans for them, later."

Camille studied him for a long moment. He could tell she was contemplating whether to take orders from him or not. But then she tugged her tank top up and over her head, exposing a black lace bra. She leaned back against the door and let him just take her in.

He did.

Finally, she kicked off her shoes, unzipped her

pants, and shimmied out of the tight fabric, leaving just brief, black lace bikini underpants. Sliding her shoes back on, she placed her arms over her head and posed for him against the door.

He was stunned speechless for a moment. Had he really thought she was plain at one time? Amazing the things women could hide from clueless men! Even with the brash red hair, she was beautiful. Sultry, even. And, yes, she'd dyed her hair down below, too, he saw through the filmy, almost transparent silk. He couldn't wait to taste it. Was there such a thing as flavored hair dye, like flavored lip gloss? Probably not. But there should be.

"Why are you smiling?" she asked.

"Because I'm happy." And that was the truth. He wasn't a morbidly unhappy person, like his brother Mordr, but living in bumfuck Siberia on the darkest, coldest nights, yeah, he knew what depression felt like. The opposite of happiness, for sure. But more than that, he now sensed what he'd been missing for all these centuries, even when he'd had all the material possessions a man could want. So, this was happiness? This warm, glowing sensation that emanated from the heart and filled the senses. Amazing! "Keep going," he said, his voice raspy with emotion.

"Turn on the stereo. I need a little music if I'm going to do a striptease. Too bad I don't have a pole."

I have one, he thought, and thankfully didn't say it aloud. He stood and went over to a stand beside the dresser. Sitting there was an old-fashioned stereo that played vinyl records. "Isn't this kind of dated?" he asked as he stacked the records that were already there on the turntable.

"Yes, but the sound is remarkably better than all that downloaded crap today."

"You have a thing for the blues, huh?" he noted. All the records seemed to be classics by old, long-dead soul singers.

"You can't be from Nawleans and not be a fan of the blues. You don't like the blues?"

"I like all kinds of music. Even vampires get the blues," he told her. Was it synchronicity that he'd just been thinking about depression and she liked the soulfully sad music?

"How about angels?"

"Oh yeah. Being good all the time definitely causes the blues."

"You're funny," she commented.

"Not the trait I'm going for!" He finally got the records lined up and hit the play button.

Immediately, Etta James began to belt out "At Last." It was a slow, sultry soul song.

He turned and leaned against the dresser.

She was singing under her breath, eyes closed. As she got into the groove, writhing from side to side, she lowered her hands and slowly undid the front clasp on the bra. For a moment she held the sides together, then she opened her eyes, dropped her hands, and let the black scrap of silk and lace fall to the floor.

"Like?" she asked.

He nodded. His tongue was stuck to the roof of his mouth, and he was keeping his lips shut tight so she wouldn't see how his incisors were already elongated with arousal. Not his most attractive feature! In fact, fangs were an affront to any Viking's vanity, but not much vangels could do about them. Vikar had tried to file his down at one point, but only succeeded in breaking the drill. Ivak had gone to a cosmetic dentist, who only laughed when asked to design a cap that would fit over the fangs and hide them. "I'm a dentist, not a magician," the dentist had said. Harek had considered having his gold plated, but that would only call attention to the orthodontic imperfections. Plus, Michael would consider it an outward sign of his greed and punish him in some way. Siberia, for a certainty.

Back to Striptease-ville. All those "crazy" songs back at the Wet and Wild must have turned him a little bit crazy. Why else would he be thinking about teeth when a near-naked woman was about to become totally naked in front of him?

Camille's breasts, which he'd seen before, of course, were pretty, that's all he could think. With her now red hair, the pinkness of her areolas and nipples seemed even brighter. The little nipples were already erect, or as erect as they would be without his further attentions, which were coming up, for damn sure.

But wait, she had her thumbs inside the elastic on each of her hips. Undulating slowly, in imitation of the sex act, she inched the garment slowly down until her red curly hairs were exposed. Then they were down her legs and off.

She stood there, wearing nothing but the red high heels, arching her brows at him.

"What?"

"Your turn."

A record dropped down and now it was Bessie Smith wailing, "Nobody Loves You When You're Down and Out."

He started to rip off his shirt.

But Camille cautioned him, "No, no! Slowly."

He smiled. This wasn't his kind of game. Or at least it hadn't been before. But, hey, he was a Viking. He could improvise. "Lie on the bed so I can entertain you."

"Think you can?"

"I can hot damn try."

And he did. Even though the Bessie Smith song was a slow one, it had a beat. He swayed from side to side. Then, slowly, he turned his back on her, bent over, and took off one sock, then the other, tossing them over his shoulder. One of them landed in the waste can. A slam dunk.

"Wow! Maybe you could do that again, later, when you're nude."

"Make a basket?"

"No, silly. Bend over when you're bare-assed naked."

What? That's the kind of thing I should be saying, not my woman. My woman? Save me, Lord. "Sure. But only if you do it, too."

"Dream on!" She laughed.

We'll see about that, witch!

Next, he rolled his shoulders and eased his T-shirt up, up, up so that more and more of his abdomen showed.

"Very nice." Camille was half lying on the bed,

braced against the headboard, with one knee raised slightly. Her hair was still held onto the top of her head with some kind of comb claw. "You must work out a lot."

"Not much else to do in Siberia. Are you going to comment on each bit of skin I uncover? It'll take forever. We'll never get to the good stuff."

"Hey, this is good stuff."

He bowed at her praise and undid the snap on his jeans and unzipped them halfway, all to the tune of "Stormy Weather." He closed his eyes and tried to find a slow beat in the music. In the end, he did a slow—very slow because he didn't know what the hell he was doing—bump and grind. Then he eased off his jeans and boxer briefs at the same time and kicked them aside.

He widened his stance, put his hands on his hips, and threw his shoulders back. *Get a good look, baby.*

She did. And suddenly she was no longer Miss Chatterbox. Instead, her lips were parted and her eyes were wide with interest.

Another record dropped down and Muddy Waters told the world, "I Just Want to Make Love to You."

I'll second that, he thought, and made a flying leap for the bed, landing atop Camille, who let out a little "oomph!" of distress, although he hadn't really hurt her, having caught the brunt of his weight on braced arms and knees. Knees that had somehow managed to land between hers and spread her wide. Just like he wanted.

"Hi!" he said, and rubbed his rising enthusiasm

against her blinking hot center. Well, it seemed like it was blinking and flame-like, the red curly hair and all that.

"I never knew sex could be so fun," she said.

It *was* fun, Harek had to admit, but then he grew serious. "Are you in love with me, Camille?" he asked. Where that question had come from, he had no idea.

"Good Lord! I hope not."

He nodded, although his spirits sank a little.

"Are you in love with me?" she inquired, tracing a forefinger over the edge of his lips, giving pause at the bumps covering his fangs.

He was going to scoff and say, *Of course not*. It would be the worst thing that could happen. Not the worst thing, but not a good thing. At least he didn't think it would be. He was the smartest of all the vangels. He was going to figure a way to escape the prison of vangeldom's restrictions. Maybe impress Michael so much that he would allow him to earn great wealth and material possessions. That was what he really wanted. Wasn't it?

Who was he kidding?

"Fangs drooling, wings over toenails, blood boiling, heart racing, dream about you at night, think about you all day. Nah, I'm not in love," he said.

He looked down at her, just waiting for the sarcastic remark.

But it didn't come. "Your eyes are all silvery, and there are wispy blue wings at your back," she told him with seeming irrelevance. "And you smell like Godiva chocolate."

"Your point?"

"I like your pretty eyes, and the wings are amazing. Most of all, though . . ."

He arched his brows at her.

"Have I told you that I love chocolate?"

She hadn't told him that she loved him, but it was close.

Harek felts swirls of a rose-scented fog envelop him. He couldn't have pulled away then if he wanted to. And he didn't want to. Not for a moment. Not for an hour or a day. Maybe not forever.

Chapter 15

Sex on a bed of chocolate . . .

That Christian Grey had nothing on Harek. The man knew things about sex. Forget fifty shades. Harek had a hundred shades of tricks up his talented fingers.

Not that she was counting.

She did remark on his skill for inducing multiple orgasms, and he replied, "Actually, we Vikings invented pleasing women in the bed furs."

"You are so full of it," she'd scoffed.

"Well, we *perfected* pleasing women in bedsport."

"I'll give you that," she said.

"What else have you got to give?"

Another orgasm, it turned out. Could a woman die of overclimaxing? What a way to go!

"Wait, wait, wait. How could I forget? I bought something today."

He got up from the bed and went over to his backpack, which he'd dropped on the floor near the door when they came in two hours ago. He was smiling widely, despite his usual efforts to hide his fangs . . . which were out in full force tonight due to overarousal, he'd explained. In his hand he held a jar and a brush.

"Wow! Chocolate body paint." And not the cheap stuff, either. This was the designer chocolate that probably cost fifty dollars a jar. "You must have been sure you were going to get lucky tonight."

"No, just hopeful. Come, stand over here so that I can paint all your good bits and then lick you clean." He waggled his eyebrows at her for emphasis.

"Oh no! You got this all wrong. I'm the chocoholic here. I'm the one who gets to feed my addiction. Not the other way around."

And she proceeded to show him exactly what he meant.

Turned out there were some things you could teach a Viking.

"I'm thinking about writing a book called *How to Make a Viking Cry,*" she said later when he sank down to his knees, facing her where she already knelt.

"Really?" He kissed her chin and murmured against her lips, "I'm thinking about writing a book, too. *How to Make a Witch Weep.*"

Turned out he knew how.

By two a.m., they'd taken a shower together to wash off the chocolate that still coated them both. More sex. Harek would be leaving soon.

Camille stripped the bed, which had many embarrassing brown stains, donned a robe, and prepared to go downstairs to run a load of laundry, while Harek was putting new linens on the bed. It went without saying that he was bending over, naked. Yikes!

About to enter the laundry room, she had the bad luck to run into Marie and Bobby Jo, who were just coming in. They sniffed the chocolate in the air, took one look at her and the sheets in her arms, and burst out laughing.

So much for her keeping her activity secret! So much for her getting him out of the house before her roommates returned!

"We're just friends," she said, which sounded lame, even to her own ears.

They burst out laughing again.

When she returned to her bedroom, instead of being dressed, Harek was back in bed, a single sheet drawn up to his waist. His back was propped against the headboard. Before she had a chance to protest, he lifted the sheet on one side for her. There was a serious expression on his face.

Still wearing the robe, she slid in beside him and he put an arm around her shoulders, tucking her to his side. "When you're in the school compound, if you're in trouble, I want you to concentrate really hard, think of me, and say in your head, 'HELP!' "

"Does that work?"

"I have no idea. Seems like it should if we are life mates or connected in some way."

She was about to say that they were not life mates but he put a fingertip to her lips.

"I don't know what the future holds for us, if anything, but I care about you and your safety."

"I've said it before and will say it again, Harek. This is what I'm trained to do. You have no right—"

"I have every right. The right of one who loves you."

She sighed deeply. "You don't mean that."

"I think I do."

Think? How can he make such a lame word so enticing?

"That was lame," he said.

"It was actually kind of cute."

"Great!"

"I'm not ready for that kind of commitment, Harek."

"And you think I am?"

A sudden thought occurred to her. "Is this mission dangerous for you, too?"

"Of course. Any time a vangel engages in battle with a Lucipire, whether it is one on one, or legion against legion, there is a risk."

"Of death."

"Worse than that. If a Lucie captures a vangel, the intent is to get him to agree to a transformation from angel to demon. That involves horrific torture that can go on for months, maybe years."

"Has this ever happened before?"

"Vangels have been caught and tortured, but they managed to escape. So far. One time Mike had to rescue Vikar, and his condition was . . . I do not want to talk about it. Like you said, it is what it is. This is my work. I would much rather talk about us." He kissed the top of her head.

"Let's not talk about love or commitment or relationships or any of that stuff. Not now. Maybe when we come back . . . I don't know. Let's just wait and see how we feel then."

"Are you saying that you don't have feelings for me?"

She sighed deeply again. "You know I do."

He nodded. "That will be enough for now. It will have to be."

Without words of love, Harek removed her robe and proceeded to show her just how much "love" he felt for her. It was a slow loving. Intense. With the soft murmur of endearments, both ways. Sweetling/sweetheart. Dearling/dearest. Heartling/my heart.

There was the usual sensual cocoon that enveloped them, but it was warm, not hot. And that was okay. Each level of sex play—kissing, touching, squeezing, talking—took them to a higher, more emotional plane. She couldn't explain it, exactly, but it was like being lifted higher and higher, outside herself. She could see the things he was doing to her and the things she was doing to him, but at the same time, she was inside her body where all the bliss emanated. Not the sharp-edged pleasure of before when his tongue plunged into her mouth, or his teeth nipped at her breasts, but more powerful in some ways for its very subtle morphing into carnality.

When he took himself in hand and guided his erection into her body, she was more than ready for him. Without asking, probably sensing there wasn't anything she would deny him, he placed his fangs against her neck and pressed lightly until he broke the skin. It didn't hurt, or only for a second. And now, with each long, slow stroke into her body, when he hit her clitoris, he took a tiny sip at the same time, and every nerve ending in her body exploded with sensation, each more powerful than the one before. By the time he'd started his shorter, harder strokes and his sipping had taken on a rhythm, Camille was mindless with nerve vibrations. Every surface of her skin was an erogenous zone. She was so overstimulated she felt as if she would go mad with her need for relief.

"Just let it go, sweetling. Let us go," he whispered against her ear. Even his breath teased her senses.

And then she did. Let go. And together they rode the groundswell of what had to be the most incredible mutual climax of all time. Wave after wave of contractions hit her and in turn grasped at him.

She cried out in wonder.

He roared his own wonder.

For a moment blood was pounding through her veins so hard, she was afraid she might have a heart attack.

Harek was panting for breath.

When she calmed down, she realized that Harek was lying heavily atop her. He finally raised his head and stared at her, "If that wasn't love, what was it?"

Good question.

Shortly after, Harek was getting dressed. It was three-thirty, and Camille was going to be picked up at four. He went into the bathroom while she pulled on a sweatshirt and shorts. Glancing out the window, she did a double take. By the light of a streetlamp, she could see the driveway to her cottage.

"Harek," she called out. "There's a man leaning against your Jeep. Is it one of your brothers?"

"Probably," he muttered.

"He's wearing a Blue Devils baseball cap."

The bathroom door flew open, and Harek had a look of worry on his face. "I know who it is, and it's not one of my brothers." He gave her a quick kiss and said, "I'll say good-bye here. See you in a couple days. Be careful." He grabbed his backpack and headed out the door. "Stay here. Don't come down until K-4 and Nicole come to pick you up."

Whaaat? After what they'd just shared, he thought he could rush out like that? Hah! She followed after him.

She eased the front door open and stood on the porch, out of sight of Harek and the stranger, but within hearing distance.

"Jasper has already dispatched two dozen Lucipires to the Sambisa Forest. That's in addition to the two dozen already there. This has been a lucrative site for him, and he's not about to give it up easily."

"Does he still plan to hit the Global School in Kamertoon?" Harek asked the other man.

"Among other places."

"When?"

"No definite date yet. Soon."

"Do you have that list I asked for?"

"I do. Check your private e-mail account. Delete it as soon as you read it. The attachment has the most up-to-date maps with hideouts shown, as well as some names and photographs. You can print out the pictures, but don't keep anything on your computer. Nothing is safe from hackers these days."

"Will do. Thanks for the info. I'll tell Mike how helpful you're being."

"He already knows. There's something else. Haroun has you in his crosshairs. If he gets wind that you're in Nigeria, he's going to be after your ass, big-time."

"What is it with Haroun? He's always targeting me in particular."

"You were both slave traders at one time, and Haroun resents what he considers your special treatment. You get to be a vangel, he's a demon."

Camille felt as if she'd been kicked in the stomach. She stepped forward and watched as the stranger walked away, in fact seemed to fade away.

Harek was opening the driver's door of the Jeep. He'd just thrown his backpack in when he looked up and noticed her in the shadows.

"Who was that?" she asked.

"Zebulan."

"A friend?"

He shrugged. "Not really."

"He's not a vangel?"

Harek exhaled loudly and disclosed, "No. Zeb is a Lucipire."

"A demon vampire? You brought a demon vampire to my house?"

"I didn't bring him here. He just showed up. There's no danger to you from Zeb, though. You could say he's a good devil."

She was not amused. "That's just great. And who is this guy Roan?"

At first, Harek seemed puzzled. Then he said, "Not Roan. Hair-roon."

"A slave trader?"

Harek's jaw went tight and he walked up to her. He tried to put his arms around her, but she shoved him away. "A slave trader?"

"Yes, he was. In the days of the old Silk Road, Haroun al Rashid was an infamous slave trader."

"And, you, Harek," her voice came out in a croak. She cleared her throat. "Are you a slave trader?"

"For my sins, I was. For a short time. Long ago."

She gasped and raised her hand, slapping him across the face, hard. "Get out!" she yelled.

"Camille, let me explain."

"Don't even try. Go away and don't ever come back. You . . . you repulse me." In fact, the scent of chocolate that still emanated from him made her sick. Much longer and she was going to upchuck on the lawn.

There was profound sadness in his blue eyes as he stared at her. Then he said, "So be it."

She stood frozen as he got in the Jeep and drove away. Glancing down, she realized that she was clenching her right hand, which still stung from slapping Harek. She couldn't recall the last time she'd slapped anyone. Yes, she could. It was

Julian . . . the day he broke their engagement and told her he'd impregnated another woman, her best friend, Justine.

This was far, far worse.

When vangels sing the blues . . .

By Sunday evening Harek was three sheets to the wind and not a wing in sight.

"She's never going to forgive me," he told Trond, who sat in his TV room beside him on a low couch. Their booted feet rested on a coffee table, something that would never happen if Nicole were around. They were watching the latest episode of *The Walking Dead*. And wasn't that a mood lifter?

They were both drinking beer, Trond's one to his five, and Harek might have already had ten. Or more.

Trond just rolled his eyes and resumed watching a zombie eat some guy's face like it was a world-class dinner. Harek got enough blood and slime when fighting Lucipires. He didn't need to see it in his spare time. For entertainment, if you could believe that!

A commercial came on, advertising some kind of fancy car. A Lincoln driven by that actor Matthew McConaughey. Maybe Harek should buy himself an expensive car, to feel better. A Jaguar. Or a Maserati. That would be fine if he didn't have a certain celestial being peering over his shoulder checking price tags and making tsking noises.

Not that Harek had heard from Michael lately. And wasn't that ominous, on top of Harek's bad ending with Camille?

"Harek, Harek, Harek. Have you not learned that some sins have a long shelf life?" Trond said, now that his attention was no longer riveted to the TV. "You cannot expect an overnight pardon."

Said the sinner to the sinner! Since when did Trond get to be all sanctimonious and lecturing? You'd think Trond was pure as first snow on a Norse fjord. His grievous sin might have been sloth and not greed, but the things he'd done had been just as bad.

Sour grapes anyone?

Was that Michael's voice in his head? If so, the archangel was getting way too modern, in Harek's opinion. And sarcastic.

"Overnight? Who said anything about an overnight pardon? More like one thousand, one hundred, and sixty-five years."

"If Mike hasn't wiped your slate clean in all that time, how do you expect Camille to forgive and forget just because you smolder at her?" Harek had made the mistake of telling Trond that Camille thought Harek had smoldering eyes. "Especially when your sin is particularly repugnant to her," Trond continued. "For a man as intelligent as you are supposed to be, you have the brains of a gnat betimes. You should have known she would find out eventually. Our life mates always do. Preparation, that is the key. A good warrior never goes into battle without planning for all contingencies."

Trond in lecturing mode was enough to make Harek puke, and he might just do that anyway if he continued to drink. As for the life mate remark, forget about that. Any warm thoughts Camille might have had about him evaporated with the first mention of slave trader.

And since when were love and war the same thing? Well, he would give Trond points on that one. There were similarities.

"You're supposed to be cheering me up, not making me feel worse. Shouldn't you be hiring dancing girls, or something? Taking me to a brothel? Buying me a longship?"

"Nicole put a ban on dancing girls when we got married. Brothels are against the law. And I've got fifty dollars, max, in my wallet." Trond grinned at him. The lackwit!

"I feel like shit," Harek complained. "What do women do when they get depressed?"

"Play sad music and cry. Watch chick flicks."

Harek looked at Trond as if he'd lost his mind and said, "I'd rather watch zombies." The commercial was over and Michonne was wielding a bigass sword at a herd of "walkers."

"Look at it this way," Trond said, taking a sip of beer. "Things could be worse. God could have made us zombies instead of vangels."

"Fuck!" Harek said succinctly.

"Precisely. You are fucked, my brother." He looked at Harek and wagged his fool tongue some more, "Ain't love grand?"

"Where's my sword?"

Chapter 16

School days, school days, good old golden . . . whatever . . .

Linda Larson was settled in at the Global School as a fifteen-year-old ninth grader, bemoaning algebra homework and talking about boys. *Did times ever change?* Camille wondered.

The school was operating at half capacity due to the constant threat of terrorism in Nigeria. Those who could afford to send their children to school outside the country did so. Those who couldn't homeschooled, if they were able. But many international families in Nigeria wanted or needed boarding schools for their children. Thus, there were a hundred and ten fifth-to ninth-grade girls, ages ten to fifteen, still there. A companion high school was located a few miles down the road, closer to Abuja.

The square-shaped building opened from four

interior sides onto a lovely garden area in the center, complete with lush tropical plants, fountains, benches, and grassy areas. Classrooms and a library were located on the first floor in front, and in the other wings were kitchens, a dining hall, a lounge for guests, an auditorium, and a gymnasium. Upstairs were the dormitories for the students, two girls per spacious room, as well as quarters for the faculty who lived in. There were also comfortable lounges for watching television or studying. Everywhere was blessed air-conditioning, a must at this time of the year.

Scattered about the complex outside were a swimming pool, stables for student-owned horses, riding paths, athletic fields, and so on, although outdoor activities were somewhat limited during these tense times.

Overall, it was a luxury school commensurate with the fifty-thousand-per-year price tag for paying students. The owners of the school could have shut it down for the duration of the threat, but everyone knew the threat wasn't going away anytime soon, whether it was Boko Haram or some other nutcase tango du jour group. And if they gave in here, they might as well do it everywhere in the world because, let's face it, terrorism was growing, not declining, and it was no longer limited to third world countries. *Can anyone say 9/11?*

It was a risk, nonetheless, to stay open. But the same was true for any school, even in the cities. Any public, or private, place really. Hotels, offices, stores, airports, restaurants, stadiums, theaters.

The atmosphere here at the school was as close

to normal as possible considering the circumstances, not to mention the bulletproof glass in all the windows and barred, triple-depth, metal-reinforced doors. The regular school security staff was in place, as well as Sly, Donita, Omar, and Camille, and the special forces units were gradually settling in the periphery.

Camille didn't want to think about Harek out there in the jungle somewhere, facing danger. Well, yes, she did want to think about him. Being bitten, maybe. Not by a snake, and there were lots of those in Sambisa Forest, but by bees, which were also plentiful. Yes, she hoped he got bitten by a big bee, one the size of a golf ball, right on his slave trading butt. Or his lying tongue. Or the knuckles of his wicked fingers. Or . . .

No, best not to waste her time thinking about the man. He was history.

Besides, the more superstitious of Boko Haram believed that the snakes and bees in the forest were their reincarnated victims come back to plague them. Bad as he was, Harek didn't deserve to be lumped in with the likes of these vile terrorists. At least she didn't think he was that bad. Maybe he was.

In any case, it was a waiting game now for Camille and others of the Deadly Wind operation, a well-orchestrated game.

Because it was mid-Friday afternoon, some of the students had gone home for the weekend after an early dismissal, about twenty-five of them, who would return Sunday evening. That left about eighty-five girls still in residence.

Age was relative, Camille soon realized on her arrival at the school on Monday, especially for girls in this age range. There were eleven-year-old girls who resembled mini-hookers and fifteen-year-olds who looked and acted like little girls.

Camille was in her room with her roommate, Cora Elton from Savannah, Georgia. Her parents were divorced and her father had a whole new family. *Sound familiar?* Her mother was the Nigerian representative, a high-powered exec, with an international beverage company.

Cora was a slightly pudgy thirteen-year-old who had a bad case of acne, which she was always complaining about, and a passion for Snickers bars, which she kept stashed in a mini-bar inside her closet, intended for fresh fruit and cold bottled waters.

The one good thing in this whole mess with Harek was that he'd cured her of her addiction. The smell of chocolate now made her nauseous. Or maybe it was the image of Cora constantly popping her zits, then using the same fingers to pop a mini chocolate bar into her mouth.

There was a light knock on the door and Else Kervandjian, a seventh-grade Armenian from Iran, stuck her head inside. "Linda, you're wanted in Miss Tinibu's classroom."

Miss Tinibu would be Donita Leone, language arts teacher.

"Uh-oh, Linda!" Cora said. "You must be in trouble."

"Nah," Camille/Linda said. "Miss Tinibu just wants to give me some assignments so I can catch up with the rest of my English lit class. A book report and a term paper, I think."

"Ugh! Like I said, trouble." Cora hated school, and the prospect of extra homework, to her, would be comparable to a ban on Snickers.

"See you at dinner," Camille said.

Else was already gone to her own room.

It took a while for Camille to make her way down the stairs and then the length of the long corridor leading toward the front of the building. Along the way she nodded or spoke to teachers and students she'd already come to know. A boarding school was like a family where everyone knew one another in short order.

When she got to the designated classroom, not only was Fatima Tinibu there, but the assistant principal, Desmond Buhari, aka Sylvester "Sly" Simms, her husband, was there as well. They made a gorgeous couple. Donita, with her close cap of dark curls, wore a short-sleeved, mid-calf dress of native fabric, vivid colors of aqua and yellow and green in a bold, original Nigerian print. Sly, whose head was shaved almost bald, was equally attractive in his own way, wearing a short-sleeved white dress shirt and bright tie with black pleated slacks.

"I just stopped in to check on Miss Tinibu's class schedule for next week. How are you getting along, Linda?"

"Okay," she said. "It'll take me a couple days to catch up. My last school didn't have advanced lit."

They had to be careful what they said to each

other, even in a private room like this. They never knew who might be listening, or what eavesdropping devices might have been planted.

"These are the assignments I mentioned," Donita/Fatima said, passing a folder to Camille. She assumed there would also be some info about the mission's status.

Camille left at the same time that Sly did. When they were out in the hall, he walked a ways beside her. "I hear there's trouble in paradise."

Camille rolled her eyes. There were no secrets with SEALs and WEALS. "Yeah. Do you know what he did?"

"You mean, a thousand or so years ago?"

"You know about that?" That shocked her. She knew how secretive the vangels were about their existence.

"Hard not to know. JAM and I were both saved by the vangels at one time."

"From death?"

He shook his head. "Worse than that. From becoming those horrid demon vampire things. Lucipires."

"What? How could that be?"

"JAM and I had been bitten, and, man, we were well on our way along the evil highway. I even ditched Donita during that time, hurt her big-time. I was a solid gold bastard."

"So I should just forgive and forget with Harek. Because he's now one of the good guys."

"I didn't say that."

"What *are* you saying?"

"Not sure. Maybe just that we are all sinners to one extent or another. Holy shit! I sound like some kind of preacher." He grinned at her.

Camille understood, but what she thought, but didn't say to Sly, was that some sins were way greater than others. Some sins were like indelible ink, no way to wash them away.

When she got back to her room, Cora was gone and Camille sat down at the desk to read through the folder. Using a predetermined code, she was able to decipher Donita's notes to her. BK was closing in. Be prepared. Any day now. Any minute now.

Camille was suddenly worried, more than usual. About herself, the girls at the school, her teammates. And Harek, blast his black soul!

She did the only thing she could. She went to the mini-fridge and took out a sinfully sweet chocolate bar. Not the itty-bitty bite-size one, either. This was a supersize one. She was going to Snickers her worries away.

And she didn't even throw up.

In fact, she thought she heard an annoying voice in her head repeating over and over, *I think I love you.*

There's hot, and then there's HOT!...

Harek was miserable. What else was new?

Seriously, what was it with these extremes in living conditions? First he froze his ass off in Siberia. Now he was burning up in some snake-infested, mosquito-swarming, monkey-chirping jungle, sharing a tent with that douche bag F.U. If F.U. told Harek one more dirty joke, Harek was going to punch his lights out.

Not that Harek didn't appreciate a good dirty joke, but the man never knew when to stop. In fact, when Harek introduced F.U. to Cnut yesterday, the halfbrain said, "You do know that Cnut is just another way of spelling *cunt*, right?" Cnut had picked him up and hefted him onto a pile of monkey dung.

In F.U.'s defense, not that the idiot needed any defenders, Cnut did trigger teasing lately with that Travis Fimmel hairdo of his, based on the History Channel's *Vikings* series depiction of Ragnar Lothbrok. It involved shaving the sides of his fool head and weaving the rest of his long hair into an intricate braid down the center from his forehead to his nape, the rest hanging into a kind of ponytail. No way he'd done it himself! Must have paid a mint in some fancy hair salon. *And Camille thinks my hair gel is excessive!*

Cnut claimed that women loved it.

"Lot of good that does you," Harek had pointed out. "You're supposed to be celibate."

Cnut had just shrugged.

Harek didn't know if that shrug meant *So what?* or *What celibacy?* He hadn't bothered to ask. He would probably get another lecture on women, just like the one Trond had given him.

They'd already killed five terrorists and taken five captives, sent off to a military jail in Abuja.

Likewise numbers for the other Deadly Wind teams in place. A mere drop in the tango bucket, according to Geek, who seemed to have the best tally on their current headcount.

In the meantime, they had time to kill, and, unfortunately, Harek seemed to be the unwilling subject of attention. Everyone knew that he'd been dumped by Camille, thanks to Trond's big mouth. And probably by Harek's pathetic, sad-sack demeanor as well, truth to tell.

As a result, they all had advice for him.

"Fuck her, there are lots of women available," F.U. said. "And women do love SEALs. Not that you're a SEAL, but you could pretend to be."

"Damn, F.U. I can't believe you're advising someone to pretend to be a SEAL. There are too many SEAL wannabes out there doing it already." This from JAM. "Have you tried prayer?" He waggled his eyebrows at Harek because he knew that Harek was an angel, having had some kind of saving encounter with Trond in the past. A vampire angel, Harek was about to point out to JAM, but then Harek supposed he *was* an angel nonetheless. Another thing he thought, but didn't say, was that if he prayed, he would just call Mike's notice to his recent sexual activities. Not a good idea!

"Give her time. She'll come around," Henry, his FBI friend, advised. Apparently both of his ex-wives wanted him back, and he couldn't decide which he preferred. Maybe neither.

"You Fibbies and your time crap!" said Brad Omstead, a CIA agent. "If you weren't always diddling around waiting for the right time, we would have wiped out Al-Qaeda, Boko Haram, and every other terrorist group a long time ago. Just bomb the crap out of them. Kaboom!"

Henry just scowled at Brad. The two of them had been at FBI/CIA odds from the get-go. No matter what one said, the other disagreed. Soon they would come to blows.

Cage offered, "Listen, *cher.* Down South, we have a motto. A belle isn't a belle until you've rung her bell. Have you rung Camo's bell?"

Holy clouds! Do these guys have no boundaries? They're worse than vangels.

"Personally"—Geek glanced up from the Motorola communication device he was fiddling with—"I think you should buy one of my penile gloves. No worries about unrequited love then. You can requite your own love in a honey sleeve."

Harek threw a clump of dried mud at Geek and barely missed his head.

Geek grinned. "I'm just sayin', my friend."

That evening Zeb showed up to give them an update. Before he left, he cornered Harek and said. "I hear you managed to lose your soul mate."

"I didn't lose my soul mate. You lost my soul mate." Not that Harek was convinced that he and Camille had been or were soul mates, but he didn't need to discuss that with his favorite Lucie. Or not-so-favorite Lucie at the moment.

"Moi?" Zeb said, putting a hand over his heart.

"Yes, you. When you blabbed that I used to be a slave trader, the night you came to Camille's cottage."

"She overheard?" At Harek's scowl, he added, "Oops."

"Pfff! I'd like to give you oops."

"Didn't you intend to tell her?"

"Eventually." *Probably not.*

"I never got a chance to tell my wife about my bad sin," Zeb confided.

Harek knew about Zeb's wife and family, and how he had inadvertently been responsible for their deaths. Mainly due to greed. Harek could certainly understand that.

"Would you have told her?" Harek asked.

"Eventually," Zeb repeated Harek's word back at him, then grinned. "And she probably would have kicked my arse out, too. See how much we have in common?"

"So, what do you think I should do?" *I can't believe I'm asking a demon for love advice. Can anyone say, "dumb as a Saxon door hinge"?*

"Beg."

Forget all the crappy advice Harek was getting. He knew what he had to do. That night, well after midnight, he teletransported himself into Camille's room at the Global School. If Michael found out he was misusing this vangel skill for such purposes, he would be teletransported all right, back to Siberia. Ah, well, *Nothing ventured, nothing gained,* he told himself. He had to try. To which Michael would probably say, *No pain, no gain,* as in painful icicle toes.

By the light of a full moon, he could see Camille's roommate snoring away, gobs of Clearasil dotting her face and Snickers wrappers on the floor next to her bed. Camille, on the other hand, came instantly awake and was reaching under her pillow for a pistol, which she aimed right at his heart.

She wouldn't really shoot him. Would she?

"You!" she said in a whisper when she recognized him. Her tone of voice was not welcoming.

He put a fingertip to his mouth. "Shh!" He motioned toward the en suite bathroom. "Come," he said.

She tucked her weapon back under the pillow and followed him inside the bathroom, where he'd already flicked on the light. She was wearing her Snoopy nightshirt. He had fond memories of that Snoopy nightshirt.

"Are you crazy?" she hissed. "You can't come here, like this. Anyone could have seen you enter the building."

He shook his head and tried to pull her into his arms.

She shoved him away.

"No one saw me. I teletransported."

"Tele-tele . . ." she sputtered. "Never mind. I don't want to know. What the hell are you doing here?"

"I need to talk to you."

"About what?"

"I think I love you."

She rolled her eyes. "So I've heard."

"I think I love you," he repeated.

"Big fat hairy deal. You're a slave trader."

"I was. For my sins, I was. It was a long time ago. I think I love you."

"I don't care."

That is harsh! "Yes, you do."

"No, I don't."

Persistence, thy name is Viking. "I think I love you."

Her eyelids fluttered. *Thank the stars! I'm making headway, or is that heartway?*

Just then, there was a knock on the door. "Linda, are you in there? I have to pee."

"Oh, great!" Camille whispered, as she glared at Harek. In a louder voice, she said, "I'll be right out, Cora. I was just about to take a shower."

"At this time of night?"

"Yeah. I just got my period," she lied, and smacked Harek when he grinned at her quick thinking. She shoved him into the shower stall, clothes and all, and turned on the faucets. Closing the shower door, she turned and let Cora in. Let Harek suffer the embarrassment of being in the same room with a tween as she peed, a thin glass foggy wall the only divider. "Don't turn the shower off," she advised Cora. "I want it to be nice and warm."

"In this heat?" Cora said.

"Yeah. It's a known fact that a warm shower on a hot night is the best thing for cooling off." *Buuuullllshit!*

"Really, I'll have to try it."

"But not now!" Camille inserted quickly, and went back into the bedroom and waited for Cora to return to bed. Then Cora wanted to talk, something about a boy over at the Global High School, who texted girls pictures of his left nipple, which was bigger than his right one. *Whaaat?* Camille told her they would have to talk later and waved a hand pointedly at her groin area.

"Oh. Right," Cora said, and climbed back into bed with a wide yawn.

Camille thought about picking up her gun again. She could shoot the intruder in the shower and no one would dare prosecute her. On the other hand, rules of engagement and all that military crap would land her in court-martial land, maybe even prison. Besides, much as she hated Harek at the moment, she didn't want him dead. Hurt, maybe, but not dead.

Instead, she returned to the bathroom and made sure it was locked before she told the man just what she thought of him. She never got a chance because a hand snaked out and she was yanked into the shower. Harek's clothes were already off and lay sopping wet on the floor, and her nightshirt was soon over her head.

He made as if he was blowing her a kiss, and she was assaulted by his chocolate breath. (*Note to self: Chocolate addiction is back.*)

He smiled at her then, a knowing smile that should have offended her, but didn't. In fact, she was reminded of an old proverb, "When a rogue kisses you, count your teeth."

For sure.

Chapter 17

Men will be men, especially Viking vampire angel men . . .

Men got windows of opportunity in the game of sex. They knew this instinctively and had from the beginning of time. Even cavemen thought, *I have five minutes max to drag Ugga into my cave, seduce her into compliance, or she'll be hitting me over my sloping forehead with a dinosaur bone.*

Harek had a brilliant mind. Maybe not so brilliant when it came to women, but, nonetheless, he knew that his window of opportunity was now. While Camille was surprised by his yanking her into the shower and amazed at the speed with which he'd removed her nightshirt. While she savored his chocolate scent lure. While she forgot the reason she was so pissed at him.

With the hot water already turning lukewarm as it showered over them, Harek lifted Camille by the waist so that her feet dangled off the tile floor. He noted with seeming irrelevance that she wore candy-pink toenail polish, an appropriate color, he supposed, for a fifteen-year-old girl, though she was looking nothing like a teenager to Harek with her pretty breasts aligned just about level with his mouth. A fangy mouth, he might add.

Bracing her shoulders against the wall, he lifted both her legs to wrap around his waist and, with no preliminaries, plunged his rampant enthusiasm inside her. Outwardly, she was shocked. Inwardly, she was giving him hallelujah clasps of welcome.

He glanced downward where her fiery tresses were blended with his blond short-and-curlies. Fire and gold, he thought. Surely, beauty like this did not just come about by chance, like those creationists wanted people to believe the world started from an amoeba. Surely, a perfect blending like they were together, in all ways, was intended to be.

Can anyone say wishful thinking? one side of his head opined.

Who says God doesn't have a romantic soul? the other side countered.

And Michael is His cupid?

Ha, ha, ha!

"Good Lord!" Camille exclaimed.

"That's just what I was thinking," he said, although he wasn't exactly sure what prompted her exclamation . . . their blended hair picture or the fact that he was twitching inside her.

(Sexual twitching was a genetic Viking trait,

some folks said. They were probably Vikings. It was a great diversionary tactic in bedsport. If there were cavemen in the Norselands, there had probably been a lot of twitching going on with Ugga.)

"Camille, I'm sorry," he said, cupping her face with both hands. She was held against the wall by the force of his hips pressed against hers, his no-longer twitching penis still inside her. (Twitching was only effective in short bouts, and truth to tell, sometimes it happened without warning.)

"For what?"

"Everything. What I am . . . was . . . how I handled . . ." He took a deep breath to calm his stammering. "I'm sorry that I was a slave trader. I can't defend myself by saying it was only one time, one shipload, which it was, because I can't say for sure that I wouldn't have continued if I hadn't died.

"And I'm sorry that I am a vangel, although I'm lucky to have been chosen for the program. I have little to offer you as a vangel. My main commitment will always be to . . ." He glanced heavenward.

"As for how I handled things. I didn't deliberately mislead you, but I knew after our trip to Louisiana how you felt about slavery. I should not have gotten involved with you, knowing my past."

"Is that all?" she asked. Her arms hung loosely at her sides. She wasn't shoving him away, but she wasn't embracing him, either. Not a good sign.

He willed his penis not to twitch again. That would be bad, bad timing. Like a giggle in the midst of a funeral.

"That is all, for now."

"And that's why you came here? That's why you have me pinned to the wall with your cock, like a human butterfly."

He winced at her crudeness, then wondered idly if she liked being pinned to the wall with his cock, like a human butterfly. *That is an inappropriate thought, considering the circumstances,* he chastised himself. *So, sue me. I'm a man . . . a Viking, for cloud's sake. That's how we think.*

He did his best to wipe his mind of its meanderings. "Not totally," he replied finally.

She arched her brows. By now her hair was plastered to her head like red spaghetti, and water dripped off her nose. Not a pretty sight. Pasta hair and Pepto-Bismol toes. Good thing he could see beyond the superficial. Ha, ha, ha. More mind meandering.

Enough! This was a serious situation, and he was going to lose his window of opportunity if he continued in this vein. The alarming thing was that he recognized his mind was drifting as a defense mechanism. He was frightened.

"For my sins, Camille, I could not stay away. I do not want to eat or drink. I can't sleep. You are on my mind night and day. I can't focus. I think I might need you."

"Pfff! Like you *think* you might love me?"

"I'm moving closer to certainty," he told her.

"Something else is moving," she pointed out.

His damn cock was twitching again. This was embarrassing. "Sorry. It has a mind of its own."

"It's actually kind of cute."

"My cock is not cute, and, no, I am not going to

engage in an argument over the cuteness of my male part. I need to know how you feel about me. I need to know if you will make love with me, willingly. I would not force you."

"Kind of late to be asking that question, isn't it?"

He started to pull out of her, but she locked her heels behind his butt. "Go ahead. I'm listening," she said.

"Can you forgive me, Camille? Can we start over?"

"I don't know. Forgive, maybe, in time. Forget, I don't think so."

His heart sank. And his cock was becoming impatient. If he didn't move soon, it was going to be the shortest fuck in history. A strokeless swive, as they said in the old days before anyone ever heard of premature ejaculation. "I have lots of time." *Oh damn! Am I begging now? Just like Zeb advised.*

"And are you offering me that time?"

"What do you mean?" he asked, even though he knew. She was talking about commitment. Was he making a commitment to her? None of that I-think-I-love-you bullshit. It was time to "fish or cut bait," as his uncle Boris used to say. Boris had been a great fisherman. In fact, he'd caught a shark one time just by holding on to his line for a full day and a half 'til his hands bled and went numb with pain.

More mind meandering!

"Camille, I have to move soon or die of testosterone overload. Besides, the water is getting cold. You have goose bumps on your goose bumps." He glanced pointedly at her breasts. "We can talk later, if you want. For now, all I can say is, I can't imagine a life without you in it."

"Good enough," she said.

Huh? It took a second for him to understand that she was giving him the go-ahead for sex. He withdrew, then plunged deep again. One, two, three times, and he was shooting his seed clear to the moon, or leastways her womb.

Turned out it was indeed the shortest fuck in history, or his history anyhow. Shorter even than his first time as a twelve-year-old when he'd had trouble finding the right hole.

He would have been embarrassed, except Camille's mouth was parted and her eyes were wide as she rode her own peak, then shattered.

She wept softly as he held her tight. Knowing her, it was probably the first time she'd let loose her emotions since Zeb's disturbing revelation. Turning off the water, he carried her outside the stall and used a towel to dry her off. He even combed her spaghetti hair into a semblance of order.

They sat on the floor then, wrapped in towels, their backs braced against the tub, his arm around her shoulders. And they talked. Softly, so as not to wake the hopefully sleeping roommate. Surrounded by the scent of chocolate and roses.

She got what she wanted, but in the wrong way . . .

Camille wasn't surprised by the quickness of her surrender to Harek. She liked sex. She especially liked sex with Harek. And, to be honest, there was something stronger, deeper than mere sex between them. Something she couldn't resist.

"Why are you so suntanned?" she asked. He looked like a California surfer boy after a summer in the sun. "Surely you haven't been going shirtless out there in the jungle."

"Hah! I would have the blood sucked out of me, not by demon vampires, either. More like vampire mosquitoes."

She smiled. It was one of the things they were warned about in WEALS survival training. Scentless bug repellents were part of the medical kits they carried.

Sensing her thoughts, he said, "A kryptonite shield probably wouldn't keep these monsters out. Henry has a bite on his knee that might be infected. And JAM claims the spiders are even worse. Personally, the snakes are my biggest worry, aside from Boko Haram. Cage killed a big black bugger this morning that was ten feet long and as wide as my arm. He said some folks make gumbo out of snakes in the bayou where he's from, but I think he's full of shit. Snakes!" He shivered for emphasis, then looked at her. "I'm blathering, aren't I?"

She nodded.

"The reason I'm so tan is—and I think I told you this before—a vangel's skin tans after killing a Lucie or removing a sinner's blood taint. I haven't saved any Boko Haram bent on becoming Lucipires, but I have destroyed several who were already in Jasper's army."

She asked how many of the terrorists they'd encountered so far, and whether their presence here in Nigeria was compromised.

He shook his head. "Not yet, but the waiting is making us all nervous. Hard to tell exactly how many are in the forest because they're so damn good at hiding."

"Do you think very many of them are actually . . . you know, those things?"

"Demon vampires?" He shrugged. "Probably not a lot. Yet. But Lucies are like roaches. They multiply. Not by leaps and bounds. One day, there may be two; a week later, a dozen. And so on."

"Sounds like a losing battle."

"Doesn't it? But, no, we're about equal at this point. And Mike is sending us more vangels to build up our army. Essentially, this is a battle of good against evil. Defeat isn't in the vangel vocabulary. Not in the Viking vocabulary, either."

"And you're one of the good guys?"

"I try to be." He smiled and kissed the top of her head. "But goodness does not come naturally to us Vikings. And then, there is my sin of greed, which often rears its ugly head."

"Greed for what?"

"Everything. Wealth. Status. Material possessions. Food. Beer. The latest, best car, computer, electronic gadget. Sex." He waggled his eyebrows at that last.

She ignored his attempt at humor and continued interrogating him, "So, you and your brothers were the first vangels."

"We were. We all 'died' within months of each

other in the year 850. The VIK, we are called. Until a few years ago, we traveled throughout different time periods, backward, forward, from the Roman Age to the twentieth century, but now we stay in the present."

"And do not age."

He nodded. "Correct. Nor do the women who married five of my brothers."

"Your very own fountain of youth."

"You could say it's one of the perks."

"I thought vangels weren't allowed to marry."

"We're not supposed to, but, well, things happened. In any case, the wives do not age, either, but they live only as long as their mates do. If Trond should die tomorrow, for example, Nicole would, too. And there will never be any children."

"Except for your brother Ivak."

"Right. Ivak is the exception for everything."

"Said with affection," she noted.

"Sometimes. Not always. When you live with someone as long as we have, people, especially brothers, can be irritating."

"Including yourself?"

"Definitely."

"What do you do that's irritating?"

"You have to ask?"

"I know what I find annoying, but what do your brothers dislike about you?"

"I think I know everything."

"Ah. A know-it-all. I can see how that would be irritating."

He pinched her arm lightly.

"Harek, I'm probably going to hate myself in the morning for having sex with you, and—"

"Point of order," he said, raising a forefinger, "I'm the one who barged in here and put you in an awkward position. No reason for guilt."

"Semantics." She waved a hand dismissively. "I could have kicked you out, if I wanted. In any case, we both know this is a bad idea. You and me. Even if the slave trader crap wasn't thrown into the equation, you're not free to commit to anything, even if you wanted to, which I obviously don't, and I've been burned so many times that my scars have scars. And yet . . ."

"And yet," he agreed. "I've had lots of time to think about us—"

"Lots of time," she hooted. "We've only known each other twelve days."

He raised his brows at her knowing exactly how many days since they'd first met, but said nothing about it, just continued, "—And while I understand that we may never get past the slavery issue, I also have to confront some long-held beliefs of my own. For as long as I can remember, I have held a conviction that somehow I will eventually beat the system, and by the system I mean vangeldom."

"You don't want to be a vangel?"

"Nobody wants to be a vangel. It is just the far better of two choices we were offered. But, in my greed or perhaps because of my superior intellect, I have chafed at being bridled. I cannot use my full capabilities. I cannot earn great wealth. I cannot live the way I want with the material possessions I yearn to have. But I have a plan, and I have been waiting for just the right time to broach it with Mike. First, Mike wants me to set up an archangel presence on the Internet, a way of bringing religion to the masses in a more modern way. It's a great idea, actually. Once I've completed that task for him, I'm hoping he will be in a good mood, more open to my veering from normal vangel rules. Timing is everything."

"And?"

"And I cannot propose such a dramatic change to my vangel rule, not right now, not even after the angel website, and at the same time, tell Michael that I have met this special woman . . . well, you get the drift."

"Oh ho! Now we get down to the nitty-gritty. It's me or a Lamborghini."

He felt his face heat. "I wouldn't put it exactly like that."

"No, you wouldn't," she said, a note of disappointment in her voice, "because that would mean you really wanted me, when you only *think* you love me."

"Time for us to lay all our cards on the table, not just mine, Camille. Do you want me to love you, Camille? Not just sex-love. Not just caring-love. But I-can't-breathe-without-you, you-are-my-other-half, we-are-meant-to-be love. Is that what you want?"

"Yes," she answered before she had a chance to think. "I mean, of course not. What a silly idea! No, no, no." She stopped protesting when she realized there was no taking back that single telling word. She raised her chin defiantly. "Yes. That's exactly what I want. It's what I deserve."

"All right, then."

"What does that mean?"

"It means, now I know where we stand. A line has been drawn. Can I tell you what I want?"

"Do I have a choice?"

"I want you to wait for me."

"Huh? Like a soldier going off to war or something? Keep the home fires burning, and all that."

"No, although there is one fire you could keep burning." He smiled as he glanced pointedly at her crotch, which was barely covered by a towel.

"Horny toad," she muttered, but she wasn't offended or anything.

"I need to get my life, such as it is, in order, Camille. Give me some time to do that. Please. Don't give up on me yet."

She sighed deeply.

"Wait for me, Camille. Please."

"All right, but I'm not going to wait forever, Harek. I'm as confused as you are."

"A week."

She nodded.

"A deal then?"

"A deal." She reached out a hand to shake his.

"Uh-uh. No way! That is not how Vikings seal a deal."

"I'm afraid to ask."

"Not to worry. I'll show you."

And he did.

Twice.

Chapter 18

The best-laid plans don't always go as planned . . .

All hell broke loose the next afternoon. It was a full-out battle between the special forces and Boko Haram, and between the vangels and the Lucipires. Caught in between were the staff and students of the Global School.

Two rickety old school buses had pulled to a screeching stop out front. That was probably how the terrorists had managed to arrive, undetected. Lying low in the vehicles, the tangos would have been hidden. No one would have questioned empty school buses traveling down the road toward the school. Now the buses sat, still running, awaiting the captives they would presumably carry away.

When the buses arrived, the tangos had streamed out, screaming "Allah be praised," "Kill the infidels," "Be Muslim or die!" And there were shouts in some local dialects, as well.

At the same time, an explosion went off near the outdoor pool where some girls were swimming under the supervision of a teacher and a security guard. Plus a fire burst into flames at a back entrance, allowing the masked militants to storm the school from three other sides. There was the sound of the school alarm going off, girls screaming, men yelling orders, gunfire, and mayhem in general.

All this Camille saw from an upper dorm window, but she was soon rushing down the stairs, calling for girls to follow her to safety.

How had the terrorists managed to get past all the special forces flanking the school? The numbers were more than could have been crammed into the two buses. They had to have come on foot from the jungle as well. Had there been a firefight? No, she would have heard something. A silent ambush? Yes, that would be more likely. Did that mean casualties . . . lots of casualties? Fatalities? What about Harek? Camille couldn't think about that now.

According to a preset Deadly Wind plan, Camille herded as many of the girls as she could into a basement storage area to hide. There were about two dozen of them, all crying and asking questions way too loud. One of them wet her pants, and another was puking her guts out into an empty coffee can.

Above, they could hear the slamming of doors,

yelling, and occasional gunshots. She didn't know who was doing the firing. Sly and Donita were certainly armed. Omar, too.

"Money? Where's money?" one terrorist kept demanding shrilly in the room above them, which would be the front office.

A male voice yelled, "Up my ass?"

A single gunshot followed, then silence.

It was impossible to tell who had been killed.

The girls began to cry even louder.

Camille kept trying to shush them, but none of them listened until she finally hissed out, "Shut the fuck up. All of you, idiots! Do you want to be taken captive? Do you want to be raped? Do you want to see your parents ever again? Then be quiet as if your life depends on it, because, dammit, it does."

They stared at her like they didn't know her. Which they didn't. Especially with a Sig Sauer in one hand and a KA-BAR knife in the other. The rubber band holding her ponytail had come undone, and her hair probably looked like a flaming bush. Her breast binder felt like it was about to rip apart with her heavy breathing. Her knee socks were bagged at the ankles. Into a wireless mike attached to her blouse, she kept repeating, "Mayday, Mayday. Red Bird to Mockingbird. Do you read me?"

There was nothing but a crackling sound. That figured.

"Okay, here's the deal, kiddos. I want you all to move back to the last row of shelves, behind those reams of paper. And Chandra, take that can of puke with you. The smell alone will alert anyone opening the door that someone's here."

The girls followed her instructions, even Cora, whose zits were standing out like Red Hots on her pale face.

"You all need to be quiet. No talking. No crying. Help is on the way, but you need to do your part. There's a good chance these numbnuts won't find you, if you're careful."

"What's a numbnuts?" one little girl asked.

"Bad guys," her friend said.

"Is it Boko Haram?" another student asked. They all knew about the native girls who had been kidnapped by this notorious group over the years. The mere name Boko Haram engendered terror, but thus far it had only been native schools that had been targeted. They had felt relatively safe here. No longer.

"Yes," Camille said. "But U.S. special forces and Nigerian military troops are out there. You'll be safe." *I hope.*

"Who are you?" one of the older girls asked Camille. It was Ruth Morgan, daughter of two TV evangelists who did missionary work in Nigeria. Camille probably looked like a wild woman, not a fifteen-year-old schoolgirl.

"U.S. Navy WEALS, honey. Will you watch over the girls while I go upstairs and see if I can round up more of your classmates?"

Ruth nodded, even though she was as scared as the others.

Camille had no sooner crept up the concrete steps and opened the door onto the first floor than she was confronted by three men carrying AK-47s, their faces hidden by long scarves wrapped around their heads and their lower faces. The air reeked of gunpowder residue. The men reeked of perspiration.

She saw two bodies lying on the floor down the hall. Caucasians. A man and a woman. Not Donita, Sly, or Omar, then. Possibly the principal and his secretary. Blood surrounded them.

"Aha, what have we here?" one of the tangos, whose bright red, oddly clean scarf was a sharp contrast to the dark skin exposed on his upper face, asked in heavily accented English. "Since when do schoolgirls carry weapons, eh?"

She aimed for his forehead and shot. Unfortunately, he jumped aside and the bullet just grazed his head, putting a neat furrow in his head scarf. She managed to take down one of his cohorts, though, a Nigerian-speaking man who had been spitting out what were no doubt expletives at her.

"What? How could . . . No, no, no!" Red Scarf said, putting a hand to the cloth on his head and coming away dripping blood. "You will suffer for that, bitch."

She raised her pistol again. He raised his rifle. But she'd forgotten the third man who'd somehow eased behind her. Last she knew, a heavy object, probably the butt of a rifle, came down on her head, hard.

In slow motion, she felt, rather heard, her knife and gun clank to the floor, and she fell forward. No one broke her fall. Her wrist, which had bent under her, was either broken or severely sprained.

At the taste of blood, she wondered if she'd broken her nose, too. *No more Miss Beauty Queen,* she joked to herself. *Oh Lord! What about the girls in the basement? Please let them be safe.*

Then she lost consciousness.

Win some, lose some . . .

Harek and his team members fought skillfully against the Boko Haram soldiers who'd managed to surprise them in their jungle hideout. In Deadly Wind's defense, this was BK's home territory, and they probably knew every nook and cranny of the dense forest. Years ago, every moveable object had been removed by the marauders from the tourist lodges that had been built when Sambisa Forest was intended to be a nature preserve. That included the buildings themselves, dismantled piece by piece. Any tourist who ventured here now had to have a death wish, or be a special forces operative. Same thing. Sort of.

He had to admit that these Navy SEALs were something else in battle. One of them could easily handle three to five of the terrorists, each, almost as good as a vangel. Henry and Brad weren't too shabby, either.

Once Harek ascertained that the other six team members were able to handle the dozen or so terrorists still standing, he slipped away to help his brothers concentrate on the Lucipires in the vicinity. He found them soon enough, and there was a whole damn nest of the demon vampires who had been holed up in a burrowed underground tunnel previously used for stockpiling ammunition and arms. They were mostly imps and hordlings and a few mungs, all in demonoid form . . . red eyes, massive fangs, scaly skin, tails. Vikar and Trond were standing back letting some of their less experienced vangels handle this crew. Now, if there were more mungs, or even one haakai, they wouldn't take the risk.

Already there were pools of sulfurous slime about, the result of being pierced through the heart by either a sharp blade or bullet treated with the symbolic blood of Christ. Although there were guns in evidence, the weapon of choice appeared to be broadswords today. Even as they watched, one new vangel, a massive former NFL football player (a Minnesota Viking, of course), swung his sword in a wide arc and lopped off a mung's head.

"Holy shit!" Harek turned to his brothers, who were also wide-eyed with amazement.

"That boy has potential," Vikar said.

"Hah! More like a Genghis Khan attitude," Trond remarked.

"You say that like it's a bad thing. Good job, boy!" Vikar was still giving his young vangel an admiring look as the "boy"—who was older than he was in human years, at thirty-five—followed through with a blade through the heart. If he had merely cut off the Lucie's head, it would have died, but it would have come back again in demon vampire form. This way, it was destined to the lower levels of Hell for eternity. A Lucipire disgrace!

"Where's Cnut?" Harek asked Vikar.

"He and his vangels have a contingent of Lucies cornered in a clearing north of here," Vikar said.

"Should I go help him?"

"No. They're picking them off easily, one by one. Afterward, we'll spread out and do a sweep to catch any strays."

"Then I need to get back to my SEAL group or answer why I've gone missing," Trond put in.

Harek was in the same situation. He should rejoin his Team Yellow, once the Lucipire situation was under control. "Any sign of Jasper?"

Both Vikar and Trond shook their heads.

"He's probably back home soaking off his scales in a hot tub," Trond said, with a bit of envy. "The beast wouldn't want to dirty his claws in an actual fight."

"Hard to tell, though. He could be here. There are clusters of Boko Haram spread throughout this damn forest, and where they are, Lucies seem to be following." Vikar rubbed his chin contemplatively. "I'm beginning to think this is not a one-day operation. Yes, safety of the schoolgirls is the mission for the SEALs today, while ours is destruction of the Lucies. But Boko Haram isn't going to be wiped out in one day, and that means the Lucies will consider this a prime feeding ground."

Trond groaned. "Does that mean we're going to have to stick around in this stinkin' jungle?"

"Maybe not you," Vikar replied with a shake of his head. Everyone knew Trond was still lazy and enjoyed his creature comforts. "You'll have to return to Coronado with your teammates. But Cnut and I will stay. And, you, Harek, once you tie things up with the SEALs."

Just then, they heard an explosion in the distance to the south, followed by rapid gunfire. Then more explosions. It had to be more than a mile away.

Harek and his brothers glanced in that direction and said at the same time, "The school!"

"Camille!" Harek exclaimed. "I have to go."

Vikar took him by the upper arm in a vise-like grip and said, "No, Harek, you do not. Your responsibility is here."

Harek was about to argue, but then he realized that Vikar wasn't even looking at him. He was staring at something behind him with an odd mixture of horror and anticipation.

It was Jasper, Haroun al Rashid, and a bunch of burly warrior Lucipires . . . at least ten in all. Mung drooled from their fangs. Blood dripped from their swords and claws. Their nostrils flared and their eyes were so red and bulging they resembled fireballs. Scales covered every inch of their skin. So much for descaling in a hot tub!

Jasper looked with disgust at the vast amount of slime about and muttered something about imps and hordlings being more trouble than a herd of hellcats.

"Oh boy!" Trond said under his breath as he took in the powerful beasts before them.

Vikar let loose with a shrill whistle, a signal to all the other vangels in the area to come at once. Jasper was in the house, so to speak. Within seconds, two dozen vangels were aligned behind them, swords and guns ready. That was in addition to the vangels who were already here, having dispatched the Lucies in the cave.

"Vikar! We meet again." Jasper's long tongue came out and licked away some bloody drool.

"Lucky me!" Vikar quipped, even as he adjusted his body and his sword to a battle stance.

"I'll have to build another cross for your torture, unless you want to join our ranks willingly." Jasper smiled, and it was not a pretty sight. Vikar had told them all of the torment the Lucie king had inflicted on him while hanging from a cross that one time he'd been captured. It had taken Michael himself to rescue Vikar, in the end. That was the first time Vikar had been given wings and what a sight that had been as he'd returned triumphantly to the castle in Transylvania, sideswiping a few trees and electric wires along the way.

"Harek," Haroun said, raising his short sword in salute to Harek. "I have wanted you to join my ranks for centuries now. We are going to be such comrades once you become accustomed to Torment. That is the name of the lavish tent city I hold in Afghanistan. I might even share some slaves with you."

"Thanks for the invitation, Roonie, but I have other plans for today."

Haroun bristled at the nickname, as Harek had known he would. High haakai like Haroun had inflated opinions of their importance, and having a silly nickname was considered beneath their dignity.

"More important things, like defragging my computer, or clipping my toenails."

Haroun roared his outrage at the insult. Lucipires had a distinctive roar, halfway between that of a bear and a lion. In fact, from deep in the jungle, a wild animal roared back, as if it were a mating call. That's all they needed. Tigers, or elephants, or some such joining the fray.

Then there was no time for thinking.

This was full-out war between the vangels and the Lucipires. Swords clanking, guns firing, growls and grunts, expletives, and death cries. There were more dead or dying Lucies on the ground than vangels, but Harek was concerned about Karl Mortensen, one of their vangels who was being picked up off the ground by Trond; the Vietnam vet had a sword wound to his shoulder so severe it appeared as if the arm was almost severed through. And him a recent newlywed, too.

"I need to get him back to the castle where Sig can treat him," Trond said, and disappeared into thin air. Thank God for teletransport.

Sig, their physician brother would probably be back at the castle before Trond got there.

If Karl's wound had even a touch of Lucie venom in it, he would be struggling for survival, just as Harek had done a few years back when he'd been near death for days from the poisonous lacerations to his body. A vangel's wound, no matter how severe, could heal; a Lucie taint in the blood could not, leastways not on its own.

One of the things that had helped Harek was having his brothers, one at a time, suck small amounts of the toxic mung from his body, then spit it out, before giving him some of their own purer blood in return, a primitive form of blood transfusion. Unfortunately, there had been no time for that here in the kill zone. Hopefully, that was already being taken care of back in Transylvania. This was one case where Fake-O wouldn't suffice. The real deal, or nothing.

Vikar was going blow to blow with Jasper while Harek was equally matched with Haroun, and, frankly, he was getting really pissed at being hounded by this particular Lucie. Enough with the slave trading already! As if he wasn't hearing enough about it from Camille!

Raising his broadsword up and to the right, he made as if he was going to attempt a head lopping, but at the last second, he raised the heavy blade high with both hands and cleaved the demon from head to gut, severing the heart on the way.

Haroun's eyes went even redder and his mouth opened wide in a scream. Then he fell to the ground and began to writhe as his body dissolved into a puddle of slime.

Jasper surveyed the scene where there were still vangels and Lucies fighting and he noticed that his high haakai Haroun was no more. With a bellow of outrage, he gave an impressive karate kick to Vikar's groin, then called out to the remaining Lucies, "Away! Away! Another day!" Jasper's karate move and his speed were impressive considering his huge size. Came from years and years as a minion of Satan, Harek supposed.

Vikar was rolling on the ground, cupping his

genitals and groaning. "I'll never have sex again. Oooh, oooh, oooh! Will you look and see if it's broken?"

"No, I will not look at *it*," Harek said with a laugh. "Stop being such a baby."

"I'll give you baby," Vikar said, but he was already jumping to his feet, exhilaration setting in over a hard-won battle. No, they didn't get Jasper, but a high haakai lord, that was nothing to easily dismiss. This was the second of Jasper's command council they had destroyed, the first being Dominique a few years back. Only a few more of his top commanders to go, if you included Zeb.

Harek and Vikar assessed the perimeter for remaining Lucies and to determine their own damages. Vikar estimated that a total of twenty Lucies had been killed, including Haroun, who counted as a huge coup for Harek. None of the vangels had been killed, although there were lots of injuries, the most serious of which were Karl's.

"We'll troll the forest for any remaining Lucies. You know that Jasper will be long gone. For now, anyhow. The coward!" Trond said. "You go off to the school. I know you're anxious to check on Camille's status. Plus you'll need to report back to the SEAL teams and tell them that Trond will be back shortly."

Harek jogged through the jungle, having to pause only once when he literally ran into a snake the size of a telephone pole, hanging from a tree. A little exaggeration, but not much. It was a big bugger and took two swipes of his broadsword before he was able to decapitate it. Yeech!

He stopped in his tracks when he got to the clearing behind the school. His heart began to race wildly as he viewed the inferno that enveloped the school. *Please, God, don't let Camille be inside.*

There were fire trucks, but they didn't seem to be making much headway. The fire was too out of control. There were also ambulances and medical personnel carrying gurneys with both injured and dead bodies. Not a lot, which made Harek wonder where the students and staff were.

He saw Brad being treated for a broken arm. When he went up to him, he could tell that the news was not good. "Henry didn't make it. The bastards slit his throat. Everyone else on our team survived, though, except for some minor injuries like mine. Some of the other teams have injuries, as well, but no fatalities. BK set fire to the school with a couple explosions, intending to burn all the staff inside, but Sly, Donita, and Omar managed to get most of them out."

"And Boko Haram?"

"Wiped out. Well, almost all of them who were here. Close to a hundred."

"Then the mission was a success?"

"Not exactly." He winced as the medical technician tightened the splint on his arm. "They got away with some of the students. Hell, they got away with a lot of the students. Close to fifty."

"Camille?"

Brad nodded.

"Crap! Where are Geek and the other SEALs?" He needed to find Camille before BK shipped the girls out of the area. Then it would be almost impossible to find them.

"They've set up operations in that garage over there."

He headed in that direction and wasn't surprised to discover that the SEALs and government operatives had already set up a command center. Buses and other motor vehicles had been removed and were parked outside. A porta-potty was located near the back door. Inside, folding tables and chairs had been brought in. Computers and communications equipment were arranged around the room, where men and a few women gathered to gain information and give opinions. There was even a coffeemaker perking away, with Styrofoam cups and napkins arrayed with condiments. Some prisoners sat on the floor at the far end of the large garage, being interrogated by Omar and an FBI agent proficient in Nigerian dialects.

"Where you been, buddy?" Slick asked him, then glanced down at his bloody sword. "Never mind. You've heard that Camo was taken with the other students?"

He nodded, unable to speak at first over the lump in his throat. "How did that happen?"

"Only a handful of the girls managed to escape. They'd been hiding in a basement storage room, under Camo's direction. Apparently, she'd gone off to rescue some other girls when she got caught."

Of course she did, Harek thought. It was an asinine thing to do, to take such a personal risk, but he knew very well that Camille would have told him it was her job.

"I want to be involved in the rescue mission," Harek said. "When do you start?" There was no doubt in his mind that the SEALs would go after the girls, especially with a Navy WEALS among those kidnapped. No man (or woman) left behind was their motto.

"It will be a couple of hours. We're putting together teams right now, and Omar hopes to get some intel from the captives so we have credible maps to go on, instead of chasing our tails in this fucking jungle."

"Hours! They'll be long gone by then," Harek complained.

"Not necessarily. The two rickety buses they shoved the girls in were seen heading inland, and I imagine the vehicles can only go so far in that dense foliage. I imagine they'll have to stop and move them on foot to . . . wherever. Can you imagine all those screaming, crying girls? They have to slow the tangos down, I imagine."

"There are a whole lot of imagines in there, Slick."

"It is what it is."

"I hate that expression. By the way, Trond had to take one of the fallen Wings operatives to a hospital. He should be back here shortly."

Slick nodded, although he had to wonder about the protocol of a SEAL taking off on his own, without prior permission. While some of the SEALs knew of the vangels' existence, Slick was not one of them.

"It was Karl Mortensen," Harek elaborated. "I think you know him. He was in BUD/S with Trond at one time."

"Yeah, I do. Good man! Is he okay?"

"He's in pretty bad shape."

"Oh shit!"

At least that drew Slick's attention away from Trond's breach of Navy procedures.

Slick turned to a newcomer to the scene, a Nigerian military officer. While Slick went off to greet him, Harek walked back to the area where the captives were being held. "Any news?" he asked Omar. At the moment, Omar was alone with about eight male captives, bound with plastic cuffs at the wrists and ankles. A few of them looked pretty banged up with wounds seeping blood. Nothing fatal. Omar's fellow interrogator, the FBI agent, had gone over to one of the computers and was typing away.

"Not much. In the old days, we could have tortured information from a prisoner. A little waterboarding and they'd squeal like stuck pigs."

Harek wasn't sure if Omar was kidding or not. Still, he offered, "I could take one or two behind the building and torture them for you. I'm not military. They can't court-martial me."

"Yeah, but they could put you in prison." Omar laughed, figuring Harek wasn't serious. He was. "Thanks, but no thanks, buddy. Listen, I've gotta hit the head. Been drinking coffee for the past hour. Can you stand watch 'til I get back?" He eyed Harek's bloody sword and advised, "You might want to hide that thing. Raises lots of questions."

"Go ahead," Harek said. He wasn't about to give up his sword yet. He saw the way the prisoners eyed it with trepidation. Guns were to be feared, but a bigass sword gave images of head loppings to this crowd.

For a brief moment, his eyes connected with one of the captive's . . . an odd shade of green. Not a native Nigerian, he would suspect. Harek knew instinctively that this was his opportunity. With a speed that had all the BKs gazing at him in shock, he was behind Green Eyes, yanking him to his feet, with one arm around his neck, under his chin. The other arm still held the sword.

"Hold on tight, buddy," he whispered into the guy's ear—he was a head shorter than Harek, but built like a bull. With a whoosh, he teletransported them both outside and to the edge of the woods.

Setting the prisoner on the ground, he cut the leg manacles with a swing of his sword. The man closed his eyes, probably figuring that Harek was going to chop off his legs, or something. When he realized that he was free, except for the hand restraints, he stood awkwardly.

"Do you speak English?" Harek asked.

The man nodded, clearly confused by his new situation.

"This is your lucky day, pal. If you cooperate with me, no one is going to get hurt. I need you to take me to your leader."

"No, no, no. They kill me."

"Not if you pretend that I'm your prisoner."

"Huh?"

"Show me the way. When we get near the camp, I'll cut your cuff and hand over my sword."

"Why? Why you do this?"

"I need to rescue the girl I . . ." He was about to say "love," and there was no longer any "think" about. He cleared his throat and said, "I need to rescue my daughter." He supposed he was old enough to have a teenaged daughter, just barely.

The man smiled knowingly and patted his chest. "Two daughters."

"You understand then?"

Green Eyes nodded. "I take you."

Chapter 19

He didn't ride a white horse, but . . .

Camille wasn't feeling so good. In fact, she hurt all over, and was fighting nausea.

And no wonder. Red Scarf, the man whose thick head she'd grazed with a bullet back at the school, took every opportunity he could to either punch or kick her. It would serve her captor right if she barfed all over him.

He was just as annoyed that she'd damaged his new scarf as he was that she, a lowly woman, had attacked him. At least that's what she'd been able to gather from his accented English. The expletives weren't all that hard to understand. "Whore!" "Crazy American!" "Bitch!" "Stupid girl!" At least he still thought she was a schoolgirl . . . albeit a gun-wielding schoolgirl. She couldn't imagine his reaction if he found out he'd been fooled, too.

She'd made the mistake of trying to defend her shooting him by pointing out that he'd been about to attack her. Her perfectly logical explanation resulted in a twist to her injured wrist, which she'd now ascertained was sprained, not broken, but might not remain that way if her tormenter kept up his abuse.

Neither had her nose been broken by her forward fall when she'd been knocked out, though it hurt like crazy. She wasn't able to check herself because her hands were restrained behind her back, but one of the girls kidnapped with her had observed that it seemed straight and only a little swollen.

Camille had been in and out of consciousness during the bus trip from the school to here, wherever "here" was. Actually, the bus had been driven into some underground bunker, where there were other equally rickety buses and all-terrain vehicles. Then, Camille and a large number of the Global School girls were frog-marched through the jungle until they reached some kind of intersecting paths where the captives were divided randomly into three groups and continued to push through the thick, snake-infested foliage. Toward evening, covered with mosquito bites but dully quiet, having cried themselves out, the girls finally arrived at a village, which had apparently been expecting them.

This might have been a tribal village at one time, but there was no evidence of families here now. Mostly men, and the downtrodden female slaves who served them, some of which Camille realized, to her horror, were the kidnapped schoolgirls the world had been looking for the past few years. By the way they averted their eyes with shame, Camille ascertained that the slaves were being forced to serve more than food to the men. Not unexpected, but disgusting just the same, especially considering their young ages.

About twenty of them were crammed into a large, single-room dwelling, which might have been a village communal meeting place at one time, or home to a large family. They sat or lay about on an immense woven carpet of once vibrant colors that covered the dirt floor and was filthy with misuse. No one seemed to care. They were exhausted and frightened into silence.

Everyone except Camille had been untied, and the others had been warned that they would die if they touched her ropes. Five-gallon buckets sat at each end of the room, serving as toilets for all of them. Another bucket, presumably clean, held drinking water and a long-handled dipper. Hunks of flatbread were their only food.

Red Scarf had taken great pleasure a short time ago in dragging her over to one of the buckets, pulling her panties down, and sitting her down to pee. The luxury of toilet paper was denied them. "Ha, ha, ha!" he'd laughed to one of his comrades. In what dumb-man rulebook did embarrassing women count as a joke? When she'd asked for water, he pressed the dipper to her mouth, and half of it landed on her face. More dumb laughter.

She took immature satisfaction in calling him an asshole under her breath.

Jasmine Olander, the Nigerian girl sitting next to Camille (her parents were foreign diplomats, who, in hindsight, should have taken the twelve-year-old with them to Paris), shared bits of her bread.

"I saw what you did to that man at the school," Jasmine said.

Camille nodded, not wanting to draw the attention of the rifle-toting guard at the open doorway.

"You're not a student, are you?"

Camille shook her head and whispered, "Navy WEALS."

Jasmine's big eyes went even bigger, the whites showing starkly against her ebony skin. "You're a Navy SEAL?"

Not exactly, Camille should have said, but didn't. It would have taken too long to explain. "Yes," she said.

Jasmine smiled, probably the first time any of them had smiled all day. "Thank you, Jesus. Our prayers are answered. The SEALs will come to rescue us!"

Lord, I hope so, Camille thought.

And then was alarmed to see Jasmine whisper the news to the girl next to her, and like dominos, the news spread around the room. The Navy SEALs were on their way. Camille only prayed she hadn't raised false hopes in the girls, who, reassured that rescue was only hours away, settled in for the night. Like a nest of puppies, they cuddled up against one another.

Too tired to stay awake, Camille fell asleep, as well. A deep, dreamless sleep interrupted only by the occasional twinge of pain from her injuries.

It was daylight when she awakened to a loud ruckus outside. There were angry shouts, arguing, what sounded like slaps and thuds, cries of pain. "You fool! Bringing a stranger here!"

"He rescued me."

"How do you know you weren't followed?"

"We weren't. Besides, he only wants his daughter."

"Idiot! He's too young to father one of the schoolgirls."

"He told me he was sixteen when—"

"He told you, he told you! I am surrounded by idiots!"

A loud slapping noise, followed by a cry of pain. She wasn't sure if it was the rescuer or the rescuee who'd been hit.

A more authoritative voice broke in, "What's going on here?" Quickly apprised of the situation in a native dialect Camille didn't understand, the man in charge said, "Bring him!" And there was the sound of a person being dragged unwillingly away. This time she was almost certain it was the stranger, not the BK member who had been "rescued."

All of the girls were awake by now, glancing toward her for answers. She looked at the guard and arched her brows. To her surprise, the man answered, but it wasn't the answer she wanted to hear, "They take man to be tortured. Aikeem good torturer. The prisoner will spill his guts. Ha, ha! Get it? Spill his guts."

That would be prison humor, Camille figured, but she wasn't laughing. None of them was.

Several hours later, after a delicious breakfast

of unsweetened, glutinous oatmeal, she got her answer. Two BK soldiers dragged in a man wearing camouflage clothing, his arms tied behind his back. One eye was swollen shut. His bottom lip was bleeding. He'd obviously been beaten, all over his battered body.

"Do not touch the enemy," one of the guards ordered the girls. "He is unclean."

Huh? If you asked Camille, everyone in this camp was unclean.

Propping the prisoner's back against the wall across the room from where Camille sat, the guard extended the man's legs, none too gently. Fortunately, because his pain must be unbearable, the man appeared to be unconscious.

Stunned, everyone in the room just gaped. Camille let out a little gasp of recognition when she realized who it was.

Harek.

He looked like hell. How bad were his injuries? Was there internal damage? She knew how these BK thugs liked to kick a body's soft parts. His hair was a greasy mess, and not the usual designer disarray. There was a bloody slash across one forearm, probably from a knife. Through his ripped clothing, she could see damaged skin. His black and blue marks would have black and blue marks. He might have chipped a fang.

Once the guards left, Harek opened his one good eye and winked at her.

Whaaat?

"Prince Charming to the rescue," he drawled.

For the first time in this horrendous ordeal, Camille burst out in tears. It was humiliating, really, and probably against Navy regulations.

A beautiful princess, she was not . . .

Camille's hair was a wild, red, uncombed bush, her freckles standing out like blinking zits, her skirt and blouse ripped in places, her socks bagged around her ankles, bruises everywhere. One shoe was missing.

Thank God she still appeared to be wearing the breast binder, otherwise she would probably be bruised in other places, too. Not that the BKers were squeamish about raping underage girls!

In essence, Camille looked like hell, but he was so glad to see her, you would have thought she was a goddess smiling down with appreciation at him. Not that she was smiling. Once she got over her bout of hysterical crying, she shot questions at him, like bullets.

"Why are you here?"

"To rescue you."

"Where are the SEALs?"

"On their way. Eventually. Maybe. I couldn't afford to wait."

"Why?"

"You know why." Along the grueling trek from the school to this godforsaken village, Harek had decided that he no longer "thought" he loved Camille. He "knew" for a certainty that he loved her. But he wasn't about to make that announcement in front of a roomful of adolescent girls and Camille looking like Little Orphan Annie's cousin from the asylum. He didn't have an IQ of 200 for nothing. Besides, it wasn't the place for romance. It kinda smelled in here.

"What's your plan?"

Definitely not romantic. "What plan?"

"No talking!" the guard barked.

Once the guard turned away to watch something outside, she began talking again. "Where are the others?"

"What others?"

She rolled her eyes, which had to hurt considering the bruises on her face, including the distinct imprint of a man's hand on her left cheek. Someone was going to pay for that.

"You came alone?"

He nodded. He was starting to get a headache with all this talking. Or it might have been that kick to the head by a guy with a red scarf. He was going to remember that red scarf.

"Can't you do that teleshot thing and get us out of here?"

"That *teleshot* thing is only for special occasions."

"This *is* a blinkin' special occasion," she said shrilly, which caused the guard to look her way and scowl. "Sorry," she said, and waited for several minutes before she hissed at Harek, "Get us the hell out of here."

"All of you? I'm not a magician." She obviously had an overinflated opinion of his powers.

"Stop acting like a dope when we both know you have the brain of a computer."

"Was that a compliment?"

"Aaargh! You're giving me a headache."

"Welcome to the club."

She gave his injuries a brief look of sympathy. Then, very slowly, as if he were the opposite of Mensa, she said, "If you can't get everyone out, all at once, how about a few at a time?"

"Camille! First of all, *teletransport* is a tool to be used in emergencies, when all else fails. I've already crossed the line with it for you. I will have many years added to my penance for its indiscriminate use, believe you me."

"I would certainly consider this an emergency."

Stubborn woman! "Secondly, it is done best alone, or with one other person. Not in multiple numbers."

"Well, couldn't you—"

Before she had a chance to come up with some other outrageous, impossible suggestion, he went on, "You are not to worry your pretty little head." *Even your not-so-pretty big head, at the moment.* "I'll think of something." In truth, just before he entered the village, he'd alerted his brothers. They would arrive before the SEALs—in fact, they were probably out there already—thus being able to clear the area of Lucipires and save any of the BK willing to repent. The guide who'd brought him here, for example, seemed a prime example of a sinner who could be saved.

His guide had informed him that the kidnapped girls had been divided into three groups, taken to different hiding places. Upon questioning about a red-haired girl, Harek had settled on this particular village, which, fortunately, had been a good choice. After all, there must have been other red-haired girls at the school.

"You could go back yourself and bring help," Camille offered in a small voice. He could tell she didn't like the idea of his leaving, now that he was here.

"I won't desert you here, not even for a moment. I won't risk these terrorists packing up and taking you all somewhere you can't be found."

She surprised him then by saying, "Thank you."

And then, thank the stars, she shut up for a while. All around them, the girls had been gaping at the exchange between the two of them. In fact, a little blond-haired pixie next to him, no more than twelve years old, with tear tracks on her grimy face, asked him, "Is Linda your wife?"

At first it didn't register with him who Linda was. Then he realized that she referred to Camille by her pseudonym. "No. Why do you ask?"

"You were arguing just like my mommy and daddy do before they go into their bedroom for quiet time." She waggled her little eyebrows at him for emphasis. The imp!

Yep. That's what he needed. Quiet time. And not the kind Blondie referred to, although that wouldn't be unwelcome. Later.

He knew that Camille must be anxious to know what had happened back at the school after she left. But she was being prudent in not asking in front of the young girls. Bad enough to know that they had been kidnapped along with a large number of their schoolmates, but they didn't need to hear, now, that the school was burned to the ground and some of the staff were dead, along with all the fatalities and various injuries to those fighting to save them.

Harek closed his eyes then, trying to tune out the soft murmurings in the room, alert for any unusual noises outside. In fact, he dozed off for a moment, only to be awakened by rustling and shushing noises across the way.

It appeared as if the girl who had been sitting next to Camille was on her knees, leaning over, her mouth nuzzling Camille's chest. Holy friggin' clouds! Harek had never entertained those kinds of female-female fantasies, but this was . . . well, interesting.

Camille was the only one who was tied hand and foot—the others had their limbs free—and didn't that raise questions about what Camille might have done to earn this special attention. But wait, the girl was still trying to burrow inside Camille's blouse.

"It's not working," the girl wailed, and went back on her haunches.

"Don't worry, Maggie. It's not your fault."

"What in bloody hell is going on?" Harek asked Camille.

"Can't you tell?"

You were about to have sex with a girl, in the midst of being kidnapped by ruthless terrorists? That was lame, he realized immediately. "Actually, no."

"My breast binder slipped and now one breast is exposed. I'm the bleepin' One-Breast Wonder."

"Oh." He couldn't help but notice, now that she'd called his attention to the fact, that she looked lopsided, with a flat chest on one side and a nice plump breast on the other. He also couldn't help but smile.

"Fix it," she demanded.

"Me? How?"

"Squirm yourself over here and use your teeth to pull the fabric back up."

Squirm? Is she demented? He tried to picture himself doing that, tied up as he was. "Are you serious?"

"Serious as a train wreck on a black op. I have to get straightened out before Red Scarf comes to take me for my afternoon pee."

"Did you say afternoon tea? Why would the BK serve you tea?"

"Not tea, you idiot. Pee, as in urine."

"Someone serves you urine, and you drink it?" These BK were more perverted than he'd thought.

"I swear, you must have lost your IQ to aliens, or the jungle heat. Red Scarf comes in and carries me over to that bucket, pulls my panties down, and put me down to pee. Is that clear enough?"

He snapped his gaping mouth shut and realized that the Red Scarf she referred to must be the same sadistic bastard who'd been torturing him. He saw red for a moment, and it wasn't any scarf, either.

"So hurry up. Squirm your pretty ass over here and put those fangs to good use."

"Fangs? What fangs?" the blond cutie next to him asked.

"She thinks my teeth are pointy. It's a joke," he explained, and glared at Camille for her careless words.

Just then, all thoughts of breasts and fangs evaporated at the loud noises outside. He recognized the roar of Lucipires, and his brothers' angry taunts.

Camille made eye contact with him, even as he was slipping a thin blade from the sole of his boot and using it to carefully slice the rope that bound his hands behind his back. "The SEALs?" she asked.

He shook his head and, now that his hands were free, began sawing at his ankle restraints. "My brothers and the Lucies." He put a fingertip to his mouth for silence.

The guard at the door was nervously watching some scene outdoors, his rifle aimed and ready to fire when Harek moved up, faster than the blink of an eye, and grabbed the man from behind. With the stink of lemon on the fellow, a clear sign he was far gone in grievous sin, Harek made a split-second decision and sliced his throat from behind, grabbing his rifle as he fell to the ground.

"Wait!" Camille yelled as he was about to rush out and help his brothers. He eyed the giant, old-fashioned key in the door, and decided he would lock the girls in for now. "Cut me loose first. I can help."

"Not a chance," he said. "You are not fighting Lucies."

"What are Lucies?" he heard the girls asking one another.

"I can at least protect the girls here."

He went over, slit her ankle and wrist ropes, then tugged her to her feet. Handing her the confiscated rifle, he gave her a quick kiss, and murmured the same words he'd said to her before, "Wait for me"—except this time, he added, " . . . heartling."

Then, with a whoosh of speed, he was gone.

Chapter 20

Evil comes in many forms . . .

Horrible noises were coming from outside. The schoolgirls huddled together in fear, but Camille admonished them to be quiet and get to work. First she untied one girl and thereafter each of them worked on their classmates until they were all free. Free, except for being locked inside their "prison." Not that anyone was willing to venture out to those violent sounds of battle.

Camille couldn't help herself, though. She pulled an empty water bucket over to a high window, upended the container, and stood on it. If she stood on tiptoe, she was barely able to see through the bottom edge of the filthy glass. She recoiled and almost fell at what she saw.

There were dozens of beasts . . . that was the only way to describe them. The same as what Harek had shown her in a cloudy fog picture back at her parents' home in New Orleans. Giant creatures, men and women, but not really human, with red eyes, scaly bodies, claws, and enormous fangs. They were fighting with swords and other weapons against what Camille knew must be vangels. Dozens of them, too.

Even if she didn't recognize Trond, and Ivak, and Harek, she would know they must be some kind of angels by the bluish hazy wings at their backs. They had large fangs, too. Except for the wings and fangs, they resembled Viking warriors of old. Belted leather tunics over slim pants. And ancient-looking broadswords and battle-axes and spears.

Even Harek had somehow become so attired. A quick change from here to there? Not possible. He claimed not to be a magician, but . . .

It was a brutal, to-the-death battle. Blood spurting out, on both sides. Slime forming as demons were stabbed through their hearts. Some vangels injured and being carried to the sidelines. Some of the demons had severed limbs and still fought on.

Meanwhile, the Boko Haram guys must be hiding or had run off, if they were seeing the same things as Camille was. Their practice of mass executions that so outraged the world must seem tame compared to this.

The girls crowded around, wanting to know what she was seeing.

"What's happening?"

"Can I look?"

"Is it the SEALs?"

"Are we being rescued?"

"No, it's not the SEALs," Camille said. "Not yet, but I'm pretty sure they're on their way. And, no, none of you are looking out this window. You would be scarred for life."

"We're already scarred for life," someone said.

And she was probably right.

As quickly as it started, it was over. Suddenly, any remaining demon vampires were fleeing the scene, and the vangels were picking up their injured and carrying them off. All that was left was a lot of slime, which smelled putrid, even from this distance. The Boko Haram began to filter out of their hidey-holes, gazing about them in confusion.

What? Surely the vangels weren't going to abandon Camille and the girls to the terrorists now that they'd destroyed their own enemy? Surely Harek wasn't going to abandon her.

But then she realized that the "real" rescuers had arrived. And another battle ensued. This time between the Navy SEALs, Nigerian military, and other operatives against the terrorists. This was a more normal type of warfare, one Camille yearned to participate in. Gunfire, grunts, roars of fury, expletives, death cries. It was what she'd been trained to do. But she also knew that protecting the girls was equally important. She stepped down from the bucket and kicked it aside. Adjusting her breast binder, she picked up the rifle and waited. If one of the BK came through that door, hopefully Red Scarf, he was dead meat.

Only a half hour or so later, they heard the key turn in the lock. Camille had her rifle trained on the door, but it was only Slick who stepped through.

"U.S. Navy SEALs. We're here to take you home."

Guess who's coming to dinner?...

Harek expected to teletransport back to Transylvania, where he would assess the day's mission with his brothers, help Karl to continue healing, and then bebop, so to speak, back to check on Camille. What he had not expected was to land on the sandy beach of his small Caribbean island hideaway.

And he was not alone.

Nope. Sitting at the edge of the beach, his bare toes cooling in the surf, was none other than St. Michael the Archangel. He was wearing Hawaiian-print swimming trunks and a white T-shirt. A gold crucifix on a chain hung around his neck. His long black hair was pulled off his face with a leather thong at his nape. No wings today, but there were obvious bumps on his shoulder blades.

Harek's first thought was *Uh-oh, my secret get-away island isn't so secret.*

His second thought was *Uh-oh, I am in trouble.*

Michael's presence here was not good news.

Harek sank down onto the sand beside the archangel, but what he'd really like to do was dive into the cool water and wash away the dirt and blood and scum of the past few days.

"Go ahead," Michael said, reading his mind.

Harek stood and shucked out of all his clothes, except for his boxer briefs. Nudity was no big deal to him, but he was oddly modest around the celestial mentor. Running out into the surf, he dived into the undertow of a wave and then swam overhand for about twenty yards before dipping under water. Then, flipping to his back, he did a backstroke horizontally to the shore for another twenty yards, going and coming, before swimming back to plop down onto the sand.

"Feel better?" Michael asked. And he wasn't even being sarcastic.

What's up with that?

"Is it not wondrous what God has created in this world?" Michael remarked to him as he stared out over the clear blue water and the coral reef that could be seen in the distance. Sea birds floated through the cloudless sky.

It *was* beautiful. That's why he'd purchased it. *Without Michael's permission.*

"Of course, 'tis nothing compared to Heaven. A veritable Garden of Eden, the Lord's home is."

"I'd love to see it."

"Only you can determine that, God willing." Michael gave him a probing look. "Is there something I should know?"

If he thinks I'm going to provide the blade to cut my throat . . . uh-uh. Later, I will broach the subject of Camille. When I have a clearer idea what's going on. He doesn't seem in a bad mood. Still . . . "No, nothing important."

"So, what have you done so far?"

What? He does know!

"Seems to me, two years is plenty of time."

Huh? "For what?"

"You Vikings are so thickheaded betimes. For a man blessed with a sharp brain, you can be very dull. The Internet, Harek. The Internet. Remember, you are supposed to be bringing us angels into the modern age so that we can spread God's word in a more relevant manner."

"Oh, that!" Harek said with obvious relief.

Which caused Michael to give him another probing survey.

Because he was so relieved that Michael wasn't here to call him on the carpet—uh, sand—over personal issues, Harek blurted out, without thinking, "That's not my fault. You can't make up your mind what you want." He immediately wished he could take the words back. Nothing to be gained by alienating his touchstone with the higher powers. Hah! He *was* a higher power himself.

Instead of taking offense, Michael gave him a short bow of apology and said, "You are right. I have been busy, but this is important. Thus, I have made special time to get the job done. That is why I am here."

"Uh," Harek said with the dullness Michael had just accused him of. "What exactly do you mean?"

"I will stay here with you until the websites, and blogs, and whatnot are set up. Day and night we can work on it until He is satisfied that the product is to His satisfaction."

Ah, Harek was beginning to understand. Michael

was the one who'd been called on the carpet . . . cloud . . . whatever.

"That could take days," Harek pointed out.

"I know," Michael said, standing and drawing his shirt over his head. He began to walk toward the water.

"Are you saying that you and I are going to stay together in my bungalow, together? It's kinda small. You'd feel cramped. Wouldn't it be better if you tell me what to do, and I can stay here alone while you go off and do angel things?"

"You don't know cramped until you've been in certain parts of Heaven. Like Disney World on the Fourth of July it is, on All Saints' Day," Michael said over his shoulder.

Harek just gaped at him.

Michael turned and grinned at Harek. What a red-letter day this was turning out to be. He couldn't wait to tell his brothers that Mike had grinned at him. "That was a jest, Harek."

Which was not funny, at all. "There's only one bedroom," Harek tried as a last-ditch attempt to save his sanity.

"You can sleep on the couch," Michael said, and waded deeper into the sea. He seemed to be studying the knee-high water, searching for something.

"What are you doing?" Harek asked, standing to get a better view of the angel who was now waist-deep and bending over to peer through the clear depths. With a swift swoop, he ducked underwater and came up grinning. Again! In his hands, he held a squirming, big-ass fish. A three-foot monster, with jagged sharp teeth the size of Lucipire fangs.

The 1970s song "Barracuda" by Heart came immediately to mind.

"Thanks be to God," Mike said. "Dinner." He tapped the fighting fish on its nostril and it went immediately still.

"I don't suppose loaves will be falling from the sky any minute?" Harek quipped. He was kidding. Sort of.

"No. I'm fresh out of miracles." Michael walked up and handed the fish to Harek.

The weight—at least fifteen pounds—surprised him, and he almost dropped it.

Michael yawned. "I think I'll take a nap. Wake me when dinner is ready."

Huh? Harek stared at the departing archangel, whose wings suddenly appeared on his back, so huge that the tips swept the sand as he walked. The modest wood bungalow was raised on stilts, a necessity against the occasional hurricane flooding in this region. Michael's wings dragged against the steps, as well, as he climbed.

Harek realized in that moment that he had not only gained a roommate who happened to be an archangel, but he was expected to be a cook for him as well, and a website designer. Who knew what else? It occurred to him then that Michael never asked about the outcome of the events of the day with the Lucipires in Nigeria. He probably already knew.

A Viking living with an angel? I will be scarred for

life. On the other hand, I am dead, so it doesn't matter. Ha, ha, ha. I am going off the deep end here.

With a sigh of surrender, Harek followed after Michael.

Not for the first time, Harek thanked God for modern computers. He needed to Google something ASAP: "how to cook a barracuda."

The aftershocks are often worse than the tragedy itself . . .

Upon return to Coronado, a debriefing was held with all team members, as usual. Even though sixty-three of the Global School girls had been rescued, even though twenty-two of the Boko Haram tangos were dead, and even though twelve BK had been taken prisoner, including two high-ranking members of the terrorist cell, even though CNN and the other networks painted the SEAL Deadly Wind operation a huge success, the mission was not deemed a success by the SEALs themselves. There were still twenty-some girls missing, they'd lost one of the Deadly Wind team—the FBI agent Henry Rawlings—and numerous injuries were sustained.

"Like I predicted, a goat fuck," Geek concluded.

"We learn from our mistakes," Slick said, though it was obvious he was as disappointed as anyone at the outcome.

They spent days going over every detail of the mission, the good and the bad, to determine what they had done right and wrong. The SEALs and WEALS would not be involved in any immediate plans to attempt another rescue; that would now be up to the Nigerian army and diplomatic efforts on the parts of various countries. In other words, probably a lost cause. A goat fuck.

In addition to the classroom exercises in Monday morning quarterbacking and woulda/coulda/shoulda, each of the team members was required to meet with the base psychiatrist, Dr. Abe Feingold, based on the principle that killing, even for a noble cause, did a head job on people. Although the jocks usually pooh-poohed this requirement, Camille realized after a week of counseling that she was having a delayed reaction to her Deadly Wind experience. Borderline PTSD. Probably it was the realization that she'd just barely escaped her most terrifying nightmare: slavery.

"I'm recommending that you take a leave of absence," Dr. Feingold told her. "Two weeks minimum, a month preferably. You shouldn't be working out with that wrist anyhow."

"But—" Camille felt a sudden panic at the idea of nothing to do but dwell on her near escape . . . and other things.

"Maybe you could go home to Louisiana for an extended visit. Let your family pamper you a bit."

Camille almost laughed at that prospect, but then she recalled that her mother and father were on that cruise. She would have the house to herself. Appealing.

But . . .

Bottom line was, she hadn't heard from Harek since he'd kissed her good-bye in Nigeria and asked her to wait for him. Trond claimed not to know where he was, said he hadn't seen Harek all week, either. Rumor was that he was in the Caribbean on a special mission.

The Caribbean? That sounded more like a vacation than a mission. A mission for whom?

Trond had just shrugged.

Camille wavered over whether to use the forced liberty to leave Coronado for a while. What if Harek came back and she wasn't here, as she'd promised. Well, he'd told her a week, and a week had already passed.

But maybe there were extenuating circumstances.

Yeah, like some island beauty.

He could have at least called her, asked how she was feeling, told her that he "thought" he loved her. Ha, ha, ha.

Am I pathetic or what?

Oh Lord, am I being dumped again?

In the end, she left word with her roommates where she would be, and was off to the Deep South. That's when her nightmares began.

He wasn't feeling very angelic . . .

Michael was driving Harek bonkers.

First of all, for a guy—okay, an angel—who

claimed to know nothing about computers, Michael had somehow managed to block Harek's e-mail so that he couldn't contact Camille or anyone else for that matter. Same was true of his cell phone. And Harek, who could probably hack into the FBI, the CIA, and Interpol, all in one click of his keyboard, couldn't figure out how to undo Michael's action.

When he asked him about it, Michael just blinked at him with innocence . . . and a bit of iron regard. "Sorry. I thought you would like privacy for work. Is there someone special you want to contact?"

He wasn't sorry at all, Harek could tell. So Harek seethed but kept his mouth shut, for now, and worked on the website, which they'd decided to call The Archangels Network. Very uncreative, but sometimes simplicity was best. They'd wasted one whole day just arguing over titles. Discarded had been Angels Around Us, Wings Away, Flutters, Heavenly Warriors, Miracles in a Modern World, Mike's Café, Messages from Above, Angelic Musings, Ladders to Heaven, and Celestial Sense. *Yeah, I know. Gag me with a feather.*

There would be the main home page with menu options, such as Q&A with an Angel, History of Angels, Blogs, Recommended Reading, Prayers, Angelic Miracles: Past and Present, even a one-on-one chat room. Harek was beginning to think he would be spending the rest of his "life" maintaining what was becoming a gargantuan website.

"Not to fear," Michael reassured him as he prepared to go off and relax on the beach, *again*, and probably catch another damn fish. Harek was sick of eating damn fish. He was especially sick of degutting and cleaning damn fish. And he wanted his phone and e-mail privileges back, dammit. "I will do my part, and Gabriel and Rafael will help, as well. Maybe some guardian angels, too. Even the pope might have some wise words."

"The pope? You know the pope?"

"Of course I know the pope. All of them. Oh, by the way, I have a wonderful suggestion for the 'wallpaper' background for our website." Michael put down his towel and rosary beads and went back to his bedroom to get something. Harek liked the way Michael had said "our" website. Not! That implied further involvement on Harek's part, and, frankly, his skills were better utilized elsewhere, if you asked him, which, of course, Michael didn't.

Harek's eyes about bugged out when he saw what Michael was carrying. It was an absolutely gorgeous oil painting of angels. In the forefront was a warrior angel, presumably Michael, and in the background, a sort of mural of various angels through history. Gabriel with the Virgin Mary, for example. The whole thing was only about twenty by thirty inches, but the details were exquisite. Even Harek, who was not an art expert, recognized its quality. Then he noticed the signature at the bottom, "Michelangelo."

Harek groaned. "Where did you get this?"

"I had it painted especially for the website. Isn't it perfect?"

"Michael! You can't just have a new painting by an Old Master show up out of the blue, without explanation."

"Why not?"

"People will wonder where it came from?"

"A miracle? After all, the website is about angels and the miracles of God and religion—"

"No!"

"Well, I'm not as fond of Picasso's work, but—"

"No!"

"Perhaps I could fix this one. Hide the signature, a dab of paint here, a dab there. No one would know it was done by Michelangelo."

Harek exhaled with frustration. "You can't ruin a masterpiece like this. Don't you have someplace to hang it for your own enjoyment? Some wall in your mansion in the sky?"

"What mansion? What would I do with a mansion?"

That's the way their conversations went over every little thing. That's why a week had gone by, and they still weren't done.

"Shall I bring a coconut back with me from one of those palm trees on the beach?" Michael had propped the painting on the floor against the wall, as if it were a Wal-Mart print and not a gazillion-dollar painting, and picked up his towel and rosary beads again. "Coconut shrimp would be good for dinner."

"We don't have any shrimp," Harek said, disgruntled.

"I'll catch some."

"There are no shrimp in these waters."

Michael gave him a look that pretty much translated to *Says who?*

Harek was alone again, tapping away on his keyboard, resigned to doing whatever Michael asked, according to his own time frame. It was futile to try to hurry up an archangel.

Harek couldn't help but worry about Camille, though. Was she all right? Was she as worried about him as he was about her? Was she still waiting for him? Was the time right to broach the subject with Michael?

How the hell did you make coconut shrimp?

That night he dreamed about Camille, and it was a really weird dream.

Chapter 21

Dream lover, for sure . . .

To her surprise, Camille was enjoying her "vacation" in the empty Evermore mansion in the Garden District. The staff had been given time off while Emile and Jeannette were away on the cruise, which was just the way Camille wanted it. No one to watch her laze about, eat junk food, watch corny TV shows, wallow. Just eat, sleep, and dream.

Dr. Feingold had given her the names of several Crescent City psychiatrists that she could consult while here, but she didn't feel the need for help, until the second night. That's when the dreams . . . fantasies . . . nightmares . . . whatever . . . started.

It was the 1850 Quadroon Ball, and she was there. Wearing a white ball gown with tiny embroidered roses and her light brown hair piled atop her head in cute ringlets, she was the picture of innocence, except for the off-the-shoulders neckline that exposed half her breasts. And she was dancing, along with about fifty other young women, some no more than fifteen, wearing beautiful pastel creations that gleamed like jewels under the candle chandeliers.

One man after another danced with Camille. Some young. Some old. Dressed the way she imagined Creole gentlemen of another era might. Tailored jackets over brocade vests and snowy white shirts, slim pants, shiny shoes, trim mustaches. One thing the men all had in common: the spark of lust in their eyes. This was after all the marketplace for buying a slave . . . a sex slave. Call it *plaçage,* call them *placées,* but the end result was the same. Was that what would happen to the kidnapped girls in Nigeria? Sold as forced brides, or sex slaves? *Is that what would have happened to me?*

But then she noticed a man leaning against the open French doors leading to a balcony, a thin cheroot in his mouth. Camille hated men who smoked, especially cigars, but she wasn't repelled by this guy, for some reason. The thin cigar seemed almost like a prop to give the appearance of lazy indifference. His dark blond hair was mussed a bit, as if he'd been running his fingers through it. He was taller, much taller than these rather short Creole men. His outfit was all black, except for the blue silk vest that matched his eyes.

It was Harek, of course. A Civil War–era Harek, but Harek nonetheless. Was he here looking for slaves to trade, or for a mistress? Each was equally abhorrent to her. And she would tell him so.

Walking up—not an easy task in about fifty yards of swishing fabric—she confronted him. "You have some nerve showing up here."

He just raised his insolent eyebrows at her. Meanwhile his eyes took in her décolletage.

"Why are you here?"

"For you, *cherie*." He tossed the cheroot into a sand-filled pottery jar and took her hand in his, leading her onto the dance floor. The band started playing a waltz.

"I'm not sure I know the steps," she said, although she'd been dancing all night.

"Just follow me."

And she did. In fact, when he smiled down at her, she would have followed him anywhere, so entranced was she. Was this how her grandmother, the quadroon, had felt all those years ago? Not trapped but loved?

The second night, the dream/nightmare started the same way, but then, instead of dancing, he led her to an anteroom, where he shoved down the bodice of her gown and made love to her breasts, just her breasts, until she was moaning out her ecstasy, while he was asking her, "Will you be mine? Will you be mine?"

"Your what?" she'd asked, and he'd just laughed.

The third night, as they rode through the French Quarter in a closed carriage, he'd knelt on the floor, flipped her gown up, and showed her that even back then, men knew what to do with their tongues. "Viking men," he'd corrected her. She'd forgotten about that. *And, by the way, oral sex with the added element of fangs was something else again. They sort of framed a part of the female anatomy for . . . well, you get the drift.* When the carriage stopped on Rampart Street, he pointed to a small, pretty cottage of pale yellow with blue shutters and said, "Yours, if you will agree." And Camille wept inside, because all he was offering her was *plaçage.*

The next day, Camille knew she had to do something. She feared what she might agree to in her dreams. She feared it would change the Camille of the future. She either had to make an appointment with a psychiatrist or find Harek and discover what the hell was going on. She decided on the latter.

Driving out to Ivak's plantation at Heaven's End, she felt a sense of déjà vu. Was she in the twenty-first century, or reliving something in the past?

When she got there, Ivak was still at his job as chaplain at Angola Prison. He would be home "directly," Gabrielle told her, and welcomed Camille as if they were old friends. She led Camille into the kitchen, where something delicious was bubbling on the stove. Crawfish gumbo, Gabrielle told her. They sat at the wooden block table, and Gabrielle served them both tall iced glasses of sweet tea with sprigs of mint and slices of lemon. There was also a plate of animal-shaped sugar cookies.

"I'm sorry to barge in on you like this, but I haven't heard from Harek in more than a week," Camille said right off. "And I'm a little worried."

"Gee, I'm the wrong one to ask. I've been so busy with my little one . . . He's down for a nap right now, thank heavens."

How anyone could sleep with all the sawing and pounding going on was beyond Camille. It appeared as if workmen were on the roof today.

"And I've been involved in a ton of pro bono legal cases for my agency."

Camille recalled that Gabrielle was a lawyer who worked for a nonprofit in the city.

"What are you doing here in Loo-zee-anna?" Gabrielle asked then. "Visiting your parents?"

"No. Actually, they're away on a cruise. I'm just hanging out in their house, decompressing from a recent mission."

"Oh my God! Were you involved with those kidnapped girls in Nigeria?"

Camille nodded. Even though Gabrielle was sister-in-law to both a SEAL and a WEALS, she had to be careful how much she disclosed.

"Well, good for you! It makes me so damn mad to see women treated like that by men, in this day and age. It's an outrage. I've donated to that save-the-girls effort, but I wish I could do more."

"I know what you mean."

"Are the conditions as deplorable as I think they are?"

"Worse."

"You said you're worried about Harek. Do you have some special reason to be concerned?"

"Not exactly. It's just that he didn't return to Coronado with the teams, as expected. He hasn't called me all week, and he promised he would. He asked me to wait for him and said he wouldn't make me wait for more than a week. And, well, a week has passed, and there are those blasted dreams." Camille could tell she was blathering and not making much sense.

"What dreams?"

In for a penny, in for a pound, Camille thought, and revealed, "I've been having these strange dreams, or nightmares, really, where it's 1850, and I'm at a Quadroon Ball, and Harek is there."

"You, too?" Gabrielle said and clapped her hands with delight. "Before Ivak and I got married, I had these strange dreams where I was a Southern belle living in this plantation house, and he came home, running up those front steps, and—" She blushed. It was obvious what came next.

"In this very house. Oh God! I hope it wasn't my grandfather you were having sex with. Yuck!"

Gabrielle laughed. "I don't think so. He looked just like Ivak. I mean, he *was* Ivak But then, he wasn't."

"Same thing for me."

"Okay, you can't stop there. Spill it, girl. What happened in your dream?"

To her surprise, Camille told her, in detail.

"Wow!" Gabrielle said when she finished. "That was some sexy dream!"

"Do you think so? It was like voluntary slavery, in a way."

"It wasn't real. And, as for your dreams, it's okay to be politically incorrect in a fantasy. Can anyone say *Fifty Shades*? I mean, I don't want to be spanked, but I don't mind reading about it . . . or watching the movie." She pretended to fan herself.

They both laughed then.

"Let's backtrack a minute here," Gabrielle said. "You mentioned that Harek asked you to wait for him. Wait for what?"

"He thinks he loves me, but he's not sure."

"Men! Dumb as dirt sometimes."

"I shouldn't be telling you all this."

"And why not? The things I could tell you about Ivak and the clueless things he's done! Know this, though, sweetie, if a Viking tells you that he thinks he loves you, he's already there. Harek just has things to iron out."

"That's what he said, pretty much."

"And if he says he loves you and wants you to be with him, are you prepared for all that entails?"

"Like what?"

"Hasn't he told you anything?"

"Some things."

"You'll never have children. You'll live only as long as he does. You can't have a normal life with friends and stuff because there's always the fear that someone will discover that they're vangels. Your life, everything about it, is secondary to a higher power. When Michael calls, they jump. They have to."

"You don't make it sound very appealing."

"Ah, but I wouldn't have it any other way. Even if we hadn't been blessed with a child . . . by accident, BTW. And can you imagine the decision I had to make, knowing I will probably outlive my child because I won't grow any older, but he will."

"Well, like I said, the question hasn't been asked."

"But if it is, you need to ask yourself something. Would your life be better with or without him? Better yet, *can* you live without him? Because if you can, you should."

Ivak came home soon after that, and he really didn't know much more than Camille did. He promised to check around and let her know.

"No one has seen him since Nigeria. He just disappeared, but someone—I think it was Vikar—heard that he might be on this Caribbean island that he owns."

"Harek owns an island?"

"It's just a tiny island with a bungalow on it. Harek considers it his secret hideaway, but we all know about it. We're just waiting for Mike to find out. The you-know-what is going to hit the fan then." He smiled, as if he couldn't wait.

"Maybe he's there with Michael," Camille offered.

"Wouldn't that be ironical?" Gabrielle said.

"I love when you use big words," Ivak said. "It turns me on."

Gabrielle looked at Camille. "Did I mention clueless?"

Camille had a lot to think about as she drove back to New Orleans. When she got there, she took a bubble bath, ate a bucket of Cajun chicken and warm biscuits, drank two glasses of wine, and went to bed, where she dreamed about Harek the sugar planter. Again.

And this time the dream was X-rated. If she hadn't already thought it before, she thought it now . . . Christian Grey had nothing on Harek in the lovemaking department, even a nineteenth-century Harek.

Could women have wet dreams?

She was pretty sure she just did.

It wasn't a Sophie's Choice, but it came close . . .

"Wow!" Harek said aloud as he awakened from a dream that was so X-rated, he felt himself blushing. Well, almost blushing. Vikings really didn't get embarrassed by much.

Camille was the star of his dream, of course, and he had to wonder if she was having the same dream somewhere on the other side of the world. Sort of life mate telecommunicating.

Does that mean I accept that Camille is my destined life mate?

What good does that do me, if I can't have her?

Is it time to have that dreaded conversation with Michael?

Yesterday, out of the blue, Michael quoted something from the Bible to Harek about cutting off your hand or foot if they cause you to sin. That was not a good sign. At the time, they'd been sitting at the table eating—what else?—fish. Harek had instinctively placed a hand over his genitals, under the table. Discreetly, of course. Michael just stared at him in that way he had of seeming to see all.

Now, Harek squirmed on the couch where he'd been sleeping, trying to find a position that was comfortable. There was none. He yawned widely, checked the luminous dial on his watch, and saw that it was only six a.m. Barely dawn.

That was when he noticed Michael sitting in the chair across the room, facing out toward the sea. There was a glow about him, like a full-body halo, outlining his white, belted robe. His hair hung loose to his shoulders where the massive wings were tucked in against his back, but still overhanging the chair down to the floor. His eyes appeared to be closed, but his lips were moving, as if in prayer.

This was strange, stranger than anything Harek had witnessed this week, living with an archangel. Michael was stronger than the strongest soldier, in prime physical condition, as evident by the fallen palm tree that he'd lifted off the shore and tossed into the sea. And he was weak as a child in his innocence at times, taking joy in the smallest things. A seagull wheeling above the waters, like a celestial dance. A bag of M&M's he'd discovered in the cupboard. A Snoopy cartoon Harek had shown him on the Internet where Linus is saying, "I love mankind. It's people I can't stand."

"I must depart," Michael said, without turning to look at Harek. He must have sensed that Harek was awake. Or maybe he had been waiting for Harek to wake up.

Uh-oh!

"What do you mean, you have to leave? You can't leave yet. We haven't finished constructing the website."

Dawn was raising its orangeish-yellow head on

the blue horizon. So Harek could see clearly now. He sat up and kept the sheet wrapped around him in the chill air.

"Thou wilt finish for me. I have been called to something more important." Michael swiveled the chair to turn toward him. There was an expression of such sadness on his face.

"What? What is it?"

"The things humans do to each other," he said on a sigh. "The Lord's work takes me elsewhere."

"But we've worked so hard on the website. We've accomplished so much. I thought you considered this important."

"I do. It is very important. I didn't realize how many misconceptions there were about angels. Every question you asked led to another and another, all of which need to be answered. Can humans become angels? No. How many angels are there? Thousands upon thousands. Can angels have sex with humans? Not anymore! Are there different kinds of angels? For a certainty. Do guardian angels really exist? Are there female angels, as well as male ones? Why does God need messengers? On and on the questions go." He sighed again.

"But . . ." Harek was confused. All this work. Ten days here working to build a site that was turning into a spectacular enterprise, if he did say so himself. And all for nothing!

"Not for nothing. Keep working on it, Harek, in between your other duties. Next time we meet, you can update me on your progress." He stood, and his wings fluffed out.

No, no, no, he couldn't leave yet. "Wait. I didn't get a chance to ask you—"

"About the woman? About Camille?"

So he knows. "Do I have your blessing?"

"Pfff! That is like asking for permission when you've already done the deed."

Harek had to act quickly. He could see that Michael was ready to leave. "In all our discussions this week about God and religion and angels, and how all these need to be relevant in a changing world, the one word that kept coming up over and over is *love*."

"Dost try to turn my words back on me, Viking?"

"I love her, Michael."

"Are you sure you don't just *think* you love her?"

Harek cringed at his word being thrown back at him. "I know that I do. I have just been afraid to . . ." He shrugged, unable to explain his hesitancy.

"Mayhap your greed still overrides everything else," Michael suggested. At the no-doubt guilty look on Harek's face, the archangel added, "Didst really think you could hide your materialistic ambitions from me?" He waved a hand to encompass the bungalow and island paradise as an example.

"I have changed," Harek protested. "Do all those years in Siberia count for nothing?"

Michael no longer seemed to be listening. Instead, his head was cocked to the side, as if listening to something, or someone. He nodded and then turned to Harek again. "I must leave. If you are asking for my blessing, I cannot give it.

Whether you take Camille as your life mate or not is your decision."

Huh? Since when was I given that choice?

"But there are consequences."

Okay, here it comes.

Michael pointed to the Michelangelo painting still propped against the wall. "The painting is yours to do with as you will. You can sell it and purchase all the things you yearn for. A palatial home. A boat. Jewels. Whatever. Consider it a reward, if you will."

Holy crap! This past week Harek had researched on the Internet the value of newly discovered works by Old Masters, even those with no known provenance, and this painting could be worth five or ten million dollars. Maybe more.

"But you cannot have both," Michael said. "Either Camille or the painting." As a parting message, he added, "Go with God."

And just like that, he was gone.

Now what?

Was ever a Viking given a choice like this before?

Harek smiled.

Chapter 22

Visitors to the right of her, visitors to the left of her . . .

After the most extraordinary sex dream so far, Camille decided she needed a cold shower. She washed her hair, brushed her teeth, and went downstairs to make herself a cup of coffee.

Time to make some decisions, she thought, as she stood at the kitchen counter, sipping the strong brew, looking over her mother's wonderful gardens. A gardener came every day to make sure no weeds dared come out and to water and fertilize the thriving plants. The roses especially were in full, gorgeous bloom.

The front doorbell rang. Who could that be at nine a.m.? A sudden hope that it might be Harek was immediately dashed. He wouldn't bother ringing or knocking. He'd come right in. Glancing down at herself, she saw that though her hair was wet and her feet were bare, she was decent in jeans and a Snoopy T-shirt. Yeah, she had a thing about Snoopy. This one said: "Happiness Is a Warm Hug."

She opened the door, and there stood Julian, holding a huge bouquet of flowers. How little he knew her. She'd be much more impressed with a ginormous box of chocolates, mixed nuts and creams, with a few caramels thrown in.

"What are you doing here, Julian?" she asked, taking the flowers from him, but not opening the door any wider.

"Aren't you going to invite me in?" He flashed her that closed-mouth smile, the one he believed was sexy, in his own overinflated opinion.

"No!"

He glanced at her T-shirt. "Not even if I have plenty of hugs to give."

Cute!

Not!

"Especially not then. What are you doing here, Julian?" she asked again, and set the flowers in the antique Newcomb umbrella stand near the door.

"I suppose you've heard about Justine," he said, and painted a sad, pity-me expression on his face. "She lost her baby."

"Oh no!" At this late stage in a pregnancy, that had to be especially heart-wrenching. As much as she'd been betrayed by Justine and Julian, Camille couldn't feel anything but grief over the death of a child. She homed in on something else then. "You said *her* baby. Don't you mean *your* baby, as in belonging to both of you?"

"Of course." He tried to look even sadder.

"What does this have to do with me?"

"We're friends, aren't we, Cam? I heard you were in town and thought you ought to know. Can I come in?"

"No, you can't come in. Why would I need to know?"

"Don't play dumb, sweetheart. You know that the only reason I married Justine was for the baby. You know I still love you. You know you love me."

Camille couldn't believe her ears. "You are a solid gold prick, Julian Breaux. Is Justine even out of the hospital?"

"Now, darlin', don't be—"

"Get out! Go away and don't ever come back. I mean it. I don't love you. I probably never did."

"Is this about that guy you brought to Alain's wedding to make me jealous?"

Camille rolled her eyes. The ego of the jerk! "Wake up and smell the roses, Julian. We . . . are . . . no . . . more . . . ever! And, by the way"—she leaned forward—"do I smell like roses to you?"

"Huh? No. You smell like coffee."

"That's what I thought." She smiled and slammed the door in his face.

When she went back to the kitchen, she was still smiling. Picking up her cup of coffee, she glanced out the window and saw a man leaning over to smell one of her mother's prized Francis Meilland hybrid tea roses, pale pink flowers the size of grapefruits.

It wasn't the gardener, Camille realized almost immediately. What gardener would wear a long white robe, belted at the waist with a gold cord? She should have been alarmed at a stranger on the property, but she wasn't. Slowly, like a domino effect across her body, every fine hair stood out on his skin. Blood drained from her head.

Oh. My. God!

She set her coffee back on the counter, and like a sleepwalker, opened the French doors to the back gallery, then stepped onto the dew-wet grass. The person . . . angel . . . whatever it was . . . didn't look up until she got closer.

She almost staggered at his ethereal beauty. Dark, silky hair. A tall, muscular soldier's body. Piercing eyes.

"I . . . I know who you are," she said dumbly.

He nodded. "I wanted to meet you, to see if you are worthy."

She arched her brows. "Of what? Salvation?"

"That goes without saying. No, I meant worthy of Harek."

She bristled. "Why aren't you asking if Harek is worthy of me?"

The archangel smiled, and it was a glorious thing. "That goes without saying, too." He fingered the soft petal of the long-stemmed, full-blown rose he held in one hand. "Do you mind?" he asked. "I would take this to Him. A reminder of just how glorious His creations are."

"Take as many as you want."

"Just one." He seemed to be thinking deeply before he looked at her again. "He doesn't know it, but Harek is one of my favorites, even if he is a

Viking. He could do great things. He will do great things if . . ." He let his words trail off.

"If . . . ?"

"If he has a helpmate who understands his primary duty in this world. If he has a helpmate strong enough to aid in his fighting both real and inner demons. If he has a helpmate whose love will lift him, not lower him. Are you that person?"

What a question!

"Would he be better off without me?"

Michael shrugged. "That is the question. Would you give him up if you thought it was for his greater good, if it would be better for his vocation's greater good?"

She hesitated, but then said, "Yes."

"Right answer," Michael said, and just like that, he was gone. No poof of smoke, no fluttering wings. Just here one moment, gone the other.

Camille had a lot to think about. It was time she got back to Coronado. Waiting around for Harek was doing her no good. She had a job to do with WEALS. Any decisions she had to make could be made there as well as here.

She shouldn't have been surprised, but she was, when she went back into house and found another visitor at the front door. Harek.

"Hi, honey. I'm home," he joked, and stepped inside before she closed the door on him, like she had with Julian. If she was so inclined. She wasn't sure about that yet. "Do you think I should develop a Southern drawl?" he asked. "Would it sound better if I said, 'Hi, darlin'. Ah'm home'?"

"It would sound better if you said where the hell you've been," she snapped, and stepped backward, putting a few feet between them. Already, the scent of chocolate was wafting her way.

"I've been on my Caribbean island," he said, and took two steps closer.

So it was true. He owned his very own island. "Alone?" She edged her way into the archway leading to the front salon.

"No, someone was with me."

Her nostrils flared and she turned away, taking several steps into the room.

He noticed her jealousy and laughed, circling around her. He was wearing black jeans and a white T-shirt under a black leather jacket. *In New Orleans. In the summer. Heck, it works for me.* "With Michael."

She wanted to laugh and cry. She wanted to smack him for staying away so long, and hug him for being here now. She wanted to do the right thing.

"I had a visitor," she said.

"I know. I saw the bastard driving away in a red Jaguar. Do you want me to go punch his nose? Or tie his tiny cock in a knot?"

He must mean Julian. "Not that visitor. Your friend. Michael."

"Uh-oh. Is that good news or bad news?"

She shrugged. "It could go either way."

"Did you wait for me, Camille?"

She didn't answer, but instead told him, "I'm going back to Coronado today."

"Can you put it off for a few days?"

"Why?"

"I thought we might get married and have a short honeymoon."

That was the last thing she'd expected to hear and her knees buckled on her. She just barely stayed upright by grabbing on to the back of the camelback sofa in front of the fireplace. "That wasn't funny."

"It wasn't meant to be funny. Will you marry me and be my life mate?"

"Why?" She felt tears well in her eyes.

"Because I love you, of course."

"All of a sudden, you know for sure," she whispered over the catch in her throat.

"I always knew, sweetling. I knew the first time I saw you coming in off the beach from your run, all sweaty and waspish with irritation. I knew when you made fun of my hair. I knew when you kissed me like I was a soldier just come home from the wars. I knew when you wore that sexy red dress and siren lipstick. I knew when you bent over in those blue denims. I knew when you looked at me like I was the sugar on your beignet when you opened the door just now."

"I did not," she said indignantly.

"Did so." He waggled his eyebrows at her, and, oh, she loved him so.

"Tell me again."

He knew what she meant without explanation. "I love you."

She threw herself into his arms and wept and laughed. He hugged her tight and groaned and smiled.

Their kisses became so frantic and their caresses so desperate that they fell to the floor and made love on her great-grandmother Octavie's antique Aubusson carpet.

He kept saying he loved her.

She kept saying she loved him.

She showed him in every way she knew how that she adored him.

He showed her that there were lots of ways to adore that she'd never imagined.

When they were both sated and still lying on the floor with several tasseled pillows from the sofa under their heads, she said, "I still want to continue being in WEALS. Will that be a problem?"

"It doesn't have to be."

"Where will we live?"

"Wherever you want, but I have this idea . . . well, I haven't thought it through totally . . . but what would you think about our home base being a Caribbean island?"

"Holy moly!"

"Don't get your hopes up, it's a small island, and if I build what I'm thinking of there, it wouldn't be as private as it has been."

"Now you have me intrigued."

"You weren't intrigued before?"

She slapped him playfully on the chest.

"We vangels—all of God's helpers, for that matter, whether they be celestial ones, like angels, or human ones, like priests—need to be brought into the twenty-first century. And I'm not just referring to computers, but that's a big part of it.

The changes in the past twenty years alone have altered the world forever. No longer is a vangel's work just carrying a sword and bludgeoning a Lucipire through the heart. We need to be able to develop computer programs for tracking Lucies and evil people, like terrorists. We need databases of where we've been and where we need to go. There is so much more we can do with the aid of technology. But that means education."

He took a deep breath.

"And?"

"I was thinking about enlarging the building on my island. In fact, putting up several buildings. A computer teaching school as well as a computer database center, command central, so to speak. A lodge for housing vangels. Perhaps some gardens and orchards to be self-sustaining. Believe me, there's enough fish to feed an army. The island isn't very big. I think the beach and some of the wooded area could be preserved, but not much else with all those structures."

"That sounds like an expensive project," Camille remarked, liking his ideas, but wondering if they could be done. "Can you afford all that?"

Harek grinned. "Have you ever heard of Michelangelo?"

Epilogue

The blue vampire was no longer blue . . .

They were married two weeks later at Heaven's End plantation. There had to be some irony in that.

It was a rushed affair because Harek kept fearing that Michael would pull the rug out from under them for engaging in sex before marriage. Lots of sex before marriage.

"We could always go celibate until the wedding," Camille had suggested.

"Bite your tongue, woman," Harek had said. "Better yet, let me."

Camille's mother almost had a heart attack when she learned her only daughter was getting married in a heated rush. In a run-down plantation once owned by their despicable ancestor? Was she pregnant? No? Why so soon then? Didn't she want a big lavish church wedding? Actually, no.

In the end, it was only her parents, Alain and Inez, and a few cousins and great-aunts who lived in the region. On Harek's side, there were his brothers; the spouses of those who had wives; Karl Mortensen, who was still healing but getting better, along with his wife, Faith; and a vangel named Armod who had a fixation on Michael Jackson as evidenced by his attire and constant moon dancing. Only a few of the Coronado contingent had been invited, including Cage and his wife, Emelie, who lived in New Orleans. And Marie and Bobby Jo, who served as her maid of honor and bridesmaid, respectively. There were also Tante Lulu's bayou family members, headed by the irrepressible old lady, who declared on hearing the news of the impending wedding, "I tol' 'em the thunderbolt was a-comin'."

"This is a disaster waiting to happen," Harek kept saying as the guest list grew larger and larger. "We have to keep our vangelness a secret."

"Then keep your fangs in your mouth. We are not eloping to Las Vegas."

The ceremony was performed under an outdoor tent by a priest wearing a pure white cassock with a gold cord belt and a gold crucifix hanging from his neck. Afterward the priest was seen to be conversing intensely with Tante Lulu, something about her favorite saint, St. Jude.

Ivak had hired a band of ex-cons from Angola to play for them. They were really good, playing all kinds of music, including Camille's favorite blues songs. People were dancing on the flagstones of the side garden. A little uneven on the high heels, but no one seemed to mind.

The men were wearing tuxes. Camille wore a long, cream-colored gown similar to the Pippa Middleton one she'd worn at Alain's wedding. Harek made a point of telling her he liked the back view, more than once.

When the afternoon was winding down, Michael, who surprised everyone by staying around, walked up to the microphone and said, "I understand the Sigurdsson men do a special dance in my honor."

There was a lot of groaning that followed as seven sets of Sigurdsson eyes turned to see who had told. Tante Lulu—who was hot to trot that day, by the way, in a red suit, red hat, and red wedgie shoes, with blue—yes, blue—hair—gave a little wave.

The band began to play that Aretha Franklin song "Chains, Chains, Chains," and the seven studly men did the snake-like dance around the patio that was made famous by John Travolta in the movie *Michael.* After that, Armod demonstrated his dancing expertise to the song "Thriller." And the LeDeux men from Tante Lulu's family, not to be outdone, showed a proficiency in the Cajun two-step with their women to wild zydeco music.

Michael was heard to tell Harek that he was well pleased with his plans for the island. And then he was about to walk off toward the trees where the demon Zebulan was watching the festivities with a sad, yearning expression on his handsome face.

"An angel's work is never done," Michael remarked.

"How about a demon vampire's work?" Harek asked.

"Doubly so. I'm thinking about giving vangels tails, by the by, so they can stop attracting females."

You could have heard a pin drop at Heaven's End then.

"Just kidding," Michael said. Angels sometimes had a warped sense of humor.

At the end of the day, Harek gave Camille a big box of chocolates. She gave him a book of philosophy called *Snoopyisms*. They gave each other additional gifts that night in the bridal suite of the Royal Hotel in New Orleans. Camille killed all her ghosts that day.

The hotel staff forever after called it the Chocolate Roses suite. No matter what they did, the scent could not be erased. And, actually, brides and grooms of the future claimed it had an aphrodisiac effect.

Go figure.

Reader Letter

Dear Readers:

Did you like Harek's story? This geeky Viking vampire angel has been a favorite of mine for some time now. I hope I did him proud.

Next up will be Cnut, the last of the Sigurdsson brothers. We don't know a whole lot about Cnut. He's the mysterious one, except he's taken to wearing a braided scalp lock sort of hairdo lately, similar to Ragnar Lothbrok in the History Channel's Vikings *series. Is this a clue to what he's been up to lately? Hmm? I have something special planned for this bad boy.*

And not to worry about that being the end of the series. I have to write a story about the tormented Lucipire (demon vampire) Zebulan who is hoping to change teams, as in become a Viking vampire angel. A seemingly impossible dream. Remember, though, that St. Michael the Archangel can do anything, if he is so inclined, but by now he's pretty much fed up with the lot of them.

After that, what's next? Well, there are still some vangels who could use a story. How about

Regina, the witch? Or Armod, the Michael Jackson fan? Not to mention lots of Viking historical romances yet to be told, like Alrek, the clumsy Viking; Tykir's other sons; the Welsh knight, Wulfgar; Jamie, the Scots Viking; and so on. There are so many choices! And don't forget the Cajun twins from Alaska, Dr. Daniel LeDeux and pilot Aaron LeDeux.

I can't tell you how much I appreciate all of you loyal fans who have followed me through these various genres. You are a blessing. These past two years have been difficult for me personally with the medical crises in our household, but your letters uplift me. Don't ever stop.

For more information about my books, check out my website at www.sandrahill.net *or my Facebook page at Sandra Hill Author. As always, I wish you smiles in your reading.*

Sandra Hill

Glossary

AFSOP—Air Force Special Operations.

A-Viking—A Norse practice of sailing away to other countries for the purpose of looting, settlement, or mere adventure, could be for a period of several months or years at a time.

Balaclava—A knitted cap that covers the head, neck, and most of the face.

Boko Haram—A militant Islamic terrorist organization based in northeast Nigeria, responsible for many deaths and kidnappings; its purpose is to institute Sharia, or Islamic law, including the ban on all Western education.

Boondockers—Heavy boots.

Braies—Slim pants worn by men.

BUD/S—Basic Underwater Demolition SEALs.

Ceorl—Free peasant, person of the lowest classes.

Cher—Dear in Cajun (male), comparable to friend.

Chère—Dear in Cajun (female).

Chéríe—French term of endearment meaning dear or darling.

Concubine—Mistress.

Coppergate—A busy, prosperous section of tenth-century York (known as Jorvik or Eoforwic) where merchants and craftsmen set up their stalls for trading.

Drownproofing—A Navy SEAL exercise that involves having the feet bound together and hands tied behind the back, then thrown into deep water.

Drukkinn (various spellings)—Drunk.

Fibbies—FBI.

Fjord—Narrow arm of the seas, often between high cliffs.

Frankland/Frankish—Early name for France.

Grinder—Asphalt training ground in the middle of the SEAL compound in Coronado.

Gunna—Long-sleeved, ankle-length gown for women, often worn under a tunic or surcoat, or under a long, open-sided apron.

Haakai—High-level demon.

Hedeby—Viking-age market town where Germany now stands.

Hersir—Viking military commander.

High and tight—Military haircut.

Hird/hirdsman—A permanent troop that a chieftain or nobleman might have.

Hordlings—Lower-level demons.

Housecarls—Troops assigned to a king's or lord's household on a longtime, sometimes permanent basis.

Imps—Lowest-level demons, foot soldiers, so to speak.

Jihad—Religious duty or holy war.

Jorvik—Viking-age York, known to the Saxons as Eoforwic.

JSOC—Joint Special Operations Command.

KA-BAR—Type of knife favored by SEALS.

Kaupang—A Viking-age market town, one of the first towns in Norway.

Keffiyeh—Checkered scarf worn about the head and neck, usually by Arabs.

Knarr—A Viking merchant vessel, wider and deeper than a regular longship.

Kudzu—Seriously invasive plant growing wild in the United States.

Longships—Narrow, open watergoing vessels with oars and square sails, perfected by Viking shipbuilders, noted for their speed and ability to ride in both shallow waters and deep oceans.

Lucifer/Satan—The fallen angel Lucifer who became known as the demon Satan.

LZ—Landing zone.

Mace—A weapon with a heavy heal on the end of a handle or chain.

Mancus—A unit of measurement or coin equal roughly to 4.5 grams of gold or thirty silver pence, also equal of one month's wages for a skilled worker in medieval times.

Martian—Alien.

Mead—Fermented honey and water.

Mung—Type of demon, below the haakai in status, often very large and oozing slime and mung.

Muslim—Follower of a religion based on the Koran with the belief that the word of God was revealed through the prophet Mohammed.

Muspell—Part of Nifhelm, one of the nine worlds in the Norse afterlife, known by its fires guarded by Sert and his flaming sword.

Nithing—A Norse insult meaning that a person is less than nothing.

Norselands—Early term referring not just to Norway but all the Scandinavian countries as a whole.

Norsemandy—Normandy.

Northumbria—One of the Anglo-Saxon kingdoms, bordered by the English kingdoms to the south and in the north and northwest by the Scots, Cumbrians, and Strathclyde Welsh.

O-course—Grueling obstacle course on the training compound, also known as the Oh-my-God course.

Odin—King of all the Viking gods.

OUTCONUS—Outside the continental United States.

Parure—Set of jewelry intended to be worn together, such as earrings, necklace, bracelet, and brooch.

Pattern-welding—Method of making a sword by forging several different metals together to form a pattern.

Plaçage—White/Creole men of New Orleans often had two families, one legal and the other to women of color, known as left-handed marriages; the system that often involved contracts, cash settlements, homes, etc. was known as *plaçage.*

Placée—Women of color who entered into *plaçage* arrangements.

Po-boy—Type of Louisiana submarine sandwich served on a baguette.

Quadroon—Person of one-fourth black ancestry, offspring of a white and a mulatto (offspring of a white and a black).
Sagas—Oral history of the Norse people, passed on from ancient times.
SEAL—Sea, Air, and Land.
Sennight—One week.
Sharia Law—Very strict law regarding Muslim behavior, especially restrictive toward women.
Skald—Poet.
Sugar cookies—Type of SEAL exercise that involves wetting body in ocean, rolling in sand, and then engaging in strenuous exercise.
Swabbies—Sailors.
Tangos—Terrorists, bad guys.
Teletransport—Transfer of matter from one point to another without traversing physical space.
Thralls—Slaves.
Torque—A collar-like necklace, usually of twisted bands of metal.
Trident—The pin earned by SEALs after completing BUD/S training, nicknamed the "Budweiser" because it is rather garish, containing an anchor, a trident, a pistol, and an eagle.
Vangels—Viking vampire angels.
VIK—The seven Sigurdsson brothers who head the vangels.
WEALS—Women on Earth, Air, Land, and Sea.
Wergild—A man's worth offered in payment.
Zydeco—Type of Cajun music.

Don't miss the next

DEADLY ANGELS

book by *New York Times* bestselling author

SANDRA HILL

The Angel Wore Fangs

Coming May 2016

Prologue

Weight Watchers, where art thou? . . .

Cnut Sigurdsson was a big man. A really big man! He was taller than the average man, of course, being a Norseman, but more than that, he was . . . well . . . truth to tell . . . fat.

Obesity was a highly unusual condition for Men of the North, Cnut had to admit, because Vikings were normally vain of appearance, sometimes to a ridiculous extent. Long hair, combed to a high sheen. Braided beards. Clean teeth. Gold and silver arm rings to show off muscles. Tight braies delineating buttocks and ballocks.

But not him.

Cnut did not care.

Even now, when three of his six brothers, who'd come (uninvited, by the by) to his Frigg's Day feast here at Hoggstead in the Norselands, were having great fun making jests about just that.

The lackwits!

Cnut cared not one whit what they said.

Not even when Trond made oinking noises, as if Cnut's estate were named for a porcine animal when he knew good and well it was the name of the original owner decades ago, Bjorn Hoggson. Besides, Trond had no room to make mock of others when he was known to be the laziest Viking to ever ride a longship. Some said he did not even have the energy to lift his cock for pissing, that he sat like a wench on the privy hole. That was probably not true, but it made a good story.

Nor did Cnut bother to rise and clout his eldest brother Vikar when he asked the skald to make a rhyme of Cnut's name:

> *Cnut is a brute*
> *And a glutton, of some* repute.
> *He is so fat that, when he goes a-Viking for* loot,
> *He can scarce lift a bow with an arrow to* shoot.
> *But, when it comes to woman*-pursuit,
> *None can* refute
> *That Cnut can* "salute" *with the best of them.*
> *Thus and therefore, let it be known*
> *And this is a truth* absolute,
> *Size matters.*

"Ha, ha, ha!" Cnut commented, while everyone in the great hall howled with laughter, and Vikar was bent over, gasping with mirth.

Cnut did not care, especially since Vikar was known to be such a prideful man he fair reeked of self-love. At least the skald had not told the poem about how, if Cnut spelled his name with a slight exchange of letters, he would be a vulgar woman-part. That was one joke Cnut did not appreciate.

But mockery was a game to Norsemen. And, alas and alak, Cnut was often the butt of the jests.

He. Did. Not. Care.

Yea, some said he resembled a walking tree with a massive trunk, limbs like hairy battering rams, and fingers so chubby he could scarce make a fist. Even his face was bloated, surrounded by a mass of wild, tangled hair on head and beard, which was dark blond, though its color was indiscernible most times since it was usually greasy and teeming with lice. Unlike most Vikings, he rarely bathed. In his defense, what tub would hold him? And the water in the fjords was frigid except for summer months. What man in his right mind wanted to turn his cock into an icicle?

A disgrace to the ideal of handsome, virile Vikinghood, he overheard some fellow jarls say about him on more than one occasion.

And as for his brother Harek, who considered himself smarter than the average Viking, Cnut glared his way and spoke loud enough for all to hear, "Methinks your first wife Dagne has put on a bit of blubber herself in recent years. Last time I saw her in Kaupang, she was as wide as she was tall. In fact, she waddled when she walked. Quack, quack. Now, there is something to make mock of!"

"You got me there," Harek agreed with a smile, raising his horn of mead high in salute.

One of the good things about Vikings is that they could laugh at themselves. The sagas were great evidence of that fact.

At least Cnut was smart enough not to take on any wives of his own, despite his twenty and eight years. Concubines and the odd wench here and there served him well. Truly, as long as Cnut's voracious hunger for all bodily appetites—food, drink, sex—was being met, he cared little what others thought of him

When his brothers were departing two days later (he thought they'd never leave), Vikar warned him, "Jesting aside, Cnut, be careful. One of these days your excesses are going to be your downfall."

"Not one of these days. Now," Cnut proclaimed jovially as he crooked a chubby forefinger at Inga, a passing chambermaid with a bosom not unlike the figurehead of his favorite longship, *Sea Nymph*. "Wait for me in the bed furs," he called out to her. "I plan to *fall down* with you for a bit of bedplay."

Vikar, Trond, and Harek just shook their heads at him, as if he were a hopeless case.

Cnut did not care.

But Vikar's words came back to haunt Cnut several months later when he was riding Hugo, one of his two war horses, across his vast estate. A normal-sized palfrey could not handle his weight; he would squash it like an oatcake. Besides, his long legs dragged on the ground. So, he had purchased two Percheons from La Perche, a town north of Norsemandy in the Franklands known for breeding the huge beasts. They'd cost him a fortune.

But even with the sturdy destrier and his well-padded arse, not to mention the warm, sunny weather, Cnut was ready to return to the keep where a midday repast, a long draught of mead, and an afternoon nap would not come amiss. But he could not go back yet. His steward, Finngeir the Frugal (whom he was coming to regard as Finn the Bothersome Worrier), insisted that he see the extent of the dry season on the Hoggstead cotters' lands.

Ho-hum. Cnut barely stifled a yawn.

"Even in the best of times, the gods have not blessed the Norselands with much arable land, being too mountainous and rocky. Why else would we go a-Viking but to settle new, more fertile lands?"

"And women," Cnut muttered. "Fertile or not."

Finn ignored his sarcasm and went on. Endlessly. "One year of bad crops is crippling, but two years, and it will be a disaster, I tell you. Look at the fields. The grains are half as high as they should be by this time of year. If it does not rain soon—"

Blather, blather, blather. I should have brought a horn of ale with me. And an oatcake, or five. Cnut did not like Finn's lecturing tone, but he was a good and loyal subject, and he would hate the thought of replacing him. So, Cnut bit back a snide retort. "What would you have me do? A rain dance? I can scarce walk, let alone dance. Ha, ha, ha."

Finn did not smile.

The humorless wretch.

"Dost think I have a magic wand to open the clouds? The only wand I have is betwixt my legs. Ha, ha, ha."

No reaction, except for a continuing frown, and a resumption of his tirade. "You must forgive the taxes for this year. Then, you must open your storerooms to feed the masses. That is what you must do."

"Are you barmy? I cannot do that! I need the taxes for upkeep of my household and to maintain a fighting troop of housecarls. As for my giving away foodstuffs, forget about that, too. Last harvest did not nearly fill my oat and barley bins. No, 'tis impossible!"

"There is more. Look about you, my jarl. Notice how the people regard you. You will have an uprising on your own lands, if you are not careful."

"What? Where? I do not know—" Cnut's words cut off as he glanced to his right and left, passing through a narrow lane that traversed through his crofters' huts. Here and there, he saw men leaning on rakes or hauling manure to the fields. They were gaunt-faced and grimy, glaring at him through angry eyes. One man even spat on the ground, narrowly missing Hugo's hoof. And the women were no better, raising their skinny children up for him to see.

"That horse would feed a family of five for a month," one toothless old graybeard yelled.

His wife—Cnut assumed it was his wife, being equally aged and toothless—cackled and said,

"Forget that. If the master skipped one meal a month, the whole village could feast."

Many of those standing about laughed.

Cnut did not.

Good thing they did not know how many mancuses it had taken to purchase Hugo and the other Percheon. It was none of their concern! Cnut had a right to spend his wealth as he chose. Leastways, that's what he told himself.

Now, instead of being softened by what he saw, Cnut hardened his heart. "If they think to threaten me, they are in for a surprise," Cnut said to Finn once they'd left the village behind and were returning to the castle keep. "Tell the tax man to evict those who do not pay their rents this year."

By late autumn, when the last of the meager crops was harvested, Cnut had reason to reconsider. Already, he'd had to buy extra grains and vegetables from the markets in Birka and Hedeby, just for his keep. Funerals were held back to back in the village. And he was not convinced that Hugo had died of natural causes last sennight, especially when his carcass had disappeared overnight. Cnut had been forced to post guards about his stables and storage shed since then. Everywhere he turned, people were grumbling, if not outright complaining.

That night, in a drukkinn fit of rage, he left his great hall midway through the dinner meal. Highly unusual for him. But then, who wouldn't lose their appetite with all those sour faces silently accusing him? It wasn't Cnut who'd brought the drought, even the most insane-minded creature must know that. Blame the gods, or lazy field hands who should have worked harder, or bad seed.

He decided to visit the garderobe before taking to his bed. He was not even in the mood for bed-play tonight. He nigh froze his balls when he sat on the privy hole, and was further annoyed to find that someone had forgotten to replenish the supply of moss and grape leaves for wiping.

When Cnut thought things could not get any worse, he opened the garderobe door and almost tripped over the threshold at what he saw. A man stood across the corridor, arms crossed over his chest. A stranger. Could it be one of his desperate, starving tenants come to seek revenge on him, as Finn had warned?

No. Despite the darkness, the only light coming from a sputtering wall torch, Cnut could see that this man was handsome in appearance, noble in bearing. Long, black hair. Tall and lean, though well-muscled, like a warrior. And oddly, he wore a long white robe with a twisted rope belt, and a gold crucifix hung from a chain about his neck. Even odder, there appeared to be wings half-folded behind his back.

Was it a man or something else?

I must be more drukkinn *than I thought.* "Who are you?"

"St. Michael the Archangel."

One of those flying creatures the Christian believed in? This was some alehead madness I am imagining! A walking dream.

"'Tis no dream, fool," the stranger said, as if he'd read Cnut's mind thoughts.

"What do you want?" Cnut demanded.

"Not you, if I had a choice, that is for certain," the man/creature/angel said with a tone of disgust. "Thou art a dire sinner, Cnut Sigurdsson, and God is not pleased with you."

"Which god would that be? Odin? Thor?"

"For shame! There is only one God."

Ah! Of course. He referred to the Christian One-God. Vikings might follow the Old Norse religions, but they were well aware of the Christian dogma, and, in truth, many of them allowed themselves to be baptized, just for the sake of expediency.

"So, your God is not pleased with me. And I should care about that . . . why?" Cnut inquired, holding onto the door jamb to straighten himself with authority. He was a high jarl, after all, and this person was trespassing. Cnut glanced about for help, but none of his guardsmen were about. *Surprise, surprise. They are probably still scowling and complaining about the lack of meat back in the hall. I am going to kick some arse for this neglect.*

"Attend me well, Viking, you should care because thou are about to meet your maker." He said Viking as if it were a foul word. "As are your brothers. Sinners, all of you!"

"Huh?

"Seven brothers, each guilty of one of the Seven Deadly Sins. Pride. Lust. Sloth. Wrath. Gluttony. Envy. Greed." He gave Cnut a pointed look. "Wouldst care to guess which one is yours?"

No, he would not. "So, I eat and drink overmuch. I can afford the excess. What sin is that?"

"Fool!" the angel said, and immediately a

strange fog swirled in the air. In its mist, Cnut saw flashing images:

—Starving and dead children.

—Him gnawing on a boar shank so voraciously that a greasy drool slipped down his chin. Not at all attractive.

—One of his housecarls being beaten to a bloody pulp for stealing bread for his family.

—Honey being spread on slice after slice of manchet bread on his high table.

—A young Cnut, no more than eight years old, slim and sprightly, chasing his older brothers about their father's courtyard.

—A naked, adult Cnut, gross and ugly with folds of fat and swollen limbs. He could not run now, if he'd wanted to.

—A family, wearing only threadbare garb and carrying cloth bundles of its meagre belongings, being evicted from its home with no place to go in the snowy weather.

—Warm hearths and roofs overhead on the Hoggstead keep.

—A big-bosomed concubine riding Cnut in the bed furs, not an easy task with his big belly.

—The same woman weeping as she unwrapped a linen cloth holding scraps of bread and meat, half-eaten oat cakes, and several shrunken apples, before her three young children.

Cnut had seen enough. "This farce has gone on long enough! You say I am going to die? Now? And all my brothers, too? Excuse me if I find that hard to believe."

"Not all at once. Some have already passed. Others will go shortly."

Really? Three of his brothers had been here just two months past, and he had not received news of any deaths in his family since, but then their estates were distant and the roads were nigh impassable this time of year. The fjords were no better, already icing over, making passage difficult for longships.

"I should toss you down the privy hole and let you die in the filth," the angel said, "but you would not fit. Better yet, I should lock you in the garderobe and let you starve to death, like your serfs do."

Ah, so that's what this was about. "You cannot blame me for lack of rain or poor harvests. In fact, your God—"

Before he could finish the thought, the angel pointed a forefinger at him, and a flash of light passed forth, hitting Cnut right in the chest, like a bolt of lightning. Cnut found himself dangling off the floor. He clutched his heart which felt as if a giant stake had passed through his body, securing him to the wall.

"Let it be known hither and yon, the Viking race has proven to be too arrogant and brutish, and it is God's will that it should die out. But you and your brothers are being given a second chance, though why, only God knows."

What? Wait. Did he say I won't be dying, after all?

"This is thy choice. Repent and agree to become a vangel in God's army for seven hundred years, and thou wilt have a chance to make up for your mortal sins. Otherwise, die and spend eternity at Satan's hearth."

A sudden smell of rotten eggs filled the air. Brimstone, Cnut guessed, which was said to be a characteristic of the Christian afterlife for those who had offended their god. At the same time, he could swear his toes felt a mite warm. Yea, fire and brimstone, for a certainty.

So, I am being given a choice between seven hundred years in God's army or forever roasting in Hell. Some choice! Still, he should not be too quick to agree. "Vangel? What in bloody hell is a vangel?" Cnut gasped out.

"A Viking vampire angel who will fight the forces of Satan's Lucipires, demon vampires who roam the world spreading evil."

That was clear as fjord mud. Cnut was still pinned high on the wall, and he figured he was in no position to negotiate. Besides, seven hundred years didn't sound too bad.

But he forgot to ask what exactly a vampire was.

He soon found out.

With a wave of his hand, the angel loosened Cnut's invisible ties, and he fell to the floor. If he'd thought the heart pain was bad, it was nothing compared to the excruciating feel of bones being crushed and reformed. In truth, he could swear he felt fangs forming on each side of his mouth, like a wolf. And his shoulders were being ripped apart, literally, and replaced with what, Cnut could not be sure, as he writhed about the rush-covered floor.

"First things first," the angel said then, leaning over him with a menacing smile. "You are going on a diet."

Chapter 1

Sister, where art thou? . . .

"ISIS? Why would any woman in her right mind join that militant group?" Andrea Stewart remarked skeptically into the cell phone she had propped between the crook of her ear and raised shoulder. Her hands were free to stir the chocolate ganache to be spread atop the Opera Cake she was preparing for tonight's dessert menu at La Chic Sardine.

The elegant gateâu was comprised of mocha buttercream spread over thin layers of cake that had been soaked in coffee syrup, topped with the ganache, then sliced into bars. One of her many specialties at this Philadelphia restaurant. As far removed from ISIS as, well, the Liberty Bell.

"How do I know why your sister does the things she does?" her stepmother, Darla, whined into the phone. "All I know is, I have a picture here in front of me, and she's wearing some kind of robe that covers her from head to toe with only her eyes peeking out."

"A burqa?" That was a switch for her sister who was more inclined toward tight jeans and skimpy shirts.

"I don't know what they call those things. They look like tents, if you ask me. I get a hot flash just thinking about how uncomfortable they must be in this heat. Thank God I'm not an A-rab."

It was summer, and the city was in the midst of an unusual heat wave . . . unusual for Pennsylvania . . . but Darla would have the AC on full blast? *Is she in menopause? At forty-five?* Andrea did a mental Snoopy dance of glee. *There is a God!* But that was mean. Darla didn't mean to be such an insensitive dingbat. She was just clueless.

Andrea set aside her whisk and adjusted the phone at her ear. Sitting down on a high stool at the kitchen prep table, she sighed and said, "Celie is going purdah? That's a new one. How is she going to show off all her tattoos?"

"That's not funny."

Actually, it was. Celie's ink, seventeen at last count, had started with a tramp stamp when she was only thirteen. Winnie the Pooh giving the finger.

"Honestly, Andy, this is going to kill your father. How much more of this crap can he take?"

Andrea rolled her eyes. Darla had been saying the same thing ever since she married fifty-year-old widower Howard Stewart fifteen years ago, when Andrea had been fourteen years old and her sister Cecilia a mere four. "Crap" was her universal word for anything the two children did to ruin her life. On Andrea's part, it encompassed everything from strep throat to a dirty kitchen due to one of her latest culinary experiments. When it came to her sister, it could be bed wetting, a low grade on a math test, or promiscuous behavior as a preteen.

Darla, a former Zuma instructor, did not have a maternal bone in her well-toned body. She'd no doubt thought she'd landed a Sugar Daddy when she met their father, a successful stockbroker, who was brilliant when it came to the market and dumb as a rock when it came to women. Little had Darla known that the Wall Street gravy train also carried some irritating baggage in the form of two kids, who hadn't been as sweet and invisible as she'd probably expected.

It was only nine a.m., and the kitchen was empty except for Andrea at this early hour. The restaurant didn't begin serving until five p.m., but employees would be trailing in soon. Andrea needed to get off the phone and get back to work. "Darla, how do you know it's Celie?"

"Because it's a video. Didn't I tell you that?"

"No, you didn't."

"Oh, well, I'm looking at it on my iPhone right now. Celie is talking about Allah and the evil United States and that kind of crap. She has black eyebrows. What is her natural hair color anyway? Oh, that's right. Blonde, like yours."

Andrea hadn't seen her sister for months . . . in fact, almost a year. Not for any particular reason.

There was a ten-year difference in their ages, and that wasn't the only difference. Celie was of average height, with curves out the wazoo. Andrea was genetically thin, rarely gained an ounce, and thank God for that with her calorie-laden occupation. Celie's hair could be any color under the rainbow, from bright purple to an actual rainbow, and styled short, long, or half-long/half-short. Once she even shaved her head. Andrea had sported the same long, blonde ponytail since she was a teenager. It suited her and her work.

Celie was the adventuresome one. Always looking for thrills (Can anyone say zip line off a cliff?), while Andrea didn't even like roller coasters. As for men, forget about it! Celie drew men, like flies or bees or whatever. Boys had been chasing her since she was ten years old. Andrea didn't even want to guess how many lovers Celie had gone through in her nineteen years, while she, at twenty-nine-almost-thirty, had had two real relationships. Three, if you counted Peter Townsend. Pete the Pervert. He had the weirdest fetish that . . . nevermind.

Back to Celie. Despite their clashes in personalities and interests, they were still fairly close sisters. They had to be during those early years of their mother's death, and their father's grieving. It was just the two of them against the world. Until he married Darla. And then, it was the two of them against Darla. Poor Darla!

They just never seemed to be in the same place at the same time these days. Celie was always traveling somewhere or other. Andrea was an ambitious workaholic with hopes of one day opening her own upscale pastry shop.

While Andrea's mind had been wandering, she just realized that Darla was still talking. She interrupted her by saying, "I thought Celie was spending the summer with that cult in Jamaica, where they run around half-naked and sell sun catchers to tourists. Led by that cuckoo bird swami person who believes that world peace will come with global warming, or some such nonsense."

"That was last year."

Celie was a great one for joining cults, not that she called them cults, and mostly they were harmless. Modern day hippies looking for the light, usually via some weed. Heaven's Love Shack. Serenity. Free Birds. Pot for People.

"Remember, I told you about her boyfriend. He's an A-rab or a Mexican, or something. Maybe Egyptian. They all look alike."

That narrows it down a lot. Darla was no dummy, but sometimes she revealed a little inner Archie Bunkerism. And Edith, too.

"His name is Kahlil, you know, like that poet guy."

"Kahlil Gibran?"

"Yes! Don't you just love his poems? They're so deep."

Talking to Darla was like trying to catch popcorn from an unlidded pot. Here, there, all over the place.

"About Celie's boyfriend?"

"Oh, right. He came to a dinner party your Daddy hosted last month for one of his big clients.

You were at that food convention in Las Vegas. Anyhow, Kahlil just frowned the whole time because we served alcohol. So rude! Honestly! Who doesn't drink red wine with Beef Wellington? And he had this dish towel thingee on his head. By the way, your raspberry torte was a huge success. Did I tell you that?"

Can anyone say Orville Redenbocker? "Yes, you told me." About the dessert, not the boyfriend. "Thanks."

"Anyhow, this Kahlil fellow talked the silly girl into going with him to a dude ranch in Montana run by some Muslim Church. Circle of Light."

"What? That's crazy!"

"You're telling me, honey. I've been saying for years that your sister is two bricks short of a wall."

"I didn't mean that Celie . . . never mind. What has any of this to do with ISIS?"

"The detective says that—"

"Whoa, whoa, whoa! You hired a detective?"

Just then, Sonja Fournet, owner of the restaurant, walked in through the swinging doors that separated the kitchen from the dining room. Hearing her last words, Sonja grinned and mouthed silently, "Darla?"

Andrea nodded and raised five fingers indicating she would be off the phone shortly. Andrea was an experienced pastry chef, but even her skills were not going to save her job if she kept engaging in these personal phone conversations while on the job, almost all of them from her stepmother. Darla thought nothing of calling up to a dozen times a day, usually about the most innocuous things, like, "What's the best way to cook lamb?" Or, "How do I clean the gravy stain off your mother's lace tablecloth?" Or, "Why does asparagus turn my pee green?" Real important stuff.

That wasn't quite true about Andrea losing her job, though. Sonja had attended the Cordon Bleu cooking school in Paris with Andrea eight years ago and was one of her closest friends.

"Listen, Darla, I can't talk right now. Why don't I come over tonight and we can discuss this, without interruption?" Fortunately, or unfortunately, her father and Darla lived in a Main Line community only a half hour from the condo Andrea had bought last year.

What was I thinking? Couldn't I find a job in . . . oh, say . . . Alaska? Or a living space on the other side of Philly? Like maybe New Jersey?

"Okay," Darla said. "Could you bring some of those yummy Napoleons with you? Oh, and a few of the chocolate croissants for your Daddy's breakfast?"

"Sure." She clicked off the phone and looked at Sonja who was grinning at her over a steaming cup of coffee. "Okay, spill. What has the wicked stepmother's thong in a twist now? I swear, girl, I wouldn't have a life if it weren't for you."

"She says Celie has joined a cult on a dude ranch in Montana that has ties to ISIS and claims she's gone all sharia complete with burqa, mainlining the usual extremist Muslim propaganda. Though, how she would ride a horse in a robe, I have no idea. I didn't even know Celie could ride a horse. Bottom line, as usual when it involves my sister, Darla probably wants me to fix things."

"Merde!"

"Exactly."

"What does she expect you to do?"

Andrea shrugged. "Lone ranger to the rescue, I guess, though I don't ride a horse, either. Or is it Julia Child to the rescue?"

"Warrior with a whisk," Sonja concluded.

Next month, don't miss these exciting new love stories only from Avon Books

Facing Fire by HelenKay Dimon

When his uncle is brutally murdered, Josiah King knows that he and his black ops team are targets, along with everyone they love. Josiah is determined to unravel the plot—until long-legged redhead Sutton Dahl becomes a dangerous distraction. Josiah and Sutton become unlikely partners, fighting for their lives even as the attraction between them flares into real passion.

The Legend of Lyon Redmond by Julie Anne Long

Rumor has it she broke Lyon Redmond's heart. But while many a man has since wooed the dazzling Olivia Eversea, none has ever won her—which is why jaws drop when she suddenly accepts a viscount's proposal. As the day of her wedding approaches, Lyon—now a driven, dangerous, infinitely devastating man—decides it's time for a reckoning.

Forever Your Earl by Eva Leigh

Eleanor Hawke loves a good scandal. And readers of her successful gossip rag live for the exploits of her favorite subject: Daniel Balfour, the Earl of Ashford. Daniel has secrets, and he knows if Eleanor gets wind of them, a man's life could be at stake. What better way to distract a gossip than by inviting her to experience his debauchery first-hand?

Give in to your Impulses!

These unforgettable stories only take a second to buy and give you hours of reading pleasure!

Go to ***www.AvonImpulse.com*** and see what we have to offer.

Available wherever e-books are sold.